THE BIG FADEOUT

By R. Jay Stewart

ISBN: 0692603875

ISBN-13: 978-0692603871

ACKNOWLEDGEMENTS

To Alexsandra, my muse.

There are debts that cannot be repaid.

I owe a tremendous one to you.

Edited by Alexsandra Silvero

Edited by Cherri Randall

Cover Photo by Allyson Stewart

Acknowledgements Inspirations:

B. Dylan

J. Cash

S. King

B. Marley

The Unexamined life is not worth living

-Socrates

I knew I had only a moment

He would surely get Jack as he ran

So I staged a "Big Fadeout" beside him

And knocked the Forty-five out of his hand

-From "The story of Suicide Sal"

By Bonnie Parker

TABLE OF CONTENTS

PART 5: THE ADVENTURES OF BONNIE AND CLYDE

To my Bonnie…

PART 1: THE STRAW

CHAPTER 1 – THE FOUNDATION

My first thought was that I had killed him.

Watching him limply slide to the floor startled me with a tinge of regret, but only after the rush of satisfaction had run its course. Before grabbing the duct tape, I checked to make sure he was breathing. I saw a mucous bubble starting to form on his left nostril. The bubble became quite large and then popped. He was still alive.

I felt minor relief for a moment before I attended to my next task. With tape in hand, I put my arms under his armpits and wrestled him back into the chair. After the first two revolutions of tape around the chair, I looked at my work and the pitiful face of my victim, who was now the possessor of a swollen red forehead.

I tore off a strip of tape and applied it over his mouth. For reasons I cannot define nor defend, I burst into laughter. As he moaned his way back to consciousness, seriousness took hold as the impact of my action began to seep into my frenzied brain.

But just for that one second.

* * * * * * * * * * *

Eight hundred billion cars may pass over a bridge, but perhaps a leaf landing at the right place and time can cause that bridge to collapse. Wind, rain, and snow pound a mountain with little noticeable effect. But beneath the surface, plates are pushing against one another with tremendous force. Eventually that force causes one tectonic plate to slip over the other. Rocks slide, mud slides, and the result is catastrophic. In these cases, the proverbial straw broke the camel's back.

The beginning of this story is about that leaf that collapsed the bridge. It is about that stress on those plates. First, we must talk about that foundation. My name is Clyde Barrow. Not my real name, but I love the symbolism of the fallen ladies' man; the desperado, the misunderstood fugitive. It suits me and I don't much care if it is 100% accurate.

So call me Clyde.

I was the youngest of a big family. It would probably be unnecessary to say I was lost in the shuffle. I was alone frequently, but that was mostly by choice. I do remember examining myself and my place in life frequently at a young age. Being from a large family had some advantages; one of those advantages was learning from older siblings. I learned to read at a very young age and this freed my mind to pursue more profound interests.

Six or seven year-olds are not generally known for deep personal examination. At least this is not popularly accepted. This introspection caused my childhood to be mostly unhappy; not tragic, but strained and different. This caused periods of melancholia followed by sudden bursts of violence over mostly trivial things.

Acceptance by others was never one of my overriding concerns. It would have been nice, but if I had to trade my real self for some babbling little sycophant, I would not have been true, not real. Therefore, while I had friends, I kept them at an arm's length. My theory was that if they wanted to be closer, they would accept me and embrace who I was. I was lonely as hell, but being self-absorbed, I really didn't realize this until much later.

I only strove for acceptance after I became the object of ridicule. In the social madness that is school, I was different, therefore, bad, therefore bullied, therefore marginalized. An outcast's life on the margins is lonely. Being outcast by choice is no less lonely and the comfort of rationalization does not compensate for this fact. Therefore, through introspection and self-examination I realized that I was what I was; an actual remarkable creature. My loneliness being mostly self-imposed, I rationalized that my completeness was only deficient of companionship.

Unfortunately for me, my social group was limited to school and all of my school acquaintances had already marginalized me. To try to fit in felt contrived. I was not going to change to fit in and that was how it was going to be. The friends I made tended to be the new kids. But even the new kids needed some concessions to how they were. I was not flexible, not pliable, and I was not going to change for them. Face it boys and girls, I am an introvert, you won't get close to me. I am inside here somewhere. In order to reach that place you are going to have to prove yourself.

So as my introspection receded, it was replaced by loneliness. As any lonely person can tell you, it is a void, completely empty. The void in my life was always there, but I failed to notice. For some the loneliness is replaced by crying, or eating too much, or drinking, or drugs. Even meaningless sex with strangers can fill that void. None of these are viable replacements for a real connection with real people. If you are Clyde Barrow, you have examined yourself and concluded that this connection is the one thing you are missing.

CHAPTER 2 – THE FATIGUE

"**Y**ou are an outstanding worker, Clyde." It was my boss giving my latest evaluation.

Mostly it concerned his own insecurities about me being smarter and more capable than him, but also his perception of me not working and playing well with others.

"So what is it this time, Del?" I asked with a bright and cheery smile.

"Oh, some of the people who work with you have commented on how you are not exactly a *team player*." He made these little quotations with his fingers on the last two words.

We were sitting in the company's classroom. It was a well air-conditioned room with ascending rows of theatre seats. Del was sitting on a raised stool next to the podium and I was slouching in a front row.

"Aaahh!" I nodded. "So can I go now?"

"No, Clyde"

"Well," I sat up, placed my elbows on my knees and my chin on my fists. “Are you going to reprimand me?"

Del cleared his throat. "I have to," he said as he paused and leafed through some papers in a folder. "You can consider this your first warning."

"Okay," I sighed. "What's this about?"

"Well," Del said as he put on his reading glasses.

Del was prematurely balding and not qualified for his current position. He had parlayed his GED and his friendships into a job as my supervisor. As soon as he reached this station in life, he began to try to get me to quit or to get me in enough trouble to get me fired. As with most situations in my life, I had not tried to fit in. I also was smarter than Del and made more money than he did. This bothered him.

"On your most recent trip you yelled at our trainee in front of the customer," Del looked up from his reading glasses.

"Oh?" I asked "Did I hurt Lenny's feelings?"

"That's not the point, Clyde," he said as he removed his glasses. "It makes us all look bad."

I sighed loudly and slid back into my seat. "Tell Lenny to grow a pair. He's too sensitive. When I learned my job, it was under more stress than this. Maybe he's not suited for tower work. Maybe he's the one you should counsel."

* * * * * * * * * * *

Lenny was Del's brother in-law; his wife's brother. Del got him a job as my protégé'. Lenny was not qualified and quite stupid. Stupid people tend to piss me off, but mostly I had it good. Our job usually involved climbing towers to install any of a wide variety of antennas. I am classically trained and very experienced in these tasks. Lenny was barely qualified for this. For one, he was afraid of heights and this caused him to become cranky and virtually useless as a climber except for the shortest of climbs. Because of this, I was the one who did most of the climbing. I would climb the towers and use him as a ground guide. On the short towers, we would both climb.

As a ground guide, he still left a lot to be desired. In fact, he left everything to be desired. He was inattentive, uncommunicative, and careless. Tangled lines were frequent and I had to hold my tongue on more than one occasion since the customer was keeping a watchful eye on our work. When the customer was not around, I could let go of the pretense. I could tell him where he was fucking up in no uncertain terms.

When climbing towers, safety is the most important concern. There is a checklist of items to be completed and they must be accomplished in a certain order. When one suffers from Attention Deficit Disorder, as I do, the checklist keeps the mind from jumping from Job A to Job C. Focus is key. As the most experienced and accomplished climber, it fell to me to train Lenny, the boss's brother in-law. So I was frequently sent on two-man climbs with this trainee.

After a few months, the trainee was expected to perform certain tasks without being instructed. One of these tasks involved setting up a pulley to ease raising the antenna to the top of the tower. It was all pretty much second nature to me. I had shown this process to Lenny several times. The pulley setup was made easier by the use of a winch on the front of the company truck. With the winch, there was minimal manual labor other than setup and keeping the lines from tangling.

On one particular job, I had to climb a 490-foot tower and install a 7-foot diameter microwave antenna. The climb itself was not particularly hard; it had a cable-guided slide all the way up. The hard part was going to be getting the antennas past all of the other antennas which were already on the tower. We had gone to the site a day ahead of time to plan our attack.

The tower was in south Texas, where there are no rises in land anywhere in sight. It is also a place where weather can change quickly. We had to make sure that we allowed enough time for the possibility of inclement weather. We had agreed in advance to meet our customer- a local cellular telephone company- at 5:00 a.m. the following day.

With his months of training, Lenny should have been experienced enough to do it all himself. Regrettably, in addition to being slow-witted and irritable, he also had a drinking problem. More correctly, he had a stopping problem. After a night of drinking and chasing women, he was hard to roust out of bed at the local motel. After I pounded on his door for a while, the door was answered by a young lady with bright blue eyes and questionable taste in men. She was wearing a sheet. I stepped right past her and pulled the blankets off a naked Lenny. This didn't wake him up. Only after I walked to the bathroom, poured a glass of water, and threw it in his face did he awaken from his slumber.

"Wake up, Buttercup," I said matter-of-factly

"Fucking Clyde!" He blurted out as he sprayed water and pulled the remaining covers over him.

I was completely calm as I turned my back and returned to the bathroom to start the shower. A hot shower to get the morning blood flowing is my best remedy for a sluggish start. I returned to the room and began to chat with the young lady.

"Hi, my name is Clyde," I stuck out my hand "What is your name, young lady?"

"Naomi," she said as she slipped on a pair of panties under the sheet.

"Naomi, a pretty name. You from here?" I asked.

"Ah, yes." She was under the sheet as she put on the rest of her clothes.

"Do you like older men?" I asked.

"You don't seem that old," she replied after poking her head out of the sheet.

"Oh, you'd be surprised," I said as I grabbed Lenny's arm and hoisted him out of bed.

I walked to the shower and tested the temperature of the water as one would for a little baby.

"Go on in Lenny," I said as I motioned with both hands. He climbed in the shower.

"You got five minutes, Rip Van Winkle," I said loudly over the water-pouring noise as I closed the bathroom door. I returned to the room. Naomi was sitting on the bed and putting on her shoes. She looked to be about twenty-one, with light brown hair, eyes that seemed to change to a dark green in the dim light, and a perfect complexion only accented by a mole over her right eye. She smiled and her perfect white teeth sparkled. I held out my hand. "Here's my card. I come through these parts quite often."

She continued to smile as she took the card and read it out loud, "Clyde Barrow- Communications God." She looked up. "Pleased to meet you Clyde," she said, holding out her hand.

"Pleasure is mine Naomi." I kissed her hand. I walked to the bathroom, opened the door, and then turned off the shower. I tossed a towel to Lenny, "Two minutes," I said as I walked back to the bedroom and sat down on the bed next to Naomi.

"In fact, Naomi, if you are not busy tonight…"

She smiled deviously, "I will definitely call you," she said.

"Cool," I said.

She grabbed my hand and started to write her number on my palm. I pulled my hand back and handed her my cell phone. "Just punch it in here, since my hand is gonna sweat all day."

She punched in the number and hit send. Her phone rang in her purse and she hung up.

Lenny was now dressing. I bid farewell to Naomi and went to start the truck. We reached the site at 5:15 and the customer was waiting. I made no excuses and no apologies. The two men wearing red Southern Texas Wireless tee shirts, matching khakis, steel toed boots, and white hardhats were waiting by their company truck with arms folded.

"Good morning, gentlemen," I said cheerfully. "I love the wildlife out here," I said as I shook each man's hand vigorously.

"What did you hit?" The older man asked.

"Nothing," I chuckled, then looked back and pointed down the road. "But I missed about fifty antelope out there on highway 90." This was only a slight lie. I had seen a herd of antelope in a field by the highway. They may have even been cows, but no matter, the tenseness of the situation had been diffused.

Lenny, for his part, was just as cranky and disagreeable as always. Mumbling, stumbling, and confused, he began to unload tools from the truck. I was already fashioning my climbing harness and ready for my ascent up the tower. I stood waiting for the rope to be attached to my back. The rope was necessary to send tools and equipment to the top of the tower. Unfortunately, Lenny had not yet unloaded the rope from the vehicle.

No problem, I was used to this by now. I retrieved the rope myself and began to lay it out on a straight line away from the tower on the side I was about to climb.

Twenty minutes later, I was at the top of the tower, secure in place. My pulley rope was secure and I sent down the end of the rope to facilitate the transfer of tools and equipment. I called Lenny on the radio. No answer.

"Lenny, this is your eye in the sky. Start sending me up some tools," I said as I started to get aggravated. No reply.

I called again. "Lenny!" I said loudly.

From my position on the tower, I saw one of the red shirt men walk over to the truck. A voice on the radio replied, "Eh, Clyde, Lenny is sleeping."

"Perfect," I said to myself. "Sir, could you wake him up?" I said into the radio.

"Hi Clyde," came the reply on the radio. It was Lenny.

"Could you send up my tools please, Goldilocks?"

"Eh, coming," came the cranky reply.

"Fucking Lenny," I said to myself as I stared off into the distance at the Gulf of Mexico and the cloudless sky.

"Oh, Lenny," I said into the radio. "Could you please send up a bottle of water?"

"Roger that," he replied.

In a minute or so, my tools arrived. Within a few moments I had my half empty water bottle.

"Lenny, did you drink my water?" I said with irritation.

"Sorry, I was thirsty," his reply crackled on the radio.

"Well, next time get your own water, Cupcake," I sneered. I took a generous drink and reminded myself that I was well paid for this job.

After thirty minutes of work, the antenna bracket was installed and I was ready for the antenna. I cannot overemphasize the importance of being delicate with this equipment. A ride up the tower for tools or brackets can be bumpy and can be done with great speed. The only caution that is really vital is the avoidance of other equipment on the tower. With antennas that sometimes cost thousands of dollars, you may not bump them on anything. You must be perfect. You get one try. I know that Lenny knows this because I have repeated this to him about a hundred times.

Immediately, upon the antenna's ascent up the tower, I sensed something amiss. Halfway up, my fears were confirmed; the rope was not only wrapped around itself, it had worked its way to the wrong side of one of the guy wires. I grabbed the radio, "Lenny Stop!" I yelled. But the antenna kept coming, on a collision-course with an array of antennas mounted 70 feet below me and most shockingly, the rope was putting more tension on the guy wire.

A word about guy wires: These are thick cables. Tall skinny towers, without being anchored by guy wires, will topple easily with only the slightest tilt in any direction. That tilt can be caused by excess weight on one side of the tower, or by wind, or by a combination of both. In this case, I was providing the weight and there was a constant 30-knot northwesterly wind. The tension on that guy wire was either going to snap that cable or pull the tower down in that northwesterly direction. As my life flashed before my eyes and before I found religion, I yelled as loud as I could, "Lenny! Stop!"

The antenna stopped its rise. The guy lines and my life were spared, but our antenna was now caught amongst the array of antennas below me.

"Sorry Clyde," a crackly voice came over the radio. I paused. I gathered my composure. A cool head was called for.

"Lenny, is that you?" I asked derisively.

"Yes?" Came the reply.

"Could you carefully lower the antenna?"

"Sure."

"Slowly. Carefully."

"Sure thing"

My life immediately flashed again as his attempt to lower the antenna caused the tower to shake violently.

"Stop!" I shouted at the radio. "I have to climb down and untangle it myself"

So down 70 feet I went. I discovered that the antenna was in no-man's land. The rope was hopelessly tangled in a guy wire and the antenna array. My only choice was to strap the antenna somewhere close, cut the rope, and to pull this 75-pound monster the rest of the way by hand.

"Lenny," I said on the radio after I had fastened the antenna to the tower.

"Yes?" He replied.

"I need all of the slack you have at your end."

"Uh, what?"

"Cut the rope from the winch. I need to pull this up by hand."

One hour later, I had worked the antenna past the array and had it at the top. I was ready for the antenna transmission cable. One problem: I had no rope to pull the cable up. I had to go all of the way down. I got all of my muttering out of my system on the way. By the time I got to the bottom, I acted professionally.

"Lenny," I said as I grabbed his water bottle, "tie the end of the cable to the ring on my back."

As he did this, I finished off his water and smiled at the two cellular telephone company guys who were now standing outside of their air-conditioned truck.

In another hour, the antenna was installed with the cable connected. In another two hours, I had finished clamping the cable to the tower as I climbed down. As I reached the ground I was greeted by Lenny who had his hand in the air ready to accept a high-five.

"Way to go Spiderman!" He said with a goofy smile.

I kept my hands at my side and glared at him.

"Is the equipment installed down here?" I asked.

"Uh, no," Lenny deadpanned as he looked down.

I unhooked my climbing harness, took off my gloves, and accepted a water bottle from the younger of the two cell phone gentlemen. Again I finished the bottle. I threw the empty bottle into the box which had once contained the microwave antenna. It was at this point that I let Lenny get to me. He was still standing there, not making a move.

"Lenny," I started, "I used to wonder how Del could ever find anybody stupid enough to marry him. But getting to know you, I think I have solved the mystery. Because, if your sister is even half as clueless as you, then she would have been easy prey for Del's unparalleled mediocrity."

I walked over and opened the door to the radio shelter. "Lenny, I am going to sit here and watch you install the equipment into the rack. I need to pay close attention because I know you are going to fuck something up. I just want to know the nature of the fuckups so I can easily correct them."

* * * * * * * * * * *

One week later I was listening to Del read my counseling statement. My cell phone interrupted his reading several times with a little tune called "Camptown Ladies." Every time the cell phone went off, Del stopped his reading and looked up. After this happened five times, I pulled my phone out of my pocket.

Message 1 was from my daughter in college; "send $$$ dad luv u." I sighed.

Message 2 was from my wife; "My car is in the shop, can u please pay mechanic?" Another sigh.

Message 3 from a lady friend; "Luv u. Miss u. Still out of work can I borrow money" A third sigh.

Message 4 is from my mistress; "tonite? me & u? u know u want it." I smile and shake my head.

Message 5 is from Naomi; "ur da best u make all young men pale in cmprsn lol thanks 4 other night when u cumin back this way?"

Only this one gives me pleasure. I wished I was with Naomi. I put my phone away and look at Del. "Can we continue?"

CHAPTER 3 – REINFORCEMENTS

When an engineer spots cracks in a bridge, he will order reinforcements. These reinforcements are temporary; they delay the collapse until a replacement bridge can be built. In my case, that bridge was represented by my sanity and therapy provided that reinforcement. The therapy was bought and paid for by my employer; the optimistically named *Sunrise Enterprises*. I had signed up for this therapy several months before my little incident with Lenny; I was seeing Dr. Marlin D. Whipple. He was a short grey-haired man with a fancy curled mustache. He had little model cars all over his desk. He seemed attentive to every word with his beady black eyes. Dr. Marlin had become my best friend over these months. He was intrigued with my mind. He was probably going to write a paper about me.

One thing Dr. Marlin wanted me to master was my fits of rage. One exercise involved my behavior when someone was yelling in my face or just giving me an unpleasant talking to. What he wanted me to do was to try to put myself in that person's place. He wanted me to try to analyze what could cause this person to be this way. At that time, I had many such instances. I had spread myself so thin in my desire to please so many people and to be thought of as some kind of super-human-love-machine-warrior-knight. This world I created in my mind was taking its toll.

As Del was reading me my counseling statement, I was imagining what kind of childhood could have produced someone of such obvious mediocrity combined with blind ambition. He was reading verbatim from the company manual. This fact did not impress me; Del was a constant violator of company policy where it suited him. So I had to analyze what factors went into the making of someone whose entire existence seemed to revolve around keeping his ass in a boss's chair.

Del had my attention, but not my attention to his words. I was analyzing whether he was an only child or a bed wetter. I knew he had a sister, but maybe she was adopted or something. Perhaps he was abused in some way. I began to sympathize with him somewhat. This exercise eased my anger and helped my mind to analyze my own situation with more clarity. I was not happy. It was my need for companionship; that need for a human connection that had led me down a trail towards a bad marriage and other impossible relationships. I was always happy to fill the void of other people without getting an even exchange of emotional fulfillment. These relationships had become a one-way street; I give and I get taken. The end result was unhappiness and despair. An observer could probably see it coming from a mile off. I suspected that Dr. Marlin did.

On our first visit, Dr. Marlin had asked me to write out my personal philosophy. On the second visit, I presented him with an essay called "The Manifesto of Misery", part of which I will quote here. Most of it is based on my own self-analysis which I covered earlier.

> *Misery is not unlike a drug; it is a comfort that is indulged in by people who seek easy answers and instant gratification. It also is frequently the result of the efforts to help such people. In my case, I think both apply to me; not only do I crave misery, but I cause my own misery by taking on the misery of others who indulge in misery creation. My intent is, on the surface, honorable, but also self-indulgent. I want to bring happiness to those who, by nature, will never be happy. This is not just a cause for concern, but also a recipe for disaster.*

This manifesto became an important release for my cynicism in the following months. I even came up with tenets of the misery addict. I probably impressed Dr. Marlin with my in-depth self-analysis, but he reacted in a much more concerned manner; Dr. Marlin recommended an extended unaccompanied vacation and prescribed Prozac. I rejected the Prozac, not outright; I accepted the prescription but never filled it. I did accept his recommendation of vacation. I spent my vacation first with my lady friend and then with my mistress. These two women were part of my misery addiction and I was part of theirs.

At the time, I was unaware that Dr. Marlin had alerted my employer as to my impending self-destruction. He was under contract to them to provide counseling to employees who might potentially flip out. There had been high attrition in my line of work; fatigue had caused many to just quit, but some had threatened violence. Tower climbing is just not for some people. In my case, I loved it. But Dr. Marlin was worried that I could harm myself and others. My employer and especially Del were concerned. They were not concerned about me, but that they would lose their best worker and someone who never said no to any job, no matter the danger or circumstance. They added Dr. Marlin's assessment to my file.

But I went on vacation. My wife was incredulous and suspicious of my motives for taking a solo vacation, but I had a note from the doctor. My mistress and lady friend were thrilled. They both loved me and mostly for the same reason; I made their ride easier. I gave to them and I kept on giving. They needed me and they came to rely on my confidence to pull them through. I was never lost, never doubted myself, and never betrayed a hint of uncertainty. I was always on top of the situation and never backed down. I never doubted their love for me, because I was just that amazingly confident.

So I went to my lady friend. Her name was Isabel. She was married when I met her, but it was a worse marriage than even mine. She was in the middle of a divorce which was caused, in part, by my insistence that things could be better for her. She had fallen completely apart in these months and relied on me to keep her from the edge. Other men had taken advantage of her situation for easy sex, but I wasn't like them. I was interested in her in totality. Sure she was attractive, but I was also intrigued by her other charms. For one, she had an amazing singing voice. I would buy her gifts and I would praise her constantly. My confidence in her never faded and she came to rely on me.

So I arranged for us to go on vacation up in the mountains. She had a man who was trying to control her and needed to get away. On the way up to the mountains I had bought her a long black dress. I wanted her to sing to me in that dress in the style of one of those legendary torch singers. I had a list of songs I wanted her to learn and I brought my own accompanying music. She obliged and it was a great ten days up in the mountains. Only after five days of her learning the songs and perfecting the vocals did I allow myself to be seduced and we made passionate love for a good part of the final five days.

The next ten days were spent with my mistress. Isabel didn't want me to go, but I had to lie to her. I told her that I had been called away unexpectedly. In reality, I had an appointment to see my girl Priscilla. Priscilla was a pro, she had clients, and she had a schedule. She had cleared ten days for me and this was going to cost me some money, but she didn't charge me anywhere near as much as she did her other clients because I was the one she could rely on. She could talk and I would listen. I would rationalize away all of the bad choices she had made in her life. Once again, it was not purely about sex; it was about misery. Shared misery was a component in all of my relationships.

But sex was definitely part of it; we were engaged in it early and often. In between, we were sharing each other's misery. She knew about Isabel and I knew about every high-falutin' big shot with whom she was involved. One minute we would be in the throes of passion, the next we would be deeply engaged in a discussion about our impossible lives. When my vacation was over, my stress had dissipated considerably. I also had become more deeply involved in the desperate lives of two of my miserable friends. Instead of eliminating these relationships from my life, I encouraged them. Not a psychologically healthy decision, but I am a misery addict. I was soon to add another collection of grief to my life; that of the aforesaid Naomi.

* * * * * * * * * *

So I sat and listened to Del finish his evaluation of my work and my attitude. He probably had Dr. Marlin's notes and my manifesto right in front of him, but he played it cool. He acted like he had saved my job and that he was my best friend in the world. In reality, we both knew I was just there until Lenny could be relied on. I knew this reliance would never occur, but to Del, mere competence was all that was required from Lenny to boot me out the door. Del summed up his counseling and stuck out his hand. I had heard only part of anything Del had said during this session. I heard words like "professionalism", "respect", and "example". All of these words made me smile. I was smiling again as I shook Del's extended hand. I was not smiling about anything he said.

I was smiling about the bomb I brought to work that morning.

CHAPTER 4 – THE BOMB

Well, it actually wasn't a bomb. Bombs require some kind of explosive and some kind of triggering device. My little contraption had only some wires poking out of my backpack connected to a toggle switch. I had rigged the thing up in haste that morning after a particularly hostile exchange with my wife. She had hurled her latest volley of insults and threats in our rapidly deteriorating marriage. The condition of our marriage was entirely my fault and I take complete blame. I should have known that I was on the road to unhappiness when this journey began, but I stayed on the stupid road against all of my better judgment and now the car was in the ditch, hopelessly sunk into the mud.

This woman I married is named Margie. Margie was not the first girl I ever fell in love with, but she was the one who was willing to marry me. It was a mistake and which was compounded a few years later by the birth of a child. We were not the perfect family, not the kind of family you see in the fairy-tale romances. But who really is? It was obvious that I married in order to not be alone and that she had married for some other reason. I never could keep ahead of her spending; no matter how many hours I worked or how big my raise, it was futility. She had to have everything and she had to have it yesterday. I resented this, but I held my tongue… at first.

Then there was the jealousy. Lord have mercy, I should have bailed on that marriage when I first was accused of sleeping with some woman who was a mild acquaintance at best. Here's a little hint for all of you people who think marriage is in your future: don't try to change your mates. First of all, they will resent it, and second of all, they won't change, unless the desire for change is punctuated with accusations. If you accuse your spouse of cheating on a regular basis, then don't be surprised that they eventually are doing exactly that. This is the old self-fulfilling prophecy; call someone a dirty dog long enough and pretty soon, it will be how they define themselves. The easiest thing for me to do was to acquiesce and start cheating.

My philandering ways were entirely my decision and my responsibility. However, I was unhappy, no defense, but unhappy people look for any port in a storm. In my case, my frequent travels provided ample opportunities for these indulgences. After a dozen or so years of being accused of being that dirty dog, I took the plunge. It was fun, it was anonymous, and it felt like complete liberation. Unfortunately for me, I felt guilty for having used this person and not telling her anything about me or learning anything about her. Again I was supplying my own misery.

My next fling turned out to be Isabel. She was in a worse marriage than me and we were quickly best friends and confidants. Soon we were lovers and intense lovers at that. Unfortunately, Isabel was quite needy and quite flirtatious. I found myself in many scrapes at many bars involving guys who had the wrong idea. I got my ass kicked once or twice, but mostly the guys backed down. Isabel seemed to get off on this. This was trouble and I knew it. It was the worst kind of trouble, but back to my wife.

On the morning of my little counseling session, I knew it was coming. Actually, I hoped to get up the courage to just quit. My wife made the morning worse because she had taken a phone call from some girl named Naomi. Yes, that Naomi. The girl was infatuated with me or something and now I had another thorn in my side. My wife was going to have me fired for abusing her and for stealing from work and for this and that. She had a whole routine worked up by now. It was a litany of supposed sins against humanity that I had committed. I was by now completely tired of this nonsense, so on the way to the car I opened the trunk remotely. Once there, I opened my toolbox and selected a nice looking toggle switch with a couple of wires attached and threw it in my back pack. I had no real plan, but there was some sinister part of my brain which told me that I had had enough.

So my "bomb" was sitting on my desk shortly after I arrived for work that morning, with the wires and the switch sitting out for the entire world to see. But the world didn't notice, and neither did Lenny, who was across the room with his head down on the work bench. He was sleeping while I was in my little counseling session. I slammed the door as I entered the room. He sat up startled and looked towards me with fear in his eyes that faded once he realized that I could not get him in real trouble. He put his head back down.

It was this singular gesture of contempt towards my importance which was that metaphorical leaf that collapsed that metaphorical bridge. I stood staring for a moment. I looked back at that sad pathetic brother-in-law-user named Lenny. As all of the accumulated stress took a toll on my foundation, I made a list of those who might come to my rescue. The list wasn't very long:

1. My daughter.
2. Dr. Marlin.
End of list.

I walked over to where the detestable Lenny sat. I grabbed a shock of hair on the back of his head. I pulled back on his head. As he took his hands from the metal bench to reach for whom or what had him by the hair, he uttered, "What the...?" In an instant I slammed his head forward with all of the force I could muster.

Bam!

I let go and Lenny kind of limply slid to the floor defenseless and barely conscious. I helped him to his chair and wrapped silver duct tape around his body to keep his arms at his side and then taped him to the back of the chair. After taping his mouth shut, I duct-taped my backpack "bomb" to him.

I sat back to admire my work as Lenny regained consciousness. As he awoke, we were still the only two people in the lab. Lenny looked at me with terror at first. I was sitting across the room with my feet up on my desk. I had taken all of his cigarettes out of the package and I was removing the tobacco from each and piling it high on a piece of paper. When Lenny started to struggle, he gained my attention. I looked up and smiled to him.

"Sorry Lenny, I hope you aren't brain damaged or anything, I needed a hostage."

Lenny said something under the duct tape and appeared angry. I got up and walked over to where he sat.

"Don't struggle too much; the bomb in your lap might be a little volatile."

He stopped struggling.

Up until this point, I had no plan, but the fact that nobody had come into the room for over an hour had allowed me time to formulate some kind of plan. I finally acted: I walked over and locked the door and made a call to Del's office. Del didn't answer. I hung up. I called the receptionist at the front desk.

"Sunrise Enterprises! How may I direct your call?" Came the cheerful reply from Anita, the perky mid-forties blonde on her third marriage.

"Hi, Anita…" I paused at a loss for my next words. I thought about how many people would be freaked out by my little situation.

"Hello? Is this Clyde?" replied her perky voice over the phone.

"Yes, this is Clyde. Umm, I am going to have to ask you to calmly ask everyone to clear the building."

"I beg your pardon?" she was confused.

"Anita, I am afraid there is a situation back here in my lab which may cause danger to everyone."

"Oh dear!" she said. "Should I call the fire department?"

"Yes!" I said without thinking. "And, and…, could you find Del for me?"

"Del is at lunch, it is 11:45," she reminded me. "I could call his phone."

"No Anita, I will call him, just clear the building and call the fire…" the fire alarm began to sound and I knew from drills that the fire department would be on the way and the building would be cleared. I hung up. Looking over at Lenny, I shrugged. "Just you and me, Len."

There was more to my Manifesto of Misery:

Happiness to us misery-seekers is a foreign concept. We have a certain idea of happiness that is defined by what seems to make others happy. There are the standard components for happiness that exist in the perfect world; a happy marriage, three kids, a picket fence, financial security, a nice car, a cool vacation home. Swell stuff for everybody to aspire to. Unfortunately for us misery-seekers, we only pretend to want these things. Whenever these things appear within reach, we find a way to prevent their realization. Sometimes we don't even get close to the realization because we have caused these things to be unreachable with our original set of choices. We make wrong choices right from the start.

We will spend all of our time explaining why we won't be able to get to that ultimate reward. "If had just chosen to go to business school, I would be set up by now." Or "If I had not married this person, I could have pursued my goals full time." It is all a ruse fortified with false information. In reality, those choices were made by someone who will never be happy unless they are miserable. Misery requires lowered expectations while pretending to aspire to something grand.

The problem with my little manifesto was that it was my attempt to explain my neurosis before it became complete insanity. I was building walls of logic where I could neatly encapsulate what my mind was really going through. It was a cry for help and I didn't know if anyone was listening. I hoped that Dr. Marlin was not too busy with other patients. I hoped he had time for my situation. Maybe he just had me write this stuff out because he was lazy. Maybe he was writing a book about loons and he needed material. All of my cynicism was working on this one. Cynicism is another tool of the misery-seeker. I decided to give Dr. Marlin a call.

"Dr. Whipple's office," A sweet female voice answered.

"Yes, could I speak to Dr. Whipple?" I asked. "This is one of his patients."

"Dr. Whipple is with another patient sir. Could I have your name so he could call you back?"

"Aaah, it's kind of an emergency," I reply.

"Could you describe the nature of the emergency? The doctor is very busy."

"Well," I paused and looked across the room at Lenny. "I have taken a hostage."

"I see," was the reply from a surprisingly calm voice. "Please hold."

The faint noise of fire engine sirens was starting to get louder.

"This is Dr. Whipple," the new voice on the phone said. "Whom am I speaking to?"

"This is Clyde Barrow, Dr. Marlin, I am afraid that I have complicated my life a little bit," I said in one of the world's greatest understatements.

"I see," said the doctor calmly. This was one calm office. Crisis management was their shtick, I guess.

"Clyde, have you hurt anybody?"

"Well, I taped a guy to a chair. But it's just Lenny. Oh, and I taped a bomb to him."

"A bomb?" he asked with a little bit of his calmness gone. This was more like the excitement I wished from him.

"Is it a real bomb?" Dr. Marlin asked.

"Not really, but nobody knows that."

"Did anyone call the police?

"I don't know, but fire trucks are here."

"Well, just untie this poor fellow and maybe you can come over to my office and we can talk."

"Umm, sure, be right over," I said with immense sarcasm.

As soon as those words were out of my mouth, there was a knock at the door.

"Is everybody alright in there?" shouted a loud professional-sounding voice from the hallway on the other side of that door. I hung up the phone and walked to the door. I unlocked the door and opened it to reveal a fireman in full fire-fighting gear.

"Are you…?" he asked. But before he could finish, I was past him and running down the hall towards the exit. I had to get the hell out of there. I burst out of the front door by the main parking lot where all of my fellow employees had gathered. I stopped running as I reached Anita. She had a quizzical look on her face and her mouth opened. She was about to ask me a question when Del stepped in front of her. He had just returned from lunch.

"Clyde? What the fu…" He stopped talking as my fist hit him flush under his left eye and he crumpled to the ground. I had now officially burned my bridge with Sunrise Enterprises.

I walked briskly to my car as some 30-plus employees and several firefighters looked on. I opened the door to my car.

I yelled, "Good day great people, it was great working with you!"

I climbed inside. I drove slowly away. Perhaps I was waiting for these people to find Lenny and call the cops. Deep down perhaps I wanted to get caught. I drove right over to Dr. Marlin's office.

I walked into his front door and I was headed straight for his office until I was accosted by the good doctor's young receptionist named Melissa.

"Good afternoon," she said. "May I help you?"

"Yes," I said. "Melissa, you remember me, Mr. Barrow?"

Melissa stood up when she realized what my visit was all about.

"Please have a seat, Mr. Barrow," she said and walked briskly to the doctor's office and closed the door behind her.

In a second, she opened the door and walked back behind her desk. "Dr. Whipple will see you now," she said while her eyes studied me.

I thanked her and walked calmly, almost relieved, into Dr. Marlin's office and turned around to see Melissa carefully studying me. I smiled and closed the door.

"Hello Clyde," he said from behind reading glasses perched on the end of his nose. He sat up from behind his desk and pulled the glasses until they fell away on the neck cord he wore. "Did you let your hostage go?"

"Sort of," I said as I sat down on the therapy sofa. "The firemen have found him by now."

"Do you want to tell me what happened?"

"I snapped, I guess." I looked over at what he was reading. It was my Manifesto of Misery. The pages had the dog-eared look of something that had been read frequently. "I think I'm going to jail for a while."

"We'll see." He said and he paused and began to read:

Humans have all the logic and reason and we use it to rationalize our own selfishness and to exaggerate our own importance. I have boiled the human condition down to that one sentence. In fact, that has been my sentiment all along. I only fairly recently found the right words to express the sentiment succinctly. Pretense is not purely a human game.

Animals in the wild are frequently deceptive. But for animals, the objective is mere survival.

Humans practice deception towards ends that they themselves cannot clearly define. Having things just to have them is purely human. Though all humans are capable of greatness, almost all shun and even ridicule those who aspire to greatness. So miserable people rule, though they themselves would not call themselves miserable. Some of them are probably quite content. But keeping that control, maintaining that power is what drives them. Their misery is in the fear of not being on top.

"My words sound better when you read them," I interrupted.

"They will sound better at your trial," he said as he chuckled.

"Do you have a lawyer?" Dr. Marlin asked.

"Do you know a good one? I asked. "One who specializes in loons?"

He reached for his rolodex.

CHAPTER 5 – JAIL

The police were waiting for me when I got home. I surrendered without a struggle. I drove my car right into my garage, left the keys in the ignition and got out of the car with my hands on the back of my head. Four policemen, each with a gun drawn and all walking towards me, asked me to get on the ground and to spread my arms and legs. I obliged.

Only after I obliged did I notice the helicopter for Channel 8 circling above. I was famous; after the drive to the jailhouse I was escorted out in front of six television news cameras and about a hundred microphones. I was infamous; I was the story of the day. My face was going to be instantly sent around the word to grandmothers watching the evening news in Spokane, Washington, to a 12 year-old girl on the internet in Topeka, Kansas, to everyone. I was The Fake

Back Pack Bomb Guy. I would soon be the subject of office humor and talk show hosts' monologues. My life, my experience, my psychosis was fodder for the gristmill of cynicism that rules the empty lives of self-absorbed dimwits. I was a clown, a fool, and laughingstock. All of this ran through my mind during the first few steps from that police cruiser. My bail hearing was scheduled for the next morning. I would have to spend the night in jail.

So they photographed me and took my fingerprints, all very impersonal and professional. If I had been in the mood for it I would have joked with my jailers, but a creeping sense of uncertainty was overtaking my mind. Maybe I was nuts. Maybe I should be locked up. I felt like I wanted to hurt somebody sometimes. But everybody has these feelings, don't they?

The mug shot that was taken of me was leaked by someone at the jail and was up on the internet within hours. There was nothing remarkable about my mug shot. It was not shameful or boasting, just a confident calm look. Maybe the coldness of my expression set people off, but for whatever reason people responded to it and I began to get fan mail. Crazy world.

That night I shared a cell with a few drunks and a couple of spouse beaters. Not one of these guys bothered to ask me what I was in for. We did get a deck of cards from the guard. A guy named Gus, who had a bleeding lip, taught me about 15 new games of poker. We played for IOUs and we stayed up all night. Most of the other unfortunates in my cell drifted in and out of the game, but Gus and I played all night. I guess both of us didn't trust anyone enough to close our eyes. We exchanged phone numbers and around 8:45 a.m. the guards came and took me to the courtroom.

I spent exactly one night in jail. Inexplicably, my wife made my $100,000 bail by putting up our house as collateral. This put me in an odd position; on the one hand, she hated me and my philandering ways, on the other, she respected me and my way with our child and my constant hard work. It was odd to feel obliged to her and maybe I should have just gone back to her and begged her forgiveness. This would have been the rational thing to do. But I wasn't sane. The part of my brain which should have seen this logic had long succumbed to the misery-obsessed part and there was no turning back.

****

I did go home, but I slept on the sleeper sofa downstairs with no sheet and a rough wool blanket, and I hate wool. I itched and slept sporadically. I wanted to be alone and I wanted to suffer. I didn't want it to last, but the discomfort made me feel real again. My temporary insanity had taken me on a ride into a world disconnected from all I had done. I had to come down. I had to take stock. The world of pretend had to take a back seat to my real troubles. I woke up late and my wife ignored me completely. Margie had an appointment of some sort to go to, but it didn't matter, because I didn't want to face her.

It turns out that Margie was seeing a divorce lawyer that morning and I got those papers the next day- special delivery, certified mail- I had to move out. The papers written by the law firm of Dockett, Crockett, & Platt, cited adultery, alienation of affections, and criminal activity. Score three for their side. I was guilty on all counts. As I sat staring at the paper I thought about my daughter. I had been calling her since I got my cell phone back from the jail property officer. She hadn't answered then and she continued to not answer. She was all I cared about, but she had probably gone into hiding after hearing about me. While I was packing to move out, the mail came. In the mail were my termination papers from my job.

Dear Mr. Barrow,

This letter is to notify you of your termination from your present position at Sunrise Enterprises for the following reason(s):

1. Insubordination

2. Harassment of fellow employees

3. Violence against employees

Enclosed is your severance pay of one month's salary minus taxes. You and your dependents will be carried on all health and dental plans for the next six (6) months. Due to the nature of this

termination, you will not be eligible for unemployment compensation. Please come to the office at your earliest convenience to retrieve your personal property.

Sincerely,
John P. Stimple
Human Resources Director

I walked from the mailbox while reading this letter and finished while walking up the stairs of the front porch. The termination letter slipped from my hand and landed next to the divorce papers on the front porch table. Leaning on my luggage, I stared at the letters and sighed. I looked around at the home I had built fifteen years previously. I looked at the papers which spelled the end of my twenty-year marriage adjacent to the papers which ended my seventeen year stint at Sunrise Enterprises. I tried to muster up some sadness or anger or some emotion that other people feel. I could only muster numbness and detachment. It was as if I had worked through the five stages of grief a long time ago and had moved on.

It was time to move on physically too; I needed someplace to stay. I called Isabel, but she didn't answer. I left a message, "Hi sweetheart, I might need to crash on your sofa for a couple of nights until I can get someplace to live. Please call me back."

I knew she wouldn't call me back, since she had probably heard about me or saw me on the news. I had always been there for her. In the darkest night and in her worst moods I had listened and comforted. Now I needed her and she was taking a pass. I finally felt something and it was betrayal. I didn't feel this about my wife and I didn't feel this about my boss, or even my daughter. Isabel was just like the rest when I thought she was different. My cynicism was fed further when I called Priscilla. At least she answered.

"Hello Clyde," came a slightly less than sweet voice on the phone.

"Hi Doll," I said in my gangster voice. "We needs to make a break for it. I need a paatna in crime. Are ya wit me?"

A long pause ensued.

"Clyde. Are you okay?"

"Well, I flipped out, got fired, my wife filed for divorce, and I have to leave my house. Other than that...,"

"I wish I could help..." The sentence just dangled there as is if she was powerless to do anything.

"I DO need a place to crash for a couple of...,"

"I can't," she interrupted. "I have clients and they...,"

I hung up. I didn't need to hear the rest. My cynicism, which I had nurtured for all of these years, had finally bore fruit. The people who had relied on me no longer thought of me as useful. Real friends and real connections really never existed. Everyone else I knew, friends, and family, lived far away. Everything was over; the job, the marriage, the house, the friendships, and my pretense of being even slightly important to anyone. I should have slipped further into some kind of depression or paranoia, but I was numb. Even the feeling of betrayal was beginning to fade. I had enough sense to take stock and examine my options.

I had a pre-trial hearing in 10 days. I had to talk to the lawyer that Dr. Marlin had arranged. I had to find a place to live. I had my savings account, my car, and the severance check. I decided that some kind of hold would be put on my savings, so I decided to go to the bank and see how much I could withdraw. I had to have a place to live and needed some cash. At the bank I was allowed to withdraw $3,000 and allowed to put the rest into short-term low interest investments. Apparently someone had put some kind of limit on what I could withdraw; it appears that I was a flight-risk.

So I passed the next 10 days in a hotel. I had accumulated some free hotel nights over the years of travel and I was glad of that. I finally talked to my daughter on day three in the hotel. She called and wanted to know how this affected her college plans. I told her that I had no income and my legal bills were going to be huge, but she could have all of the money I had left in the bank once there was a way to get to it. She was crying the whole time and I probably should have cried too, but the numbness was still there. It was a cold realization that I was a mere object of financial support to some people, emotional support to some, and perhaps sexual gratification to others. I accepted these as facts years ago and was not surprised by it. On the contrary, I was at ease in feeling completely right.

I was vindicated.

Misery was the great comfort in those days. I didn't even drink nor do drugs to alleviate the suffering. I just wallowed in my misery. I stared at my face in the hotel mirror for long periods, perhaps hours. I looked at my phone and read old text messages from various lovers. They all made me smile now, a big broad ironic smile that I would stare at in that mirror. These messages were all lies.

January 9, 3:26 PM from Isabel:

I dont no wat i wud do without u luv u ☺

February 3, 1:14 AM from Priscilla:

Hey stud u left ur umbrella here. Hope u dont get 2 wet, luv u<3

I would read them and laugh and look at myself in the mirror. I didn't drink, but I ate well and often. Perhaps I was thinking that they wouldn't lock up a fat guy. The hotel had a free breakfast buffet. I ate as much of it as I could every morning. When they started to take the food from the buffet, I would grab a plate, pile it up high with what was left, and take it to my room. For dinner, I would go to all-you-can-eat buffets and do just that. In those ten days, I probably gained 30 pounds and none of my clothes fit except my workout clothes so I stopped wearing anything else. My mirror-staring ritual revealed a fat pathetic loser who didn't care. I gave myself over to whatever fate awaited me.

CHAPTER 6 – THE SELF-DENIAL PRETENSE

The descent into madness was accompanied by visits to Dr. Marlin. He was like my buddy and he loved reading my little manifesto. It made him feel like he was really in my mind, I guess. In the ten days of my stay at the hotel, I visited Dr. Marlin five times. In each session, he would dissect my written words and try to decide what it was that made me tick. It was proving to be quite annoying. But I had to indulge him; he was my ticket to getting out of this mess without prison time. He was my star witness, my only witness.

"Tell me about the women in your life," he said to open my next to last session before my hearing.

"Well," I started, "Naomi still calls me all of the time. She really is sweet, but she's younger, you know"

"Younger?" he interrupted.

"Yeah, I have about 20 years on her," I continued. "She started as a one-night stand, but she seems to want to understand me. Funny, I just took her to be a bimbo."

"How do you mean?" Dr. Marlin asked.

"Well, she slept with Lenny, and then jumped right in with me. I even asked her about it.

She just said Lenny had some good weed and that she regretted meeting him. I told her that made two of us. We laughed."

"Why do you think Naomi is still around?" The doctor asked.

"I asked her that also. She said that I rocked her world, her words. But she appreciated that I listened to her feelings and thoughts. I treated her like a fellow human being and not a piece of ass."

"Does she know about your troubles?" asked the doctor.

"She knows all about them, and she said she would stick by me through my prison sentence. I am not sure what that meant. Maybe she's one of those chicks who gets turned on by convicts or something."

I paused as the doctor began to write furiously.

I continued, "She'll forget about me in a month if I get locked up. Women like sex and they like to be held especially. I can provide neither."

"We shall see, Clyde," Dr. Marlin said as he looked from his notes with his reading glasses resting on the end of his nose. "I want you to write something for me."

"More writing, doc?" I asked. "Are you getting bored with my manifesto?"

"No Clyde, I want you to add to it. I made a copy of it so you can reference it." He handed me the pages. "You promised me some tenets of the misery-seeker."

"Indeed I did," I said as I took the pages. "Does this conclude our session?"

"No, it doesn't, not quite. You haven't told me of the other women in your life."

So I told him of my wife and our complete emotional disconnect and the way she bailed me out when I didn't expect or ask for it. I talked about my daughter and how she was going to have to quit after next semester or work three jobs to stay in school. I talked about how Isabel was just using me as rest stop and how Priscilla was just as superficial as I feared she was. My major disappointment in both of them was what I expected all along. This was a result of my cynicism; one of my tenets of the misery-seeker.

The Tenets of the Misery Seeker

1. Cynicism- Good things are never what they appear to be

2. Happiness cannot last

3. Never do things that are expected of you

4. Find something wrong with every situation, then dwell on it

5. Try to please everyone even though you know it is impossible

6. The self-denial pretense- Try to be a super hero who disdains the accolades, but then feel as if you should get accolade

7. Despair over others' happiness

8. Despair over others' unhappiness

9. Despair over virtually everything

I stopped at nine tenets. It seemed proper to leave the good doctor wanting for more. I could have added perhaps twenty more items, but it seemed to me that I was just writing his next thesis for him and he would get published in the *Journal of Psychiatry* or some such trade periodical and I would just be Subject A. I also felt that there was little else to add to this list other than variations on the original nine.

So during my last pre-hearing visit, I presented Dr. Marlin with my list and watched him chew on it. He made several notes in his little book as he read my simple little list. He then looked up from those reading glasses perched on his nose.

"Why nine?" He asked.

"You need more?" I replied.

"No," he paused, "I just wonder why there are nine instead of a nice round number like ten."

I smiled and grabbed the list from his hand. I wrote on big block letters on the neatly typed paper,

10. THE REFUSAL TO CONFORM TO THE ORDER OF THINGS!

I handed the paper back. He read it and sighed. It was hard to make Dr. Marlin laugh, but I did detect a faint smirk.

"Clyde," he continued, "have you been taking the drugs I prescribe?"

"I don't need them," I said. "They make me sick and feel like another person trying to be accepted. I gave up trying to be accepted a long time ago. I only seek acceptance so I can refuse it. Haven't you been reading my manifesto?"

"Yes, of course," he said as he finally removed the glasses, "But if the court knows you are being treated they may be lenient."

"I am being treated," I insisted. "I spout off to you and it makes me feel better. Some drug you give me is only masking my inner beauty." At this he even smiled.

"Yes, but you want to be cured…"

"Cured?" I interrupted. "What does that mean? Have you ever cured anybody?"

I had him and he knew it. It all played nicely into my theory of the medical and mental health profession: They seek no real cures and keep you coming back to fill their pockets. A racket… if you please. Dr. Marlin knew my feelings well on the subject and he was not in the mood for another lecture.

"I can only keep you out of prison if you let me help you." He put his stupid glasses back on his nose and reached for the prescription pad.

"I am prescribing you Thorazine," he said as he scribbled his doctor-scratch indecipherable jargon on the pad.

I stood up and walked behind his desk to the bookcase where I picked up a volume entitled *Prescription Drugs: A Doctor's Guide.* I thumbed through it to the T's and found what I was looking for. I read out loud.

"Thorazine or Chlorpromazine is used to treat the symptoms of schizophrenia." I paused and looked up. "Schizophrenia?" I raised my right eyebrow.

"There's more, I am sure," Dr. Marlin replied.

"So there is," I continued reading. "Schizophrenia- a mental illness that causes disturbed or unusual thinking, loss of interest in life, and strong or inappropriate emotions." I looked up again, "Doc, I think you may be onto something."

I continued. "Thorazine is used to treat other psychotic disorders including conditions that cause difficulty telling the difference between things or ideas that are real and things or ideas that are not real. Also used to treat the symptoms of mania in people who have bipolar disorder."

I closed the book. "It looks like you are covering your bases," I said. "If this doesn't work then it's leeches, right?" I got another smile.

"Clyde," he stood up and let his glasses slide down on the necklace that dangled on the front of his sweater-vest. In the same motion he handed me the note pad page. "Take these and we will see where you stand in thirty days."

I grabbed the paper and stuffed it haphazardly into the front pocket of my jeans. Just like a crazy person would. I left the office and drove right over to the pharmacy in my car which I could no longer afford and had the prescription filled. I drove back to my hotel and took one pill as instructed. I went to sleep almost immediately and woke up 12 hours later at 4:45 in the morning.

It was the day of my hearing.

CHAPTER 7 – THE HEARING

I had met with the lawyer that Dr. Marlin suggested for me. His name was Elvin Williams. Mr. Williams was a smallish man, about 5-feet 7-inches 130 pounds. He spoke with a lot of certainty like a religious huckster from the south. Three days before my hearing I finally got a chance to talk to him. Since he was working pro-bono, I had to wait. I walked into his mahogany office and found him sitting on the edge of his desk with his feet dangling inside of some slick grey rattlesnake skin cowboy boots. He wore one of those bolo ties and he was dressed in a sky blue suit. He looked like he was waiting for his daddy to get back to the office. My mind immediately said to me, *you have got to be kidding*! I stuck out my hand.

"Howdy, ya must be Clyde." He shook my hand vigorously for what seemed like a minute as he grinned and looked into my eyes. I retrieved my hand. "My name is Elvin, but you can call me Tex or Mr. Williams."

"Hello, Mr. Williams," I finally decided to call him.

"Call me Elvin, I was kidding about Tex," he laughed a little.

It was at that point where I decided that ALL I would ever call him would be Tex.

"Clyde," he said. "We are going to plead temporary insanity. Then the judge will set a trial date and we will work on getting your head straight and getting you on the right path."

"So... so what do I do at the hearing?" I asked.

"You just sit there and look contrite," he said. 'You have committed a crime that you don't quite remember and you are quite remorseful. You are seeking help and have sought help in the past. The company you worked for is quite aware of this. They are complicit in this also. But we will save that for the trial, Clyde."

"When will there be a trial?" I insisted.

"Well, I would say two to four months. The witnesses are established, the time and date. All that needs to be cleared up is the degree of guilt." He scooted off the desk he was sitting on and walked towards the door.

"And we want to prove that I am not guilty because I am crazy?" I asked as he motioned me out the door.

"Essentially, Clyde," he said while he slowly closed the door. "Now if you excuse me, I have a class action lawsuit meeting. I am suing a drug company." He closed the door. I stood there and peered out the front window of his little mini-mall office as the sun came blazing through the open blinds. I fished in my pocket for my sunglasses and put them on the end of my nose just like Dr. Marlin and his reading glasses. I looked to my left where the receptionist sat. She smiled and I smiled back. I walked over to her desk, grabbed a pen out of the pen holder and wrote my number down on the enormous desk calendar.

I looked up at her over the top of the glasses and said, "You can call this number to reach me at any time. But don't forget that I am crazy." I pushed the glasses back on my face and left the office.

****

Three days later I was awake early after my record-setting Thorazine-induced slumber. I was not wide awake and I don't think anybody who saw me that day would call me wide awake. I got up from my hotel bed and stumbled across the carpeted floor into the bathroom and looked at my face in the mirror. I looked like a red-eyed basset hound: big bags and my painful eyes alerting all as to my general condition. My condition was that of a half stupor. I just needed to throw up and get back to sleep. Neither one of those things happened. In spite of my best efforts, my stomach did not produce anything of substance. All I did was cause my guts to churn and my head to hurt even more.

I then tried to take this pounding aching head back to bed with my big droopy red eyes. The best I could do was to remain motionless, but sleep never came. I lay there until around eight o'clock. I got up and put on my best business suit which was still in the plastic from the cleaners. I looked like a well-dressed basset hound by the time I finished tying my tie. I went down to the hotel lobby to see about getting breakfast, but found that I had no appetite. Everyone who passed by me on my way out of the hotel gave me looks that ranged from wonderment to fascination to revulsion. I did grab a cup of lobby coffee on my way out and took a small sip. It was only at this time I was able to accomplish what I had failed at earlier; I threw up… right behind my car in the hotel parking lot. More looks from passers-by, this time all of them were revulsion.

After my little incident, I climbed into my car and drove to the courthouse. On my way there, I became quite hungry. This was too bad because I was already running late. My hearing was scheduled for nine o'clock and I was flying through traffic desperate to be on time. As I pulled into a parking space, I glanced at myself in the rear-view mirror. I looked horrible; skin yellow, bags still under the eyes, and eyes even redder, if that was possible. I sighed and gathered what was left of my half-numb wits and climbed out of my car.

I sort of half-ran to the courthouse and ran up the steps. There was no media this time. The hot story of a few days ago had died down. Fake Back Pack Bomb Guy had faded into legend and unless I did something else crazy, I would remain a footnote. I arrived at courtroom three and opened the door to reveal an almost empty room. A few spectators and some other folks and their lawyers sat in various pockets around the area. Some reporters were there to see what remained of me. I had nobody present to support me. This probably should have depressed me, but I was even more numb than usual. Only Dr. Marlin was there along with Tex, the short dime-store-cowboy lawyer. The prosecutor was a quite attractive brunette with her hair in a bun and wearing a smart gray business suit with a long gray skirt. She was actually a knockout; if I was even half of my normal self, I would have been angling to talk to her after the hearing.

But the Thorazine had taken some of what I had left of my personality and was reluctant to return it. I was about two minutes late. They went in alphabetical order by last name and there apparently weren't any A's; as they started with Barrow, Clyde. Every head in that courtroom turned as I entered. The pretty prosecutor shook her head and looked down. Almost everybody else looked disgusted or disappointed except my lawyer. Tex just sat with a stupid grin on his face as if he knew something that none of us knew. He didn't know shit; he was just an idiot. I just stood there and took it in.

My eyes eventually found their way to the judge. He was a middle-aged ordinary white-haired white guy who looked like he was born in those robes. He was looking out from behind some beady little black eyes and his face had a look of impatient consternation. This was not going to be fun at all.

"Are you Mr. Barrow?" The judge finally said.

"Huh?" I managed, as I realized that I had not spoken a word to anyone that morning. My voice barely worked.

"Yes, sir," I squeaked out in some voice I used to have when I was maybe fourteen.

"Have a seat Mr. Barrow," the judge motioned towards Tex, the grinning idiot.

I walked past the judgmental eyes of those people gathered for this occasion and I stumbled next to Tex who sat at this little table in the front row of seats. The beady-eyed judge stared at me the whole time as if he expected some kind of show. I considered doing a little tap dance for his amusement, but in my condition I could barely get my muscles to respond to the commands. I just slumped into my seat and tried to be invisible.

"Mr. Barrow, please rise," the judge commanded.

After sitting for all of two seconds, I stood up.

"Mr. Barrow, you have been charged with kidnapping, assault, reckless endangerment, and terrorism." He looked up and continued.

"Kidnapping carries a penalty of from 5 years to life and a fine up to $100,000. Assault carries a sentence of up to 10 years and $50,000. Reckless endangerment has a maximum sentence of 5 years and $25,000." He looked up again. "The terrorism is a federal charge and this is a municipal court. I just want to make you aware that those charges are pending at another court at another time. I also want you to be aware that a conviction for certain violent crimes in this state requires a minimum sentence of five years."

I looked at Tex for some sign that he was in control of something. He was in a half-grin and this inspired no confidence.

"Mr. Barrow, are you represented by counsel?"

My mouth began moving, but Tex spoke, "Sir, I am Mr. Barrow's attorney for these proceedings."

Good for you Tex, you can talk, I thought.

"How does the defendant plead?"

"Your honor," Tex replied, "we plead not guilty by reason of temporary insanity." He held up one of Dr. Marlin's files. "We earlier provided the court with Mr. Barrow's psychiatric records."

The judge nodded, "Indeed, quite fascinating. I did read them."

The judge folded his copy of the files and spoke, "Mr. Barrow, your trial date is set for October 3rd, which is roughly two months from now. Until that time, you will be confined to the state mental hospital for further observation."

It was at this point that I felt something. It was betrayal; dirty underhanded rotten unforgiveable betrayal. I wanted to squeeze the life out of Dr. Marlin and this stupid fucking lawyer he had set me up with. All I could manage was to go weak in the knees and collapse onto my bench seat. Tex sat down and whispered into my ear. "Relax, Clyde. This is the only way we can keep you out of prison."

"F-f-f-fuck you, Tex," I managed under my breath.

Tex backed away in disappointment. "You will thank me for this. You could get 50 years in some maximum security prison."

I just glared at him through my baggy red eyes. Two officers began to walk towards me. Behind them was THE proverbial man in the white suit and he was carrying what looked like a straitjacket. I thought of resisting the officers, but I was aware enough to recover with the thought that my insanity was supposed to be temporary. Perhaps they would see how normal I was in a few days and let me go home until the trial. They led me to a squad car, opened the back door and let me climb inside, no handcuffs or any restraint. The man in white climbed into his big van behind us. He followed as we pulled out of the rear of the courthouse parking lot and headed towards the interstate highway.

I looked out from the back window as my former life disappeared forever.

CHAPTER 8 – OBSERVATION

The state hospital was not far from Dr. Marlin's office. He followed me there and stayed with me as I checked in. I was in no mood to talk to this betrayer and con man. I kept my cool because I realized that choking my psychiatrist would lead to long incarceration. Instead I pretended that I didn't hear his words of advice.

"Clyde this was the best that could be done under the circumstances, blah, blah, blah, …" he counseled in his reassuring tone that disintegrated into blather.

I stared holes through him in response.

"This will keep you out of prison, Clyde," he said. Then he went on about the rules of visitation being more convenient for him. I looked away towards a long corridor that led to my future; a future of being poked with needles and fed with pills and interviewed by numbskulls, interrupted by periods of being completely ignored by everyone. My cynicism was being fed, and this was the kind of thing it gorged itself on, disappointment, disillusionment, and impending doom.

I was led away from Dr. Traitor and escorted to a private room by two large bald orderlies, one white and one black. Once in that room, I was stripped of my clothes and what remained of my dignity. I was issued a pair of boxer shorts with which to hide my shame and I was asked to sign a paper which declared that all of the contents of my pockets did indeed come out of my pockets and that, yes, I would like them back when declared non-insane. I was then handed some blue pajama-looking garb with the logo of the state hospital emblazoned over the left pocket. They were real comfortable PJs and I secretly hoped I could keep them when I left. I also got some real comfortable slippers to wear.

I was then taken to another room where a man stood behind a counter. The man looked down at my feet and then looked at his clipboard. He walked back to a back room for a few moments and reappeared with a contraption with lights and a lock. It was a monitoring bracelet; this I did not expect. He spoke to me.

"Mr. Barrow, you are being given a chance to be a trustee of this institution. This bracelet will sound an alarm if you go beyond 10 feet of the perimeter of the hospital grounds. You will be given one chance and one chance only; beyond that, you will be treated as a confined inpatient..."

I interrupted, "Did you say impatient?"

"No, sir," he smiled, "IN Patient, opposite of outpatient."

"I see, so that means that I have one chance to escape and get the hell out of here before this gadget gives me away."

"Sir, we would prefer if you just relax and treat this as an opportunity to get better."

This guy had an easy-going reassuring manner. I hated that. *Just be an asshole dude, because that's what you are to me; another asshole to cause me problems.* So Mr. Easy-Going snapped the monitor around my ankle and asked if it was too tight. I said it was fine. He told me that it was water tight and I could shower wearing it. I told him that I planned on showering several times a day to test that theory. The dude laughed at me again. I had a fan of my derisive sense of humor, swell for me.

Mr. Easy-Going turned me back over to the giant orderlies who led me to that long well-lit corridor. After passing perhaps three-dozen doors, they led me into what would be my room for the next couple of months. It had one bed, which was good, and a television inside of shatter-proof glass. The floor was soft and the room was warm. The biggest and ugliest orderly told me to push the red button next to my bed if I needed anything. He then left the room, closing the heavy steel door with a loud ominous slam.

I was alone and still hungry.

I pressed the red button by the bed. During the something like fifteen minutes before another large orderly came, I familiarized myself with my surroundings. I yelled "Hello," and heard no echo. I was in a padded room. I scanned the ceiling and spotted a small camera that was mounted conspicuously in the corner where a chunk of ceiling tile had been broken off. Not a professional job, I noted. I was being monitored. I could not reach the camera, as the ceiling was a good eight feet high. All of the furniture in the room had been nailed down, so moving something to stand on was not an option. I had a bed, a night table, a chair, a small table, and a dresser. I walked off the dimensions of the room and found it to be twelve feet by twelve feet. I also had a small bathroom with barely enough room to turn around. The bathroom had no door.

At this decidedly sad time in my life, I was not desperate; I was cold and calculating. It was as if I had always expected this. Isolation was not new to me, but this was an officially-sanctioned type of isolation. It was different, but I was ready. They would not break me. Cynicism is funny that way; if you practice it enough, it will bear fruit and you shall feel vindicated. A small victory for some, but to the cynic, it is a bittersweet irony that tastes like the blood at the back of your throat after a punch in the nose; awful to the unprepared, but a feeling that is almost welcome to the misery enthusiast.

In those fifteen minutes, I basked in the exquisite misery of that taste of bitter defeat and isolation. I was interrupted by another large bald orderly opening my door. I would have to learn to distinguish between these giant people by their name tags. This man's tag read "SIDNEY".

"You rang?" came the booming voice of this abnormally large human.

"Yes, I haven't eaten all day," I said. "Could I get something? Anything?"

The large orderly sighed. "I will see what I can scrape up," he said. He then closed the door with a heavy thud. In a minute, he was back with an egg salad sandwich wrapped in cellophane. He opened the door and walked over to where I sat on the edge of the bed and handed me the sandwich.

"Here," he said. "All they had. I am Sid." I took the sandwich from his catcher's-mitt-sized hands.

"Thanks, Sid. I'm Clyde."

He gestured towards the bathroom, "There's drinking cups in there for water. We can't give you anything else." With that he turned and left the room with that big heavy door slamming behind him. I sat and ate that stale sandwich like it was the manna of the gods. I ate slow and enjoyed every bite as if it was a thick ribeye steak for my last meal.

In a few minutes, Sid was back with a pill. It was a bright yellow pill, so I knew it was Thorazine. I took the pill eagerly, knowing that I would sleep for a long time. If I could sleep until the trial, it would be fantastic. I asked Sid if I could have another as soon as I woke up. He laughed and said that it depended on when I woke up. He left the room and soon I was asleep. As I slept, I dreamed.

****

In my dream I was little boy. I was that same withdrawn contemplating child that I was in real life. But in the dream, I could also see what others thought of me. My siblings were an open book in real life, so there was no revelation when I discovered that I was insignificant to them. I did discover that I was also a nuisance to them. I read the thoughts of my school mates and found out that they thought I was dirty and unpleasant. The girls whom I was interested in were repelled by me. Everyone I encountered in this dream had thoughts of my obvious inferiority. I was not shocked by this observation. In fact, it comforted me to a great extent to know that little was expected of me.

Every person I talked to had the same type of response; I would ask a question and get a passive answer followed by a comment about me personally; "How are you?" would get a response: "Fine, but I think that you are a filthy unsavory person." This was not a normal response to anyone in everyday conversation, but in my dream it was typical. In my dream it made so much sense. I would thank each of them for their honesty. There were people in this dream I had only met once and only casually; a person on an airplane or at a bus station. But they all felt the same about me.

I felt this was the key to my existence and the misery I believed that I needed. Maybe having my perceived shortcomings pointed out to me was required somehow. I wanted to be scorned, I wanted to be undesirable. Don't praise me, because you don't mean it. In summation: The ones who praise you are phonies and the ones who ridicule you are real, but not to be trusted; a cruel game of the mind that paints one into a corner. I had to write this down. I had to enter this into my Manifesto. But first I had to wake up.

* * * * * * * * * * *

Day two of my "observation" began around noon and it began rather groggily. I opened my eyes to my padded room with the not-quite-hidden cameras and tried to rise to my feet. I really had to urinate, but my brain had not alerted my feet that I was awake and my first step out of bed sent me to the floor where I slept for another few minutes.

I awoke to find myself being carried to the toilet by another large bald orderly. I felt like a baby and I really didn't like the feeling of helplessness. I struggled to get out of his control and he gave up and set me on my wobbly feet. He supported me as I walked the rest of the way to the bathroom where I did my business. When I was done, which was maybe three or four minutes, I asked the orderly if I could get some more Thorazine.

"No, Mr. Barrow, you have an appointment to see the doctor," he replied.

"I don't want to see Dr. Marlin anymore," I said with my eyes blinking and legs shaking as I walked back to my bed. "He betrayed me." I sat down.

"You will be seeing one of the staff psychiatrists today; Dr. Marlin is not on our staff."

"Look…" I paused to look at his name tag. "Look, Brad I don't want anything except to sleep. Short of that, I would like some paper and some pens. I have to finish my manifesto."

Brad looked at my chart and sighed. "You are not allowed sharp objects." He said.

"Because I am criminally insane?" I asked.

"Just a precaution."

"Is there a computer where I can write?"

"You can visit the library at some point."

"So when do I see the new brain doctor?"

"It says here that you have an appointment at 1 o'clock"

I had no reaction to this news. I just sat on the edge of the bed and stared at my feet. I was still quite dull-witted and was in no mood for any more conversation. Brad left and I just sat there until he returned with a wheelchair. I gladly accepted the ride since my wobbly legs and even more wobbly brain were not speaking the same language. We rode that chair to an elevator, where Brad hit button 3. On the third floor, he wheeled me to a dimly-lit room with a couch and a chair. In between the couch and chair was a small table with a lamp and vase with fake flowers. The decor itself may have been vibrant and new, but the lack of light made the room appear pastel and neutral. Being already groggy, this setting made me nearly comatose.

"You may sit where you like, Mr. Barrow," he said as he parked the wheelchair.

I got up and plopped down on the couch and lay down so I could drift off to sleep. This small journey, which required almost no real exertion, had left me exhausted. I slept until I was startled by a female voice. It was not from my dreams, so I stirred awake. I turned my head towards the sound and in my bleary-eyed state began to focus on a female form sitting in a chair. It took me several attempts at blinking to even make out her face. She was young; perhaps in her late twenties or early thirties. She had sharp green eyes and a nice smooth white complexion broken up by a small mole under her left eye. She was quite attractive and this definitely stirred my interest. In my groggy half-doze, I managed to say "H-h-h-ello..."

She smiled a little. "My name is Monica…," she paused as if to compose herself, "Dr. Caulder," she continued.

"Hi Monica," I said as I attempted to sit up. "I am pleased to meet you," I said as I eventually managed to stick out my hand.

She took my hand and said," I am here to begin your initial evaluation."

"I will save you the trouble Dr. Monica," I said. "I am completely sane and I am here for a vacation."

"I see," she paused and looked over her clipboard. "It says here that you are accused of kidnapping and terrorism."

"Don't believe everything you read," I said, trying to lighten things up some more. She didn't smile.

"I have extensive notes from Dr. Whipple," she said as she picked up a pack of papers that I could tell was my manifesto.

"Oh, that," I said, 'he's just going to have me locked up and then plagiarize my notes so he can make a fortune."

"You don't trust Dr. Whipple?"

"I don't trust anyone," I said as I lay back down. "Let the evaluation begin."

Dr. Monica pulled out a little digital audio recorder and pressed a button.

"Tell me about your childhood Clyde," she said.

I let it rip, telling her all of the tales of my self-imposed childhood exile, I told it all and it took quite a while and she interrupted frequently with questions where you would expect them and she was quite the professional. I really didn't mind opening up and sincerely wanted to be cured of whatever was wrong with me and I always was a sucker for a pretty face anyway. I hoped above all else that it would soften the ultimate punishment which was headed my way.

When I had finished with all of the unpleasant details of my sad childhood, I sat up and said, "So you see, I am completely normal and I should be allowed to go back to my normal life."

Monica smiled. "Clyde that is our ultimate goal."

For that brief flash while that smile was on her pretty face I felt something that must have been hope. It faded fast. After she concluded our session by pushing a button on the chair and standing up, I fell back into doldrums. When Brad arrived and opened the door to let her out, I felt worse. By the time I was escorted back to my lonely room, I was downright depressed. Even the fine meal of meatloaf and mashed potatoes didn't improve things. After the meal, I was given my medication and I drifted off to another long slumber; so ended day two.

CHAPTER 9 – MENDING FENCES

Days ran together for me in those two months. I had some activity, some exercise, I got to talk to Dr. Monica some more. I also talked to some other doctors, but none got me to talk like she did. Dr. Marlin got nothing out of me except stone silence. He had lost my trust and he had betrayed me. It was to Monica I would talk and really no one else got into my brain. In any event, I imagined she could play her recordings of the sessions for anyone and she could share the notes I gave her.

I confided in her about my new dreams. I wished to have them interpreted and I hoped I could find some way to sanity. I still was not trusted with a pen or pencil, just crayons. It was a silly rule in a silly world full of silly people looking after sillier people. A manifesto written in crayon deserves all of the derision is receives. So when the dreams were fresh in my mind, I asked for access to the library.

Then there were the puppet dreams; I was on a set of strings and someone was controlling me. All I could see above me was a giant smile; a big set of teeth between some big red lips. It was always a smile and The Big Smile was having me do some pretty strange things. I would sit down at a table with bread and peanut butter and jelly and make endless numbers of sandwiches. This was one entire dream; just me making those damned sandwiches over and over as The Big Smile smiled at me and pulled my strings. I was exhausted when I woke up and I was not hungry for a couple of days after that I couldn't stand even to hear about peanut butter, let alone eat it.

When I was awake enough to function after the PB & J dream, I hit the button and one of the large bald gentlemen escorted me to the library where there was an old computer with word processing capabilities. I went into painful detail about the dream hoping that the lovely Monica would help me out of the dark forest of my own mind. It was something like hope again and it was foolish to think this. I probably knew it at the time, but lying to myself had become my favorite coping mechanism.

`But the doctor I visited the next day was a balding older gentleman by the name of Dr. Smedley. He was another staff shrink, smelled of mothballs. My disappointment at not seeing Monica was probably very visible to the good doctor and he may have mistaken my mood for depression. I was depressed, but it didn't help that they were playing musical doctors with me.

"I see you have some notes for me," Dr. Smedley observed as he sat crossed-legged on the chair.

I sat, hunched forward and shuffled the latest installment of my manifesto and my notes on my vivid dreams, which I wished I had not printed. I was almost sure that the staff would just take it from the computer in any case, but this did not comfort me.

"I, I… I was going to give these to Mon…, Dr. Caulder. She asked for this," I heard my shaky voice and stopped.

"I will make sure that she gets them," he assured me. "Now get comfortable."

I handed him the papers and sat back on the couch. He grabbed the papers and paid no attention to them as he inserted them in a folder with big letters on the tab: C. BARROW. I lay down on the couch.

Dr. Smedley began where Dr. Monica had left off, which was my childhood tainted with my deep introspection. I was not quite open to this stranger as with Monica since I now suspected that they would replace him with someone else. I hoped that somebody would at least see that I was not crazy and that this whole thing was just a reaction to events. I hoped that my manifesto would convey the message that I was just like everybody else, except that I thought deeper than most. After the session, I went back to my room and took more medication. I think this was the end of my first week in captivity, but the days had begun to blur.

It became a comfortable routine for a while. I would wake from my Thorazine stupor, write about what I remembered of my dreams, and then eat. I would then gather my crayon notes and follow one of the orderlies to the library where I would transcribe my notes. Then I would visit the doctor of the day around noon time. They would then feed me and I would get a pill with my meal. Then I would get some outside yard time, weather permitting. I would snooze hard on these pills. I wouldn't usually eat the meal they brought in the evening because I was off in Dreamland. In this fashion, my pre-hearing girth was beginning to subside.

Dreamland was a wondrous mix of confusing symbols and people I didn't know. One feature that seemed to always be there was a particular voice. It was a female voice and it was unfamiliar, but she seemed to know me well. She seemed to know my nature. She was sometimes reassuring, sometimes critical, but the voice was always right and always confident. After a few of these dreams, I started looking forward to the voice. In one dream I was mending fences as I once did back on the farm. I used to help my mother and it was tiring and thankless work that seemed to never end.

The voice was there as I mended the fences, "This is humble work, Clyde." The voice said. "Work never ends. You learn more from work than from any book," the voice said.

It wasn't my mother's voice. It was a sweet voice, but firm and wise-sounding. It was reassuring and calm.

"Clyde, the world is a big place. But there is no room for selfishness. There is more to life than your selfish needs." She was always saying things like this. She was like a mentor I never had in real life, a mentor without a face.

In another dream I was climbing a tower. She was there to tell me to take things one step at a time so I didn't do something careless. She was there in the dream where I was driving my car. I was on a long drive to somewhere important, although the reason was unclear.

She kept saying, "Stay awake Clyde, it is important. You have to make it there." I drove on throughout that damn dream. I made it to the destination just to wake up.

Even my P B & J dream was accompanied by the voice, although less clear. I mostly remember the smiling puppeteer from that one. I talked to the various staff psychiatrists about these dreams and the voice. They all asked if the dreams existed before the Thorazine, and I had to admit that they didn't. They all took notes on the subject, but they didn't change my medication. I came to expect the dreams and even look forward to them. This whole imaginary world became my social life and the voice became my guide. The voice knew the better side of me and made it okay to struggle. I was a little boy in the dreams and that didn't really seem too bad. But the voice wanted me to be a man. The voice told me that there was more to the world besides me. When I talked to the doctors, they seemed to only want to know about me.

CHAPTER 10 – DIVORCE

One does not stay married to someone for a couple of decades without having some kind of attachment. I make no excuses for my philandering ways; I just didn't have the depth of feeling for the person I was married to. This happens all of the time, I am almost certain. Divorce rates bear this out. People make mistakes and sometimes those mistakes are compounded by children. This was the case with our marriage.

My wife may have had some depth of feeling, but I had no sense of this. To me it just felt like control. She had control of me at one time and I would hear her brag to her friends about how I was completely under her spell. I knew this to be not true and I did rebel against this type of mentality. At some point the child becomes the only reason to stay together and the one who pays the price for this obligation is the child. You stay together for the sake of the child, but to tell the child that fact is to risk causing him/her to feel guilty for making everybody unhappy. It is a big stew of misery and it fits right into that manifesto I kept adding to.

Sometime during my first month, my mail caught up to me. Included was my final divorce decree. It seems that divorces can be rushed through when one of the parties is locked up and suspected of being nuts. Good enough for the legal system. My wife was free from her bad marriage and she had control of all of the property. I was under suspicion, and would be under suspicion for the rest of my days.

Also in that pile of bills, credit card offers, magazines, and assorted junk, was the paperwork removing the lien on my house that was held by the bail bondsman. There was also a letter from my wife which contained no hint of feeling, no anger, no sadness, just facts and the settlement proposal. She was selling the house with 30% of the profits to go towards my legal defense. This was good news for the lawyers, but it didn't mean shit to me. I figured that I would appeal any decisions and hire a lawyer that wasn't free and wasn't recommended by that quack Dr. Marlin. If the money was not used for my legal defense, it would be used for my daughter's education. She did not detail what would happen with the other 70% of the profits.

Also in the mix of papers were two letters from Naomi. The first one was probably written before my little kidnapping episode. It was all about her life in Texas and how her father controlled her and she would like to get away. She told me she wanted to live where I live. She said that her family had money and she didn't have to work. She made jokes about sex with an older man and that she was tired of boys.

The second letter was written after my troubles began, well my legal troubles anyway. She began by saying that she thought I was set up and that she understood if I didn't write back. She asked if I needed money for a lawyer. The letter gave a brief glint of hope in a mostly hopeless situation. I also realized that she had no idea what she was talking about or what was really involved. I appreciated the loyalty, but I knew that it was based on good intentions, bad information, and wishful thinking. It reminded me of schoolgirl's letter to Santa Claus. The hope faded quickly.

I had by this time begun to write my little diatribes in crayon. I had to relieve my boredom somehow and if I had something good in my brain, then I needed to write it down. I could not wait for my turn in the library.

I also started to meet some of the other inmates. It must have appeared that I was no threat to other patients, because in a few days one of the tall bald orderlies, I think it was Brad, entered my room and said, "Good morning Mr. Barrow. It's social hour." I looked up from the crossword puzzle, put down my crayon, and followed Brad down the long corridor towards a door marked "LOUNGE". I was in one of my Thorazine dazes, which I normally was. But small sparkles of reality were starting to shine through to my brain. I was coming out of it. Good timing, Brad.

As Brad opened the swinging door and guided me in, I was greeted by the smell of coffee and cinnamon pastries. In a smallish, dimly-lit kitchen, four normal-looking men in pajamas similar to mine were sitting around a well-lit rectangular table and playing cards. I say normal-looking because none of them were presently drooling on themselves. I had no idea what occupied them when they were alone. But they seemed to be not too involved with their card game and more with their current argument. I took a seat in the chair at the opposite end of the table from them.

The argument revolved around car stereos. One man who was older, perhaps 70, was giving a detailed history of the car radio. He wore a pair of reading glasses and he had a round head with only small patches of hair on the sides. He talked with a sense of urgency. His name was Barney.

"You see the Motorola was the first car radio. Moto for motor and the rola part was just what they called everything I guess. You know the original phonograph was a Victrola by RCA…"

He was interrupted by Vic. "Yeah, but we are talking about quality of sound here," said Vic. "The Blaupunkt was the best system I ever had back in the seventies and I could get the babes with that sound quality."

Vic was hairy. He was one hairy dude. His arms and neck and just about everything else was covered in hair. I seemed that I could see the hair grow on his face as he talked. He had a New York/New

Jersey accent, I don't know which, but it didn't matter much. It seemed Bronx-ish perhaps.

Amos, the black man at the table, interjected, "I always had a Pioneer. It sounded good to me and I did alright with the ladies."

Amos had a Southern accent, perhaps Louisiana. He was probably mid-forties by the look of the tufts of grey hair which had appeared on his balding scalp. He was also very twitchy. He looked crazy. Shifty eyes, too; twitchy and shifty. I don't mind telling you that he made me nervous.

The fourth man in this little group, whose name was Alvin, spoke up. "My first good car stereo was a Kenwood," he said.

This man had an Australian accent and he was chomping on gum and he seemed to lose his accent occasionally as he talked. This made me think he was either faking it or he had begun to lose it after years in the States.

"My Kenwood did me alright, Mate," he said as he patted the older gentleman on the back. This made the orderlies stand up in a gesture intended to prevent any physical contact between the inmates.

Barney responded, "All I know is that I miss my Bose system in my Mercedes."

They all nodded and went back to the card game. I shifted my chair closer to the table and the screeching sound made everyone look towards me at once. I nodded. My meds had worn off sufficiently by this time for me to utter complete sentences.

"Hi, my name is Clyde," I smiled one of my crooked half-smiles and they ignored me and resumed the game.

I have no idea what game they were playing and maybe they didn't either because they just kept picking up cards off the top and discarding unwanted cards and placing impossible bets. Vic would bet the Eifel Tower, Barney would raise him the Great Wall of China, Amos would offer the Taj Mahal, and Alvin bet the crown jewels of England and they all folded. *Crazy people are crazy*, I thought.

Barney, as he gathered the cards, looked over his glasses at me, "Can we deal you in partner?" He asked with a kind of bounce in his voice.

"I would like to play, but all I have to wager is the Statue of Liberty," I deadpanned.

This was followed by howls of laughter from all present, including the orderlies. I had made instant friends. This did not fill me with any other feeling except relief. At least they weren't enemies.

We played some game I never quite understood for the rest of that hour and talked about the best cars, the best cities, the best cigars, the best steak; the best everything. Things we could no longer attain. Everybody, including me, avoided the topic of our own particular psychosis. When it was time to go back to my room I walked away with Big Ben, The Kremlin, The Golden Gate Bridge, The Pyramids, and several other treasures. I also had gained a sense of something else: belonging. I felt a kinship with these whackos.

This did not comfort me one single bit.

In the time between lawyer meetings and psycho-analysis sessions with various staff psychiatrists, I did get to meet with these gentlemen in my lucid moments. I had two months between being sent here and going to trial. My interactions with them helped to pass the time. I had to inquire about them indirectly through the large bald orderlies. My situation was dire and I had surrendered myself to the idea that I was thoroughly doomed to be locked up and alone for a long time. Maybe I just wanted to see what their prospects for sanity and freedom were when compared to mine.

I found out that Barney had been in World War II and then Korea as a pilot. I garnered some of this from his war stories that he would allude to occasionally, but he never seemed to go too much in depth. He would say, "I prefer brunettes to blondes, except Germans, but that's another war story." I learned that Barney was committed here by his daughter after he was arrested on the front lawn of her house in his boxer shorts, waving a lawn mower blade at the neighbors. The neighbors would not drop the charges of attempted assault unless the daughter had him committed. According to Sidney the orderly, it was the most tearful and sad scene when Barney's daughter dropped him off at the hospital.

Before the lawn mower blade incident, Barney had just missed his VA appointment where he could have gotten the right medication for his waning sanity. He had since been diagnosed with the beginning stages of dementia. He was at the local state-run metal facility because the VA hospital was too far for his daughter to visit regularly, and she did come regularly.

I was able to learn all of this from the orderlies. Everything else about Barney, I learned from Barney himself.

When Barney talked he would look you straight in the eye, and he would phrase things as if that information was filled with irony and wonderment. "Planes are easy to fly, you know," he would say as he slammed the deck of cards on the table and looked me straight in the eye. "Even takeoffs are easy, Claude," he loved getting people's names wrong. I think it made him feel superior or something. "But landing them on a moving ship is damn near impossible. I don't know how I did it." He would move his face closer to mine during this last bit. Barney didn't seem crazy to me. At least not any crazier than any other old pilot I had met.

Vic, the hairy guy, had once been muscle for some northeastern crime syndicate. He was the guy who would get people to pay their debts. He would shake down local merchants for protection money. He was a goon, if you will. To me, he just seemed like another troubled young man, but the orderlies told me that he was certifiably insane. He had killed people, they assured me, but they had no proof.

In my interactions with Vic, he displayed that clichéd false bravado of someone whose confidence was derived from how many people he could scare. He didn't scare me, not even one little bit. It always seemed to me like he was a lost little boy. Without clinical training, I couldn't really diagnose what his real issue was.

Vic was scared and that was apparent to me. He had been locked up here after he started threatening everyone he came in contact with. He apparently just woke up one day, grabbed his gun and started waving it in everybody's face. He threatened the mailman, he threatened his fellow thug friends, finally he threatened people at the grocery store and someone there called the cops. His mob lawyer convinced the judge that it was just stress, so he was locked up in this loony bin for 90 days.

Vic's little display of aggression seemed so much worse than mine, but I didn't have the connections to get such a light sentence. I was facing a lengthy stretch in the Graybar Hotel and Vic was in here, taking pills, and playing cards. His future employment was assured as long as he kept his bosses happy. I'm not sure if I fully resented Vic, but I do remember wishing that I was a scary killer type accustomed to getting his way. Though I was being treated that way by everyone I knew and the news media, it was far from the truth.

Vic, who may have killed or maimed dozens of people in his life (he didn't talk about these things), was anonymous to the world. He would go right back to what he was doing until the next time he snapped. I wasn't sure that there would be a next time, but even with my limited knowledge of psychosis, I could tell that 90 days here wasn't going to cure him.

Alvin, the guy with the fake Australian accent, was a classic schizophrenic. Australian guy was just part of his repertoire. I don't know if he or his doctors had names for any of his personalities, but it would have been a fun game to name them because he seemed to never be the same guy twice. I am not even sure that his name was Alvin; it may have been just the guy I met the first day. The guy I met that first day playing cards was considerate and interesting, both calm and positive. Even the fact that he was obviously faking that accent didn't bother anyone.

Every time I met up with Alvin, Barney, Amos, and Vic it was in the same setting and around the same time of day. My circumstances were always the same; I had just come back from a trip to Thorazine-land. I may have seemed the same to them every time, or they may not have even noticed. Alvin, though, was unpredictable. He was sometimes a petulant child who got mad when he lost and threw the cards or insisted on dealing every time.

Alvin's story was as hard to untangle as his many personalities were. He had spent so many years traveling that he may have developed these personalities as a defense mechanism for missing most of his children's lives. They grew up while he was gone and they never seemed to adjust to him when he was home. He may have compensated for this by becoming a different person every time. He may have been a different person in every city he traveled to just to protect his family life. Alvin was a roadie for several rock bands; one of those guys that showed up before the concert to set up and stayed after to tear down. He was gone for sometimes two months, sometimes six months; he was a stranger at home and eventually a stranger to everyone.

If I had to choose what kind of crazy to be, I would choose Alvin's way, since he seemed to have everyone guessing and it seemed like a game to him. I asked the orderlies how many sides of Alvin they had seen. The answers I got varied from a dozen, to fifty, to unlimited, so I decided not to count them and just enjoy the ride.

After all, I had my own problems.

One of Alvin's personalities tried to kill him. He was locked up in this happy place because he had stabbed himself over forty times with a screwdriver. I didn't know if the personality that performed this deed was ever in my presence. The truth is that I didn't want to know. I never approached my fellow patients about their particular madness and I didn't want them to approach me. If they were curious about me, they could just ask an orderly, like I did.

I did learn that Alvin's sickness had been under control for a while and it took over three years before they allowed him to interact regularly with the other patients. He was in his early fifties and he was also probably going to be institutionalized for the rest of his life.

The fact that he had no hope of freedom had no real effect on me personally. I didn't feel bad for him because I knew he was a potential menace out there if he missed his medication. I felt worse for myself because I was being lumped in with his type of person. It was unfair and I felt that I could become a pariah because of this association. These associations also bothered me because of my limited contact with the outside world. My visitors consisted of my lawyer, my shrink, and no one else.

Amos was from Mississippi; a little town somewhere around Biloxi and Gulfport and he grew up working on shrimp boats and oyster boats. His psychosis was not obvious, so again I had to dig. Amos was raised by his mother and a series of foster parents. He rarely saw his siblings and never saw his real father. A few of his stepfathers abused him to some extent. I don't want to add more to his story than I actually know; so I won't delve into those specifics, I just want to fill in what I was able to learn from the big bald orderlies.

Amos was probably in his mid-forties and he had those eyes that always seemed to be looking somewhere else. He was looking into the past or into the future, but it was never quite where I was. He would smile at things I said, but otherwise never respond to them directly. If I said, "Nice day today," he would say something like, "When I was a kid it rained five inches one day." It wasn't a direct response, but it was weather-related.

Life was hard for Amos and it was something he accepted long ago. From home to home, then back to mom and a boyfriend or husband who was typically a total stranger. I could only imagine. If I was capable of sadness at that time, I may have even cried for him, but I had come to accept misery as part of the human condition. People were miserable bastards; I knew this to the bone. It was accepted by me long ago. Others who hope that it will change are fooling themselves. Those idealistic buffoons who think that humanity is about to turn the corner where true happiness reigns and we accept each other… well they are just in for disappointment. I wasn't going to tell them all though. Let them find out the hard way like me.

But back to Amos, a victim of hope. Hope is a child's word. It is based on things coming together just right at the right time and going exactly right for a short period of time. This concept was revealed to me over and over through years of small victories that felt empty almost immediately. Amos and his hope depended on somebody actually giving a damn about a young man in a desperate situation.

Very rare are those people who reach out to the desperate. I am one of those people, but I am a misery addict and the snake oil I sell is false hope based on my expectation that you will accept my misery. Very few people will accept this bargain. The recipe for misery is like the recipe for chili; everybody's process is different. I will add a pinch of cumin where Amos would add molasses. Amos and I couldn't be more different and we became friends instantly. As doomed as we were, we would exchange horrible tasteless offensive jokes until we could think of no more.

So while these guys were not destined to be integral to the story of my life, they were my crew during the months I awaited trial. I was anxious and lonely and desperate for something in my life besides uncertainty. I was a vulnerable mess in a place and time that I was completely unprepared for. Nobody ever tells you about these kinds of situations because nobody knows about them. The only ones who know are considered crazy.

And nobody listens to crazy people.

CHAPTER 11 – UN-TETHERED

In between my card-playing escapades with my new-found friends, I attended therapy. Apparently, the higher-ups had decided that Dr. Monica was the best medicine for me. This was just about the best news I could have hoped for. I wanted to be cured and I wanted to open up to somebody, but I trusted no one. At least Monica was good to look at. I know this sounds superficial, and it is to a certain extent. However, if there is one thing that extracts my deep feelings it is a pretty face. I confess to being superficial in this way and I believe this admission makes me more genuine.

So Dr. Monica appeared one day in my usual therapy room. She was sitting on the chair cross-legged wearing a smart white blouse and a gray mid-length skirt. I paused as I entered the door with my orderly-escort. I smiled widely with genuine delight.

"Good morning, Dr. Monica!" I said with enthusiasm. "I was afraid that I had scared you off."

She looked over at me and she was all business. "Please take a seat Mr. Barrow," she said as she waved her hand towards the couch.

I noticed that she had my updated manifesto in her hand. I had added more to my volume while cooped up and it included my observations of others. I had decided that I was mentally distressed, but I was not sick. I was in a defendable position with regards to my misery addiction and that the stress existing in my life, while being a result of my personal choices, was largely external and that all people had this issue.

In my new writings, I included my informal interviews with orderlies, nurses, doctors, patients, janitors, and anyone else I had come in contact with. I had written these down on paper in crayon until I could transcribe them in the library. My conclusions in this essay were backed up by my interviews and I had concluded that I was normal and accumulated stress was the cause of my actions which led to my kidnapping/bomb threat stunt. It was a pressure-relief valve. After I took my seat, Monica began to read my words back to me:

Any person with a so-called normal outlook on life can be subjected to stress. Seemingly, the factors that cause stress are universal. I conclude from my interviews that the major external stress factors are work, relationships, family, and money. While I make no claim that this is a scientific study, these seemed to the most common stress factors in my observations. Wherever these exist, there must be a mechanism in the mind which can help the brain cope. Some people avoid them, which keeps these stress factors at bay, but also can cause them to build or get worse.

Confronting the stress factors is obviously the right thing to do, but not necessarily when the wrong approach is used. From the people I have interviewed, the most overwhelmingly successful method for dealing with stress factors was compartmentalizing these factors and dealing with them one at a time. This approach is smart and effective. The wrong thing to do when confronting these stress factors is to confront more than one of them simultaneously without prioritizing them. This makes things worse and it will eventually lead to the solution being part of the problem.

As a misery addict, I have chosen the avoidance method and have paid dearly. As my stress factors grew, I became more detached from them. These factors did not go away, but changed and became unmanageable. As they grew, I began to add even more stress factors from external sources. Other people's problems became mine. I avoided these peoples' problems also while playing as if I was really engaged. Instead we were sounding boards and a receptacle for each other's problems, as I found out when my stress led to my rather impulsive actions and these people were nowhere to be found.

So here I have identified four internal stress factors plus the possibility of endless external factors, both large and small. Additionally I have identified three coping methods; 1. Prioritized confrontation, 2. General confrontation and 3. Avoidance. In my interviews, although a small sample, it seemed that both sane and insane people practiced avoidance and general confrontation, while the technically insane had sometimes practiced the preferred prioritized confrontation. These results prove to me that "sane" people make bad choices and "insane" people are capable of dealing with stress. I, as a misery addict, dealt with stress improperly and paid the price, but I contend that my research and interviews provide evidence that my reaction was more of a normal reaction to accumulated stress than it was the actions of an insane person.

In short: It could happen to anyone.

As Monica read my words, I sat and stared at those bright green eyes dancing across the page. Her mouth was slightly crooked and her voice, while trying to be clinical, became seductive, at least to me. I started to become aroused; I crossed my own legs and then awkwardly lay down.

After she finished reading, she asked, "Why should anyone believe that you will never harm anyone again?"

Startled, I sat up. "I have never harmed anyone in the past; I say it was my avoidance of stress that led to my actions. I have learned there are other methods. It won't happen again."

"You need to say that on the stand," she said with a sort of positive firmness.

Monica and my new friends made the rest of my stay a positive experience. I look back on it now as a sort of home: a sanctuary where I could be free and be myself. As my trial date approached, I found myself dreading how things would turn out. I figured that I could be locked away in prison for a long time or sent to a mental hospital for a long time, or perhaps a short time. I wanted go back to the place where I found Monica, Barney, Amos, Alvin, and Vic. These were my people and that thought no longer depressed me. I was headed for a cure. Unfortunately the "trial" reversed that course.

* * * * * * * * * * *

It is now my considered opinion that trials are held in order to make members of a community feel as if they are solving a problem. You have a judge who is either elected or appointed, but never claims the power himself. The judge is legitimized by having been chosen by someone else. You have a prosecutor, usually appointed by a local politician who has to answer to society. This lawyer's job is to convict someone of something. If he/she does not get a conviction, then he/she has failed. If the conviction is of someone very famous, these lawyers can themselves become popular and perhaps run for office or get that big appointment, maybe even become a celebrity.

The defense attorney is there to make sure a defense is actually attempted. Some defense attorneys are assigned by the court and some are paid for by the defendant. In either case, they function to give the appearance of fairness. The old saw, "innocent until proven guilty" is just a theory. In practice, everyone believes that if you are on trial, you must have done something wrong.

The last component of the trial is the jury. Again, these are set up to make people feel good about justice. The local government selects a dozen or so local citizens from the voter rolls to pass judgment on total strangers. The jury selection process is deeply flawed because it selects people who have nothing better to do. You almost have to WANT to be selected for a jury and that makes you a very dangerous person; you want to be selected because you want to pass judgment on people.

Add to this mixture the news media which are constantly looking for a sensational story and you have a recipe for a serious miscarriage of justice. They can call it what they want, but it isn't fair, not even in the least bit. The deck is stacked against the defendant and almost everyone; the attorneys on both sides, the judge, and most of the jury, want a quick settlement. Only the most desperate and judgmental jurors want a long trial, the defendant wants a fair trial and the news media wants a story.

When the day of my trial arrived, I was awakened by an orderly named Carl. He was big and bald like the rest. He came in and told me it was time to get dressed for my trial. Tex had arranged for a nice suit of clothes for me to wear. I was in good spirits on that day because I started to trust my lawyer again. After all, Tex had gotten me to this place where I had begun to feel that I could ease myself back into a normal life. I had a good breakfast that morning and I changed into my new suit. I would still be living here during the trial, so my room would still be there for me.

As I sat in the front waiting room, I saw a police squad car pull up in front. Suddenly I began to feel a sinking sensation. There were rocks in the pit of my stomach and my legs were weak as I stumbled towards the door with my orderly escort. It was a feeling of dread. It was the loss of control. I guess I knew that this day would come and I thought that it would just be another day. When faced with this, I just wished for the numbness to return, I wished for the Thorazine which had worn off. I was not prepared. For the first time in a long time I was scared for myself.

As I rode in that squad car, I found myself looking out the window and admiring the scenery. I had been locked up for sixty days and even though I was allowed time outdoors, it was always the same trees and the same yard. I had declined to attend the jury selection process in my condition of protracted divorce from reality.

I absorbed the variety of the scenery and sampled the assorted joys of ordinary life that I had not even attempted to appreciate previously. It was not freedom, but it was a luxury that was previously taken for granted. On that first ride to the courthouse, I vowed not to take my freedom for granted ever again. However, I had to prove that

I was not a danger to others and I had no idea how this could be demonstrated

To my delight, those trees on that October morning were every color in nature. They flew by on the highway and they stood still for me during the frequent stops after we left the interstate. It was a cold crisp morning with the smell of dried leaves in the air as I stepped from that car and approached the rear entrance to the courthouse. There was no media crush and I was grateful.

My gratefulness was destroyed by the scene I soon faced in the courtroom.

The lighting in this particular courtroom was dim except where the judge sat and where the defendants sat with their attorneys. These areas were lit by spotlights. I don't know if this was done for dramatic effect or if it was random, but it made it seem like a stage. In the dimness, two bailiffs stood with a stenographer seated at a small table between them. I walked up to where Tex sat and he looked up with his stupid smile and my confidence was completely shattered. *Why didn't I fire this clown?* After I sat down next to him, he whispered in my ear, "I'm trying to work out a deal." This news doesn't make things better. *A deal? What river is he sending me up now?*

I looked over at the prosecution table that sat to my left in the relative darkness. They were allowed to hide in the shadows while I basked in the limelight of my minor celebrity as the tragic villain. Perhaps bask is the wrong word. I just wanted to hide somewhere. I swallowed hard. I swallowed hard a number of times. The numbness that I usually felt this time of day was notably absent and my heart was beating rapidly. Soon a bailiff escorted the jury into their seats. I looked over at them for a moment, and then turned away. I guess I just didn't want them to think I was studying them.

As soon as the jury was seated, the door behind the judge's bench opened and the bailiff announced, "All rise, the honorable Judge Roy Bailey presiding."

Through that opened door walked a smallish silver-haired man. Judge Bailey took his seat and motioned to the bailiff. "Please be seated," the bailiff told the gallery and the gallery sat.

Judge Bailey began. "This court is hearing the case of the State vs. Clyde Barrow: I see that the jury is seated. Will the defense and prosecution please rise?"

Tex stood and I rose to my shaky feet. I guess the prosecution rose also, but I didn't look into the shadows. The judge continued.

"Mr. Barrow, you have been charged in this court with assault and kidnapping, and as the federal charge of terrorism has been dropped, this will be your only trial dealing with these events."

The news of the feds dropping the terrorism charge was a joke to me. The only thing that bugged me about this was that I suspected once again that Tex was not sharing information with me.

"It is the court's understanding that a plea of not-guilty by reason of temporary insanity is to be entered," the judge said, addressing Tex.

"Yes, your honor," Tex answered. He again seemed to be grinning.

"Very well," the judge looked down. "We will begin with opening statements. Will the prosecution please present their case?"

A female voice from the prosecution bench answered, "Your honor, may I approach the bench?"

The judge waved his hand in a come-forward motion. "Very well," he said and both the prosecution and Tex headed for the bench. Tex turned towards me and flashed another stupid fucking grin before he joined the others. Once he arrived there, much low murmuring took place.

I sat there again; clueless and powerless, I had grown used to my situation of being just some guy about to be condemned to some sort of sub-human status, but it did not make the waiting and wondering any better. It was probably ten minutes before both sides returned to their seats. Tex had an even wider stupid grin on his face. Again, no comfort, he just seemed like a clown to me. The judge spoke again. "This trial cannot proceed until the defendant's competency can be established. I have received a plea offer from the prosecution that has been accepted by the defense. The jury is dismissed. I will hold the meeting in my chambers tomorrow, at which time I will take testimony from the witnesses attesting to the defendant's state of sanity." He banged his gavel, "court is dismissed."

"All rise," the bailiff bellowed. We rose and the judge left.

I looked over at Tex and he was actually looking serious. "We need to get Dr. Whipple in here tomorrow," he said. "He was on your witness list anyway. This will just move the date up."

"Tex, what is going on?" I asked.

"I made the offer to have the two sides' experts testify as to your mental state and let the judge decide what will happen based on what he hears."

"Well I want Dr. Monica here for that," I said.

Tex raised an eyebrow, "Who?"

"Dr. Caulder, she interviewed me at the hospital."

"Oh," Tex said, "She works for the state, so she will testify for the prosecution."

I don't know what I felt about this. I trusted Monica more than my own shrink, but she was on the other side. This did not mean that I trusted her much at all, but at least she had made me feel like I was getting better. I never felt like Dr. Marlin Whipple was doing anything for me other that fulfilling a contract with my employer. This whole thing felt wrong.

"So there will be no trial?" I asked.

"It doesn't look like it," Tex replied. "I asked for you to be set free, the prosecution asked for five years in the mental ward at the state prison, I balked; I wanted five years at a minimum security mental facility. The judge took both into consideration.

"Five years?" I asked in a hushed tone, almost to myself.

"In this state, violent crimes require a mandatory minimum sentence of five years. The judge told us that he had read the affidavits from the witnesses and he had read Dr. Whipple's notes. He had also read the notes from the state's psychiatrists. He told us that we need to present both sides' recommendations tomorrow. This is good news, Clyde."

"Okay Tex," I said. "I guess it could be worse." My anxiety had dissipated somewhat as I realized that at least I wouldn't have to look at Lenny or Del on the witness stand. It may have led to more violence on my part.

"Can I get assigned to the place I am at now?" I asked.

"Possibly," Tex smiled. "That would be pretty neat huh?"

I had to admit that, yeah, it would be neat. I had friends there and I would be able to talk to Monica more and get better. Two police officers were suddenly in front of me; they were there to escort me to a squad car and drive me back to my temporary home. I went without a struggle.

As I walked towards the back of the courtroom, I scanned the faces of the few spectators for a friendly face. The only face I found turned out to be a pleasant and beautiful surprise; it was the bright blue/green-eyed perfect face of Naomi, the sweet girl all the way from south Texas. I stopped in my tracks and my escorts attempted to nudge me on. Naomi and I locked eyes and she began to move towards me. One of my police escorts stepped between us.

"Please, a moment?" was all I could manage. He stepped back and let her come closer to me.

In all of my experience with people this was indeed a rare occurrence, a revelation really. She had come all of this way on her own, with no communication from me. She had just followed the case in the media, thrown caution to the wind, and appeared at my court date to support me. We had only a few seconds for me to absorb this act of kindness and for her to express her feelings. She managed to communicate, I didn't.

"Clyde," she said as she reached me, "I had to see you; I have never been around anyone who has made me feel important. I feel so alive around you. I have been thinking about you every day for months. Can we be together?"

I was stunned, I had no answer. I could only tell her where I was staying and when the visitors' hours were. "I can put you on my visitor's list."

But that was all I could say as my guards moved me through the back of the court. Naomi scrambled towards her belongings and announced quite loudly, "I will follow you!"

And I believed she would, but I knew they would not let her in that day, but maybe in the future…

The trip back to the nut house had a completely different feel than the ride to the courthouse. I still watched the trees with wonder, but now I had a feeling that somebody cared. This sensation was coupled with a feeling that Naomi might be quite troubled and more untethered than me. As a misery addict, I had grown unaccustomed to taking people at face value. It is a pathetic no-win game I play with my own expectations, my own recipe for misery that spoils everything. I decided that romance with Naomi was unwise and that I would treat her as a sort of guardian angel.

Back at the hospital I was taken to my room and I collapsed on the bed. I had decided that life can be good, but my fate was in the hands of a judge and two shrinks: one theoretically on my side who was supposedly going to help me get off easy and the other on the opposite side who was ostensibly looking out for society in general. I trusted the opposing side more and this did not comfort me, nor did it worry me. It all just seemed like what my life always was; an unexplainable mess. Now added in was the lovely Naomi, who would walk through walls to please me, if given the chance.

The orderly came in with more Thorazine and soon I slept. While I slept, I dreamt. In my dream I was with all of the women I have ever known; my wife Margie, Isabel, Naomi, Priscilla, and all of the others who had once brought passion into my troubled life. They were all feeling pleasure in this dream. They were all laughing and enjoying themselves. But I sat on a stool in the midst of them, numb. It was an erotic dream in that it was sexual in nature, but I felt nothing; no longing, no yearning, just flat-line indifference. Naomi would beg me and I would defer. Priscilla would offer her services and I was aloof.

When I awoke I was strangely relaxed and rested. I was calm with no more fears. What they were going to do to me had already been decided. The die was cast and I felt as though my life was going to be the life on an inmate; the life of a number, of a test subject. I would be featured in papers and case studies. I would become Joe Doe or some other pseudonym. Clyde Barrow would be medicated, analyzed, and journalized out of existence. I was an animal in a test lab. All that remained to be decided was what type of cage I would be kept in.

The orderly named Sidney brought me my dinner and I ate whatever it was. The thought of a last meal did enter my mind. Most of my thoughts were a million miles away. I was analyzing again in my calmness. I was thinking about how many people like me were out there who will never be locked up. I remember thinking that I was the only one in such a circumstance. I analyzed that what I did was wrong, and how I could have handled things better. I analyzed my misery manifesto and I analyzed the analysis of my manifesto. I worked my mind around every corner of my current situation in a clinical way. I detached myself from myself and it led me to conclude that I had painted myself into this corner on purpose. What that purpose was, I had no idea.

Soon Sidney returned, took my food tray, and escorted me to my card game.

****

As I walked through the door to the break room, I was met by Vic, Barney, and Amos. They were sitting at the card table and all three smiled when they saw me. Vic even got up and pulled out my chair. It was evident that they had a sense that I wouldn't be back. This saddened me some, but I had a feeling I would be seeing some of them someday. I sat down and Barney, who had been shuffling, slammed the cards down in front of me.

"Your deal," he said.

"Should I deal or wait for Alvin?" I asked.

Everyone at the table just kind of stared off into the distance. It was a signal that all was not right with Alvin. I heard later that one of his destructive personalities had returned and tried to slash his wrists with a plastic knife. Alvin was recovering. I didn't know this while I dealt cards and suspected that none of my friends knew the details, but from their reaction, I knew it was not a routine absence. I finished dealing and we played several uneventful hands before Barney broke the monotony.

"In my old unit, it was customary to send someone off with a remembrance of the time he spent with the unit." He motioned to Sidney, who went into a store room and came back with something covered by a cloth napkin.

"Clyde, in your short time here," Barney continued, "you have taught us many games of poker and you have laid claim to many of the world's treasures." We all laughed. "I can speak for our little group when I say that we consider you a friend and we hope you feel the same. Therefore, since we all feel you will be set free from here or at least will go onto another place of extreme scrutiny, we present you with this token of our high esteem, appreciation, and in partial payment of our gambling debts," Barney waved at Sidney, who pulled back the napkin to reveal a plaque. On the plaque was a picture of the Eifel Tower with a certificate underneath. Sidney walked over and placed it in my hand as I put down the cards that I was holding.

"Read it," Barney ordered. I obeyed.

To Clyde Barrow:

This certifies that you are now the proud owner of France's most prominent monument. It is with sadness that we part ways with our national treasure, but being French, we thrive on sadness and loss. Please take care of our tower and use it only for good. Please send us pictures of it from its new location and always remember that it is very tall and sometimes attracts annoying crowds. This situation is part of the curse that comes with an object of such grandeur. Please accept our congratulations on your monumental poker win. Vive La France!

Sincerely,

The People of France

I smiled and looked up at my friends and they all smiled back. I laid the plaque on the table and announced, "So, who wants to try to win this back?" The table erupted with laughter.

We played cards for the rest of the hour and I lost the Eiffel tower once or twice and won it back eventually along with the Brooklyn Bridge, Grant's Tomb, and The Alamo. It was a fitting farewell from these strange characters who had made my stay in this impossible place at least manageable.

The euphoric feeling wore off soon as I was escorted to my room for the final night. I lay in bed for a long time with all of the lights on. I guess I hoped the cameras would record my last few nights of counterfeit happiness and borrowed contentment. I drifted off to sleep at some point and dreamt that I was still that little boy who was quiet and introspective, but instead of being shunned I would be respected and appreciated. A small short beautiful dream of impossible things, but after all, that's what dreams are.

CHAPTER 12 – JUDGMENT

On my last day at the home that I called home, Sidney the orderly startled me awake from my blissful dream and a shot of cruel daylight stunned me back to reality. I was awake and I was scared; at least for a moment. "Clyde, let's get breakfast," he said. He pointed to the rolling rack which carried my court wardrobe. I got up and began the change from the absurd institution pajamas to the court costume designed to make me appear respectable. In a few minutes I was eating a terrible breakfast of tasteless eggs and overcooked sausage. I brushed my teeth after I finished and Sidney took me to the front waiting area where I met my two officer escorts and began the journey to the courthouse.

Upon arrival, I left the squad car with the two officers and began to walk across the rear parking lot to the courthouse. Out of the corner of my right eye I spotted Naomi headed our way. I turned my head in her direction and smiled at her.

She smiled back, "Clyde, I'm here for you. I will wait for you." The two cops chuckled.

"I will call you when I get a chance," I said as they tugged at my arms to guide me up the steps to the rear entrance.

I looked over my shoulder at the poor delusional girl as she broke down into tears. *What did I do to inspire such loyalty?*

The three of us entered the judge's chambers where he sat at his desk. Seated in facing chairs to my left was the prosecution attorney, next to her was Dr. Monica. On the right were Tex and Dr. Marlin. In the middle, but set back a few feet from the other chairs, was an empty chair. "Please be seated Mr. Barrow," the judge motioned with his palm facing upwards. I walked forward and sat in the chair. I tried nudging it forward as to align it to a more equal status with the other chairs. The chair didn't move much.

An extremely awkward silence was finally broken by the judge, "Mr. Barrow, I have dismissed the jury because your attorney and the prosecution have entered into a plea agreement. The last detail of that agreement will be my decision. I will let the prosecution make their case for their side and I will let your defense make their case. Are there any questions?"

"Will I get to testify?" I asked barely above a whisper.

The judge looked at Tex. Tex shook his head one time and looked down at his feet, and without his customary dumbshit grin, he looked like a lost schoolboy. "No, Mr. Barrow, your defense and the prosecution have decided that the only testimony in this proceeding will be provided by analysis of you counseling sessions with the psychiatrists present here today."

I looked coldly to my right at Dr. Marlin, who I lost trust for a long time ago, and to my left at Dr. Monica, who I vainly hoped would rescue me somehow, but neither looked back at me. I sat up in my chair.

"Do you understand, Mr. Barrow?'

"Ye... yes sir," I said, again very hoarsely.

"Dr. Caulder, will you please read the statement for the prosecution?" The judge folded his hands like a smug version of Solomon deciding the fate of mankind in conjunction with the devil.

Monica opened her file folder and began to read, "Dr. Whipple and I have compared our analysis' and have combined our diagnosis into one testimony," she glanced over at Marlin. I cursed both of them silently.

"Anhedonia is the inability to experience pleasure. At some point, a person who used to enjoy activities will find these are no longer enjoyable. Anhedonia prevents feelings of happiness. Instead of happiness, the person feels nothing. Activities that used to excite, energize, calm or relax now offer no positive reward. Life seems boring, not enjoyable, and empty."

As the lovely Monica spilled out her diagnosis of my troubled mind, I found myself feeling sorry for the guy she was describing. If this was a compassionate judge, he would surely see that all I needed was a little medication and some depth of understanding. Judge Bailey sat unmoved and didn't seem to blink. I avoided looking him in the eye too much since I thought he might think of me as permanently insane, so I would look at him in flashes as I looked about the room. Monica continued:

"Mr. Barrow has gone through a stressful stage in his life and I will say that his course of action was extreme. He did not consider the consequences because he didn't recognize that the consequences existed. He consistently throws himself into situations which seem desperate to the outsider, but to him they seem heroic. He sees himself as a narrator of the condition of life. He examines things while not experiencing them to the full extent. He seeks reaction, he seeks rejection, he wants to shock and even astound others with extreme behavior that he sees as dreary."

Dammit, Monica, I thought, *I am beginning to sound like a monster.*

She passed the diagnosis baton over to Dr. Marlin Whipple, who I sensed was going to throw dirt on my fresh grave.

"A few months ago," he said as he paused to put his reading glasses on his nose, "I asked Mr. Barrow to explain his feelings to me in writing." He opened up a big folder. "In response, he wrote down what he calls his 'Manifesto of Misery.' I will read a rather revealing passage from this manifesto."

We sufferers will crawl from the muck of our own despair to occasional success while not enjoying this success to its full extent. While the success lasts, we will sow the seeds of our own downfall. The downfall is not a tragedy to us, but an expected outcome. We plan for the fall. We live for the crawl in the muck. We seek success only to shun it. We hunt accolades only to refuse them.

The judge's stone face just rested there on the end of his wrinkled neck as he listened to these words. At least I think he was listening, though he seemed dead. I could detect some breathing, but as I said, I didn't want to stare at him. Marlin continued reading.

The situations I have put myself into in my life have been done without any encouragement of others and without regards to the harm I might cause myself. I may have wanted others to see that I was desperate, but these other misery addicts were desperate also, so their self-absorption may have masked any real concern they had for me. Only after my arrest and incarceration did I realize the totality of these people's indifference to my suffering. I am a true misery addict and a true misery addict suffers alone.

Dr. Marlin looked up after he let his glasses slide off from his nose. "Your honor," he said, "I recommend that Mr. Barrow receive treatment for his condition in a mental health facility. He can be a productive member of society with proper psychiatric care."

Judge Bailey blinked, and then turned towards Monica. "Dr. Caulder, do you agree with Dr. Whipple's recommendation?"

"Yes, sir," she said.

This made me smile a little. The judge turned to face me as if he saw that trace of a smile on my face. He looked through some of his notes for a while and looked up at me. "Mr. Barrow, you have committed a crime. It is unlawful to hold another person against his will. Your victim suffered head injuries which could have been serious. You have committed a violent felony. Your mental condition, according to the law, must be considered. I have considered this argument seriously." He paused and looked at the two shrinks one at a time, then continued, "This court is bound by statute that violent crimes must serve a mandatory five-year sentence. Therefore, I have decided that you will spend the next five years in the state penitentiary."

I sat stone faced as I heard these words. I knew there had to be more.

"You will not spend that time in the general population, but in the psychiatric ward under the care of the staff therapists and psychiatrists."

I just sat silently and tried to wrap my mind around this new situation in my way. I knew I could handle the isolation of prison, but the injustice of what was taking place was beginning to sink in. I had said goodbye to my institutional friends and I had no regrets about anything I did there. Again my misery addiction kept me from taking this as the end of hope, mostly because hope was a silly concept to me.

I was helped to my feet by Tex and I moved forward to sign the plea agreement of the judge's desk. The details of the agreement were foggy to me then and remain foggy to this day. My rage, so evident during my attack on Lenny, somehow found no reason to question this injustice. After I signed, one of the two police officers who had escorted me to this place, grabbed my arm and the other put handcuffs on me. I just stood there and looked at my wrists bound in those metal bracelets. I stared downward as I walked out into the back alley behind the courthouse; where I heard Naomi's voice.

"Clyyyyyde!" she shrieked. "Are you alriiiight?" I looked over towards her. She approached me.

"Can I have a moment?" I asked them.

"We really shouldn't," one said.

"I'm in cuffs," I lifted my hands up. "You have guns. You can shoot me if I run."

"Okay," the other one said.

I left them and walked over to Naomi. "Naomi, why are you here?"

"I am here for you, because we belong together," she said in a schoolgirl voice.

"Naomi, I am going to prison. I don't know how this can work. I am a mess. I am a criminal," I held up my cuffed hands.

"No," she interrupted, "You are a kind generous man. I love you. I love y...,"

"Stop!" I said. I looked into those eyes and that perfect face.

"Why?" I asked. "You are so young and pretty. I am going away."

She looked down at her feet. I had no hope that she would ever stay with me. I was not anything but a dead end. I would leave her unfulfilled. I decided to acquiesce.

"Naomi, dear sweet girl, I am going to the state prison. Please write me. Please visit me. I do want you in my life."

She looked up and kissed me and I kissed her back. It had been a long time since I had touched a woman in this way and it filled me with wonder and I fell deeply into a sort of passion I hadn't felt in a long time. The next thing I felt was the hands of my guards grabbing my shoulders.

"Let's go, Clyde," one said, "We have to go to the hospital and get your belongings so we can transfer you to state prison."

I pulled away from the fair Naomi and I felt the beginning of a tear. Was I going to cry? For her part, Naomi was drowning in tears. She cried my name, "Clyde, oh Clyde, I will be where ever you are."

I looked away from her and towards the car. What a weird scene! Bizarre as my life had become, this was exquisitely and profoundly unexpected. I had some young girl head-over-heels obsessed with me. It was flattering and scary. It was pleasant and embarrassing. It was the perfect fit for my impossible life.

Once inside the car, my two police escorts had much to say on the subject of Naomi.

"Looks like you got yourself a jailbird junkie," the one driving said, "and a young pretty one too. Good for you Clyde, but be careful."

"Why? What do you mean?" I asked.

"She'll have an angle," he said, "They all do. She's not wired right and she seems desperate. She probably hates her parents." He looked back at me before he started the car, "I mean she probably reeeeeealy hates her parents." He started the car.

"Yeah, I think she does," I said, "I think that may be what this is about. But this is extreme, she lives in Texas. She has no job here as far as I know. I really didn't expect her to be here at all. I only slept with her once and that was more of just a fling. She's either gone on me or doing a great acting job"

"Nah, she's nuts!" Said the cop in the passenger seat as he looked back at me, "I've seen them before; they all have father issues." I nodded slightly.

Then I just became really quiet. I knew this new situation was dangerous and I should have been concerned or scared, but I kind of liked it. It was nice to have someone who was stuck on me. I had no idea how real it was, but I had no feeling of dread or foreboding. I actually relished it. *Good for me,* I thought. I was quiet as I looked out at the trees that lined the interstate flying by on my last day on the outside.

I took in every part of the view that I could.

PART 2: BROKEN

CHAPTER 13 – A PLACE OF EXTREME SCRUTINY

State Prison Facility 3 was a stone monument surrounded completely by swamp. Mosquitoes were thick as hell in the summer. It made you wish for the bitter winter winds screaming across those almost-treeless swamps. The front gate was iron and about 40 feet tall. The entire place was drenched in the smell of sweet rotting vegetation. It was a humid stew in the summer and a frozen bowl of guacamole in the winter.

I was stripped of my suit that I wore to court and I was told that I was Inmate Number 679842. At first I had a cell to myself. It was six feet deep by ten feet wide with a heavy iron door, a small barred window, and a little flap at the bottom through which the guards would slide food trays. I was separated, but not quite isolated from everyone in the psycho ward of the prison. This was always welcome by me, but most particularly in these circumstances. I had to adjust to another place. Adjusting to other people could wait. I was not completely cut off, since I could hear the other various mumblers, criers, and ranters who occupied this strange hotel. One man seemed to be persecuted by voices who told him to kill them all.

Another mumbled bible verses to himself and praised himself for remembering the verses. "And this is the condemnation, that light is come into the world, and men loved darkness rather than light, because their deeds were evil!" He would then say something like. "Testify!" Or, "Tell it brother!"

Yet another inmate would let loose blood-curdling screams in the dead of the night. The sound of "Yeeeeooooow! Make it stop! Make them stop!" was enough to get me so unsettled that I couldn't sleep for hours.

The jailers would come by a few times a day to bring food and medication. Everyone in my section got twenty minutes in the exercise yard alone. It was a silly place on a rigid schedule. My new doctors prescribed Clozaril and I knew it wasn't anywhere near the same as Thorazine since I stayed up all night the first night. Instead of making me drowsy, it made me restless. The change was not welcome at all. I complained to the guards, so they changed my medication. In fact, they changed my medication seemingly on a whim.

There was no psychiatrist interviewing me or asking if I felt better. It was all so surreal and pointless, so I stopped taking any of these drugs. The guard would slide a soft plastic cup of water and a cup with a pill through the barred window. I would put the pill under my tongue, swallow the water, then pass back the empty cups. When the guard left, I would flush the pill down my little corner toilet. I wanted to get better, and I could not become a psychoactive brain stew mixing and melting chemical reactions in my brain with unpredictable results. Fortunately, I soon had a roommate who wanted all of my extra drugs.

His name was Clarence. Clarence was about 5 foot 11 and medium athletic build with graying brown hair and wild brown eyes and a crooked mouth that made him seem to always be about to burst into either laughter or tears. He looked crazy. He was one of those people who heard the voices. The psychiatric world is thoroughly convinced that the voices do not actually exist, but are an invention of the mental patient's own malfunctioning brain. Clarence nearly convinced me that the voices actually came from somewhere else. He claimed the voices were in the news broadcasts, in the electrical appliances, and even in the small animals and insects. He heard them everywhere.

Clarence and I had one thing in common and that was violence in the workplace. One day the toaster oven or the blender told him to take his gun to work and shoot a bunch of people. They even told him to shoot himself when he was done. With widely-scattered shots, he managed to wound three people through ricochets before someone stopped him from reloading to do himself in. He was sentenced to 20 years for all of his troubles and he was given a break because of his mental condition. He had been in prison for six years when I arrived.

Clarence was talkative, which I didn't mind, he had lived an interesting life; he had been a West Point Army cadet at one point, but didn't make it through. Among other things, he had been a pilot and a cook, which finally allowed him to land a job as the assistant head pastry chef at a large resort. There are lots of appliances that talk to you in the kitchen of a hotel and Clarence told me about all of them. He really hated the big ovens. The big ovens were always taunting him, he told me. When he went to work that day he was going to kill those ovens. He didn't intend to hurt any of the people there, but he had to make those ovens stop their taunting.

I made sure I never taunted Clarence, and I always gave him my extra medication. It was from him that I learned the ins and outs of the institution that I found myself living in. He told me that mental patients were pretty much treated the same as regular inmates with a few exceptions; one was the medication, a second was a visit by the staff psychiatrists, and another was the isolation. Regular inmates were always two or more to a cell, but psych ward people were either isolated completely or two to a cell. Some prisons preferred to pen them up- even a dozen in a large cell- but according to Clarence, this place had found that method counterproductive and it normally led to violence.

Clarence was clearly not sane; he would hold conversations with ants, roaches, mice, rats, and common house flies. They all seemed to have a lot to say to him and he had a lot to say back to them. The topics of the conversations would range from sports to politics to the guards' personal lives to his new roommate. He was entertaining and I could appreciate that. Whatever my own problems were, I could at least see the value of being in the company of someone whose journey back to normal was going to be much more difficult than mine.

"So when do I get to see my shrink?" I asked him one day early in my incarceration as I lay on my mattress on the opposite side of the room from his mattress.

"Let's see," he paused, looking up at a spider, "How many times have I seen a shrink?" He paused again as he listened for the answer. "I have seen the shrink about ten times in six years."

"So they give us drugs and they don't even know what effect they are having?"

"Yes, Clyde, I would say that is a fair assessment." He said this as he looked over at me.

"I don't think I will be taking my drugs then. What's the point?" I asked, sitting up. I stood up and walked to the door of the cell. When I was sure no one was listening, I whispered, "I stopped taking my medications when they stopped giving me Thorazine. At least that stuff let me sleep."

"Well, you can give them to me," Clarence said, "I like the drugs, they sometimes take me places." Now he sat up "I get nothing out of seeing the doctors anyway. The doctors only ask me if I stopped hearing the voices. They think the voices are in my head and they keep asking me if they go away. What can I say? The voices talk to me; I can't stop them anymore than I can stop the rain. If I could stop them, I could work in the kitchen instead of the library. Even there I can only work with the books; I don't want the computers there to even see me."

"Do you ever get visitors?" I asked Clarence.

"Yes, my wife and my grown children come to see me." He pulled out a folder to show me pictures of his wife and his two sons. "My wife has stuck with me all along, but my sons talk to me like I'm an infant."

I looked at the pictures; his wife was an attractive brunette in her mid-forties- at least in the picture. His sons looked exactly like him with the same wild look in their eyes. I suspected that each of them would one day be hearing voices too. This would explain their impatience with dad; they feared ending up like him and this helped me excuse my own daughter's reluctance to even acknowledge my situation with a call or a letter. I began to wonder if I would ever see her again.

"How about you, Clyde?" Clarence asked. "You have family?"

"My parents are dead, my siblings are strangers, my wife divorced me, but I have a daughter. I hope she visits." I paused at the candor contained within this statement. I really did need to see her. I had been calling her since day one. When she did answer, it was short, awkward and sad. I had written her a letter on my first night in prison to let her know where I was and to tell her that visitors were allowed on Sunday. She hadn't written back. I tried to call her during my weekly ten-minute phone call, she didn't answer, so I called nobody. I just sat and stared at my reflection in the shiny chrome that lined the inside of the phone booth.

"What's her name?" Clarence interrupted my deep thoughts.

"Uh, Annette, Annette is her name," I blurted out. "She's uh, she's in her third year of college." I reached for the only picture of her that I had and handed it to him.

"She's young here," he said as he studied the photograph.

"Yeah, twelve, she was getting ready for her first concert, she sings like an angel."

He handed back the picture. "She was away in college when my troubles began," I told him as I stared into those twelve year-old hopeful eyes. Those eyes saw a man who was her hero and protector. He was going to help her achieve her dreams and he was going to be by her side like a best friend as she knocked down those obstacles in her way. Dad was going to be everything all of the time because it just had to be that way. He was never going to melt down and take stupid actions that served no purpose.

"Huh!" I uttered. I had become a stranger to her. I had drifted to become some kind of monster and that was all she would ever see. I was an embarrassment to her and I wouldn't see her on Broadway and I wouldn't see her win awards except on some small TV in some institution somewhere surrounded by men who talk to rats guarded by men with clubs in rooms built like cages. I had fucked up. I blinked and held back the stupid blubbering that was inevitable.

"I doubt she visits me at all," I finally managed.

"Anyone else?" Clarence Asked.

"Just a young girl infatuated with me, Naomi." I replied.

"Young huh, well that's something," he said

"Yeah, I know. I barely encourage her. I guess she will be here next visitor's Sunday."

"Clyde, you need to have her in your life even if it is not the real thing," Clarence looked at me without the crazy look I had become accustomed to. "She is willing to visit and willing to stick by you, I say you need her even though it may be scary. Do you have a picture?"

I reached in my big envelope of papers and handed him one of the pictures that Naomi had already sent me since I my incarceration.

He grabbed the picture, looked at it, then looked back at me. He did this several times and the crazy look returned to his eyes. He stood on his mattress and showed the picture to the spider.

"What do you think?" he asked his arachnid friend. "I think so too." He stepped back down to the floor.

"Clyde," he said as he handed me the picture. "What's her last name?"

"Jones," I answered, "although it could be made up."

"It's not made up, Clyde. Naomi Jones is an heiress; her mother married a billionaire Texas oilman. She's a trust fund kid, she stands to inherit a huge bundle when her stepdad croaks and he is probably ninety now. Ever hear of J.J. Cowling?"

"I… I guess," I was stupefied. I stared at the picture of Naomi.

"Her mom was a beauty queen who had a child at a young age, but she married the rich guy about 15 years ago when he was a young and vigorous seventy-five." His serious-non-crazy look returned. "Cowling owned the resort I worked at. They stayed there a few times. Fussy eaters, sent everything back. Dang, Clyde, you have hit the jackpot here. Don't let this one get away."

I was now in some kind of surreal perplexing situation. I tried to piece things together in my mind. Somehow, Lenny, who is as charming as a rattlesnake, had won over this young heiress enough for her to go home with him. Almost as startling; I have done an even better job of winning her over. This was not quite computing in my analytical mind, so I had to add a few more variables. She was clearly unhappy, but why? The American dream was to get rich, at least for some people. Was she being controlled too much by her mother or her stepfather? My quest for answers to these questions and a few others became my mission.

I decided to call her the next time I had a chance. If she visited me, it would be better. I definitely would write her and try to keep her in my life. Clarence was right: I had a golden opportunity to secure a lifeline and I wasn't going to be stubborn and stupid about it anymore. I was under no more stress or pressure and this place was far more relaxing than my outside life had become. Naomi was my ticket. She was confused and young and that part would pass, I was sure. Why else would she hitch her wagon to a loser with no future?

In my cell, with the now familiar sounds of Clarence's dialogs with his voices, I began to once again attempt to steal a little hope from a dark hopeless future. I slept well that night as I anticipated what the future could bring; high priced lawyers and early release. I had no idea what I would do after that, but in Naomi I had a possibility and that was something. In my mind she had transformed from young delusional girl to a sort of superhero.

CHAPTER 14 – MOST PEOPLE SETTLE

It was three weeks before I was allowed any visitors on Sunday. I don't know why this rule existed. I also had not been able to call anyone. I was just fed my pills, which I gave to Clarence. He loved the moods he would get in with those different combinations of psychoreactive drugs and I found the conversations he would conduct with the voices to be quite entertaining. I asked for a phone call twice a day and I was ignored. The guards had become quite proficient at ignoring us crazies. I can't say I blame them. If I had to listen to some of the impossible requests that inmates spewed daily, I would also just learn to not listen. Some guy kept asking to speak with Winston Churchill and another would beg for a bottle of cognac to wash down his pills.

I wrote Naomi several letters to make sure she knew that I wanted her to come visit me. I sincerely wanted this, but now I had a new reason for this. I tried really hard to sound sincere, but I may have laid it on a little thick. On my third Sunday I was awakened by a guard. "Mr. Barrow, you have two visitors," he said through the little bars that served as a window on my heavy steel door. "One is named Annette Barrow and the other is a Naomi Jones. Both of them are real pretty." The guard seemed impressed. "Which one do you want to see first?"

I really wanted to see Naomi and I didn't want to risk discouraging her affection for me, but I had to see my daughter. I hadn't seen her since she returned to college. I really risked losing her forever if I made her wait. So I told the guard to send Annette first and I hoped that Naomi would understand. I really had no doubt she would, but my perspective on her had changed dramatically since learning that she could be my key to freedom.

The meeting area for visitors was open enough, there were no screens between us, just a room with 16 picnic tables with benches attached on either side. These tables were contained in a room surrounded by bars. Half of the tables currently had inmates and visitors seated. It was like a company picnic in a cage with no food. Annette entered and I walked quickly to embrace her. When we pulled away after the long clinch, I studied her face. She looked strained and worried, as if she had aged ten years in the few months since I had seen her. She strongly resembled her mother, but with my blue eyes and my crooked smile. She also had Margie's curly hair, but it was light brown like mine with streaks of red.

"How are you Dad?" she asked as we both clumsily found seating on opposite sides of the table. "I wished I could come sooner," she continued without waiting for my answer, "but I don't know. I… I felt awkward. I didn't want to face this."

It hurt me to see her in such a situation. I felt like an ass for putting her through all of this and I realized that it was hard for her to face. I missed her these months when I needed a friend and felt completely abandoned. While this feeling fed my misery addiction, the betrayal felt still somewhat unfair coming from my only child. Upon seeing her face, I forgave everything almost immediately.

"It's okay, Doll, I have put you in a tough spot. I can't expect you to put everything on hold to come see me in my craziness."

"Dad, I should have come, I didn't realize how bad things were. I think about you every day, but I thought if I avoided this, I would be able to continue at school without falling apart." She looked down for a second, then back up at me. "When they locked you up here, I could no longer continue. I took a week off to come and see you and…well, to see how Mom is holding up."

I grinned slightly, "How is she?"

"She's okay, I guess. She sold the house, but your lawyer put a lien on your share of the money. She paid the rest of my tuition and moved into a small condo. She sold your car and paid off what was owed and had some money left over, which she gave to me. It was about $2,000."

"Okay, so what happened to my stuff?" I shocked myself with this question; I had not really thought much about all of my belongings since I had been detained, but I was quite irritated at Tex for promising to work pro bono, then making a money grab. I guess I wanted to take inventory of what I really had left in my life.

"Mom put your stuff in storage and paid two years' rent in advance," Annette told me. "She said to ask you if you wanted to give me anything."

"Take my guitar and amp and my recording equipment, for sure," I said earnestly, "I don't want some thief to get those or some rat to chew them up."

There was a long pause while she studied her shoes some more and I looked at the top of her head. She finally looked up and broke the silence, "Dad, I'm sorry," she said as tears trickled down her face.

"Me too," I said, as I could no longer hold back the tears. I reached out for her hand and we held them together for a long time and alternated between looking at our clasped hands and each other's faces. The rest of the conversation was about what we were doing during the last three months. I told her about the mental hospital and the people I met there and I told her about Clarence and his voices. We laughed a little.

Annette told me about school where she was majoring in the performing arts. She was already a beautiful singer, but she was learning all of the disciplines. She had no steady boyfriend at the time and really didn't date much anyway. It was not any time to get serious, she said. This led her to ask about her mother and me.

"Dad, did you stay married because of me?"

This is a question I had expected but feared for a long time. I knew the answer was an unqualified yes, but simple answers can be hurtful and can create more problems than they solve. I decided to qualify my answer; "It isn't that simple, sweetheart." She looked disappointed in my answer.

"Babe, I could lie and say we would have been together this long if we didn't have you, but I won't do that. We were in love once, but it… her love wasn't the same love as mine. I can't speak for her, but for me I think it was just time to find somebody willing to put down roots and she was there for me and never seemed to want anyone else. I could have married a dozen others I guess, but none of them were willing to be exclusive with me, so I settled for the one who was through with dating also."

"You settled?" she asked with a skeptical voice.

"I settled," I answered.

"Everybody settles, Dad," she said with more anger than disappointment.

"I suppose," I replied.

"But you didn't stop dating, Dad," she said a bit loudly.

"Honey, it's more complicated than that."

"Enlighten me!" she was now hostile.

"Annette, don't be angry," I said in a hushed tone, hoping to also bring her volume down. "She accused me of affairs constantly from day one. I admit I had a wandering eye, but that's all. It was years before I did anything, but I succumbed to the pressure of being pronounced guilty of something I wasn't doing." I paused while I searched for the way to make her understand. She was still looking at me like I was the criminal I was dressed as.

"Look," I resumed in the same hushed tone, "You know I was always being accused of everything. You probably had to believe it yourself. I don't know what she said while I wasn't there, but she accused me of things in front of you for years...,

"Dad, that's lame," she interrupted. "You didn't have to do anything. You could have just played it off."

"Easier said than done," I said. "I was accused of being a playboy, and in your eyes I'm sure there were doubts about me. I began to feel as if I couldn't win, so I gave in. It was the easiest thing in the world. I just started doing what I was accused of, it was liberating to some extent. It didn't make my life easier, but I definitely felt justified. It felt like being sprung from a trap. Of course that led to another sort of trap."

"How do you mean?" she asked.

I began to explain my misery addiction and my manifesto, but the guard stepped in. The hour was up and it was time for my little girl to leave. We tearfully embraced and she was led from the room looking over her shoulder. "I love you, Dad. I will be back as soon as I can." She promised. "I get Thanksgiving break in a couple of weeks."

"I love you baby," I answered. "Take care. Please write me."

Annette left and I was alone. I had a pitiful feeling in my stomach. My visit with Annette had been useful and cathartic, but it was incomplete. I was also pissed at Tex for being such a flim-flam man. I was glad that Margie had moved on and actually taken care of things quite seamlessly. My feelings were a mix of stuff that would keep me occupied with self-doubt on most days, but I had to get my mind ready for my next visitor.

CHAPTER 15 – NAOMI THE HEIRESS

Soon, the familiar bright face of young beautiful Naomi was walking through the door of the visitors' cage. I was absolutely delighted to see her. She was not only my lover, she was my potential savior. We embraced and kissed full on the lips for at least a minute. I felt her desire and she felt mine, but this wasn't a conjugal visit, it was just a chat. I did make a mental note to ask about conjugal visits, though. We both sat down at the table.

Naomi slid off her shoes after she sat down. She started running her foot up my leg. She was flirtations as hell and this visit was not going to be easy to get though if I had to spend all of my time aroused. I looked over at the guard who probably had seen this a thousand times. The guard smirked and he shook his head.

"Ma'am," he said. "Please restrict your contact to greetings only."

Naomi withdrew her foot from my upper thigh. After my emotional visit with my daughter, I had to compose myself to attempt to get Naomi Jones, the attractive young woman to reveal herself as Naomi Jones, the attractive young heiress. If I let on that I knew she might reject me outright.

"Clyde, I have missed you so much," she said quite convincingly.

I became instantly uncomfortable. I was not in love with this girl and I doubted not only her sincerity, but also her sanity; even more than I doubted mine. I hated having to mislead her into to thinking I loved her, but I had no idea how else I was ever going to dig myself out of this hole I had stumbled into. I needed her loose grasp of the circumstances to last long enough for her to help me. I wished I had known she was rich right from the start, because I could have faked loving her and gotten away from my wife and job a long time ago. Now I had to fake something to get something; not an admirable act, but desperation does not tend to shine the best light on people.

"Good god, I have missed you Naomi," I feigned sincerity the best I could.

"I know Clyde, but they can't keep you here forever, can they?"

"No, but I fear someone here may do me harm," I said as I looked around with a scared look.

"Oh, darling, I wish I could get you out of here and we could start a life together," she said, thoroughly convinced that she was in love with me.

"But what can we do?" I asked. "You probably spent your life savings getting here. How do you eat? Where do you stay?"

She paused a long time. I sensed that she didn't want to divulge her wealth, but maybe something in her pulled at her sense of right and wrong. If she was going to love me, she had to be honest. I knew before she even spoke that she was going to tell me her secret.

"Clyde, I have to tell you something about me," she grabbed at my hands and held them.

"What is it, doll?" I asked.

Naomi shot a glance in the direction of the guard and whispered, "My father is very rich."

I pulled back and slid my hands from under hers. "I don't understand." I shook my head slowly. "You are rich and you want to be with me?" I asked with all honesty, since I was actually confused on this point. My tension eased as she was now on the defensive. Her secret was out and even though I was still trying to use her situation to my advantage, she was on the defensive; she had been holding back.

"Clyde, I had to know if you loved me for me. I had to know that it wasn't the money. Men find out I'm rich and they change, they start worrying about what my dad is doing and how my dad thinks. I don't even know him that well, since he's my stepdad and I was raised by nannies and servants. To those men I am a spoiled rich kid who always gets her way."

I sat in the silence that followed this explanation. I was beginning to see the light. I now knew what I was; I was revenge on her mother and stepfather for their neglect, and I may even get her disowned if I wasn't careful. She broke the silence.

"Even my real father, he didn't care about me until Mom married into money. He is another opportunist. I had to get away from him too. I don't trust any men. But you Clyde, you see me and love me and accept me, you might be my last hope."

I began to feel guilty about my plan to use her. In true misery addict fashion, I started to doubt my sinister plan. The plan wasn't really that sinister, but I knew it was less than honest. Truly evil people do worse stuff every day just to get a parking space.

"Naomi, I love you for you and not just because you stood by me," I said, there being some truth to this. I hadn't known about the money, but I did need her friendship and she provided it and then some. More guilt worked its way to my conscience. "I just hope you are prepared for a bit of a wait."

"Clyde, I can do more than wait, I can hire the best lawyer in the world if you want. But...," she looked down.

I sat there, head tilted, and raised my eyebrows, "But... but what?"

"I would have to ask my stepdad and that would mean crawling back to him and my mom. I told them I didn't need their money.

I sat with my hands at my side. I had completely surrendered to the sincerity of this pure creature. I don't mean pure in the virginal sense, but pure in the motive sense. She truly wanted to do something real and good. She sincerely wanted to make her mark on the world. I knew right then that she would do all she could for me and that I was her last hope for good in this world. I felt that old familiar tinge of getting into something I didn't understand and something I didn't even want to contemplate. As a misery addict, I knew that this was just the way it had to be.

Naomi and I sat and talked about what we would do with our time together which we thought would be soon and she seemed to think would be forever. With my vain and freshly-found optimism, I also entertained such thoughts. My thoughts were of a far off land and a big ranch with a modest house in the middle of the big spread somewhere. We would live simple and have no worries and we would pursue interests that were ours together and individually. A life based on mutual respect, but no worries about money and possessions: my paradise.

Naomi's thoughts were similar, although she hoped to accomplish this without the aid of her stepfather's wealth. She was a perfect candidate for the misery-fest that my life had become. She dreamed impossible dreams made impossible by her own stubbornness. She adhered to a code that she could explain, but not defend. Her honor was her greatest possession and would not be sacrificed for mere money. She wanted to save a hopeless crazy man, and then live in paradise forever with him, but without any source of outside help, even though she had access to the resources to make this come true. Her misery was grand in scale and monumental in its hopelessness. She was unique among my small tribe of sufferers.

She explained that she stood to gain a large fortune upon her 25th birthday, but she must return to the fold and participate in the family business. To me this seemed easy to do. Just be on the board of directors and show up for some votes on this and that. Maybe go to business school. This stuff all seemed easy to a working man like me who had to struggle for any bit of anything.

I admired her all the same. I wished that I had the chance to shun all of that stuff, maybe not shun it upfront and open, but I would do it some cunning way that caught everyone off guard. I fancied myself as a virtuoso of misery; a maestro, if you will. Naomi just took it to the limit from the start. She had no cards left to play; she would just be stubborn and consistently deny the wealth that was coming her way. She had played the stubborn card and would continue to play it.

So we talked of paradise and dreams and plans. The more we talked, the more impossible they seemed. Soon I just started to feel like a fool. I wasn't a kid anymore and I wasn't going to fall for plans that made no sense. But I had to indulge her. I had to make believe that I thought it was all possible. I had to suppress the instinct to call the whole thing bullshit and laugh at the audacity of it all. I held my tongue and held her hand and promised that I would join her wherever she wanted me. I also expressed my dearest wish that she stick with me through my incarceration.

On this wish, I was sincere.

CHAPTER 16 – THE MIX

As soon as I was back in my cell, I returned to the routine of being handed pills and giving them to Clarence. The routine of letter writing and exercise yard visits. I was getting letters from Naomi, as usual, but I was also getting letters from my daughter. Annette was keeping me up to date on her singing career and her schooling. Naomi would just write about a future that only she could imagine. Her future was with me in a paradise where work and money weren't required. If the prison people were ever to send a shrink around and I showed him these letters, he would probably prescribe her some nice medication.

For my part, I would get a rainbow of colored medication which I passed on to my roomy Clarence, which often provided me with entertainment. He would hold long discussions with himself and whatever objects available. The toilet, the light bulb, the spiders, just whatever was in the room. They talked to him he talked to them and he talked to himself. It may sound cruel, but I enjoyed this. Sometimes he did Shakespeare; sometimes it was a Broadway musical. I didn't hear all of the lines, but his long pauses made me think that the other characters were speaking. But he took the leads. In Hamlet, he was Hamlet. In Richard III, he was Richard. The winter of our discontent, indeed. His mind may have been abnormal, but it stored a whole bunch of great stuff.

One night, not long after my first visitor's Sunday, I lay awake listening to Clarence babble in the corner. This was not his usual disposition. I could usually decipher the words that came out of his mouth, but this was way different. He seemed to be speaking some made up language. He seemed to be in a full-blown hallucination. His murmuring began to sound like anger. Soon his angry babbling foreign-tongue turned loud.

"I see how it's gonna be!" Clarence suddenly shouted at an apparition that I couldn't see.

"I have to be the one! I have to sacrifice! I have to put it all on the line! Nobody else sees what I do for you! If they did they would be on my side!" He was now shouting and standing on his bed.

This turn of events was quite surprising and was more entertaining than any of his previous shows. In fact, my amusement was beginning to transition into genuine concern. My concern didn't last long, however, as it was overtaken by terror, then self-preservation. All this happened in a matter of seconds as Clarence traversed the short distance between our mattresses and was on top of me trying to choke me. Apparently I was the boogie man in his current hallucination.

"I will show you!" He shouted as he leapt upon me and clutched my throat. "I will take you down."

I am not the type of person to take this type of attack lightly. My instinct was to end his life in one of many various ways, but I knew Clarence was just nuts and it could have been my pills that caused this freaking out. So I simply over-powered him and twisted his arm up behind his back to where his hand was between his shoulder blades. I then slammed him face down into the floor. This, to me, was the least violent thing I could do without getting my ass kicked by the guards. Unfortunately, it turned him into a victim.

"Get off me! Get off me!" He screamed.

"Calm down, Clarence," I whispered, "It's me Clyde. Calm down and I will let you up."

"Help! Help! He's trying to kill me! Guards! Guards!"

So this ranting lunatic, who had attacked me, was now painting me as the aggressor. In a few seconds the guards were on top of me and pulling me away from Clarence, who I had not harmed. I was merely restraining him. The guards, however, thought it was proper to do me harm. One baton blow to the kidneys and a kick to the nuts later, I was subdued. They dragged me by my feet out of the cell as Clarence continued, unmolested, to yell obscenities at me and his fucking voices.

The guards dragged me by my knees and I struggled with them until one talked into his shoulder radio mic, "We need sedation in ward C." I stopped struggling and tried reason. "I was attacked, I was defending myself." I said in a loud voice. This brought down the baton on my other kidney. I was done protesting. In a second, a man in a white lab coat came through the door at the end of the corridor and he was holding a needle.

He injected whatever happy juice it was into my arm and my brain completely shut down.

****

The next thing I remember was waking up on a mattress on the floor of a dark room accompanied by the scuttling of a small creature in the corner. I do not know how long I was out, but everything ached. My kidneys, my nuts, my head, and my feet all were sore. I didn't move for a long time. I just lay curled-up on that musty mattress and took inventory of my new situation.

I was in solitary confinement; that was obvious. At least it was quiet, except for my furry friend off in the dark corner. No more rants from Clarence and he would get no more of my drugs. I hoped that Clarence got his ass kicked by the next guy. Not everybody is entertained by their roommate talking to voices. Some people are irritable and react with much animosity to such things.

Another thing I realized was that prisoners in solitary get no visitors. This distressed me greatly. I had to see Annette and I really had to see Naomi. I had no idea how long I was in here for, or what the damn rules were. Nobody was going to tell me either. I just lay there, moaned and hoped that I would heal. I wished for anything to stop my feeling of helplessness. I slept again.

In my sleep I dreamed. It was the return of the voice. I had not dreamt of the voice since I stopped taking Thorazine in the state hospital. I was waterskiing in the dream and I was not much good at it. I kept flipping over and losing my skis. The voice was there to help me and to guide me.

"Clyde, you cannot be defeated by your fears," said the unfamiliar, but authoritative female voice. "Your enemy is fear. All things are possible if you conquer your fear."

I got on the skis again and again. Each time I got a little farther. I kept at it until I was able to stay up all the way across the lake. Soon I was doing tricks; I stood on one ski, I spun around working the handle through my legs, and I was soon skiing on my hands, then barefoot. I did every trick I could think of. I was the most confident acrobatic water skier in the world. I was so confident that I quit. I let go of the rope and coasted to the shore. Once on shore, I set fire to my skis. Never mind that they were wet; this was a dream.

The voice implored me, "You are a success. Why do you walk away?"

I had no answer. I just kept walking away from the flaming skis.

The voice called after me, "Clyde you have only won half the game. It is only halftime. Your fears will own you if you do not move to the next level."

I woke up not long after that. I was sweating and I was still sore, but at least the room was no longer dark. I moved against the pain I now felt everywhere. I sat up from my musty mattress and looked around in the pastel light. On the wall was a window to the outside world. It was very small and up about 10 feet and blocked with thick metal mesh. It shone light down on the door to my cell which had a small flap at the bottom for food and a small barred window at the top. In front of the flap was a metal tray with some kind of food that was currently being enjoyed by a quite healthy rat.

Looking around the room, I saw a shadowy toilet. This was important because I was about to lose whatever contents were in my stomach. I rolled over and crawled in that direction. When I reached the bowl, I heaved a couple of times. In the dull light I saw that the puke was quite colorful, my guess was red, but I couldn't be sure. Next I relieved myself and that proved to be one of the most painful things I had ever experienced. I could tell that this was bloody. I wiped a sample of some of the urine with a tissue and took it into the light. It was red. The rat ran over my bare feet and I shuddered a bit. Even that was painful. The guards had really done a job on me.

I still didn't feel any kind of despair. *There are no highs or lows with me, folks. I just analyze.* I clicked into my analytical mode and began to assess the situation. I had been here at least all night and been fed at least once and the food remaining on my tray felt cold. My guess was maybe two nights since the last thing I remembered on the outside was late afternoon. I woke up from the happy juice at night and now it seemed like morning. I guessed it was Friday. It was also very quiet where I was, so I guessed that I was in some sectioned-off space of the nuthouse area of the prison.

I figured they would keep me here a few days unless they moved me to the infirmary, which I knew was where I belonged at this particular moment. I decided I didn't want the infirmary- I wanted a regular cell and I wanted to see my visitors. I also didn't know if I would get my mail. I couldn't read it in this room anyway, there was no light bulb. And it sure was quiet, except for the chewing and scuttling of the rat, who I decided to name Rex. Rex the Rat. *Fuck it,* I thought, *I might as well start talking to animals and appliances like Clarence.*

My brain eventually drifted to how long it would be before I saw Naomi again. This circumstance was a definite setback to my plans with her. I wasn't discouraged, but felt that I was somehow vindicated.

I announced in a proud voice, "Tenets One and Two of the Manifesto of Misery: Good things are never what they appear to be and happiness cannot last. You hear that Rex?"

I looked in the direction of the rat-like noise in the corner behind the toilet. I looked at the sunlight on the door, which was now lower. This meant that the sun was rising. It was morning. Maybe they could bring me breakfast soon and I could ask some questions. Maybe I could even eat. *At least maybe Rex could eat.* I thought, and then chuckled to myself. Even that hurt.

The silence of my world was shattered when the guard brought me breakfast. I could hear a metal door creak open, then slam shut and footsteps coming my way. I counted fourteen boots-on-concrete steps and estimated he walked 30 feet until he stopped. I knew my cell was ten feet wide which meant that he passed 3 cells on each side of the hall. He didn't stop until he got to my cell.

The bottom flap on my door opened and he pulled the tray out. He slid a new tray in.

"Breakfast, Barrow," he announced.

"Thanks," I replied.

"You feeling better?" he asked.

"I'll live." I answered. "What day is it?

"Friday," he answered.

"How long am I in here?" I asked

"That's up to the discipline board," he replied. "They will see you on Monday. Do you need to see a doctor?"

"I'll manage," I said. I just wanted to be alone. I imagined they would have to let me see the doc soon anyway.

"Suit yourself," the guard said. "Your medication is on the tray." He walked away another fourteen steps to the door which slammed behind him.

I walked over to the tray and examined my food. It was warmed-up mashed potatoes with green beans. There was some kind of meat gravy on the potatoes and there was a small roll. I picked up the medication from the tray and examined it in the light; it was yellow. I guessed it was Thorazine and I washed it down with water.

Swallowing was painful, but I comforted myself that I would soon be asleep. I tried the potatoes and green beans a little, but gave up. I was not well and I knew it. I slid my tray over to where I thought Rex might be and lay down on my mattress, waiting for sleep to come.

CHAPTER 17 – TERMS

On Monday I was roused awake by a guard. This one wasn't bringing breakfast. He was coming to take me to the Discipline Board. The name of this board was one of the things that made me sleep restlessly all weekend long. The name implied that I lacked discipline and that they were there to deliver it to me. The term "Discipline Board" sounded so sado-masochistic; I imagined women in fish net stockings with whips and chains. As it turned out, that would not have been so bad.

I had spent a great deal of my idle non-drugged weekend imagining that Naomi and Annette were each somewhere waiting for a letter or a phone call from me. I imagined Naomi showing up for visitors' hours on Sunday and being turned away. I imagined that the prison people would tell her that I was a "discipline problem". In between considering these troubling scenarios and the more troubling term "Discipline Board", I dreamt and I added to my manifesto.

I had nothing to write with, so I had to commit my words to memory by reciting them over and over out loud. I soon figured out that no one else was in this section except me, so I was free to say whatever I wanted without reservations. In my dreams is where the manifesto wrote itself, with the help of that mysterious voice that I had begun to call Thora. Thora was a wise and calming presence in these dreams and I believed she was part of some unconscious state of awareness that I had now discovered.

In the dream world, I was typically engaged in some task that at first seemed difficult, but I was soon able to master with the guidance of Thora. In all of these dreams I would persevere and succeed. When all was going well and I was a master of a particular skill, I would blow it all up and walk away. This part of the dream represented Misery Tenet number 3: Never do things that are expected of you. Tenet number 10: Never conform to the order of things, was also in play. In fact, all of the tenets were in play; they always were.

On Saturday morning I began to recite the newest addition to my manifesto. I could not write this down until weeks later so I had to commit it to memory. Even then it was not word for word:

> *The self-fulfilling prophecy is another part of the misery addict's repertoire; if you expect things to turn out a certain way, then all actions will be geared toward that result. The misery addict will be correct or be damned; and being damned really is no concern because that also can be a desired result. Failure is success, success is failure. Love is hate*

that hasn't happened yet. Happiness is tragedy delayed. It is a stew of impossibly contradictory logic that emits from one original thought: "I will not do as expected."

For years and in private I have taken apart and examined all of my own observations. I know my mind and what makes me happy. Happy, not in the form of outward delight, or an expressed smile, or a laugh; happiness in misery. Misery is the goal. Misery is all that there is. Pleasing other people also brings happiness, but only if I cannot share in that happiness. I know that I am capable of ruining everyone else's happiness and I know that I will do so out of instinct. I will turn your good news on its ear, so best not to expect me to celebrate with you.

The good news is to be shared with those who will just mindlessly celebrate as if this condition is permanent. I know it isn't permanent and will move directly to the post-celebration; where elation comes crashing into the banal or even into despair when the ultimate emptiness of the small victory is realized. You want clowns and I give you harsh medicine. You don't want me at your celebration. It is best that I shake your hand, pat you on the back, and say, "Congratulations," as I depart.

The old saying goes, "Hope for the best, but plan for the worst". In the misery seeker's world, the saying would more accurately be, "Know that the best is possible, but avoid considering it because the worst will inevitably happen, so accept it". The best part of being a misery aficionado - and I mean this sincerely- is our practicality. We do get things done and we are reliable. The greatest harm we misery enthusiasts cause is to ourselves. Our mission, our sacred mission, our calling, our purpose, our function, our absolute reason to be- is to be miserable. We plant seeds daily that lead to this condition's ultimate fruition.

These thoughts were written down in long form much later, but they were in my head as I sat there on Saturday morning waiting for whatever nothing was going to happen to me. I expressed these thoughts in some form to Rex as he sat on my tray and finished my breakfast. I also remember telling him how lucky he was to be a rat. I remember remarking that he was also named after a giant dinosaur with a small brain.

I'm not an expert on spirituality, but there are eastern religions that believe in reincarnation. They believe that your path of enlightenment moves in stages as you die as one form of life only to reborn as a higher form as you become enlightened. Conversely, if you live a life and do not get enlightened, then you must go back a stage or two. I am pretty sure that they don't believe that humans are the final stage in the progression, since this would make any religion quite unpopular. There has to be something much higher than this, right?

My thought on this religious exploration was that perhaps the rat is ultimately enlightened in that he strives for the simple and attainable instead of pretending that there really is some great purpose in all of the bullshit. I remember feeling proud of my conclusion as I sat there alone in a dark dank cell in some stone building built over one hundred years ago. On that one lonely day, I felt that all I could do in this world was to define the world for other people. Mostly I could define things for people like me. I felt I was gifted and I could explain all of the universe if I could just be alone the rest of my life. I was also still sore from my beating at the hands of the guards and, after my meds, I drifted back to sleep until it was dark.

Sunday was filled with trepidation; I knew Naomi would visit and I hoped that she wouldn't think too harshly of me. There's that word again- hope. I was actually entertaining hope. There was a part of me that saw this as progress, but deep down I knew that hope was what kills. I always bury hope as soon as it appears. I had to live with what was. I had made bad choices and continued to make bad choices. I didn't have to give Clarence my drugs and I didn't think about the consequences. I had done what I always do: which is to set myself up for failure in advance.

I had talked to my friend Isabel about such things often. When we met, she was in an awful marriage to a terrible guy. He cheated on her and openly bragged about it. He was able to make her feel like she had no other option but to stay with him. He was always calling her dirty and making fun of her intellect and telling her that no one would tolerate her behavior. He made her feel undesirable except as a sex object. If she gained a pound, he called her fat. If she took a drink, he called her a drunk.

When I met her, Isabel was considering doing herself in. She felt trapped and useless. I took on her misery as my own. I at first tried to make her feel good about herself. It was important to me that she didn't give up. I was there for her when she needed it and I believed that I did make her feel special. She would sing to me and it made me feel special. She saw where I was in my life and she told me to expect more from people.

We became best friends and then we became lovers. I never let up in my praise for her. I believed that it was important for her to know what she meant to me. I thought we had a breakthrough. For a short time I even thought we would end up together. In her case, she was done feeling tied down and wanted to date other men after her divorce. I can't say that I blame her, since I was married and perhaps too generous in my praise of her and maybe too good to be true in a sense.

Her "dating" lasted exactly one relationship before she fell for a guy who was even worse to her than her husband. He would take her out to places and leave her there with no money and no way to get home. She would call me for a ride and I would pick her up and take her home, sometimes even my home. I was still a loyal friend.

Sadly, Isabel kept going back to this guy. I had more than one confrontation with him on the phone and a couple in person. He would say the wrong thing and I would go after him. I have no fear, so if I got my ass kicked a few times, it came with the territory. She knew I cared about her, she knew I would fight for her, but in the end it didn't matter. She always went back to the abusive asshole.

She would always say, "All men are assholes, so what does it matter?"

To which I would reason that I wasn't an asshole, and she would say that I was the exception to the rule. It was all so pretentious; her claiming to want happiness, and then setting herself up for misery. Of course she was playing that self-fulfilling prophecy to the tee.

The end of my friendship with Isabel came when I really needed help. Predictably, once I was locked up, she decided I was too much for her to handle. After that first time I called, she changed her number. I sat on that mattress in that solitary cell and thought about her and what she was doing and who she was with. It made no difference that I thought of myself as a better person than whatever guy she was with. I knew she would always go back to the asshole and the asshole would never find a reason to change.

In my cell, in the dark, with my new friend Rex, I wouldn't trade my misery for hers in a million years.

****

On Monday after breakfast, the guards came for me. They entered my dark cell and one asked me to stand. I stood and he asked me to put my hands out. I held my hands in front of me and he slapped handcuffs around my wrists. He told me to sit and I sat on my floor-mattress. The other guard produced manacles for my legs. I chuckled a bit as I realized that I was going to be presented as a violent criminal who was likely to go on a murder spree if given even the slightest hint of freedom.

The guard slapped on my shackles and I did a little shuffle out the door and down the hall of the solitary confinement area. I emerged from that door to bright sunlight. It was a late autumn day, but it was unseasonably warm and sunny. I was blinded to anything that could have possibly been outside on that day. I was blind and I was shuffling and I was still in a lot of pain. Now I was going to be presented to what they called a "Discipline Board".

Upon entering a building on the other side of the compound, I was dragged up two flights of stairs to a set of big wooden double doors that opened inward. One guard opened one of the doors and the other escorted me inside a large meeting room. On the opposite side of the room from the doors and facing me was a large table. At the table sat three individuals. All three looked up as I shuffled through the doorway.

The board consisted of two women and one man. The man, who sat between the women, looked like an intellectual; he had round glasses and a balding scalp with gray patches on the temple and wore one of those brown corduroy jackets with elbow patches. He wore no tie. If he had worn a bow tie he would have resembled a professor. He had a slight chin and he fidgeted with what looked like an expensive pen. He had mild brown eyes and he dropped his pen when I first made eye contact with him. "Please, be seated Mister…," he looked down at the paper onto which he had just dropped his pen. "Mister Barrow." He finally managed to say.

I shuffled forward to a single curved plastic chair that sat about six feet in front of these three people. I looked up and scanned my evaluators. The lady on my left was a bit pudgy, but one could see that she may have been attractive in her younger years. For now, she had a large light-brown puffy-curly hairdo and she wore a little too much makeup and she had eyeglasses on one of those eyeglass necklaces. She was dressed in a blue and white striped dress that was being stressed at the seams in some areas. She had long fake fingernails and she looked down when I made eye contact with her.

The lady on my right was slim, but her face was not attractive; at least to me. Her nose was long and thin and she had no lips to speak of. He chin was even slighter than Mr. Elbow Patches. Her hair was jet black with some gray and it was shoulder length. Her brownish pant suit just hung on her, as her body had no definition. She may have weighed 95 pounds. She stared at me without blinking. Mr. Elbow Patches spoke again.

"Mr. Barrow, we are the Discipline Board and our function at this prison is to decide what action to take when an inmate violates any of the major rules of this institution."

He gestured to his right, "This is Miss Eleanor Delancey." Ms. Delancey smiled at me and looked back down.

He gestured to his left, "This is Miss Janice Caldwell," Ms. Caldwell didn't show any expression as she continued to stare through me. This chilled me some. I speculated that this lady was probably responsible for a few executions.

"My name is Theodore Grundy," he continued. "I am the chairman of the board. We will be deciding on a suitable punishment for your offenses."

I was a little stunned. *My offenses?* I was guilty already without any pretense or presumption of innocence. I had no lawyer or anybody to speak for me. My defense was going to be… me, if I was going to be allowed a defense at all. These characters were going to add to my sentence when my only crime was giving my unwanted medication to my nutty cellmate. I began to coldly look into Janice's cold eyes in an effort to make her stop trying to penetrate into my soul.

Theodore continued, "Mr. Barrow, On November 14, you attacked your cellmate, one Clarence Hollings. Mr. Hollings suffered severe head trauma due to your attack and is now in a coma." I never took my eyes off Janice as Theodore read these words. She never blinked.

Theodore continued, "Mr. Barrow you will be allowed a statement in your defense before we decide on your penalty." He looked up as he paused for a few seconds; which I took as my cue to begin talking.

"I didn't attack Clarence," I began calmly. "He attacked me. He was choking me and I pinned him to the cell floor. If he hit his head on something, I am unaware. He was still babbling as I was dragged out of the cell…,"

"Mr. Barrow," Janice interrupted, "He was kicked in the head and knocked unconscious." Her voice was nasal and annoying and made me wish I was deaf.

"Well I didn't do it." I replied. "Maybe one of the guards… they were pretty violent with me…,"

"Are you accusing the guards of assaulting him?" interrupted Eleanor.

"Ma'am," I answered, "All I know is that I was dragged away and he was still conscious."

The three board members exchanged looks and they looked at each other's notes. I didn't know how to take this; I was assaulted by both my cellmate and the guards and now they were going to charge me with assault or possibly attempted murder. I shifted in my horribly uncomfortable seat.

"Mr. Barrow," Theodore said after the little note-reading session, "the Discipline Board is given authority to extend sentences for up to six months." He lifted his arms to acknowledge his fellow members on either side. "However, in cases where the inmate's mental condition is in doubt we sometimes defer to a professional to determine any mitigating factors." He looked down at his notes again, and then looked up at me. "When is the last time you visited one of this institution's staff psychiatrists?"

"Sir, I have yet to visit with any doctors at this facility," I said, trying to sound as clinical as possible. Again, the board members went searching through their notes, Janice looked up at me.

"Well Mr. Barrow, it appears there has been an oversight," she admitted. "I think we can adjourn this meeting until we can gather more information as to your mental state. In the meantime, I think you should remain in isolation." She looked towards the rest of the panel. "If the other members agree, we can proceed to have a meeting set up with the prison's psychiatric staff."

Both of the other members nodded their approval, and then Theodore nodded to the guards, who helped me to my feet. I resumed my awkward shuffle back to my isolated cell. On the way back, I was still mulling the absurdity of my life. I had the key to happiness somewhere out there in the hands of a young confused heiress, but I didn't know when I would see her again. I was accused of attacking a guy who attacked me and I was being held in an institution run by morons of a high degree. Somehow, it all made sense. The thought that things were as fucked as always gave me a perverse comfort. As I eventually shuffled into my cell and had my restraints removed, a trustee inmate entered with my mail, and there was just enough light to allow me to read.

CHAPTER 18 – SISTER NAOMI

In my mail were five letters from Naomi and a statement from Tex the lawyer. I decided to read the really bad news first. Tex sent me a legal document with all of the fancy lawyer words which essentially informed me that I was not going to get a cent from the sale of my home. I silently put Tex at the top of my shit list. In fact, he was the only person currently on my shit list. He misrepresented himself as working for free and now he was going after my only real asset in the world. I gave his legal document the proper respect it deserved; I smeared it with oatmeal and I fed it to Rex.

The five letters from Naomi were only slightly better. Sure, they were bright and optimistic and were bulging with plans for the future; our future, but they were written pre-solitary. All five letters were nearly identical and they would have lifted my spirits had I not been locked in a hole. Knowing that that these letters were written before I was locked in this hole made them bittersweet. The letters did not depress or anger me, since bittersweet is pretty much what misery addicts thrive on.

The fifth letter was almost exactly like the first letter. Only the details of our future plans changed slightly. In letter one; she planned on us living in a small house on a ranch somewhere out west. By letter five, she had changed the ranch to an island and though the house was still small, it was part of a large compound occupied by many people. The letter was hand written on light green paper with blue ink:

Dearest Clyde,

It is Friday and I anxiously await our next visit. I think about you all of the time. I think about our future. I want to be with you because I see a magnificent man who does what he wants but also thinks of other people. I may seem naïve falling for someone who has so much trouble in his life, but I feel something about you. I feel your deepness. I feel like I've known you for years. I feel like I have known you in another life. My life has been leading up to meeting you and I will do everything in my power to make sure we are together.

I have been thinking about what we will do and where we will go. I think an island is the best possible world for us. Not only can we be away from those who would control us, we could do many great things. I want to start a home for terminally ill people and people rejected by society. I also want to help injured animals. I want a sanctuary, Clyde. I want it with all of my heart.

Anyways, I will talk about this with you when I see you Sunday. I haven't seen any of your letters yet since Tuesday. I guess the mail gets delayed where you are staying. But I will see you on Sunday. Only a couple of days away. I can't wait to feel your arms around me. I love you dearly.

XOXOXOXO,

Naomi

I folded the letter and put it with the rest under my pillow. I didn't know what to do with myself. Her words gave hope, but they drifted off into a tangent world where we would provide sanctuary to unwanteds and cripples. I had no real desire for this, but I would gladly do so for this girl. She seemed sincere and she actually had the wealth to make it happen. But how patient would she be with me now that I had assaulted another inmate? After a few hours of lonely contemplation, a guard brought my drugs and I drifted off to sleep.

* * * * * * * * * *

On Tuesday I had an appointment with a staff psychiatrist. After breakfast, I was taken to the showers first and given a change of clothes. After my "freshening up" I was taken to wait in an office adjacent to the library. It was one of those old offices in the older part of the building. Everything in the office was made of wood. I could smell the antiquity as I entered through the barred door with frosted glass and the word COUNSELOR stenciled in black on the front. Inside the office, the guard sat me down in a rather plush leather couch left over from early last century. The office was decorated very tastefully as if the Great Gatsby himself was entertaining here. It was too tasteful for a prison.

The guard walked over and sat in a chair by the door as we waited for the doctor to show. In a few minutes, a short chubby balding man wearing rumpled clothes walked in and took a seat in a chair across from me. He never even looked up from his notes. At long last, he looked over his shoulder towards the guard. "You may leave now; I will call you when I need you." With those instructions, the guard got up and left, closing the door behind him. The doctor turned his attention to me, but not his gaze.

"Good morning, Mr. Barrow," he said as he looked over his notes and fumbled for his reading glasses. "I see here you have been before the Discipline Board." He paused for an answer I didn't give, and then continued to shuffle papers.

"Mr. Barrow, can I call you Claude?" He finally looked up at me.

"Sir, you may call me Claude, but I answer to Clyde," I answered.

"I see," he replied with no hint of amusement.

"Clyde," he said, "I have good news. Your cellmate has regained consciousness. You may not face murder charges."

This news amused me.

"Is Clarence back to talking to bugs and blenders?" I joked.

The doctor paused over his notes, "Clyde, I do not joke about patients' mental conditions. Would you like it if people made fun of your mental condition?"

This was actually a pretty good question. I had to think of a good answer. All along I thought that people made fun of my mental condition. I was an infamous character and a cult symbol for crazy workplace violence. I knew for a fact that people found humor in my certain brand of crazy. I knew this, but I decided to word my response carefully.

"Doc, I understand the serious nature of your business, but I am not responsible for Clarence's injuries."

"Clyde, what medications are you taking?" he moved right on to the next subject as if my proclamation of innocence was a mere nuisance. His manner was completely dismissive, as if I was a child. I didn't like this guy at all. For one thing, he still hadn't told me his name. He wore no name tag and made no introductions. Maybe he was playing a head game or something I decided to draw him out.

"Doctor…," I paused, waiting for him to fill in the name, he didn't bite. "Doc," I said finally. "I had been taking Thorazine until I got here, then somebody changed me to some other stuff, I think Zoloft, Prozac, Clozaril, and some others. I didn't always take them."

"Clyde," he looked up from his notes. "You must take what we prescribe you. It is very important."

"Some of them made me jumpy, Doc." I replied.

I was really beginning to resent that he knew my name and he wouldn't tell me his fucking name. It seems like a small thing, but I was tired of being patronized and subjugated. I had to treat this as a test; it was too weird not to be.

"I see, Clyde." He scribbled something on a small notepad. "Do you prefer Thorazine?"

He seemed to only care about drugging me, not my childhood, not my relationships, not my goddamned Manifesto of Misery!

"I guess, Doc," I said. "I sleep better. My dreams are more vivid."

"Well, then." He concluded as he got up from his chair. "We will keep you on Thorazine." I left him a wide opening to ask about my dreams and he just walked away.

He continued to the door and called down the hall for a guard. It was then I caught onto his game; he wasn't telling me his name because he really wasn't any good at his job. He just dispensed drugs to losers who got stuck in this place. There was a reason he was here and it probably wasn't because he finished at the top of his class. He wasn't here to cure me or anybody else. He was here to punch a clock and collect a paycheck. It made sense that he didn't want me to know his name. He wanted me to forget about him as soon as possible.

The guard came and Dr. What's-His-Name left. The guard took me to my cell. I spent another week in that cell before the Discipline Board decided to go easy on me and return me to the general psycho population. I received word that my sentence was extended the full six months that the board was authorized to add.

I said goodbye to Rex and left much of my old food for him. He didn't even look up from the oatmeal buffet. Even though he never seemed to warm up to me personally, I felt like a traitor for abandoning him. Returning to my old cell, I found Clarence wasn't there and none of his stuff was either. I had the cell to myself and I had mail; it was a short note from Naomi saying that she was disappointed in not seeing me, but understood. She said she would come and visit when I was allowed visitors again. She also said she had big news.

I wrote her immediately with a tingling anticipation. The news of my extra six months would mean little if I had a real lawyer in the real world. I had my ticket to freedom and she wasn't giving up on me. I wrote and told her that she could visit the following Sunday. I wrote that I loved her very much and I really wanted to see her and that I had not been allowed to write in my solitary-confinement cell. It was a cheery letter and writing it cheered me even more.

I was so cheered that I sat down and composed a letter to my daughter to explain my current situation, leaving out any mention of Naomi. The letter was optimistic and cheerful and was full of future plans of seeing her sing on Broadway or perhaps at the opera. I sealed both letters and passed them to the trustee who picked up the mail when he made his rounds. I was in a good mood that day, which was surprising for a guy who just had six months added to his sentence. My good mood even lasted a few days; it lasted until visitors' Sunday.

When Sunday came I was escorted to the visitors' room where Naomi was already waiting. The smile on her face had a sort of majesty to it and her face had more color. Her entire appearance had taken on a kind of holiness. I walked to her and we embraced. This time there was no flirtatious rubbing and pressing of the flesh. It was a sincere, tight, and loving embrace, but not sexual in any way. She pulled away and that majestic smile was still on her face. She sat down on the bench seat opposite of my side of the table.

"Oh, Clyde, I know what I am going to do," she gushed. "I am so excited!"

"I am excited for you, sweetheart," I grasped her hands. "What is the great news?"

"Let's see, where should I start?" she turned her eyeballs upward as if the answer was written on the ceiling behind me. "Two weeks ago, I came to see you. I got here early because I didn't want to make you wait. When I got here, the guard up front told me that you weren't allowed visitors for a while. I was disappointed and I felt let down, but I knew there would be a good explanation."

"There is, Naomi," I cut in. "What did they tell you?"

"They told me that there was an altercation with your cellmate, but I knew about him because of your letters. He hears voices and probably attacked you."

"That's right," I said with a touch of excitement. Naomi was golden; I began to think that I really did love this girl. I mean, she stood by me and believed in me even when the whole world was kicking sand in my face.

"Well," Naomi continued, "I was about to leave disappointed when I spotted the chapel entrance to the right of the door to the visitors' rooms."

I nodded. The chapel was right next to the visitors' rooms and was very popular. Inmates and their families were encouraged to worship together.

"Well, Clyde," she started talking in a sort of serious low voice, "you know how they say things happen for a reason?"

"I do," I answered even though I really didn't subscribe the so-called "fate" line of thinking.

"Well, I decided that since I hadn't been to church for a while, it might be good for me to seek absolution for my sins." She leaned forward and whispered with the same smile she hadn't lost since I got here, "I am a bit of a lapsed-Catholic."

"I see," I said. I had begun to get that familiar feeling that I was going to be let down. It seemed inevitable sometimes.

"Well, I watched the service. It was a Catholic service and the priest's name is Father Quinn. He was really good. Have you met him?"

"No, I really have never been much for religion."

"I know, Clyde, but you are spiritual. You are deep. You transcend religion in so many ways."

"Thanks, Naomi. I am glad someone finally noticed," I said sarcastically.

"Stop it Clyde, I am being serious." She continued, "After the service, I approached Father Quinn and asked him for advice on my plans; you know, the island and the sanctuary. I told him about my wealth and my stepfather. Well, we talked and talked for a long time and he counseled me on my plans. Well, to make a long story short, I have big news."

"Yes, you said so in your letter," I smiled, "What's the big news?"

"Clyde, I am leaving on Wednesday for a retreat." She paused.

"A retreat?" I asked.

"Yeah, up in the mountains somewhere," she stood up. "I'm gonna be a nun!"

A nun? I sat silent and composed my thoughts before I expressed them. This was my style. People who know me have learned this and understand that patience is required to wait for my response. Impatient people tend to want to force the issue and this drives me deeper into thought while I make them await my answer, if I give one at all. Naomi was one of those who knew to be patient for my response.

It made sense that she would decide on this course of action. She was pure of heart and her love for troubled people was unquestionable. I hadn't pegged her as the type to lead a life of celibacy; in fact, I hoped we could find our way to a few conjugal visits while I was here. I actually was proud of her decision, but worried about where that left me. She was presumably going to be incommunicado on her retreat in the mountains and I worried she would forget about helping me get out of this mess.

"How long is your retreat?" I finally asked.

"I think it is six months or as long as it takes for me to decide what I am going to do."

She paused and sat down. "Are you going to be alright?" she finally asked, looking down at the table

"I don't know, doll," I said, grasping her folded hands. "This is kind of hard to take. I mean, I thought we would be together. I thought maybe we would raise a family."

The family thing was sort of a lie. I knew it was possible, but I really didn't plan it. If it happened, it happened. The truth is that I was still regrouping from the stunner she had delivered. I was attempting to pull her back to domestic life with me. I was hoping that she was just being flaky and that this would pass. The truth is I didn't have anything to offer her but my devotion. A mountain retreat would probably do her good. It would give her time to think and reflect. I hoped she would realize that she was going to be with me, but I knew hope is a silly thing. I suspected that she would likely just come to her senses, go back to her rich family, and forget me altogether.

"I won't forget you Clyde; I will help you all I can." She was still looking down. "But Father Quinn suggested that I search my soul for the answers and pray on the solutions. He thinks I have acted hastily and he thinks you should visit him too. I promised I would try to get you to go to church. You are down here on Sunday anyway. I don't know if this is going to work out, but I won't know for sure unless I try. I love you and care about you, but I don't know if I can be the woman you want."

This speech was sincere and I knew this was the way she felt. I knew she wasn't exactly the woman I wanted and deep down I suspected that woman probably didn't exist. I was stuck with who I was and the impossible expectations I must put on people. Naomi was a kid. I was much older and maybe she thought that she had to be a super woman or something. In reality, I had no idea what kind of woman I expected her to be. I started to feel like a clown who was using this poor girl.

"Naomi," I tugged at her hands that I was still clutching, "You do what you think is right for you. I cannot hold you back from this. If I did, you would resent me for the rest of your life. I hope you can write me. I will write you."

She looked up. "Only Father Quinn can get letters to me. I have no idea where I will be. So the mail will reach me through the church couriers."

"So you are going to make me go to church, huh?" I said this with a smile.

"Yes, Clyde," she smiled broadly, "Your heathen days are over."

"As if," I said and we both laughed.

"Clyde, I am so excited. I am sorry if I gave you false hope, but I have to get things right in my head. I have met mostly phonies in this life and I need to find out what else there can be. Do I have your blessing?"

"Naomi, you have my blessing," I said out of reflex.

I really did not put much value on my blessing, but it seemed to mean a whole lot to her, so I gave it without reservation. For the rest of our visit I told her about solitary confinement and Rex. I told her about the Discipline Board. I talked about the dreams where I kill my own success. We talked about my dreams while in real life another one was about to walk out. When the guard told us that our hour was up, we both got up and embraced. I told her that I loved her. She told me that she loved me and that god loved me. I stood and watched the guard escort her out. She looked over her shoulder and blew me a kiss. Then there she went…

Saint Naomi.

CHAPTER 19 – STIR

Alone in my cell, I was able to conduct an inventory of my situation and, most importantly, my feelings about the situation. I had not expected such a large dose of bad news. My situation had not really changed since I woke up on that Sunday morning, but my optimism had certainly diminished. I had foolishly let myself think that the future had promise, so I had to suffer the dashed hopes and try to adjust my expectations. Naomi had her own issues to work through and I was not going to be much help. I was going to be out of reach for a while. She decided to take herself out of reach while she examined the state of her own mind. I could neither hate nor blame her. In fact, I admired that she could do something like this.

My examination of my misery continued by examining it from a new angle: Faith. I had transcribed all of my recent memorized entries to my manifesto and I was ready to add more chapters. Just in time, I had confronted a new cause of misery. I now had to address faith and more specifically, blind faith:

Religious people seemingly accept things as they are written in a book or as they are interpreted by a holy man or woman. This fact might lead me to conclude that these people are less prone to being miserable. In my opinion, it would be a mistake to describe the devoutly religious as being happier than the typical non-religious misery addict. Jesus, after all, took on the suffering of many miserable people only to be betrayed and nailed to a cross. He acted humbly and is sanctified because of it. That fits the description of a misery addict quite closely.

The religious people who do not fit the mold of the misery addict are the ones who don't question and pass the word on to others. The religious zealots, who say one thing and then do another, are also not afflicted with this curse. They just happily con the world and feel no remorse. Then there is the blind faith that some embrace; this unquestioning belief frees them from the responsibility of examining the nature of their faith. If I, as an inquisitive person, am told that god will answer my prayers, then I question why he doesn't answer everyone's prayers. If my prayers are true and non-selfish and for the good of all mankind, well, he should answer them, shouldn't he?

Happiness is, in large part, determined by expectation. If you expect the world to be on board with your wants and needs, then you are going to be unhappy. If you just want be accepted, then it is best to go along with the expectations of a large group. If you seek acceptance and acceptance equals happiness, then religion is your ticket; just accept whatever principles they lay down for you. If one examines religion at all, it is more about control than anything. Some people like to be controlled. Some people need to be controlled. Sometimes the mechanism for that control is religion. Likely the people in control and the people being controlled are not misery addicts.

Naomi did not fit my definition of a misery addict. I had to put her in the category of someone capable of blind faith. Unfortunately for her, such faith had seldom been rewarded. She certainly had an uncommon trust in me. After I examined what was going on, I had to conclude that any sign of her faith being rewarded would send her down that road to a future as a holy woman. She needed to see good in people; she craved this, it was her curse and that wasn't going to change during a mountain retreat. I began the process of slowly letting her go. I decided that I would still write her, but I would no longer keep alive the hope that she was going to help me get out of here. Acceptance was my only weapon in this dank bleak place, and no amount of wishful thinking was going to change anyone's mind.

****

The days started to blur for me right after Thanksgiving. I was kept busy with a grueling job in the prison laundry. Annette did visit me on the Sunday after Thanksgiving and the visit was pleasant, but strained. She commented on how I didn't look too bad and I told her about my dreams and my visit to the Discipline Board. I told her about my visit to the strange doctor with no name. I told her how they added six months to my sentence and about my lonely boring useless days filled with walks in the exercise yard and meals and medicine. I wanted to know how her world was. She was full bore involved in school and had learned some exercises to strengthen her voice and she was going to audition for a Christmas musical staged by the college. She had been in school musicals in the past, but now she was going to try for the lead role. I was happy to hear this and apologized for not being a real father and she let me off the hook by saying that I had raised her well and had been a great father.

Then she broke down and cried.

I got a letter from Annette a few weeks later saying that she had gotten that lead role and that she would not be able to visit during Christmas vacation and that maybe after the first of the year, before the semester started, she could stop in for a visit. She also gave me the address of the storage unit where my stuff was kept, plus the codes to enter. I half-expected the news that she wouldn't visit me and I moved into a state of mind that I had become useless to virtually everybody. I did visit Father Quinn each Sunday. I talked about my totally secular life and he surprised me by opening up about himself. I passed notes to him that could possibly find their way to Naomi.

I heard nothing from Naomi as the winter months dragged on.

My free time was a routine of monotony and writing in journals. I only added to my Manifesto when I was inspired. I wrote of other things: songs, poetry, and observations about the daily routine of nothing that my life had devolved into. I had little interaction with other inmates. I found it curious that I was theoretically expected to return to society someday, but I was mostly kept isolated and I never saw a psychiatrist after my session with Mr. Doctor/Counselor What's-His-Name. I did not see Annette in January either, although I did get a letter where she expressed her regrets, but she had taken a few more singing gigs. I heard nothing from Naomi even though I kept writing. I stopped expecting anything except for people to forget about me.

In early February, on the coldest day of the year, I was walking around the exercise yard trying to keep my feet from freezing when I struck up a conversation with another inmate/mental patient. His name was Kyle Jackson and that's how he introduced himself.

"Hi, my name is Kyle Jackson," he said as we both entered the exercise yard.

The exercise yard was about the size of a football field; 100 yards wide by 50 yards long. It was divided by a 15-foot high chain-link fence every 10 feet or so. The guards would typically roust 20 or 25 of us from our cells and march us to the doors that led outside to these exercise pens. We were allowed to exercise how we saw fit. Each pen had a basketball hoop on the far end, although some of these were in disrepair. The wall under the hoop was made of cinder block where one could play handball or something. An inmate could request a basketball, a small rubber ball, or a soccer ball. Sometimes inmates would use the soccer ball to play a form of volleyball over that 15-foot fence.

Mostly, though, the inmates paced back and forth and socialized a little. On this cold day, there was nothing else to do. It was about 15 degrees Fahrenheit and standing still was out of the question. So I was pacing quite briskly when Mr. Kyle Jackson made his introduction.

"Hi Kyle," I responded, "My name is Clyde, Clyde Barrow."

We both began pacing slower to continue the conversation.

"What are you in here for, Clyde?" Kyle asked me.

"I beat up a guy at work and taped him to a chair," I said with a certain pride of accomplishment. "The D.A. called it kidnapping."

"I killed three people," Kyle proclaimed with more pride than I ever had about anything. "I followed two women and one man from a bar to a hotel. Before they reached the hotel back door, I ran them down with my car. Then I got out of my car and dragged them to my car and threw the man in the trunk and the women into the back seat. I made sure they was dead before I took them to my house. That's where they found me. The whole thing was caught on the hotel security cameras."

I was a little shocked; not by the crime, since everybody there had done something crazy. I was shocked at how easily and matter-of-factly the confession poured out of him. Kyle was nuts. He was the scary kind of nuts and I hoped he would die in this place. I didn't want to be his friend.

"When they found us," he continued, "we was playing cards. I was winning all of the money." He then let loose an unmistakable hillbilly laugh that went: "Haw hawhawhaw, hic, haw hawhawhaw, hic."

"N-nice to meet you Kyle," I said as I made a mental note to avoid any interaction with this goofball.

"Did you hear? They's gonna shut us down?"

"They what?" I stopped in my tracks and shivered while rubbing my hands.

"They's shutting down the prison." He said as he stopped and leaned towards me on the chain link fence.

"I hadn't heard that," I answered while doubting that this loon knew anything about anything. "I never heard of them shutting down a prison unless they had somewhere to put...,"

"They's gonna move all of the inmates up to the new private prison up in Cedarville," Kyle boasted

"Private prison? I...,"

"They's cutting budgets and the new prison was built with private money. They also will not have to buy insurance for the guards and all of the insurance liability goes to the contractor running the prison. I heard it from my cousin Norman; he's a helpin' build the new place."

Kyle, in spite of his ridiculous accent and butchering of the English language, sounded convincing. I decided that there was enough merit in his ravings to ask somebody who really knew. I decided to ask one of the guards.

I had really only gotten to know one guard well enough to ask him questions. His name was Tyler Finnegan. Tyler was about 6-foot 5 inches and quite burly. He had a crew cut and a round face. Tyler had an affable nature and was strong as an ox. He wore an easy smile and was often amused at how ridiculous some of the psychos acted. I apologize for using the word psycho, but that's what everybody in the prison called us and it's what we called each other.

Tyler had been a radio operator in Marine Recon and I had heard that he was a war hero of some repute, something about carrying his commanding officer through a hail of bullets during a firefight to a medevac helicopter. Tyler was respected by everyone, even us psychos. If you didn't respect him for his war-hero status or for the fact that he could snap you in two, you respected him because he treated you with respect, even us psychos.

A few days after my little talk with Kyle, Tyler Finnegan was escorting me and some other psychos back to our cells from exercise.

He had his usual half grin as he good-naturedly unlocked and locked cell doors for the inmates. I was the last to go in, so after I walked in my cell and he closed it with a clank, I spoke up, "Where are you going when they close this place down, Tyler?"

"What have you heard?" he asked as grin disappeared. I knew I was on to something.

"Just some crazy ramblings from Kyle," I replied.

"Oh, well Kyle probably got it all wrong, but there is talk of cutbacks and such."

"Are you going to lose your job?" I asked with genuine concern.

"They are opening a private prison up in Cedarville," he was talking loud so everyone in the section could hear him. "The thing is, if I work there I have to apply to a private contractor and lose my seniority, maybe my pensions, maybe my benefits aren't as good. Plus, I either move my family or I commute three hours in the morning and three hours at night." He made a forward motion with his palm flat and pointing downward.

"Dang, Tyler," I said. "That is a big change. Why are they shutting this place down?"

"A few years ago," he began, "they sent the head of the Department of Corrections down to Texas to study how they were able to save money within their system. Turns out, they were able to hire private companies and save tons of money. They just pay the company a set amount per-head, per year. The company pays the salaries and benefits and all of the costs of operation."

"That works?" I asked.

"It works in cutting costs, I guess." Tyler continued. "But the guards are paid less and are less qualified. Some of the prisons were converted warehouses or old military barracks. Some of these companies went real cheap on security and they housed like four inmates to a cell sometimes. Sometimes they lived in tents like that county out in Arizona. But the politicians only care about the bottom line until somebody gets hurt or somebody escapes."

"Does that happen?"

"It does happen, it is bound to happen, but the contractors who run these places run their own internal investigation on the minor incidents and most are covered up and never made public. Escapes are hard to cover up, but the few they have had were minimum security people. The really dangerous people are still kept in the state pen… for now."

"What are they going to do with us… mental cases?" I resisted the word psycho.

"I think the more dangerous ones will go to the maximum security state penitentiary; guys like you will probably go to private mental health facilities."

"I see," I said as I started to think of my next question.

Tyler continued, "Before this state passed the law allowing private prisons, they made sure that the private contractors built real prisons. That's what is going on in Cedarville. Some of it is subsidized by the state, since they had to build a new prison in any case. Places like this are falling apart."

"Yeah, this place is pretty old," I paused. "When do you think we move?"

"Warden says construction should be done by the end of the summer. Harder to build in the winter." Tyler lowered his head closer to the bars and whispered. "I think early fall for the regular inmates. The people in this section are going elsewhere, so I think it will be on a space available basis. But you didn't hear it from me."

I nodded. I was surprised and a little flattered that Tyler would confide this information to me. In my view, it meant that he had noticed that I was not going to run at the mouth to everyone. It was a small gesture, but the kind that makes a person feel like part of humanity instead of some sideshow curiosity. My family had given up on me, my friends had vanished, my potential redeemer had gone off to find herself, and my misery was in full bloom. My misery was consuming me and my sanity was being slowly sucked into a hole of endless despair.

Tyler nodded back, and then walked away. He was a genuine person, not the least bit pretentious and I hoped he could find a better job than this. But perhaps he liked doing this. Who am I to judge? I was just barely hanging on anymore. The news about possibly moving to a private mental health facility at any minute was both good and bad. Good, because I could maybe get the help I needed. Bad, because it made me anxious and worried, and that is not my best posture. Good, since I would no longer be locked up in some century-old prison that smelled like a musty cave. Bad, in that I was uncertain if I would go to a private loony bin or just get locked in another prison, possibly a worse prison.

Tyler did say that the dangerous cases were heading to the maximum security lockup. I didn't know where I fit into this. I didn't know if he knew that I had six months added to my sentence for being violent. My so-called violence had at least allowed me to have my own cell. I spent that spring in a strange limbo; I escaped into my dream world when I could. I wrote when I was inspired. I was preparing for a big change, but an unknown change. I had no maps and I had no guidance and I had nowhere to hide.

Change was going to find me.

CHAPTER 20 – MODIFICATIONS

Up until this point, this has been about Clyde Barrow. It has been Clyde Barrow's mind, Clyde Barrow's mistakes, Clyde Barrow's solitude, Clyde Barrow's misery, and the crack in the foundation of Clyde Barrow's psyche that led to his downfall. It has been the story of one set of principles and the consequences of their cumulative effect. It has been, up until now, The Clyde Barrow story.

But within my mind, in these days of waiting for news of a transfer, as I examined the sum total of my hopelessness, I considered the plight of those also confined within these walls and most were worse off than me. Some of these people would die within these walls. Their last moments and thoughts would probably be in the infirmary in the care of doctors similar to the pill-pushing nameless one whom I encountered in the Counselor's office. Some would die alone in a cell. Many of these poor souls would be buried in dignified, but largely anonymous graves. Their funerals would be attended by few, if any non-inmates. They would be remembered by their families as the person they used to be. Those people on the outside had moved on a long time ago from the undesirable rabble of the fallen souls who got shipped to this grim depot.

For those people I had pity and some sympathy. I have always recognized that I am fortunate compared to some, though I had never owned that feeling of privilege, mostly due to my self-absorption. So as the days turned to weeks I went through the hollow prison routines and listened to those misguided people who made the mistakes that required them to be removed from polite society. All of the stories seemed to be of abuse and neglect by relatives or some type of traumatic events. Most every man in this hole had a tale of a woman who did them wrong.

I came to realize that my situation was unique in nearly every way. For one, my wounds were almost entirely self-inflicted. Also, even though I had used others as they used me, I was not a deeply psychotic person. I had snapped and acted irrationally. My punishment did not fit the crime. I felt as if I had suffered enough, I knew this. The entirety of my consciousness consisted of these facts. It added to my misery, so I hoped to remain conscious as little as possible. Thorazine had become my friend and in my dreams, Thora was always there.

Without my Thorazine-induced dreams, reality would have been kicking my ass. I hadn't heard from Naomi and even my daughter stopped writing me. In my dreams I was a hard-working soul guided by the voice of Thora, she who boosted my confidence to where I was the master of all I surveyed. The dreams were all so real that I wished I could remain there forever and find the reason why I always self-destructed at the end. When I was awake, I wished to hear that voice, I wished to be sleeping so I could discover the person behind that voice. If I had to live in reality, I wished I could meet the person behind that voice.

In actual reality, I had become more isolated. Mid-summer, I got a letter from Annette in which she said the she had joined an alternative rock band called The Travelled. She was going to be their new singer and she had written some songs for them. In the letter, she said that her name in the band was Gypsy Rae. Rae was her middle name and she sometimes used it as her name in middle school. I was excited by the news; I couldn't wait to get out so I could see her perform. I wrote a letter to her expressing this sentiment.

A few weeks later, I got another letter from Annette, aka Gypsy Rae, telling me that she did not think it would be a good idea if I attended any of her concerts. I was stunned; I knew there was a stigma attached to being the daughter of a crazy man, but I thought she was beyond such prejudices. I doubt the world would care too much if I was a little off-center. I decided that it must be some bad advice she was getting. I always assume people who do not like me are getting bad advice. I wrote another letter saying that it was silly that I could not see one of her concerts.

About a week after her second letter, I got another letter. It was from one of those law firms with four names. Inside the envelope was a restraining order barring me from coming within one hundred yards of Gypsy Rae or Annette Rae Barrow. I took this news in stride; I should have predicted it really, I was going to be completely cut off now from everything I loved. It was Clyde Barrow being torn down to the bare floor. The world was going to push me in a corner and pretend that I never was. It was the saddest of all possible things and I never shed a tear. I just stared at the letter that told me in large legal terms that even my freedom wasn't worth much.

I continued to visit Father Quinn, although my visits were down to about once a month. I hated going near that visitors' center with all of the lucky bastards who had family, friends, and lovers. When I did go, I would pass to Father Quinn the five or six letters that I had written and although I doubted that he was forwarding them, I would still talk to him because I needed some sort of release. However, my goodwill towards him had faded since I had not received Letter One from Naomi. During my last month there, I didn't write her at all.

****

One August morning, just past the one-year anniversary of my crime, I was sitting in my cell, composing my random thoughts into a rambling treatise on the sublime pointlessness of insightful thought and unique personality. I was completely lost in my thoughts and listening to music on my cheap headphones. I didn't hear Tyler Finnegan approach, but he did get my attention when he banged on the cell bars. The clanging startled me, so I dropped my pen and removed the headphones.

Tyler was standing there with a big grin, "Clyde, you are one of the lucky ones," is all he said.

He pushed a piece of paper through the bars. I stood up, then walked over and grabbed the paper. It was a legal-looking form and it was written on the letterhead of The Department of Corrections. I looked up at Tyler who just kept smiling as he walked away. I read the letter to myself.

TRANSFER ORDERS:

Subject: Psychological patient/inmate Clyde Barrow (State Inmate #679842)

Action: Transfer to a private mental health facility

Memo:

Mr. Barrow is deemed to be of low to moderate danger to his self and others. He is a first- time offender who has been observed to display mostly good behavior and has been counseled frequently by the prison chaplain. The chaplain has written a letter of recommendation that Mr. Barrow not be transferred to

the state maximum-security prison with the violent psychological inmates and the repeat offender psychological inmates.

Due to closing of obsolete prisons, some less violent offenders are being sent to privately-run institutions.

Effective September 2nd, Mr. Clyde Barrow (State Inmate #679842) shall be confined to the Angelina Tallhill Memorial Wellness Center for the remainder of his sentence, subject to any parole hearings and mental competency evaluations.

Signed,

Doug Turgeon

Department of Corrections

I stood with this paper in my hand, not quite knowing what to make of it. I did not feel vindicated, but did feel like I was saved. I did feel a little ashamed of how I had misjudged Father Quinn. I knew there was a big difference between the maximum security lockup and a mental institution run for profit. I was not going with the Class 1 nutjobs like Kyle Jackson and the people who really needed to be put away. I had a chance to be redeemed. I wanted to tell somebody. I wrote Annette. I wrote Naomi. I wrote Annette and

Naomi again. I made plans to visit Father Quinn and thank him properly.

I had a letter with good news. I had something to look forward to. I had new things to consider. I had the unmistakable feeling of something slowly building within me in spite of all of my efforts to resist it. The feeling tingled and burned through all of the defenses I had built into my psyche to protect myself from folly and foolishness. The feeling arrived and took hold as my efforts to suppress this alien sensation failed and I confronted, then embraced that devil; that confounding trickster known as hope.

PART 3: BONNIE

CHAPTER 21 – THE ANGELINA TALLHILL MEMORIAL WELLNESS CENTER

It was an all-white compound in the middle of a 275-acre estate donated by a millionaire named Daniel Tallhill. I learned from my research at the prison library that Daniel Tallhill was three-quarters Shawnee. His mother, Angelina, was committed to a state institution back in the glory days of shock therapy. From his autobiography, I learned that Daniel was never convinced that she was really insane, but his father wanted to move on with his life and his business of making a fortune selling cars in the early days of the automobile. Daniel's father was half-white and he had a knack for selling cars and turning a profit. He wasn't going to let his wife's drinking get in the way of his success. He had her committed and then divorced her.

Angelina Tallhill died lost, alone, and forgotten. By the time Daniel was allowed to visit her in the asylum out in the mountains, there wasn't much left of her mind. She had no recognition of Daniel or any of her surroundings… and she seemed to have no personality whatsoever. Daniel so wanted to see the pretty young woman who used to sing him to sleep with tribal songs and bake him cookies. What he got was a shell of a person who babbled about where she could get matches to smoke a cigarette. Daniel was convinced that electroshock had ruined her and he vowed that he would build a place that would help people who were broken and maybe a little lost or addicted. Before he died, he donated the 275 acres and the funds to build the Wellness Center and staff the place. In his will, he also set up a generous endowment for continuing operations.

Along with the endowment, private donations funded much of Tallhill. The rest of their revenue came from patients who were there voluntarily.

With the privatization of prisons and real mental-health reform, Tallhill was one of the many private institutions who accepted thoroughly-investigated mental patients from the state at a per-head rate and on a space-available basis.

I knew a great deal of this before the white van pulled up to the prison gate to transport me and a few other inmates to Angelina Tallhill Memorial Wellness Center. I learned that Tallhill housed female patients also. This intrigued me as I imagined the days occupied with female voices in the breezeways and corridors. There was also the fact that they referred to all of the patients as members, as if it were some kind of bizarre Club Med. The guards called the place Tallhill and I remember liking the way that name sounded. So it came to pass that one day I climbed into the white van with three other inmates and we made the four-hour journey to Tallhill.

There were no side windows in the van and none of us transferees were much interested in talking, so the journey was a quiet one. I believe that the nervous anticipation and uncertainty had drained all of our imaginations. I know this was true for me. We all just exchanged looks of some sort of secret acknowledgement as if we realized that small talk was useless and pleasantries would be fake. Better to be silent and get your own mind straight than to feed the already-biased opinions of your relative sanity.

In those four hours of that windowless trip, I do not recall talking or even hearing anyone talk except the guards in the front seats. Even they only talked about the route and the exit they would take. If they talked about anything else, I don't remember. I just remember thinking. In my thoughts it was kind of an endless loop of the possible outcomes of this newest adventure.

In the first scenario, I was treated, cured, and released. In another, I was ignored and marginalized like I was in the prison. In another scenario, I became part of some strange new experimental treatment where things didn't go quite right. In all of the scenarios, my fate was left to others who didn't know shit about me. In all of the scenarios, Annette was still going to be distant and Naomi was still going to be a nun on some mountaintop somewhere.

That white van did eventually arrive at the gates of Tallhill. As I gazed through the windshield from my vantage point in the back of that van, the driver rolled down his window and announced our arrival to a speaker/microphone mounted on a concrete pedestal.

"Four new inmates from downstate," he announced rather loudly, "This is Sergeant Wilson."

The gates slowly opened and the van drove into the compound. Our view of the compound was limited to what we could see through the windshield, but what we did see was impressive. The hedges were trimmed immaculately. There were fountains and arches and fruit trees. From that back seat, I saw people, both male and female, working on the grounds. I assumed that these people were all patients, since they wore jumpsuits; the women wore purple and the men wore green. I cannot speak for my fellow passengers, but I found this development to be pleasantly surprising. I like to work and if I could get outside and interact with the opposite sex, then life had more in store for me than drugs and therapy.

Looking out the back window, I noticed the glaring lack of barbed wire on the fences. This meant that escape would be relatively easy, so I wondered what the other security measures would be. I assumed that there would be electronic bracelets used, a guess that would soon be verified. After the two-minute slow ride down the driveway to Tallhill, we stepped out of the van to take in the view of a grandiose mansion of white. On either side of the large sliding entrance doors were the obligatory children-pissing fountains that gave the place an air of faux class. The portico had a large arch decorated in plaster flourishes of flowers. Our guards followed us through the automatic doors to the reception area.

Behind the desk of the reception area stood a man in customary all white garb. The guards filled out a bunch of forms while my companions and I stood around the vast lobby admiring the paintings and the sculptures. I have no pretention of knowing what constitutes good art, but I remember thinking that they were over-doing it a bit. Every available inch on the walls were covered with paintings, mostly landscapes and seascapes, which I imagine were designed to calm people's moods. It probably worked on a good number of people, but in my case, I was still anxious as hell.

After the guards finished their paperwork, they waited for members of the staff to arrive before they removed our handcuffs. These staff members, who soon entered through swinging double doors, consisted of an authority figure in a gray business suit and what appeared to be four orderlies. The man in the business suit was tall and skinny with brown hair graying at the temples. He wore John Lennon glasses and stood in front of us and thanked the guards, who left without saying anything to the four of us who had been in their care for so long. I found this odd and a little disappointing. I was being treated as if I was a package being delivered or maybe the trash being left on the sidewalk for pickup.

The man in the gray suit spoke to us as a group, "Good afternoon, gentlemen and welcome to the Angelina Tallhill Memorial Wellness Center. My name is Doctor Ben Simons." He said these words with great enthusiasm and with a smile that was almost too charming. It was one of those smiles that people have when they know about something really funny that you haven't been let in on. In fact, the four orderlies had similar grins. It was as if they were all sharing some kind of psychic joke.

"These gentlemen are our associates who will help you with your processing and your introductory tour." He motioned to the four men in white uniforms who stood off to his left.

"Just a word about our place before we start," he continued. "This institution was conceived and designed to be like a home. It was created by the mind of Mr. Daniel Tallhill to be a place where our members are treated with dignity. This is not a place of punishment or a place of experimentation. This is a place of healing. You are here because what we call 'polite society' has decided that you have the potential to be cured and to be returned to that society. Please try to make this place your home. I and my associates here consider this our home and we are here to make your stay here as comfortable and rewarding as possible."

I began to fight the feeling that I had recently known as hope. I quickly replaced that creeping feeling with cynicism, which to me was more familiar and easier to wrap my mind around. I felt more comfortable disbelieving this presentation as a con and that I was being drawn into a false sense of belonging. I have been fooled before. The good doctor requested that we feel at home and my home was misery and skepticism.

"My associates will now take you for processing," Dr. Simons continued with that same knowing smile. "After your processing, we will get you something to eat and we will start our tour and our indoctrinations." The doctor then turned around and walked through the swinging double doors from whence he came.

I began to like Dr. Simons immediately, but I reserved my enthusiasm for a more complete assessment of what the tour of this new home was going to entail. I had been drawn in recently by false promises after I had carelessly let down my cynicism guard. I had made the state hospital my home and accepted some of those patients as friends and they had been taken away. I had accepted Dr. Marlin, then Dr. Monica as professionals interested in curing me and I had been let down. I had accepted Tex as a sincere country lawyer and he turned out to be a greedy shyster. I accepted Naomi as my salvation and she disappeared in my hour of need.

I was fully prepared for another disappointment.

* * * * * * * * * * *

After a bathroom break, each one of the four orderlies took one each of us "members" to separate rooms. I was taken to a decent size room by a blonde smallish young man who seemed to have borrowed Dr. Simons' smile. In the well-lit room were an examination table and two chairs.

"My name is Glen," he said. "I see from your paperwork that your name is Clyde Barrow." He stuck out his hand.

"Hi, Glen," I said as I shook his hand. "Are you people for real?"

"What do you mean, Clyde?" he said as if he'd known me for years.

"I mean, it seems like you all are in a cult or something," I said with my own sly smile. "I keep expecting Jim Jones or Charles Manson to be prowling the place."

Glen laughed, "That's funny Clyde; we actually have had several members here with a sort of messiah complex. But I assure you that we are not a cult. Our doctors, nurses, and orderlies are thoroughly professional and interested only in helping our members. Disrobe please."

Glen pulled a pair of latex gloves from a drawer and began to slip them on. I took this as the cue that my person was about to be invaded in a quite unholy way. I disrobed and the unceremonious invasion took place. With this indignity completed and my nether regions proclaimed free of all contraband, I was given a new wardrobe which was more like a green workout suit than anything else. I was made of some kind of polyester and fit loosely. Glen then fitted me with a security bracelet.

"Clyde," he said as he adjusted the bracelet and snapped it shut around my leg just above my ankle. "This bracelet is going to be part of you as long as you are here. I learned from your dossier that you are technical-minded. Therefore, you should comprehend how this bracelet works; it continually sends a radio signal that fades as it gets farther away from this facility. Approximately one quarter mile outside this compound, the signal is lost by the radio receiving the signal in the control room. When the signal fades enough, an alarm will sound. If the unit's batteries run down, an alarm is triggered. If the unit is tampered with or cut off, an alarm is triggered."

"I see, I better conform then," I said with a smile.

"Conforming is easy here, Clyde. This is a great place," Glen said as he disappeared into a walk-in closet. When he came out he had a stack of bed linens and several more workout suits.

"Clyde, these are six more changes of clothes, including boxer brief underwear and socks," he said, and then went back in the closet. When he re-appeared he had a pair of loafers and a pair of Velcro-fastening sneakers. "I want you to put on some socks and pick a pair of shoes for the tour." He paused and pushed the sneakers forward. "I suggest these; you have a lot of walking to do. Size 10 is alright I hope."

"Yeah, size ten is just right actually," I raised an eyebrow and tilted my head to the side as I said this. I grabbed the shoes and sat down to try them on.

"Super," Glen said as he watched me put on my shoes. "One more thing Clyde, I will be your personal trainer."

I looked up from my shoe fastening with a confused look, "My personal trainer?"

"Well, yeah, one of your personal trainers, but your main one." He sat down on the other chair in the room which faced me. "It's going to be explained as part of you orientation, but I don't mind telling you now." He scooted his chair closer. "Each member has a team of associates assigned to him or her. You will have a psychiatrist in charge of your case and he will have some associate doctors assist him or her. I will have help also; I can't be here all day. I will help with your physical training and determine what you eat. I will also consult with your doctor on which medication, if any, works the best for you."

"I am really starting to become impressed with this place," I said.

Glen smiled that same sly smile he had before. "It is a proven method, the sound mind and body and all; they are all connected. Frequently mental capacity can be affected by poor nutrition, vitamin deficiencies, or poor physical fitness. For instance, did you know that a lack of vitamin D can trigger depression and that vitamin D cannot be synthesized without sunlight?"

"Interesting," I interrupted, as I thought of all of the depressed people in prison who got very little sunlight.

"You will also be assigned a mentor from among the members who have been here for a while."

"A mentor?" I asked

"Yes, Clyde. It is part of the whole body healing we practice here. You will also be a mentor someday, if all goes well. We won't recommend discharge from here unless you can willfully help others."

I was contemplating all of this new promising information when there was a knock at the door. Glen opened the door and Dr. Simons walked in and announced that the tour was ready to start and that the other new members were ready. We walked out of the room and into the hall where we joined the other new members and their personal trainers. Our first stop was in the beginners' wing of the building, where we dropped off our bed linens and clothing.

Dr. Simons gave us a thorough tour of the building after lunch. We stopped at the theatre and saw a slide show about the history of Tallhill and its institutional philosophy. We stopped at the huge gymnasium and watched all of the activities we could become involved with. There seemed to be so many possible activities I could sign up for. We toured the library which was fully digitally wired for the internet. We took a fairly long walk around the outer perimeter of the facility, which revealed several gardens growing vegetables that were to be harvested to supply the kitchen, where meals were prepared for members and staff. We toured the dining area.

Our last stop on the tour was a room called The Members' Catharsis Center. As we walked down the hall leading up to the place, I could hear a female voice. It may have been the effects of a long afternoon and the long walk in the sun taking its toll on my brain, but I swore that I knew that voice. The voice was firm and authoritative, but friendly. The voice made me feel confident and welcome. It was the voice from my dreams.

It was Thora's voice!

As we drew closer, the voice became louder and drew me in more. The voice was being amplified by a microphone. We came to the door of the Catharsis Center, which was slightly ajar. Dr. Simons pulled the door full open and we all went inside the room. As the others took seats in the back row, I stood transfixed and staring.

On the stage, in a wheelchair, was a young woman. She was quite attractive, with short black hair cut in one of those flapper cuts where the front is longer than the back. She wore a modest amount of makeup, but she sparkled. No, she radiated. He dark eyes burned sincerity and purpose. I was smitten. Tears trickled from those dark eyes which she occasionally dabbed with a handkerchief as she spoke. It was her words, spoken with firmness and humanity that had the room enthralled:

"It takes one look into the eyes of a dying child to realize that you have been a fool. Those piercing eyes that tear away the pretense you have worked so hard to construct. The child may not know you are a fool playing pretend, but you know. You know and you feel embarrassed. The answers are no more within your reach as they are within this child's reach. But the trust displayed is obvious; you are the grownup, the adult, the one with all of the experience and knowledge. You wipe away the tears and conquer the fears. You have seen it all."

But you have not seen death. This little body is going to see that before you and the acceptance is apparent in the firmness of the smile. "'It will be alright,'" she says to comfort me. I weep. I am made of nothing but what I pretend to be. I am comforted by one who is about to lose everything. Every drink of water and every breath is precious and dwindling."

Small things are now important, the last song on the radio, the bird on the window sill. I hold a hand that will soon be cold. I hear the cough, the whispered voice, and coldness slips in. The breathing stops. I still hold the hand. I cry, but not for this short life that has ended. I cry for me, I cry for the beauty of what I now know. I cry because I realize that I can be free and this child has led me to know this. I will be better than I was because I know that what I have is not permanently warm. It is temporary, it is borrowed. The hand turns cold in my grasp. I let it go."

I looked around me and the entire audience for this catharsis reading was in tears. This included Dr. Simons, the associates, and the new members. For my part, I had tears, but I was on to another emotion, being stricken with a feeling that I had not known of before. As I watched this magnificent woman with the voice from my dreams being wheeled from the stage, I had a feeling that can only be summed up by the four words that kept repeating in my head:

I have found her!

CHAPTER 22 – THE ROUTINE

Clyde Barrow was in trouble; he had performed a desperate act which had landed him in jail, then the mental hospital, then prison, then finally a private asylum. He had lost all of his friends and lovers. He had lost his wife and his daughter. He was in a sort of trance waiting for the next kick in the stomach that life would deal him....

This was hand-written on a thrice-folded note taped to the outside of my door as I was starting the first day at Tallhill. In my former life I would think somebody was just toying with me, but here I took it as some sort of therapy. I was still curious about who wrote it, but I was going to keep my investigations to myself.

I had awoken this morning refreshed but stiff. I was invigorated mentally. I had witnessed with my own eyes the face and body that belonged the voice of Thora. I may have tricked myself into thinking this, but I was possessed with a magical thought that it all was real.

Was my real salvation this beautiful woman in a wheelchair and not the flighty Naomi? It took a few splashes of cold water on my face to shift to thinking that my new-found hope was actually delirium.

This was before I walked to the door, which was unlocked and unguarded. I opened the door and found the note and read it. I took the note back to the nightstand by my bed and put it in a drawer. In a moment, Glen was there to tell me that it was breakfast time and he had a list of food he wanted me to eat; mostly fruits, but also four eggs over medium.

"Clyde," he told me, "I have several members who I train. I will be your personal trainer, but not exclusively. I have menus here for the whole week; all three meals." He handed me a small binder. "I will give you this once; I will take you to the dining area once. I have the rest of your schedule here." He handed me a laminated paper.

I looked at the Schedule:

0800 Breakfast

0845 Work area

1130 Lunch

1215 Therapy

1315 Physical training

1415 Work area/Mentoring

1600 Personal time

1800 Dinner

1900 Personal time

2200 Lights out

I looked up from the schedule. "This doesn't seem too bad." I looked back down. "It says work area- slash- mentoring…?"

"Yes," Glen interrupted, "Those hours will become flexible depending on your work area."

"What is my work area?" I asked.

"That is up to what you want to do and what is open," he said as he looked at his watch. "We will get you assigned after breakfast. Remember, this is the only day I will guide you through this, after today you are on your own, you have your schedule." He motioned towards the door. "Now we need to get you breakfast and after that we will see what jobs are open."

Glen kept talking as we walked down the hall, "I or one of the trustee members will take you to your work supervisor, who will guide you through the fine points of that job then take you and your co-workers to lunch. I believe that one of your psychiatrist's assistants will get you from there."

Once we arrived at the dining room, Glen escorted me to a table marked by a large B in the middle. I sat down; a lady in purple brought me a tray of food.

Glen stood next to my table and examined my tray, then said, "Eat slowly Clyde," then he excused himself and left. I had grapes, strawberries, slices of melon, orange juice, milk, and four over-easy eggs. I ate slowly and drank my juice quickly. The juice was refilled promptly and I drank my milk. I had to admit that this place ran like a well-oiled machine. I even had time to sit and reflect since I had read that my schedule had me here for another half hour.

I analyzed my soft landing in this seemingly amazing place. I had truly lost everything and then some. Just a few days previously I was looking at a lonely future that probably would end alone in some gray hotel with other unfortunate dingbats. I would go to my grave dreaming about a mysterious woman and hoping my daughter would visit and wishing I knew what happened to Naomi.

However, things had changed. As I looked around at my new surroundings, I took stock of my few new blessings and my still-clinging troubles; I had a brighter outlook and I seemed to have found that dream-voice. My cynicism told me that my new home was too good to be true and it instructed me that believing I had found Thora was just wishful thinking and sleep deprivation. My troubles consisted mostly of my daughter's self-imposed estrangement. I was also still confined against my will and being ordered about. I had appointments and places to be for every hour of the day. I liked none of these things. But I could have landed in a worse place.

I looked around the cafeteria to where other members were coming and going and being dropped-off and received by associates and even other members. This new place was like a bee hive of activity and it seemed as if no one was complaining or protesting. It didn't seem like any of them were crazy, for that matter.

At precisely 0845, a man in green garb such as mine approached my table; he had short dark hair, a sly smile, and a patch on his shoulder that read, "TRUSTEE".

"Mr. Clyde Barrow?" he said he reached my table.

"Yes," I replied.

"My name is Steve," he said. "I will be taking you to your work area. Do you have any problems working outside?"

"Only when it's cold," I said.

"Hahahahahaha," he laughed, "you have a good sense of humor. Just leave your tray here. One of the members who works in the cafeteria will get it"

One of the things I had begun to understand about Tallhill was that they dealt in positive reinforcement. I had not heard one negative comment about me since I arrived. I guess this was good, but a very strange good. We began walking away from the cafeteria down a flight of stairs. On the lower floor we walked down a long corridor to a set of double doors that said "Garden Shop" on the outside. Steve produced an electronic card that was hanging from his belt by a retractable string. He passed the card over the card reader next to the door and the doors slowly opened.

Inside the garden shop there was a variety of lawn tractors and machinery to my left, stacks of bags containing fertilizer and seeds to my right, and a counter in front of us. Behind the counter stood a woman dressed in purple with a patch labeled "TRUSTEE". She was standing in front of several sharp tools; shovels, hoes, rakes, clippers.

There was no guard or associates in sight. I smiled to myself as I thought- *the inmates are really running the asylum*.

"Hi, Martha," Steve said, "This is Clyde. We will be starting him off in the garden crew. Could you get him some work gloves?"

"Of course," said Martha with a sly smile that was apparently the mascot for this place. If Tallhill had a football team- and I wasn't so sure they did not- it would be called the Tallhill Sly Smiles. Martha, with dirty blonde hair and major crow's feet around her blue eyes, had what looked like a slashing scar on her right check. She gave me a nod of approval as she turned to get a pair of gloves from a bin located behind her.

"Here, Clyde," she passed them to me over the counter. "You may keep these unless they get too dirty or tear. If that happens, just bring them back and you will get a fresh pair."

"Thank you," I said, as I reached for the gloves and momentarily touched her hand as we made eye contact. She gave me another look of approval and I became slightly aroused. It was an unexpected sensation that I had to quickly suppress, but it did make me wonder how much action it was possible to get in a place like this. I looked down on my schedule which rested in Steve's hands. *Nope, no sex on the schedule just yet.* Another secret laugh to myself.

Steve and I walked between the lawn vehicles to the outside door which he opened with his card. A bright shaft of sun light from between tall oak trees glared down on my face and I squinted. I shaded my eyes.

"Okay, Clyde," Steve said. "I will be dropping you off with an associate who will supervise you."

We stood and looked around. "Your supervisor will tell you what is expected of you," he continued. "He will tell you how to report for work in the future." He looked up. "Here he comes now. This is where I leave you." Steve stuck out his hand and we shook. "Good luck, Clyde," he said and he was gone before the supervisor arrived.

* * * * * * * * * * *

The supervisor was an older gentleman who wore white coveralls that had brown stains on them. He wore shaded safety glasses and he was removing his gloves as he approached me. He stuck out his hand and I shook it.

"My name is Charlie," he said. "I will be your supervisor." He had that same sly smile and he had a very wrinkly face. I was guessing that he was about seventy years old and he was kind of smallish- maybe 5 feet and 6 inches- and not powerful looking at all.

"Nice to meet you Charlie," I said. He handed me a pair of shaded safety glasses with his very next motion.

"Let's get you a hoe, Clyde," he said as he scanned his card over the card reader by the garden shop outside door. "We are going to take one of these tractors to the outskirts of this place," he said as we entered. "You are going to be turning over a row in one of the gardens where we have already harvested the food. It's hard work, but good honest work. It helps to keep you occupied. It makes the days go much faster."

We walked over to where Martha stood and she already had a hoe in her hand. I signed for the hoe in the property book and Martha told me to have her hoe back by the end of the day or she would come looking for me. She said it with a smile so I laughed and thought about her sexually again. Again I suppressed this feeling instantly. Charlie jumped on one of the garden tractors and Martha opened the large garage door that led to the outside. I put on my shaded safety glasses as the sun stung my eyes.

"Jump on the back, Clyde!" Charlie shouted over the sound of the tractor.

I obeyed and sat on the back, facing outward like a little kid going on a fun ride with grandpa. As we rolled out the door, Martha waved goodbye and I waved back as she disappeared behind the descending garage door. We rode that tractor for a good twenty minutes before we arrived at the outer reaches of the compound. On the way I saw members everywhere running lawnmowers, clipping hedges, pulling out stumps with tractors, hoeing gardens, raking, working on sprinklers, spreading fertilizer, and other tasks. Almost all of them had sharp tools at their disposal. I only saw two or three associates supervising them and none of them seemed big or powerful. It didn't take much of an imagination to think that this was a tragedy waiting to happen. As I watched the workers dedicated to their tasks, I recalled that in my previous research, I had not uncovered any reports concerning a violent incident of any kind at Tallhill. It was truly an amazing place.

Upon arrival at my patch of dirt, Charlie shut off then dismounted the tractor and I followed. I stood there, holding the hoe with the blade up. Charlie walked around the tractor to my side and put his hand on my shoulder.

"Clyde, this garden has been harvested," he pointed out with his palm pointed down and made a broad sweeping gesture. "I need you to go up each row and bring all of the dirt from the underside to the top. Then work the next row the same way on your way back" He looked me in the eye. "Each row should take about fifteen minutes."

He slapped me on the back and walked back around the tractor to take his seat. Before he started the tractor, he said, "It's 9:15 now; that gives you two hours. I expect eight rows by the time I get back here." With that, he started up the tractor, put it in a higher gear then sped away.

I stood there for a moment under the realization that there really wasn't much to prevent me from walking away. I scanned the trees for cameras and found a few, but I reasoned that I would be over that fence before anybody watching a monitor could react. *Maybe the fence is electrified,* I thought. I shrugged. I could escape later and I really had no plan and nobody on the outside to help me. So I hoed my eight rows to the best of my ability and in two hours Charlie was promptly there to pick me up, this time on a golf cart with two other male members dressed in green, one in the passenger seat and one in the back.

Charlie scooted out of the drivers' seat of the cart and walked over to examine my work, "Nice work, Clyde," he smacked my back again, "Very thorough." He smiled and grabbed the hoe, which he slid into a golf bag on the back of the cart. I slumped into the vacant back seat of the cart and we whirred away in the electric cart.

We rode back to the garden shop, where Steve the trustee was standing with that Tallhill smile on his face. He took off walking towards the door and the three of us members followed. Once inside the door, one of the men in green stopped to open the garage so Charlie could drive in. I stopped for a second too, but Steve kept walking towards the counter where Martha still stood, smiling. I followed and smiled back at her as I approached the counter.

"Wash your hands over there, Clyde," he said as he pointed to a deep sink. I stuffed my work gloves in my pockets, washed my hands and dried them. I smiled at Martha again as I followed Steve out the door.

"You have lunch for the next forty-five minutes, Clyde," he said as he walked briskly and I kept up. "After that someone will take you to meet your therapist. After today, you will reach all of these destinations on your own. So pay attention."

As we walked down the hallways, I marveled at the activity that went on all around us. People whizzed by me in the hallway, some with that by-now familiar knowing smile and some with just determination. There was not much talking. I had read that they had no escapes, but that could have been just marketing. If true, it was like some kind of miracle as far as I was concerned. People have a million reasons to want to leave, but at Tallhill I guess the theory was to make the everyday drudgery seem like a mission. I decided I would stick with that theory until my mind changed.

My lunch was also regimented. It was lean roast beef piled high with a generous side of mashed potatoes smothered in brown gravy and very buttery Brussel's sprouts. I ate greedily at first until I remembered Glen's admonishment to eat slowly. *Sound mind and sound body,* my mind repeated the mantra as I realized that I was becoming one of THEM. The bizarre thing was that this thought did not trouble me at all.

* * * * * * * * * * *

At precisely 12:15, a man in a nice black pinstriped and vested business suit strolled up to my table. His hair was combed back on his head and he had kind of a slick shuffle walk, which made him appear to be gliding. He had a kerchief in his left breast pocket like some kind of holdover from the 1940s, when all of the gentlemen dressed this way, at least in my imagination. He also had that smile that was beginning to grow on me a bit.

"Clyde Barrow, my name is Dr. Sinclair Baxter," he announced as he glided into my immediate presence.

Of course it is, I thought.

"Pleased to meet you," I actually said as I stood up and shook his outstretched hand.

"I am going to be your principal therapist," he said as he sat down. "You may call me Dr. Baxter, but my friends call me Silk. It is a play on the name Sinclair. You may even call me Dr. Silk if you please."

"Okay, Doctor, I guess, I will call you Silk then," I said

"Very well then, Clyde, let us get started," he stood up and started walking away. I left my mostly-empty tray and followed.

We walked down another long corridor to an office that had a frosted-glass window on the door. The lettering read: Dr. Sinclair Baxter, Chief Associate Psychiatric Counselor. Silk opened the door for me and I walked into an office that had soft light and mellow music playing. I guess the desired effect was to get me to relax, but after hard work and a meal, Silk was going to have trouble keeping me awake.

"Take a seat wherever you like, Clyde," the doctor said as he closed the door behind him.

I went straight for the couch and stretched myself out quite readily. The couch was probably more comfortable than my bed- which was damned comfortable.

"Clyde," I heard Silk's voice say, "I see here that you have been on Thorazine for a good while."

"Yes, Doc… Silk," I said as I scooted up a bit on the couch.

"What effect has it had, in your opinion?" He asked.

"Well, at first it put me in a daze, then it became the only thing I could rely on to get me through the day, you know… sanely." I looked over at him to see if that was a proper clinical term. He didn't react. So I continued. "In prison, it was my only real relief; I had the most amazing dreams too. If they had taken Thora away from me, I probably would have cracked. I tried other stuff but…,"

"You said Thora," he interrupted. "Is that your pet name?"

"So I did," I said as I realized how I really felt about the drug.

He didn't respond, so I went into quite specific detail about my dreams and the voice. I talked for the rest of my session about these dreams where things were difficult at first, but the guiding voice had helped me overcome the obstacles just so I could dash my own hopes by tearing down my own accomplishments. Silk let me talk with few interruptions and when my session was over, he stopped me.

"Clyde, the clock on the wall rules around here, so I will have to end our session, I am going to discontinue your medication. I think you have been relying on it too much. I think you will find real tangible help here that will help the real you escape from all of the fences you've built. I believe you will see that the harm you have suffered is self-inflicted."

I sat up in amazement at this spot-on diagnosis. In the soft light, I could see that he had that smile on his face. I didn't have much to add to his words, so I remained silent. I was conditioned to think that people were just trying to trap me, so I let his insight just hang in the air. I wanted to think about this alone so I could decide what exactly I had revealed that this doctor understood much better than Dr. Marlin ever did after reading my manifesto.

The slightly uncomfortable moment passed when a knock came at the door. Silk opened the door and there stood Glen, right on schedule. He had six members with him- three male and three female.

"Hello, Clyde," he said. "Ready to exercise?

The truth was that I wanted to go to sleep, but I knew by now that this was not scheduled.

"Sure, Glen," I managed to say. "Thank you Silk," I said. Silk nodded and we all walked quite briskly to the gymnasium, which seemed like a mile away.

Inside the gym, which was massive, people were playing volleyball and basketball. Some were hitting a heavy bag and some were just stretching. Glen and the rest took off walking towards a door at the opposite end of the gym, so I followed. We reached a door marked YOGA, which was next to a door marked SWIMMING POOL. Again, I was amazed. This place was like a resort.

Once inside the door, the other members went to exercise mats placed in rows and began stretching. The door closed and no sound could be heard outside the room. Glen motioned to me and I sat down on the closest mat to me.

"Clyde, this is your first day," Glen said. "Have you had any Yoga training?"

"Some," I replied.

"Good," he said as he handed me a chart which diagramed Yoga positions.

"So you know we are going to do a whole lot of stretching."

I began doing the same stretching that the others were doing. Yoga is about finding your center and being limber and it can be quite trying and invigorating. Just to say, that by the time I left there, my fatigue had been supplanted by some sort of energy that I didn't understand.

At precisely 1415, Glen told us that the session was over. I was in the cobra position at the time. The cobra involves lying on the mat in the prone position with palms flat, back arched, and the head tilted back. I had my eyes closed and I was in some quiet place. When I heard Glen, I opened my eyes to see the smiling face of Steve the trustee standing near the door with a clipboard in his hand.

I relaxed my posture and Glen handed me a towel. I stood up and toweled myself off as I walked towards Steve.

"Hi, Steve," I said. "I guess it's time for more yard work."

"Actually, Clyde, it is time for you to meet your mentor," he said as he bounced onto the balls of his feet a little too excitedly.

He turned and opened the door and I followed him through. We walked the country mile back to my room as I alertly remembered the route for future reference. Anticipation was the feeling I remember as we approached the final steps towards my quarters. Upon reaching my door, Steve excused himself and left. I opened the door.

Inside, next to my bed, in a wheelchair, sat that lovely girl with the comforting voice. She was looking through pages of a sizeable three-ring binder. She looked up at me, but not with the house-approved smile, but a genuine-looking smile of satisfaction and eyes of expectation.

"Clyde Barrow, I presume," she said.

I stood for a moment in the doorway, stunned, then walked on wobbly legs towards her as my will and my heart melted.

CHAPTER 23 – BONNIE

Bonnie (not her real name) had been a dancer. She told this to me within the first few minutes of meeting her. A dancer in a wheelchair is like a bird without wings; a grounded and flightless victim of some unexplained calamity. But Bonnie is not an object of pity and not an object at all. She is an alive vibrant wonder and a tribute to the human spirit.

I walked into my room and sat on the edge of my bed next to the young lady in the wheelchair.

"Yes, I am Clyde Barrow," I replied to her inquisition and stuck out my hand. "And who do I have the pleasure of meeting?"

"You have the pleasure of meeting Bonnie Parker," She smiled broadly and gasped my hand harder than most men would or could.

"What are you reading?" I asked as I cocked my head to the side to get a better look at the large binder which rested on her lap.

She kept smiling at me in a sort of almost-laugh and said, "It is the brief and chaotic history of a recently declared lunatic named Clyde Barrow."

This sort of bluntness was not the least bit insulting coming from… from that voice. It was disarming and charming even. I would not have been more defenseless if I was naked in a nest of crocodiles. I had to think quickly to keep up with the droll humor of this conversation.

"I think I read the beginning of that book," I managed. "Don't tell me how it ends."

"I am to the part where he meets his match in the young feisty brunette in the wheelchair," she said with those laughing-smiling eyes.

"I hear that's the best part," I shot back at her.

"I am hoping so, because up until now this guy just seems to be getting tough breaks and is too caught up in his own self-pity." As she said this I started to feel a little hurt. "He even wrote long diatribes trying to figure out what he should already know."

"You seem to know a lot about this poor fellow." As I said this I slid away from her and reclined on my bed.

"I just know a hard case when I see one," she said in a more serious tone.

"Miss Parker, I was asked to analyze my misery by this doctor I used to visit," I said with a tiny bit of irritation. "I did the best I could. I tried to give the reader a perspective on my life."

"Please, call me Bonnie," she said in an even more somber tone. "I think I have struck a nerve."

"Not really Bonnie, I just have been introspective for my entire life and I poured my feelings on to those pages so I could be taken seriously. I occasionally want too much from people for some reason. I operate under the belief that people are basically selfish and pretentious, but then I am somehow disappointed when this is actually proved out. It is quite confounding."

"I see," she said as she closed the book. "I think I see the real Clyde and he is very close to the surface. The real Clyde is proud and beautiful. The real Clyde holds people up to impossible standards while calling those standards a fantasy. You want to have your cake and eat it too."

"What about you, Bonnie?' I asked as I sat up in the bed.

"What about me?" she asked surprised.

"Yeah, your story," I said.

"You mean why am I in a nut house and in a wheelchair?'

"Well, that, plus everything else," I replied. "I want the whole Bonnie Parker story. You know so much about me and I just know that you are pretty, smart, funny, and in a wheelchair."

I could see that she was not expecting this, but I was feeling cornered and exposed. I had to get to know where this creature was coming from before I let her take me by the hand. I had never had a mentor and I didn't like people having the upper hand intellectually, which she clearly did at this point.

"Clyde, I will start by telling you the story of my parents," she began.

"My parents were born and raised in a small town out on the Great Plains. My father was the son of the town locksmith and my mother was the daughter of farmers. My father was the one who was going to get out of that town by going to college. His mother died young and his father took every job imaginable to see that his son had a better life. My father, whose name is Benjamin Parker, also worked hard at everything. He was the top of his class in school, he was the quarterback of the football team and he was the valedictorian. He won a scholarship to college to play football, but also earned a law degree.

"My mother was the youngest of seven kids- three boys and four girls. Her brothers were all going to inherit large sections of the farm and the girls were all going to marry local boys and never leave. But not my mother; not Rosemary. Rosemary was the dreamer and the romantic. She saw the limitations placed on her as someone else's issue. She loved to dance and she played several instruments and even sang. She was quite beautiful. Her father had met her mother in Spain during World War II. He was in a part of the war that few people knew about. But that's another story. They married and she followed him to the states after the war, where he took over a struggling family farm. He took it over and made the farm a success and raised a beautiful industrious family that was going to stay in that Great Plains town and do like he did."

"Except for Rosemary," I interrupted.

"Yes," she stopped and smiled at me. "Not Rosemary. She knew she had talent and she knew she was pretty. She had many suitors, but they were all going to stay in that Great Plains town until they died. She wanted to go places. She was two years younger than Benjamin, but she could see that he was her ticket out. He was not going to inherit anything from his father but unpaid bills, a sore back, and calloused fingers. He was going to play football at the state school and study law. They started dating during his senior year in high school. By the end of his first college year, he proposed, but I think she might have been pregnant also, because they got married in a courthouse in that university town."

"The baby was you?" I interrupted again.

"Clyde," she admonished me, "I won't get through this story unless you stop making me lose my place."

"My mistake," I said. "But at least you know that you have my rapt attention. Please continue."

She stared at me for a moment with a furrowed brow before she continued. "Dad had to limit his classes as he took a job to help support his prospective family. He still finished law school, but it took him a little longer. When he graduated, he took a job as clerk for a big city law firm. By then I was probably six or seven."

"My mother put off her dreams of being a dancer, but at least she got out of that town that her sisters were condemned to. They had all married and had broods of kids, but hardly set foot outside their home county their entire lives. I kinda liked to visit that little town sometimes, but I digress."

Once I was old enough to go to school full time, my mother took a job as a dance instructor. She started out at a small studio, but her number of clients grew in a few years, so she started her own studio and hired assistants. I was at her side most of the time; learning to dance. She took a great deal of her earnings and enrolled me in a top-flight ballet school. I was going to be a ballerina, Clyde. I had the talent and I had the discipline."

"What happened?" I asked, not realizing that I had interrupted until she shot another furrowed-brow look.

"Chandler happened," she continued, "Chandler Chadwick the Third. With the pretentious name and the striking good looks, plus the charm honed over generations of manipulating people. His dad was a full partner in the law firm my dad worked for; 'Chadwick, Fox, and Silkwood'. My dad had passed the bar by then and had become a hard working lawyer who was always on top of his game. He was a star and on his way to becoming, hopefully, perhaps, maybe a junior partner someday."

At this point, she wheeled herself over to the water cooler in the corner of the room and poured herself a paper-cup-full and drank it down before re-filling and repeating the process. She wheeled back over to me and started again. "Clyde, I realize that my story has a lot of should-have-beens in it so far, but I want you to get the full picture of what I was like in my former life before I tell you the cause of my current condition."

As she spoke, I was thinking about the calm measure of her voice and comparing it to the voice in my dreams. I was sure they were the same, though I cannot tell why I was convinced of this. I do not believe in kismet or fate or the supernatural, so I had no coping mechanism to rationalize these thoughts. I just accepted her as the one from my dreams and fell under her spell.

"So one day, I am attending one of the law firm parties with my parents. I rarely went to these, but I was by then in my late teens and they perhaps thought that they could show me off to the society types running in that circle of friends that the top lawyers found themselves in. This particular get-together was at the Chadwick mansion. I remember walking in that door and being overwhelmed with the opulence of it all. I didn't know it at the time, but my parents were considered to be social climbers by these folks. We weren't of their class and everybody there knew it.

"The only thing I could tell you about that night is about Chandler. Other people talked to me and I was introduced to showbiz people, and industrialists," she waved her hand with a rolling motion. "And movers and shakers, and shakers and movers. Their names and faces are a blur now, as they were then. At one point I was talking to a couple of the assembled splendid luminaries when I stole a glance over the shoulder of one of them and saw Chandler. We made eye contact and he immediately excused himself from the small group he was with and walked right over to where I stood.

"'Hello,' he said as he grabbed my hand, bowed, and placed a kiss on the back. 'My name is Chandler and I believe that I am in the presence of the beautiful Bonnie Parker.'

"Goddamn, he was charming. I was defenseless. I didn't need to do anything the rest of that night but stand and sit by his side. We were left alone for much of the night; he took me on a tour of the house and the grounds. He made several witty comments to which I politely laughed. People nodded approvingly at us at every turn. When the band began, we danced every dance we could and by the end of the evening, I was in love and there was nothing but approval of this development coming from all quarters, especially my parents."

As these words lingered in the air, a knock came to the door. I opened the door to Steve the trustee. He was still in possession of the institutional smile.

Bonnie looked up. "I have successfully wasted our time talking about myself, Clyde. I think I will finish this in out next session. Is to-morrow okay?"

"Yes," I replied with disappointment at having to wait any longer to discover the Bonnie Parker story.

"Same time, then Clyde," she said as she wheeled herself through the door which was being held open by Steve.

"Wait," I said as I looked at my schedule. "Do I come here every day or do I report to my work area?"

She pivoted in her chair, "I will re-do your schedule, I don't think that they need you for yard work as much as you need to find out how you are going to get better. You will be with me every day, if that's okay with you. You always have the right to refuse a mentoring."

"I will see you tomorrow, Bonnie," I said as I placed my schedule on my bed and headed out the door, still being held open by Steve. "Can I push you anywhere?'

She shot a surprisingly cold stare out of those dark eyes, "No thank you, Clyde. I am very capable and this is good exercise."

"Very well," I said as I closed the door behind me. "I eagerly await our next encounter."

She wheeled herself away towards the elevator as Steve took off in a brisk pace in the opposite direction. I followed.

CHAPTER 24 – FREE TIME

The term "free time" implies that I could do anything that I wanted. Free time for the people at Tallhill was limited to inside the building and the outside breezeway area. Members could sit in their room and write letters; they could visit the library and use the computers. There was a chance to do laundry. There was also the break room.

Steve took me directly to the break room. I had seen the break room on my initial tour. The room was large enough to accommodate eight big screen televisions, four pool tables, four ping-pong tables, six computers with half-hour time limits, and other minor distractions among several large comfortable chairs and couches. It was clean and well organized, with only small groups formed and those people talking in low conversational tones.

I walked into the break room and immediately my eyes went to a black man sitting in a large chair watching a baseball game on television. He wore a Houston Astros' baseball cap and he was watching a

Houston Astros' game. It was Amos, my friend from the state hospital.

Steve put his hand on my shoulder and said, "Clyde if you want to, you can spend your free time here, dinner is at 1800. You could also go to the library. I could also escort you to the outside breezeway..."

"I will be fine here," I cut him off and began to walk towards Amos while wondering what his impressions would be of this place.

"Very well," Steve said over my shoulder. "You can find your way to the cafeteria?"

"I can," I said as I turned around.

"Super," Steve said with that unfailing smile as he disappeared through the break room doors.

As I walked up to where Amos sat, he looked up and a faint look of surprise appeared on his face and then he returned to his normal thousand-mile stare. I walked over and sat down on the chair next to him.

"Hello Amos, you look well," I said somewhat cheerfully.

"I'm alright Clyde," he said as he looked at me momentarily before returning to his television gaze.

"Houston Astros, huh?" I asked.

"Versus the Atlanta Braves, playoffs at stake," he deadpanned.

I instinctually knew to keep my mouth shut until there was a commercial. There were two outs with runners on first and third in the eighth inning. The Braves led 3 – 2, but the Astros were threatening. As the Astros pulled off a double steal to tie the score, Amos leapt from his seat, slapped his hands, and let out a little "ha-haaaaaa".

"Good managin' there, Clyde," he said without taking his eyes off the screen. "Put pressure on the defense."

The batter popped up the next pitch and the inning ended with the score tied. I saw an opening.

"So Amos, how long have you been here?"

"I got a break a while back when it was found that I was the victim of a fraud involvin' a prescription drug that wasn't tested too well," he answered in his non direct way without looking at me. "I had a psychotic reaction which landed me in that state hospital."

He looked over at me, scooted forward in his chair, and then crouched down to talk in a whisper, "My lawyer got me a big settlement and I got treatment for my brain problems paid for by the big drug company." He slid back on his chair.

"Interesting, do you like it here?" I asked. But the game was back on he had drifted back to watching balls and strikes.

"I guess I been here goin' on five months now," he answered my previous question after the first out was recorded.

I waited, hoping that my next question would be answered after the next batter, but instead he changed the subject back to baseball.

"My daddy was a baseball player for the Astros' farm team up in the northwest. I never knew him." I was getting the answer to my first inquiry. "But that's not why I am an Astros fan. I always liked Nolan Ryan; that dude would just make batters shake, ya know?"

"Yeah, he could bring the heat," I off-handedly remarked.

A batter reached base and the Astros made a pitching change. This left another opening.

"They found my daddy swingin' from a hotel shower in Idaho when I was just a kid. I guess he kilt himself. That's what they say."

"Sad," I said with a complete lack of anything else to add. I was not about to ask another question for fear that I would lose track of the unanswered ones.

"I figure I like Tallhill alright. I gets treated like a grownup here," he said as he caught up to my questions. "In six months you can become a trustee. I have a month to go, I figure. How long have you been here, Clyde?"

"Just got here yesterday," I said as the relief pitcher took the mound.

"I thought I saw you yesterday with the tour group," he finally looked at me and smiled. "I work in the kitchen. It's good to see you made it through penitentiary life."

"It wasn't too bad…"

"Someday, you'll have to tell me about it," he said the next batter stepped in.

I sat there as the inning concluded and looked around at people calmly and politely playing games, reading, and surfing the internet.

When the Astros finally won the game in the 9th, Amos finally turned his attention to me.

Clyde," he said "I guess I have been lucky after such a hard life."

"You hear anything from Vic, or Alvin, or Barney?" I asked, expecting him to answer much later.

"Vic is doin' hard time," he answered directly. "He kilt his next door neighbor for parking in front of his house. I think we all knew he was not cured when he left. I like the way the Astros played that eighth inning tonight."

"Yeah, it was exciting," I threw in. "I'm not surprised that Vic snapped again, either."

"Alvin kilt himself," Amos continued. "He was on the same medication as me; he sliced his arm up the long ways, hard to stop that blood from pourin' out from that. He didn't have my lawyer either. "

"That's horrible," I said. "Who is your lawyer? Maybe I can hire him."

"Barney got sent up to the VA hospital," Amos continued. "The state cut the budget for the state hospital and they found that the VA could take him off their hands. Barney is a great guy, I miss him. I hope he doesn't lose his marbles."

"Wow, so all of my friends are gone now and you are here," I said with amazement.

"Elvin Williams is my lawyer's name," Amos said. "Little guy always wears a cowboy hat."

"No shit?" I asked, shaking my head. "Fucking Tex."

"Yeah," Amos said anxiously. "He joked about me calling him Tex at one time."

"Yeah, well Tex was my lawyer, too." I said with no small irritation. "I guess he's better at suing than he is at defending."

"Why you say that?" Amos asked.

"He got me a stretch in prison," I said with some rage boiling. "Then, after saying that he would work for free, he put a lien on my house."

"I guess I will change the subject then," Amos smiled at me. "How 'bout my 'Stros?!"

I had to laugh. The same guy who screwed up my defense and betrayed my trust was Amos' savior. But somehow we both ended up here; Amos by choice and me by a strange series of events.

"Amos," I finally said, "I never asked you what you did that got you in the state hospital." I usually don't ask such things, but for some reason I thought he would open up.

"I never asked you either Clyde," he responded.

"I don't mind telling you, Amos. I was famous…or infamous for a while. I held a co-worker hostage."

"He musta pissed you off," he said.

"He did. Lenny was a real asshole." I laughed, "I imagine he still is."

Amos laughed, "I had assholes in my line of work. I always thought about quitting because of it, but instead of attacking them, I just took off my clothes one day and started walking around naked."

"Wow," I said

"Yeah," Amos said as he shook his head, "but I was medicated. I had started seeing a doctor for my depression a few weeks before that. He prescribed me Polychlorophilitin or some such thing. Anyway, it was one of those miracle drugs that wasn't quite tested out fully. It caused hundreds of people to do crazy things. Some jumped off bridges, some drove cars into crowds, some went on shooting rampages. I guess I'm not the violent type, 'cause I just got naked,"

"So you got locked in the state hospital and Tex got you a sweet settlement?" I asked

"Yeah, I don't ever have to work again," he said proudly. "People won't hire me anyways but part of the deal was that I still had to get better. So I picked a place to get better. This place is great and I don't know if I want to leave even if I get better."

"What did you do for a living?" I asked, "If you don't mind me asking."

"This place has it all mapped out for you," he was back to not answering my immediate question. "I am in the best shape of my life. I like working in the kitchen. I got me a sweetheart there. I will be a trustee soon, so maybe I can have more responsibility."

"I wondered about romance in here," I interrupted.

"I was an airplane mechanic," Amos answered. "But I could never do that again. I was also learning computer programming. I never sat still on my learnin', Clyde. If I stood still, I drifted into depression. But for some reason, I am content here." He scooted closer again. "And no medication either."

"Fascinating," I looked down then looked back towards him. "So you have a mentor, too?"

"I like working in the kitchen," he replied "I get up early and make breakfast for y'all. I also prepare lunch, I don't do dinner though."

"Huh," I managed as I began to lose track of the number of questions I had asked.

"But me and Bernice, we are getting closer," he started again. "We talk and laugh, she's from New Orleans, so we talk the same type of southern nonsense." He laughed and shook his head.

"Bernice is your mentor?" I asked.

He looked at me with a crinkled-eye confused look. "Bernice is my sweetheart. We works in the kitchen together. My mentor is a white guy named Dan Johnson. Straight up hero he is. He was a Special Forces guy a while back. He helps me more than my doctor. More than anyone I guess, except Bernice, heeheehee."

"I really like my mentor, too," I said. "It is like we've known each other forever, or in some past life."

I stopped talking; I caught myself talking in terms that I very rarely use. I usually only discuss spiritual matters as they apply in theory. If I had known Bonnie in a separate life, then it made sense that her voice was in my dreams. This was my first day at this wondrous asylum and so much had happened. I had not had a real moment to collect my thoughts. *Maybe that is their secret.* But before I could dwell on it any more, Amos produced a deck of cards from his pocket and slapped them on the end table between us.

"Well in this life," he said "I believe you still have that Eifel Tower that I have had my eye on."

I laughed heartily and grabbed the cards. "Only if I get the first deal."

"Deal!" he said with his own hearty chuckle.

We played cards for the remainder of my free time. At 1800, we both got up and walked to the cafeteria, where we ate our specially regimented meals and talked about our past lives and our future plans. I was going to try to reconcile with my daughter and maybe try to find Naomi. Amos was going to use his money to buy a ranch in Mississippi, but he seemed to think that dream was silly even though he had the money to do it. His immediate plans were to get Bernice alone.

After dinner, we headed our separate ways. I went back to my room and found another note on the door. It had been a long day and I had almost put the first note completely out of my thoughts. This note was written in the same storytelling third-person style:

Clyde Barrow was beginning to discover the hidden part of himself, allowing him to grow and stop examining things too closely. He will learn that the key to happiness is to accept that some things cannot be changed and to seek peace within the structure that is presented. Every problem may have a solution; however, the solutions are not always for us to find. He will learn to leave that crooked picture on the wall alone. He will learn to let people fail on their own. He will learn to walk away from the treacherous temptations. He will heal.

Once again, I resisted the temptation to get angry at the note writer. Although I had to admit the audacity of this person was beginning to bug me. I opened my door and took the note inside my room and placed it in the nightstand drawer with the first note. I noticed two new things in my room; one was a pair of green pajamas laying on the bed with a shaving kit next to it. The other was a laundry hamper on wheels by the bathroom door. I shrugged, grabbed the pajamas and the shaving kit. As if programmed to do so, I disrobed, and started the shower.

I took a hot shower and brushed my teeth. The whole time I drifted back into my old analytical mind. I was in a place where I felt completely accepted and I had new friends and even an old friend. I had fallen into a kind of bliss, but that nagging cynicism just kept kicking in the door to that comfortable place I had reached in my mind. I fully intended to write down these thoughts, but as I reached my bed, fatigue overcame me and I slept deeply and dreamlessly.

CHAPTER 25 – BONNIE CHADWICK

It would be monotonous to detail every day at Tallhill. Suffice to say that seemingly not one single minute spent at Tallhill was wasted. However, detailing the everyday aspects of this life would become repetitive. I will say that my second day was much like the first and the third day was like the second, and so on. All had challenges and bright spots and physically challenging activity and mental acuity exercises. The days were full and interesting. Eat, work, therapy, exercise, and rest describe the routine, but do not even come close to adequately presenting it.

The second day began with a small alarm clock next to my bed playing soft music. At first the music played low, but gradually got louder. I rose from my very restful slumber and found the off switch for the alarm. With the alarm silenced, my eyes jumped towards the door. I scrambled out of bed and opened it wide. There was no note this time. I shrugged. Perhaps last night's note was intended for today. I went back inside and began my day by changing into my daily green uniform.

I ate breakfast alone, four over easy, a carafe of orange juice, and plenty of bacon, compliments of Amos. Then I reported to my work station in the garden shed where Martha flirted with me a little and I flirted back a little. Charlie assigned me some rows to hoe and I did as I was instructed. I ate lunch, then I talked to a doctor other than Silk in my therapy session; he was an older gentleman named Dr. Cooper. My physical training session was stretching followed by basketball. Basketball was something I excelled at all through school, so I quite enjoyed this, even though I was still out of playing shape. After my exercise I took a shower in my room. Toweling myself off while walking out of the bathroom, I was pleasantly surprised to see Bonnie sitting next to my bed.

"C'mon Clyde," she said cheerfully, "we're behind. You take long showers."

I continued, in my unclothed state, to dry myself as I searched for a change of clothes.

"Goodness, Clyde," she continued, "There is a lady present. Have you no shame?"

"I sometimes wish I did," I said as I wrapped the towel around me. "Besides, you knew the shower was running when you let yourself in. If you expected me to jump back in the bathroom like an embarrassed child, you may have misjudged. I have little to be apologetic for and nothing to be ashamed of."

"Indeed, Clyde," she leaned forward as I dressed, "you have nothing to be ashamed of."

This was considered full-blown flirtation, and in my former life we might already be in the throes of passion, but it wasn't my former life, it was casual, but clinical and in no way conducive to romance. There was also the matter of the wheelchair and her unfortunate condition. It just hadn't crossed my mind to think of her sexually; at least it hadn't up until that point. I pulled on a pair of boxer-briefs and slung the towel over my shoulders.

"Thank you, Bonnie," I finally said with a big toothy smile. "Coming from such a beautiful woman, I take that as a high compliment."

"It is sincere, I assure you," she said.

"I believe you," I said as I sat down on the edge of the bed and continued to towel-dry my hair. "I think you left off yesterday with you meeting Chandler."

She stared at me for a moment, as if I had scared a thought out of her head.

"Oh Clyde," she said and turned her head away from me and began staring off into the distance. "What is it about you that makes me want to let you in on all my secrets? We are swapping roles here. I want to remain mysterious to you, but I feel like you need more from me than just an ear."

She turned her chair forward to face me and began, "Chandler and I became inseparable. I was only seventeen then and he was twenty-four. I was inexperienced in everything and he was a man of the world. The words that romance novelists use: dazzled, impressed, charmed, captivated, fascinated, enchanted, enthralled, beguiled… use whatever word you wish, I was in that bewildering defenseless state. I had only dated school boys up until then and even those dates were movies and dinner and quickly home to a watchful mother and father."

This relationship was totally different; my parents let me stay out late with him, they let me go to night clubs. They saw this relationship not only as my future; they saw it as their key to getting to the top. Rosemary was signing richer clients. She moved into a bigger studio and hired more employees. Benjamin was chumming it up with big shots of all stripes and from all over. They were on the rise and if Chandler married me they would both be ecstatic."

"You call them by their first names?" I interrupted.

"Yes, it makes the story more objective for me, I guess," she said. "Do you mind?"

"No, you go ahead," I said.

"So eventually…," she sighed. "Chandler proposed to me not long after my eighteenth birthday. What was I going to say?"

"You married him?" I asked

"I did," she said. "But I would have been crazy not to, right?

I let this question go. The answer was not as obvious to me and it probably was a rhetorical question in any case. Instead I shaded my answer with another question.

"Well, how well did you know him?"

"I knew what he put forward," she said in a slightly hurt tone. "He was tall, handsome, and charming to all outward appearances. He was a prince; he was popular. My parents treated him like the son that they wished he was and I was young and impressionable."

Her voice was a little shaky at this point and she took a moment to compose herself before she continued.

"We took a long honeymoon, he just asked me to spin a globe and pick four places. We hit San Tropez, Vienna, Venice, and Rio before we returned to the states. Life was awesome in every way. I continued dancing and perfecting my skills. My parents continued to climb that social ladder and I fell in with the country club set. Clyde, it was all in front of me."

"But it didn't last," I said, like some kind of assistant narrator.

"Obviously," she said as she motioned with both hands at her lifeless legs. "We were complete. I was in love; maybe not completely in love with the man, who was still a mystery, but in love with the life and with the sensation of being part of something wonderful. I volunteered for charities with these well-placed women in this elite set. I was much younger than most of them and the older ones took me under their wings."

Once again Bonnie's voice betrayed an emotional creakiness, so she stopped and wheeled over to the water. I sat quietly as she composed herself. She stayed by the water as she continued her story.

"We were married for four years Clyde," she said. "Early on, we decided that we would have children. At our ages, and with our wealth, we were in a good position to give everything to any child. At first we just thought it would happen naturally. After a couple of years, we decided that something was wrong. Chandler had his sperm count checked and it was found that he was normal. I had myself checked and it was discovered that I had underdeveloped ovaries. It was unlikely that I would have children. This news was not horrible or tragic, since at least I could continue my dancing career without interruption and I might still conceive someday. Instead of having my own children, I decided that the charity I would focus on would be children with cancer."

"The speech I saw you give the other day," I interrupted.

"You saw that? That's good I guess, so I won't have to break down here," she said as she wheeled herself back towards the bed. "Well I continued with my dancing and charity and my social obligations and Chandler was not around me much in that fourth year of marriage. He was busy with this legal briefing and that out of town meeting. I was busy with my dancing and my charity work and my new found high society dames. We actually stopped trying to have kids. I don't want to get too personal, but we weren't even having sex. Well..., at least I wasn't."

I raised an eyebrow and waited for her to continue with the salacious details to support her last statement.

Instead she got philosophical, "You know, Clyde. When people get married, there is a lot of stuff that each brings to the situation." She looked over. "You were married Clyde, you know what I mean."

"I know what you mean, Bonnie." I said.

"Of course you do," she smiled. "People marry for a variety of reasons, mostly comfort level. But sometimes things are overlooked. Sometimes the reason one person marries is different than the reason the other person marries. In my case, I married for prestige, money, and comfort. Love was down the list a bit, but it was definitely there; just not storybook head-over-heels love. There just wasn't a connection, ya know?"

"I do know," I said as I self-consciously examined my own failed marriage. "What did Chandler want out of marriage?"

"Well," she looked down a little, "I used to be a knock out. He liked having me on his arm, he liked showing me off. He even liked it when I talked to other men, so he could walk up and make them slink off; and they always did… always. But to put it delicately, Chandler was more experienced than me sexually. Actually, I had no real experience. He expected certain things that I was not good at. I even watched adult movies, but they just made me uncomfortable.

"Looking back, I guess I noticed the looks on the faces of the ladies in my charity circle. They were always so damn sympathetic. If I was older and wiser I guess I would have caught on. But I was like a freaking Stepford wife; all naive and unquestioning, trying to please."

Bonnie's voice started to crack again, so she stopped and dropped her chin to her chest and closed her eyes. I could feel her presence; her pain became mine. My eyes started to moisten, so I closed my eyes and swallowed hard. She continued.

"I caught him one day," she said dryly as she lifted her head. "I had a charity event scheduled at the country club. It was a fundraiser for the children's hospital. It was a golf tournament, we were going to wheel the kids around in golf carts and watch the action. We even had some real pros show up. But it got rained out. I ended up driving seven kids back to the hospital after we gave them lemonade and they got some autographs from golfers they never heard of.

"Clyde, it was a disappointing day for me and the kids, but we tried to make the best of it. These kids were all dying and they had so little pleasure in their lives. It was sad that they had to miss an event that was going to be so much fun. I had been deeply involved with the planning and I took this hard. As I drove that mini-van full of sick kids back to the hospital, I thought about how little time they had left. I promised them all that I would plan something else even more fun real soon. I had no idea what I would do, but I had to make them feel better. By the time I dropped them off and said the long cheerful goodbyes, I was feeling the stress of this small but significant failure coming down on me."

She again stopped and wheeled herself over to the water and took two long slow drinks. She looked over at me with those sincere dark eyes and began again. "I was only twenty-three, Clyde. I was a little self-centered, but I genuinely wanted to help everybody who ever had anything go bad with their lives. I had been raised by people who thought that wealth was their way to happiness, but they also raised me to realize how lucky I was. I was lucky, you know, luckier than almost all the rest of world. But I was distressed that day; not for my lot in the world, but for these kids who would never have the chances that I had. They just wanted stuff like a pony or maybe a remote-controlled car before the days ran out."

She wheeled herself back to where I sat on the bed. "I will continue this tomorrow, Clyde," she said. "I have to go swim in a warm pool to help my legs and I don't want to be an emotional mess and drown myself in despair."

I sat like a kid who was waiting for a dessert that wasn't coming. "Our session isn't over," I said in an almost sheepish tone.

"I need to cut it short, Clyde. This story is... well... hard to tell," she said. "I need composure and lucidity. I was about to start throwing things and using profanity. Not lady-like and definitely not mentor-like."

"Can I push you...?"

"Clyde," she cut me off. "I am stronger than you know."

So I got up opened the door for her and she wheeled herself out.

CHAPTER 26 – EDGES

As I began to circulate among the general population at Tallhill, I started to collect observations. My manifesto was terribly neglected during my stay there. I really didn't need it in any event. My psychiatrists would occasionally read from it and Bonnie eventually became fond of quoting it. I had the general ideas in my head for reference; so naturally I was constantly looking for an angle on Tallhill. Things that look too good to be true usually are.

In my observations, I focused on the universal contentment bordering on happiness bordering on euphoria of all of the members and associates. I never heard a raised voice or a disagreement. Even Amos just fended off any arguments that I attempted to start. He would dismiss arguments about sports, which I would purposely start. For instance, I knew he was a big Muhammad Ali fan. I raised the point that Frazier was actually a better fighter, but he lost the mental game. Amos just played it off with a casual, "You may have a point, Clyde."

The Amos I knew form the state hospital might have challenged me to a duel.

Tallhill had something alright; they prescribed no drugs as far as I could tell, they kept everyone on rigid schedules and seemingly everyone just showed up where they needed to be in a timely fashion. Even I- the most contrary person you could ever hope to meet- stayed on schedule and adjusted to every change without a complaint. I just showed up at the appointed time on my schedule. This place was a miracle, and I was beginning to think they would cure me. But, being the misery addict that I have declared myself to be, I set about listing the negatives of the place.

The first negative was that I was constantly monitored. There were cameras everywhere. I suspected that they were even in the bathrooms, but harder to detect. Everyone also wore the ankle bracelets, with the exception of Bonnie; who I guess was considered not much of a flight risk. She did have a tracking device on her wheelchair, however, so she was technically covered.

Another thing I counted as a negative was the complete lack of non-conformity. I wondered if I was the only one who thought this way. I wanted to ask the three prison inmates who were transferred here with me, but I didn't even see them for the first few months. I think this was intentional so we couldn't compare notes and comment about how odd everyone seemed. In any event, I found it amazing that they could keep us from even accidentally running into each other for so long, if that was their intent. I do not know if they saw each other, but I was actively looking for them and did not see them.

After trying to provoke an argument with Amos, I decided to ask him about the contentment phenomenon.

"Amos," I said as he was watching a game show in the break room. "Have you ever seen anyone argue here?"

He sat up in his chair and gave me a puzzled look. "No, Clyde. I don't think I have even seen anyone talk loud or complain. I've seen people cry, but it seemed to be happiness tears. I think people are really genuinely happy to be here. I know I am. I love this place."

"Why do you love it?" I asked.

"Well, Clyde," he leaned over a bit to talk quieter. "I was raised in a dozen homes with all varieties of people; some of them nice and some not so nice. Whether it was a foster home or another one of my mother's friends or husbands, I always felt like a stranger or an interloper. Those houses was sometime dumpy apartments and sometime pretty decent houses, but none felt like a home. Here, I feel like I am at home."

"I see," I said. "When are you scheduled to leave?"

"Well, they evaluate you after six months to be a trustee," he replied. "That's the first step. Then I guess you are on the way to getting better. But, hey, I can live here the rest of my life happily. I have enough money to pay for it. The outside world just kept taking chunks outta my ass. None of that here; here I have certainty. Here I have community. I may have even found true love. I may never want to leave."

"Do you know of anyone who has left?" I asked.

"Clyde, you ask a lot of questions." He went back to his pattern of not answering directly. "Just be happy and accept what a great place this is. Before you know it, you will be cured."

"But people do leave here, right?" I persisted.

"I don't know anyone who has," Amos admitted. "I think that the people who die get to leave. But I really think that most people think like me; the world is unhappy for them and this place is like the womb, it is like a mother and father. But better, because we are not treated like children."

Amos had properly explained Tallhill to me succinctly; it was the mother ship, it was the womb, and also a father who expected us to behave, so we did. It was filled with people who probably needed that in their lives because they had not had that nurturing parent.

However, there was one important difference between Tallhill and an excellent parent; parents let their children leave the nest and spend years preparing them for that eventuality. Tallhill was creating a kind of slavery to a routine. Slavery was in fact what it was, free labor, in fact some of the members were paying good money to work for free. After I had adjusted my body and mind to the routine of Tallhill, I decided that I would write Naomi through Father Quinn and I decided to write Annette, hoping the letter would be forwarded since I had no current address. It was probably week two when I finally had the time and was not too fatigued to think. I wrote both of them almost identical letters telling them that I was on the road to recovery and that I missed them and loved them.

I received one piece of mail in those first few weeks and that was forwarded from the prison. It was from Margie, stating that the sale of the house was final and that Elvin Williams, aka Tex, had settled our accounts in the amount of $15,342.16. I cursed that crooked bastard under my breath and suppressed the urge to chew that statement into a thousand pieces. Instead I walked over to my night stand and opened the drawer to put it with my door-notes.

This action reminded me that the notes had stopped coming right after I met Bonnie. I smiled. I found it odd that I hadn't thought much about the notes after I started hearing her stories. I guessed that maybe she had misjudged me and that she really was benefitting more from mentoring me than she thought she would. Maybe if I did leave she would come with me. This thought gave me some foolish hope.

Knowing it was foolish did not dampen my mood, however. I smiled and felt good. Tex, the huckster ambulance chaser, had taken me to the cleaners and I was absolutely okay with that. As long as Bonnie was around, I was okay. I slept the sleep of kings that night. I had no reason to be content or even optimistic, but I was happy. I was happy a slave in an artificial womb. But the real world demanded nothing more from me. For what that was worth.

* * * * * * * * * * *

"We lived in large house on a cul-de-sac at the end of Fairlawn Road," Bonnie began our third mentoring session with these words right as I opened my door. "I got home early that day. I got home hours early. It was 2:45. I remember seeing the time readout on the dashboard as I pulled into my driveway. In the driveway was a yellow Porsche Carrera GT with the license plate FOX E LANA. It belonged to Lana Fox. She was the semi-attractive daughter of one the founding partners of Chadwick, Fox, and Silkwood. She was the mid-thirties daughter of Chandler's dad's partner. She was part of my charity circle and she was divorced with three kids. She had also been absent from my little golf outing."

"I pulled my minivan next to her car and just sat in the driveway, trying to rationalize what she was doing there. In the mood I was in, I wanted just to be with Chandler, who even though we were not sexually compatible, was always kind and understanding; never cruel, never condescending. I just wanted him to tell me that I would see better days and hold me and stroke my hair. Instead I was shocked into the real world; I got out of the car and marched swiftly to the front door, which was unlocked. Once inside, I heard the unmistakable sounds of a bed creaking and people moaning. I heard the sounds of passion and they were coming from my bedroom."

"Oh shit," I said as I began to see where this was going.

"I don't even remember my next actions. I know that Chandler kept these ceremonial swords over the archway to the dining room. They were too high for me to reach. I must have pushed a chair over to reach them. I somehow made it up those stairs to that open doorway. I can still see her on top of him grinding. I lunged forward. Lana's back was to me; but Chandler must have seen me, because he shoved her aside as my thrust reached her. I missed badly and the sword went deep into Chandler's neck.

Clyde, it was horrible. She was screaming and naked and he was bleeding everywhere and looking at me with bulging unbelieving eyes and trying to talk. He only managed whispered words; he said 'Bon, Bon, Bon…,' and not much else. I didn't even think about saving him, I just thought about getting her. She was running down the stairs. I pulled the sword from his throat and began to chase her. It was raining hard by this time; she got out the front door and slipped on the wet pavement and I was close behind. I lunged at her and slashed her in the shoulder. I fell and she got back up and reached her car. In a couple of seconds she had fired the engine and was backing out of the driveway. I leapt onto the front of the car with my bloody sword in one hand and my other hand holding under the hood where it met the windshield. She turned on the wipers and I tried to grab one of them with my other hand as I dropped the sword. I held that wet wiper which was now going full speed. I held that wiper with everything I had. She shifted into forward gear and sped away. I lost my grip on the wiper and I kind of slipped over the roof and onto the pavement on the street in front of my house."

As Bonnie related this, I sat staring at the television set in the corner of my room. The television had not been turned on since I arrived in this place and I truly had never noticed that I even had a television. I was just concentrating on something to avert my eyes from looking at Bonnie as she described this pivotal event in her life. The silence that followed compelled me to turn towards her and ask a question.

"So that is why you are…," I froze.

"Crippled?" she finished for me. "Yes, Clyde, I sustained an injury between the sixth and seventh discs of the thoracic region of the spinal cord. I was told that I will never walk again. I landed quite awkwardly on the street; I landed on my lower back and skidded for a few feet. I tore my clothes and peeled off some skin. I remember lying there semi-conscious and helpless. I did manage to roll over and drag myself to the side of the street.

One of my neighbors, Greg Jarvis, came running out and told me that an ambulance was on the way and he tried to help me up, but it was no use; my legs were numb, they didn't work."

Bonnie looked down at her legs. "They still don't"

This whole story that Bonnie related triggered several questions in my mind. But I held my tongue since I knew she wanted to tell me her story in the proper sequence. This was obviously the most significant thing that had ever happened to her. I considered her a vitally important person in my life; she was the voice, she was the ticket to me finding what marbles I had left, she was Thora for god's sake! If she was going to think of me as a serious person, I would have to withhold any frivolous inquisition. I put my curiosity in check as I sat rapt on two pillows at the head of my bed.

"You know, Clyde," she began again. "As I lay there on the pavement waiting for the ambulance, I hoped to walk again, but I thought about everyone this would affect. I first thought of Chandler, whose betrayal I had already forgiven. I wished he could hold me. He was by that time either already dead or close to death. I had struck his carotid artery and that drains the body rather quickly. I thought about Benjamin, who was going to be a junior partner, but now his daughter had killed the senior partner's son and slashed another senior partner's daughter."

I thought about Rosemary," she said with misty eyes, which she wiped with her sleeve. "I wished my mommy was there to hold me and tell me it was all okay and that we would come back from this. I thought about how her dance studio would suffer because she was the mother of a killer. I thought of those poor sick kids who would now not get the great charity event that I had promised, but would just get something ordinary or maybe nothing at all.

I thought of my charity circle ladies and what they may have known about this affair and I began to understand their somewhat sympathetic tone towards me even though I thought I had the world at my feet. I wondered how many of them just accepted the indignity of having infidelities in their marriages while quietly enduring it for the greater good of being wealthy. I lay there and looked at that bloody sword lying on the driveway and I wished I could reach it. Because I had started to finally think about myself and what the rest of my life was going to be like. Clyde, if I could have reached that sword, I would have plunged it through my own heart."

Bonnie looked up from telling the story and cocked her head to the side. "Why do I open up to you? It must be your kind eyes or your easy manner or something. I have only told my therapist that part about thinking of killing myself. I was not raised as a quitter. I was raised to always achieve and never make excuses. Self-pity is not a comfortable feeling for me. I realize now, I actually realized pretty quickly that defeating my own will was not an option. In a few minutes, the ambulance arrived and I told them about Chandler upstairs. One of them checked me over as another ran down the driveway towards the house. They loaded me into the ambulance as the police arrived. The last I saw of that nice big house on Fairlawn Road was through the back window of an ambulance. Even then I only saw the upstairs windows; behind the middle one was the bedroom where my Chandler was lying lifeless."

At this point Bonnie stopped talking, she had drained all of the emotion from the story and what remained was a long awkward silence. My mentor had gone through hell in a very short time. She had gone from a perfect life to a condemned and sad life that needed complete rebuilding. She had lost all of the comforts of wealth and she had lost her legs, she had lost her one great expression; she lost her ability to dance. I was dumbfounded for what to say. I trusted her beyond all doubt and she trusted me, this was apparent. A bond was forming and we both were aware of it. I decided the silence was more than I could take, so I changed the subject.

"I wish I could have seen you dance," I said.

"You will, Clyde," she responded with not a hint of irony. "I will dance under the stars someday. You will be there and it will be glorious."

I smiled and she smiled and I guess that was the best way to end our little mentoring session. I impulsively crossed a line at that point. I got up from the bed, walked over to her, and kissed her on the forehead. She smiled even broader at that point.

"Thanks, Clyde," she said. "How did you know that that was exactly what I wanted?"

"Just a guess," I said with a big smile of my own and walked to the door. "Now if you will excuse me, I have a card game to go to, would you like to join me?"

"No thank you," she said as she wheeled out the door. "I have physical therapy for the next hour. They strap me onto these machines that move my legs for me. It is torture, but it keeps the muscles active."

"Well, can I push you somewhere?" I asked. I just felt the need to be with her.

"Stop it Clyde," she said as she wheeled herself away. "No pity Clyde!" she yelled from down the hall. "I don't feel it and I won't accept it."

I just stood there in the hallway with my hands in the pockets of my green uniform.

With that stupid Tallhill smile on my face.

CHAPTER 27 – THE PARIAH

I was not like most of the Tallhill members in that I felt no need to be nurtured or to be taken care of. All I sought in this place and in the world in general was someone who understood and accepted me. I wanted love and understanding. I also wanted freedom. I began to believe that Bonnie was that love and understanding and I began to convince myself that she felt that way too. However, Bonnie felt a purpose at Tallhill; she was loved and admired by all. In the outside world she was a pariah to most of her family and all of her old friends. Even the ones who still talked to her treated her like an invalid. At Tallhill, she was a pillar and a goddess beloved in every way.

Bonnie had been at Tallhill for almost eight years. She was in her early thirties and still young. I was convinced that the staff thought she had nowhere else to go. I thought differently. I was convinced they thought she would be the thing that kept me there. This may have been true if I thought she wanted to stay here, but I thought maybe she thought about the outside world quite frequently. In our long talks, she let loose some emotions about seeing some of those old places where she had felt at home.

Bonnie and I were kindred spirits in many ways. One thing we had in common was that we were not clinically insane. We had both snapped due to stress and performed irrationally violent acts. If given the choice one thousand more times, we would certainly act differently. That was the truth fifteen minutes after our violent acts and it was the truth years later.

"I still hear from my father," Bonnie began our fourth mentoring session. "My mother is another story."

I had just changed into my clean clothes after a workout and a shower. On this occasion, she had not let herself in, but had simply waited outside my door. After I dressed, I opened the door and she was there smiling. We had not seen each other for a few days, so on those days I had reported to my work station where I performed more exhausting work. But I began to realize with her opening words that she felt that she needed to tell her personal story completely before she could help me.

"Clyde," she continued. "I took away a son from a prominent family. I attacked the daughter of another prominent family. I ruined my father's chance at a partnership. I scared away clients from Rosemary's dance studio. Within six months, she had to cut her staff and within a year she couldn't renew the lease on her big downtown studio. She had to move to a smaller studio near the inner city. Her dreams were dashed and I only remember her visiting me once in the hospital while I was lying there helpless. Clyde, it was the worst time of my life and my own mother treated me like a common criminal or worse. Even during that one visit, she talked mostly of all of the bad things she was experiencing. It was cold. It was as if only her life had been affected."

As she spoke these words, Bonnie had wheeled herself to the one window in my room. The window overlooked a small courtyard that was filled with different varieties of bird feeders and small fruit trees. It was a pleasant view, but I had spent little time at that window. Bonnie just stared out as she told this part of the story. I guessed this meant that it was harder to tell than most of it. Maybe she didn't want me to see how hurt she was.

"But Benjamin was there for me," she continued, using first names again. "He took a leave of absence from the law firm, where he sensed his presence was now much less welcome. He visited me every day and would spend hours reading to me and talking to me and reminiscing about my childhood and how great it was going to be when I got better. I had ruined his chance at the big important law firm and we both knew it, but he never talked about it. A few months later, he resigned, but he never told me about it; I found that out during Rosemary's one visit. He had decided to take a job at a law firm that helped poor people. It meant less money and it meant that they had to move out of their big house and live a more modest lifestyle. If this was a strain on their marriage, he never let on."

"Did he represent you in court?" I asked.

"He did," she said as her gaze remained on the courtyard. "But there was no trial. We pled not-guilty due to temporary insanity. The prosecution was not interested in prosecuting a cripple in a hospital bed who had acted in a crime of passion. I was committed to this place until I got better; whatever that means."

"Are you better?" I asked.

"Clyde, I was never sick. I did what I did, but it was a reaction to events. I really never had a jealous incident in my life, I just felt such betrayal. I guess what I had to overcome was the sense that I couldn't trust anything or anyone again. My mother made it worse by ignoring me. I have forgiven her, but that took time. My father has apologized for her over and over, but I just tell him not to worry about it. He tells me that she is in therapy, which I think is a good thing."

Bonnie left the window at this point and wheeled back over to me by the bed. "Then there were my social friends; the people in my Charity circle. I was new to them and much younger than most of them. I sensed that they all agreed with what I did and never trusted Lana around their men, but none of them visited me either. I asked Benjamin if he would inquire about my charity work, but he said that they would not take his calls. When he went to the country club to possibly talk to them, he was told that his membership was revoked."

"Some cold people out there," I deadpanned.

"Yes sir, Clyde," she said. "I had even lost my charity work with those beautiful children with no future. But as soon as I could get around at the hospital, I visited any sick child that I was allowed to. I needed to feel like someone needed me again. I was a pariah to all I had known except my father. He was the one who kept me trying. He was the son of a man who never gave up. He told me that his father once fell from a tower and nearly broke his back, but never gave up working. He just did things a little slower until he got better. He never made the excuse and he never blamed the people he worked for. I guess I get my determination from them. If not for Benjamin, I would have given up."

"So why are you still here?" I asked.

"I have had my sanity assessed several times and each time they tell me that I am not ready to join society. I guess it has just not stayed important to me after all of those times. I have it pretty good here; people like me, people trust me. I am important. I still get to visit sick children. I help people in here."

"But freedom…,"

"Freedom would be nice," she interrupted, "but it would let so many people down if I left. I guess someday, but it would be hard to leave. I would be here every visiting day anyways. Might as well stay. I get the physical therapy that I need here and I really can't back out like I could out there." She made a general pointing motion with her hand in the direction of the window.

"But, you see," she continued. "I took someone's life. I killed my husband, my Prince Charming, my friend. I do not deserve freedom. I took away any chance of having children. I did everything wrong and

I can never make it right. If I was free, I would be cheating. I would be stealing time."

"But you were found to be temporarily insane," I insisted. "It isn't like you are a career criminal and a danger to others."

"Aren't I?" She asked

"You reacted," I said. "Probably 99 out of 100 women would act violently in that situation. I think you are being a little hard on yourself."

"Clyde," She said. "I have had twelve years to think about this and I will continue to think about it. I have dissected every move and every motion. I remember everything clearly except actually pulling the sword from the wall. It was like I was standing there shocked one moment and then walking up the stairs the next. When I examine what I did, I realize that I could have turned back. But I felt a sense of entitlement. I felt that I was going to defend what was mine. I wanted to show that I was not going to be taken lightly anymore. I wanted these rich and powerful people to know that I was significant."

Bonnie grabbed my hand at this point. "Clyde, I can feel those feelings today. I have examined these feelings for twelve years. I have discovered, through therapy and through my own contemplation, that I feel righteous about all of these feelings. I had suppressed my individuality for the sake of others. I was subservient to my parents' ambitions and goals and totally consumed by Chandler's persona.

Only in those few moments did I become a complete being. I was expressing myself. The fact that it ended tragically does not change this fact."

She gripped my hand tighter and looked into my eyes. "Clyde, I have never felt so alive and so in control. I wish I had just pulled hair or something. The part I don't remember is grabbing the sword. But after that I WAS in control. For the first time, I was in control. It felt good and I have come to accept that."

"So do you think you could kill again?" I asked

"Hard to say," she answered. "Life is full of complications, well, life out there, anyway." She made a sweeping motion with her free hand. "Tell me Clyde," she said as she let go of my hand, "What led to your violence?"

As I contemplated my answer, I felt a little drawn-in by her tactics. While she was holding my hand, I felt a real connection and a part of her world. My understanding of her was made more complete by this gesture. As she let go, I felt a rush of abandonment that was fleeting, but real. I guessed that she had learned this technique from years of psycho-analysis. I recovered from this condition in a few seconds, but the effect that it had was for me to actually feel those conditions that had made me snap in on that day at work. It also fed my cynicism. I was opened and laid bare. Bonnie was a master surgeon of the soul and I was defenseless on the table.

"I guess my expectations of people wore my patience down," I began. "I have always given to people and given generously. I have given time and money to them. I expected some kind of return on my investment. I wanted to feel as if I was appreciated beyond all of the empty gestures that people make that serve only to make their own selves feel better."

I stopped and noticed a smile of recognition as Bonnie nodded to my words. I continued:

"I wanted to strike out at all of them, but I chose the next one."

"The next one?" Bonnie asked.

"Yeah, the next one who took me for granted, the next one who questioned my importance and viability, the next person who looked upon me with any disdain."

"The next one was a co-worker?" She asked.

"It was," I responded. "Although it could have been any number of people; I chose the one who was clueless as to my importance to the point that it really got under my skin. I rigged a fake bomb to scare him into realizing that he was taking many things for granted. He took me for granted, he took his work for granted, and he took his very existence for granted.

"I had piled upon myself a burden of responsibilities that really weren't mine to take. But I made them mine and it caused me to neglect all of my real duties to some extent until all of these chickens came home to roost."

"What responsibilities did you take on?" Asked Bonnie, as she shifted in her chair.

I got up and walked towards the window to avoid looking her in the eye.

"I had taken on a few lovers. Not just for sex, but for the companionship and the shared misery. All of them troubled. I am not going to tell you that I was faultless or blameless, but more self-indulged than narcissistic, if you can see the subtle difference."

"What is the difference?" she asked, as she turned her chair slightly to look at me.

"A narcissist is in love with his own beauty," I said as I watched a man in green clean the bird feeders. "I was obsessed with my own pain. I never thought of myself as particularly appealing. But I did want others to see my sacrifices and my pain. I was alone in this when I thought I had company. But it took my fake bomb stunt for me to see this"

"Clyde, I won't lie to you," Bonnie interrupted, "I have seen all of your files; your arrest records, your psychiatrists' notes, and your manifesto. It is all very compelling and troubling. I have read them several times, in fact. I wonder if you would allow me to provide a new perspective."

"I would welcome it," I said, turning around to face her.

"You have used the misery excuse for all of your troubles. You put yourself in this box where you limit your own choices by design. The fact that you realize this does not help. It only shows that you analyze everything, indeed, over-analyze everything. You can laugh at a joke for ten seconds and then spend forty-five minutes analyzing why the joke is funny. You are a kill-joy. You are a downer. Your dry sense of humor is quaint at first, and self-deprecating to a fault. You seem to think you are misunderstood and that allows you to stay in your shell. I realize that I am being harsh, but to analyze a life is to not live a life."

"I analyze for sure," I said as I began to feel even more vulnerable. "I have always done that. But it hasn't hurt me. The thing that has me here is my impulsive action."

"Was it impulsive?" she asked. "You had a fake bomb and took it to work. The idea must have been there for at least a little while."

"It was one of many sketchy plans that were squirming around in my head," I said, as I sat down on the bed. "I also had an idea where I just took off and worked on a fishing boat. I had an idea that I would just withdraw my savings and be a drifter. None of these were real plans. The bomb was one of these vague fantasies. It just so happened that the bomb fantasy turned out to be the one that I acted upon. It was impulsive and not well thought out."

"But you have analyzed it since then?" she asked.

"I have, but not much," I replied. "I did it and it is done. I will admit relief that I did not kill the man. While he was unconscious, I thought that this might be the case. But, I had not acted impulsively before this. I had made some moves based on instinct. My instincts about a person can sometimes be very strong, yet very wrong. I guess I am attracted to people who are bad for me and they are attracted to me. So the clash of similarities with the pain and hurt are inevitable."

"There you go," she interrupted. "Analyzing the analysis. When you take what should be raw emotion and break it down into its component parts, you are cheating yourself."

"You think I cheat myself?" I asked, a little startled.

"If you don't believe in happiness, then you are just faking any disappointment or hurt feelings; unless you are faking the whole nonbelief in happiness." Bonnie said these words as she left my bedside and wheeled towards the door. Once there, she pivoted around to face me. I stood and walked over to look into those deep black eyes which were at that moment reflecting my own face to me.

"Bonnie," I said. "I accept what you say and I realize that it is almost all completely true. I know my mind and I know I just make reasons to deny happiness. I have to know why this stuff is in my brain."

I paused, mostly because what I was about to say next might cross a line.

"Bonnie," I said. "You killed your husband and I knocked a guy out and held him hostage. These actions landed us here. You came straight here and I came here through a more circuitous route. But I have heard your voice before."

I stopped to study her reaction. She sat motionless with one hand on the door knob and I didn't see a trace of surprise.

I continued, "I started having dreams a little while back after my doctor prescribed Thorazine. The voice was calm and reassuring. The voice was a female voice, but it didn't come with a face. I finally saw the face my first day here.... it was your voice I heard coming up that corridor that led to that Catharsis Center where you were telling your story."

Bonnie's face now betrayed a flash of recognition. It was there for maybe one-tenth of a second, but I caught it. It was enough to make me believe that she believed what I believed. It was enough for the time being. I changed the subject.

"Well, I guess you have to go now," I said as she had recovered from the little strangeness I had thrown her way. "You have your hand on the door knob and I know how this place is loyal to the clock. Will you visit tomorrow?"

"I will Clyde," she said. "We have had a real breakthrough today and I want to keep churning things up. It's healthy."

I said nothing in return as she helped herself out the door and it closed behind her. I sat for a second and again began to analyze- like I do. I let her in on my dreams because she had unexpectedly delved into my psyche. It was a shock. I spent the next few minutes curled up on my bed, crying like a baby that has just been slapped for the first time.

****

That night I dreamt about Thora for the first time since I arrived at Tallhill. I dreamt about her for the first time without medicine. I found myself in what used to be a forest in the mountains. The forest had been clear cut and was now a landscape of stumps. I wandered through these hundreds of stumps guided by Thora's voice.

"All is not lost, Clyde," she said. "You are now realizing that your enemies are powerless to stop you if you realize that you are your worst enemy. To be happy is to be free is to be happy to be free to be happy," she said, redundantly.

It was both profound and silly and was followed by a laugh that was more like a schoolgirl giggle. I saw a flash and turned in that direction. Standing on the highest stump in that whole range, in a plain white dress, stood Bonnie.

"Clyde," she said, in that same voice I had been hearing in my dreams. "What are we waiting for?"

CHAPTER 28 – THE TRAVELLED

The mentoring sessions with Bonnie were becoming more important to me than the therapy provided at Tallhill. The more I thought about it, the more I realized that this was done intentionally by the staff. I think the process of being examined by a professional dehumanizes people to a certain extent. For instance, one does not hesitate to disrobe for a physician. One would hardly feel comfortable doing that for a banker or the plumber. Well, most wouldn't. At the doctor's office we accept that we are but one of the many slabs of meat he or she will see that day. We even dehumanize ourselves in advance of the doctor's visit.

A similar dynamic is at work with doctors of the mind; we open up to things we would not discuss with friends or lovers. We want them digging through our darkest little corners looking for where the damage is located. But this candor and this openness does come with the requirement that we submit to authority. It is a situation where one person is firmly in control and the other is relegated to subject status.

Tallhill's mentor program pairs up people who are equal in the respect that they both have lost their marbles to some extent and can definitely relate. I cannot speak for all of the members, but Bonnie and I could definitely relate. If this mentoring affected most of the people in Tallhill in this way, then it is no wonder that nobody ever seemed to want to leave. The therapy itself was less invasive than other places, but the mentoring was absolutely nurturing.

If I had met Bonnie when her life was easy, she would have been no help to me. I would have noticed her beauty, but we probably would have exchanged pleasantries and moved on. As the tragedies unfolded in our lives, we found that we were vulnerable and dangerously so. Our behaviors led us to be institutionalized and all of the professional mind doctors in the world could not put themselves in our places.

The time I had spent on the outside adopting other people's problems had led to my tangled web of over-obligation, but it had also given me a glimpse of other people's psychosis. My former mistress Isabel was hopelessly drawn to abusive men, but she also volunteered at a suicide hotline. She had a keen insight into what goes wrong with people's minds when they find no reason to continue. She was good at telling these people things to cheer them, or at least give them perspective, but she was extremely proficient at screwing up her own life. She also could never help me… and I needed help.

It wasn't as if I helped everybody who was miserable. In some cases I thought it would harm my psyche to get involved with people who clearly needed help. Lenny, my unfortunate "victim" was one. He was stuck in this world where he just drifted along being half-effective and getting away with it. I didn't know the technical term for it, so I just used the colloquial "fucked-up". That suited me fine. That was my diagnosis and I prescribed for him a smack on the forehead with a work bench. I have my doubts that it did him any good, but I am not a professional.

Then there was my old boss Del. Del was one of these people who would pick out a personality trait or some detail about a person and use that information constantly. For instance, if a person once wore cowboy boots in Del's presence, then he would become "Mr. Cowboy Boots", "Urban Cowboy", or some variation on that theme. These things amused no one but Del, and were annoying to most, but he did these things presumably to assert some kind of power. He frequently called me "Goggles" or "Goggle Man". One time I insisted on wearing goggles for a tower job- which was the safety requirement in the company handbook- so he bought a pair of cheap strap on goggles and I donned them with a smile. But from then on, he called me "Goggles" and he thought it was funny as shit. All it got from me was a sneer.

Part of the reason that Bonnie was my mentor, in spite of being over a dozen years younger, was because she had learned to trivialize the trivial. By that, I mean she could see through the façade I had erected in my manifesto that allowed me to excuse my self-inflicted solitude. She was on top of the situation at once. Perhaps she was always this intuitive; maybe she had gained wisdom at a rapid pace after losing her ability to walk. In my opinion, it was both of these, but her talents were brought into focus when she realized the true nature of people. Her world came crashing down and instead of rationalizing the problem away, she investigated the nature of things.

Recently, I investigated Tallhill's methodology and realized that bringing Bonnie and me together was not pure happenstance. I was brought from prison to Tallhill because of my mental condition, or lack thereof. When accepting people from state institutions, Tallhill only accepted the non-violent types or the first-time offenders. I fit into this latter category and so did Bonnie. There were probably some indicators in my profile which made me a perfect match for Bonnie. There had to be. In any case, Tallhill never appeared to cure anyone; they just made them mentors and kept collecting members and building additions and adding to their reputation.

The upshot of this philosophy and methodology was that nobody ever wanted to leave. Life had been difficult for some, cruel to some, and downright tragic to some others. Tallhill, as I have stated, provided certainty that some had seldom seen and others had never seen. I had not developed a real attachment to the place, but I wasn't unhappy either. I had seen the underside of being cast into a group of hopeless loonies and I wanted no part of that. I could ride things out at Tallhill for the foreseeable future with no complaint.

This attitude soon changed.

Two things happened in one day that broke my complacence and acceptance of my circumstance. In mid-October, the baseball season had ended and I was only aware of this fact when Amos took to watching the entertainment news in the afternoons when he used to watch baseball games or baseball news or other sporting events. I was a sports fan in my former life, but over time, I began to find the games mundane and pointless so I sort of drifted away. It was probably a symptom of my impending collapse, but I stopped following my teams and pretty much any sports.

Amos watching the entertainment news was the circumstance and the situation which existed at that point in time that found the both of us sitting in the lounge one afternoon. Between the features about celebrity marriages and movie premieres, the blonde lady on the television made mention of an upcoming segment about a new exciting folk-rock group called "The Travelled". My attention, which at that point had been concentrating on Amos's speech about which celebrities he would like to meet (Mohammed Ali and Clint Eastwood), suddenly was all on the entertainment news.

Blonde Lady returned to the screen after a few commercials and began her feature about this new exciting group. They had started out as a road touring group that would pile into a van and go from town to town without notice and try to drum up work. They caught on after a while and started to build a following. Their repertoire consisted of songs that weren't folk songs that they converted to folk songs.

Among the songs the blonde lady mentioned were "Born to be Wild", and "Paranoid". The group featured a talented young singer who called herself Gypsy Rae.

According to the blonde lady on the television, Gypsy Rae had an amazing vocal range and was the main reason for the band's success. The band's following had apparently become quite large and these fans had taken to following them around the country like latter-day Dead Heads. The band soon had a manager booking them into venues well in advance. The venues became larger and larger and the caravan of vehicles following them became larger until they decided to buy a tour bus. The last part of the feature was an interview with their exciting young singer, Gypsy Rae.

Up until this point, I was sitting there semi-aware that Amos was talking about something. When I saw Annette's image on the screen, I held up my hand in Amos's direction to indicate that he should be quiet.

"What is it?" He asked.

"Listen," was all I said.

"We are not trying to be trend setters; all of us in the band just have eclectic tastes in music. We were all raised listening to different types of music. We have our style and we incorporate the songs into our style. Our goal is to entertain and if we draw big crowds it is because people are entertained. Our success has been mostly word of mouth, but I think now with the hiring of a manager, we will get more promotion."

"When asked if success will spoil them, Miss Rae replied with candor," said the blonde lady's voice.

"There is always that danger. You see it over and over. Success breeds excess, they say. We will try to keep a level head, but it is not about our success or how much stuff we can buy. At this point in time it is about the music. No telling whether that will change. But I can't think about that. I think about things like taking care of my voice and the next gig. "

"The Travelled's first album, with mostly original material, is due to go on sale on the first of November," the blonde lady said as she wrapped up the segment.

"Pretty girl," Amos said as the entertainment show went to commercial.

"Which one?" I asked.

"The singer," he said.

"That's my daughter," I said, "and thank you."

Amos, who never focused on anything I said, changed the subject.

"I got good news Clyde," he said as he scooted up and leaned forward on his chair.

"I have been made a trustee," he whispered with a smile on his face.

"That's great!" I whispered as I was leaning forward to share his news.

"I am going to be an apprentice for building maintenance, electrical mostly, the generators, the cameras, the security stuff..."

"That IS good news, Amos," I said as the seed of a plan was planted in my brain.

"She has a lovely voice," Amos said, pointing to the television.

On the TV, they were ending the show by playing a clip from one of The Travelled's recent shows. There was Annette in a simple white dress with her hair back singing "Paranoid" while being accompanied on acoustic guitar by a man with a goatee sitting on a stool.

"I need someone to show me the things in life that I can't find.
I can't see the things that make true happiness, I must be blind"

The lyrics clearly meant something to her. I had heard and seen her sing hundreds of times, but never with so much emotion. Even the most jaded music critic could see there was something there. The range of feelings that I went through in that moment were complex and numerous: pride, fear, abandonment, sadness, hope, and anger, among others. My head was swimming and I needed to just be alone to think about this. It was my personal time, so I stood up and congratulated Amos, then excused myself and headed back to my room.

Once there, I contemplated my feelings in the context of my situation. My dear sweet Annette was on the verge of stardom, perhaps superstardom. I was on the verge of something I understood little about. My little girl wanted no contact with me and had her manager/lawyer send me a restraining order. My emotions were tangled into a cloud of confusion. I was in a place which promised a cure to my troubled mind and had already delivered a sublime creature to me who seemed dedicated to finding the virtue in me.

But I wanted out all the same.

Freedom would seem to be one of those simple words to define. When I was young, freedom meant breaking free of my parents. Later, I got married and forgot what it meant to be free. Maybe I was scared of freedom and married for security and certainty. In any case, this reinforced to me that love was not freedom of any sort. For a certain time after I married, I really didn't care about freedom. Certainties eased my mind, but make no mistake, it was a trade. After a while, what I traded seemed more valuable.

No, the word freedom is defined by those who own it. For Amos it was freedom from doubt, even if it meant spending days in an institution. For Naomi, it meant that she was free from the control of a rich step-father and her status-seeking mother. For Bonnie, it was perhaps freedom from her wheelchair (I wasn't sure). For Annette, maybe it was freedom from me. For Clyde Barrow, it meant freedom from other people making decisions for him; it meant freedom from the people who used his misery addiction for their own benefit. This definition also included freedom from Tallhill.

The fact that my daughter was now famous combined with the fact that she wanted me at a distance began to tear at me a bit. I wanted to be detached and unemotional, but I began to feel alien from the one life I had created in this world. All parents probably know this feeling to some extent. I wished I was a bigger part of her success. I knew I was part of the foundation, but I felt as if I was being cheated on the spoils of her ultimate success. I sat in my room for those few hours, stewing in my own misery. It was beautiful and tragic at the same time.

The tragedy was my situation, but the beauty was that I could do something about it. Amos had triggered something in my brain that started to form a plan. Amos was now a trustee. The fact that he had access to information about the security systems was especially important. I decided that my plan depended entirely upon Amos's ability to be my confidant. He definitely didn't care about his own freedom; he had found love and certainty at Tallhill. What I didn't know was how he felt about helping me.

CHAPTER 29 – LETTERS

Alone that night; I sat up chewing my fingernails. Not because I was fearful or alone, but because I wanted to be somewhere else. I wanted to be where Annette was. I wanted to be there to tell her that I was sorry for the thousand errors I made as a father. I wanted to tell her that she need not be ashamed of me because of this temporary condition I found myself in. I needed her to know that her father is not an object of pity. I needed my little girl to not feel the object of circumstance. I wanted to hold her and feel her feel my warmth and protection.

I began to form a plan in my head that involved Amos. I could not let him know because I decided after careful contemplation that he may have divided loyalties. He was absolutely happy to be at Tallhill and I considered that he might just turn on me, friend or not. The objective of my plan was to escape from Tallhill. More correctly, my objective was to see my daughter and try to convince her to allow me the dignity to be a real part of her life. Toward that goal, I had to work on details; money, transportation, and shelter were major concerns.

The very first detail I needed to work out was to find out where "The Travelled" were appearing in the near future. In the library, I could find the group's tour schedule to see when they were going to play close to Tallhill. I had to be careful though; everything at Tallhill seemed to be monitored. If I did a search on the internet, it could possibly be surmised that I was planning on attending that concert. For this part of my plan, I decided to use Amos.

Amos was in a phase of his life where he was starting to recapture past glories. In his life before clinics and asylums, he was a master airplane mechanic. He loved to tinker with things. He had a technical mind; in this respect we were very much alike. Not long after he became a trustee, I found him in the break room on a computer. He was studying the workings of the ankle bracelets and their associated circuitry. I pulled up a chair behind him and looked over his shoulder at the virtual manual he was studying on the computer monitor. He seemed completely oblivious to my presence as he was when he was watching baseball. But I knew that he knew I was there.

"This stuff is very interesting, Clyde," he said after about three minutes of my eavesdropping. "Do you know that these bracelets are constantly sending a signal back to at least one of several receivers that are located beyond the grounds?"

"I guessed something like that, yes," I answered honestly.

Amos just looked over his shoulder at me and raised his right eyebrow. He turned back to the manual and continued his tutorial, "You can cut these off quite easily, but once the circuit inside the bracelet is broken, the signal is no longer being sent and the system goes into alarm. A little blip appears on the screen which shows the bracelet's last known location. It triggers the cameras for that sector and the pictures from those cameras are displayed on another monitor that the security people watch. The video of those cameras is recorded and there is an immediate alarm for all members to return to their rooms."

I sat amazed that this institution was trusting an inmate with this much security information. My amazement lasted until I realized that I was also being trusted with this information by Amos. Perhaps Amos knew instinctively that I wanted to leave and he was slyly letting me in on the secrets of Tallhill. He didn't want to leave, but keeping me here was not in his best interests either. He wanted contentment, since his formative years had been filled with change and he would happily stay here to live and love. Clyde Barrow and his impossible dreams were not part of that picture.

I absorbed all that Amos taught me about the security system and the backup generator that day. I learned that the backup generator would power up the security system before almost all else, but that meant about a two minute delay before the systems was fully operational. He also taught me that only half of the cameras operated under emergency power. All of this was valuable information for someone wishing to escape. I asked no questions during this time, just listened and absorbed.

Before Amos logged off that computer that day, I asked him one question; I wanted to know the tour schedule for The Travelled. He found the schedule quite easily and was ready to print it for me. I grabbed his hand before he clicked on the print button. Not wanting to leave an electronic trail, I grabbed a pencil and copied down the closest concerts to Tallhill: December 9- Maplewood, December 11- Carlisle, December- 13 Chancellorsville. He closed the window and I excused myself. I had less than six weeks to get my plan right.

****

During the period of planning my escape and the few weeks before, I solidified my relationship with Bonnie. She was a sincere person, but full of regret and she frequently told me that she was paying her penance for her evil deed. I did my best to ease her mind and reassure her that her pain was in no way going to be eased by continuing to act like someone or something was keeping her in check.

"Your dreams are your dreams," I said. "Your dues were paid a long time ago. Feeling guilt and regret isn't going to change any of the past."

"Wait," she interrupted. "Just, who is the mentor and who is the mentee here?"

We laughed. In reality, our roles had started to change somewhat. I fed on her optimism and I had begun to see that I was going to find my way back to normal. Our sessions had also changed the way she acted. It was less noticeable at first, but soon she was displaying signs of vulnerability. She showed up at my door one night after lights out and cried herself to sleep in my arms. She had been dreaming about her mother and she kept repeating how she wished her mother was in her life, wishing that she cared enough. I sat in a chair next to her and stroked her hair until she cried herself to sleep. Once she was asleep, I carried her to my bed, tucked her in, and then fell asleep in her wheelchair with my feet propped up on a chair.

A couple of weeks later, we were sitting in the break room just talking. It was not an official mentoring session. She was wearing a pair of diamond earrings that her father had bought her with his first raise when she was quite young. She told me that she hadn't worn them since her arrest and that she had to have her ears re-pierced to wear them. I took this as a sign that she was coming out of the doldrums and didn't ask her any questions about them. I just let her open up.

"I am glad you are here Clyde," she said after a long pause.

"Thanks, Bonnie," I said. "I am glad I found you here."

"I can tell you," she replied. "This relationship has been rewarding for me also. I never suspected such a thing was possible. I have been on my guard to prevent anyone getting to me. But something about you makes me want to get on to the next thing."

"It must be my undying charm," I joked.

"It might be that, but I think you are healing me in some way," she said.

We were sitting across a small table from each other. There were other people around, but our gazes barely left each other. It was apparent to me by that time that we were in love, but the idea scared me. I had impossible love before, but this was insane. I was planning my escape, but she wanted to stay here. Furthermore, she was in a wheelchair; making her escape difficult and mine next to impossible if I tried to bring her. Still, I quickly added her to my escape plan. I would come back to get her. But this would take some convincing.

At this moment, she was sitting there with the earrings, a new hairdo, and she absolutely shone brilliance. I had resisted thinking of her as a sexual being up until that time, but my thoughts became even more clouded with the complications. We never talked about being together and the night she cried in my arms was not mentioned afterward. It was just that way with us. We were reasonable people, we were done with romance. But reasonable people also want to feel desired.

The following morning, I woke up and took a shower; my normal morning routine. As I opened the door to leave I noticed that a note had been slipped under the door. I had not had a note at my door since those first couple of mornings. This one was similar in size to the others and was written on the same type of paper. I suspected where the notes came from, but only upon opening the note was my suspicion confirmed:

Dear Clyde,

I want you to make love to me.

-Bonnie

I stood there for a moment, staring at these words that further complicated things. I felt flattered, then confused, then scared, then amused, then eventually happy. I walked back and sat down on my bed. I looked up at one of the cameras that watched my every move and sighed. I placed the note in the drawer next to the bed with the others. I got up and took myself down to the cafeteria.

That day was a blur. I performed my yard work and exercised. I was not conscious of anything but thinking about seeing Bonnie that night. I was not scheduled for a mentoring session, and since I didn't see her in the break room that evening, I expected her to visit after lights-out. But she did not show; I even stayed up late waiting for her. I just eventually drifted off to sleep alone. I did not see her the next day; nor the day after that. Those were two long days, but soon my mind was back on my escape plan.

I had recently begun a new job as a groundskeeper for the golf course. Have I mentioned that Tallhill had a golf course? It was only nine holes, but it was kept in immaculate condition. This new job was also crucial to me getting the lay of the land as far as escape routes were concerned. I had mapped most of the security cameras in my head by now and I knew that the golf course had fewer cameras than most of the grounds. The wide open spaces allowed for that. Every hole had three cameras; one on the tee box, one out in the fairway and one near the hole. If there were a power outage, then only half of them were going to work.

I had to learn this thoroughly and file this information in my mind for future use. I couldn't write any of this down without risking discovery. My time in solitary confinement memorizing my manifesto had sharpened my mind. I had also made a mental map of the distances from Tallhill to the concert venues to be played by The Travelled. Maplewood was 48 miles to the northeast, Carlisle was 53 miles to the west, and Chancellorsville was 71 miles to the south. I found them easily on a road atlas in the library and took to memorizing the routes to each town. I would go to the atlas and refresh the route every couple of days. I even used a different atlas each time so the pages I was memorizing didn't seem used too much. You just can't be too careful in a place with so many assets devoted to monitoring.

On the third evening after finding Bonnie's note, I returned to my room after dinner. I found a stack of eight letters sitting on my bed. They were all addressed to Clyde Barrow in care of Father Quinn. The dates of the letters started from February and were roughly one month apart, with the last one being in October. The first six were postmarked Riddle, WV, and the last two were stamped with an overseas postmark from The Bahamas. They were, of course, from Naomi.

Most people would tend to want to read letters in order that they were written. But I really wanted to know what happened that caused her to end up in the Bahamas. I have never been too much for mysteries, since my life was already a play of the absurd. I decided to skip to the end and read the last three letters first. The July letter was written in her sweeping fancy boarding-school cursive:

Dearest Clyde,

I have not heard from you in a while, but I have exciting news. I have been praying and praying for guidance. I have learned much here in my solitude in these mountains. One thing I have learned is patience. I now understand that I must give my worldly desires over to the lord in order to serve others.

I know that you remember my plan to build a ranch on an island. Well, my stepfather actually owns an island in the Caribbean Sea that he's giving to me for my dream. It is about 800 acres and it has a few houses, and I am going to go and check it out in a few days.

I am almost done here, and I think I am at peace with who I am and I have forgiven those who have wronged me. I also thank you for being such a beacon to me. I do not know if I could be brave enough without your help. I do not know where you are right now since you stopped writing, but I understand why since you probably didn't hear from me for a while.

I just wanted you to know that you are welcome at any time on my island once you get out and find the world is not treating you right. I will write you as soon as I get there.

Love,

Naomi

This letter excited all kinds of possibilities in my mind, so I opened the next letter as soon as possible.

Dearest Clyde,

I arrived at my new home 2 days ago. The place is called Russell's Cay. I think he was a pirate of some note. The buildings here need a lot of work. There seems to have been some hurricane damage and there is no fresh water since the water pump in the well is not working. I am contracting out for someone to fix all of the problems and I hope that with a little hard work, we can get this place up and habitable in a few months.

I still haven't heard from you and I do not know if you have even been seeing my letters. I hold out hope that one day I will see you again. Perhaps I am too much of an idealist for most people to take, but I think you know I am sincere and I am going to make my dream happen. I have hired a boat and a driver to get to the bigger islands for supplies. I am going to take that trip in a few minutes. I just wanted to let you know my progress. I will write you soon with more news.

Much Love,

Naomi

So Naomi was building her refuge. I knew she had it in her and it didn't surprise me that her stepfather owned an island. I knew she would give everything she had to make it work and if nothing else, it would be a spectacular learning experience. Letter number eight made the picture even more complete.

Dearest Clyde,

Things are happening very quickly here at RC (Russell's Cay). I have had a new well drilled and we now have fresh water. Most of our power is going to be supplied by windmill, which is being erected and should be complete in a couple of weeks. We will also make use of the sun with solar panels. I have had to read several applications for residence here. I will probably accept them all (laugh). However, I cannot currently house anyone but myself and my few workers. I have unlimited support from my stepfather, who is quite old and is probably trying to buy his way into heaven (laugh).

I wish you could be here to see this place take shape. I still haven't heard from you, but I trust Father Quinn delivered the previous letters to you. I miss your calm presence. I miss your smile. I know distance has separated us, perhaps forever, but I hope someday you will visit me in my paradise. I am renting a P.O. Box on one of the main islands here and one of my workers goes there twice a week for provisions. I am including my address, so please write.

I will conclude by saying that you have touched me in many ways and have improved my life and my outlook. I am firmly in your camp and I love you forever.

Yours Truly

Naomi

So there it was. Naomi was living her dream. She was making it happen and she gave me way more credit than I ever thought I deserved. I had thought of myself as one of those people trying to take advantage of her wealth. I had hoped that maybe she could get a team of lawyers to have me set free. Maybe her rich daddy could bribe a judge. Instead, she was using me to bolster her confidence. I was in the right place with the right attitude to allow her to throw off all of her self-doubts.

She no longer needed me, but I still maybe needed her. I needed her not for her wealth or her stepfather's power. I needed her as a refuge. Naomi was now part of my plan. The plan that was coming together in my head. The plan which seemed to get more complicated each day, but also had potential to succeed, now more than ever.

I held onto the remaining five letters from her without opening them. Perhaps they would make me see a more complete picture of where she was in her life. I just didn't want any more complications at that point in my life. Emotions are dangerous things and Bonnie had recently thrown me a curveball that I was having trouble adjusting to. For the last three days since her enticing note, I had not seen a trace of her and there was no follow-up note.

I was beginning to grow weary of wanting love or sex. I took all eight of Naomi's letters and shut them in the drawer with Bonnie's notes. I sat down on my bed and stared at my feet and started to sort out the complications in my mind. I decided that I was going alone and that was the only way.

As I got up to go brush my teeth and retire early, there was a knock on the door. I opened the door and there she was in her wheelchair; Bonnie Parker, beautiful as ever. She had a wide bright smile and she wore those diamond earrings and a Tallhill issued night gown.

"I am here Clyde," she said. "Be gentle."

CHAPTER 30 – DELICACY

I was not surprised that she was there. I had been expecting… nay anticipating her arrival at my door ever since I read her note. I was tingling with excitement and fear of discovery. I was like a school boy skipping class to smoke a joint. It was like prom night or something.

Bonnie wheeled herself inside and I just stood there and let the door close. My thoughts ran wild as she smiled and blinked her eyes at me. This is where the awkwardness took over. I had not been with a woman in the over 14 months that I had been locked up. I thought about it often and dreamed about it frequently. In none of my thoughts or dreams was there a girl in a wheelchair involved. At least not up until the last few days.

I also had up until recently thought of Bonnie as a sort of victim. She had murdered, but immediately before and for some time afterward, she was a victim of what others did to her. She was helpless in a hospital bed and she had been shunned by her social circle and her mother. She was a beautiful woman in her early thirties, but she was a victim. Having sex with a victim is not only predatory, it is downright sick.

I also thought of this situation from her point of view. I had not the nerve to ask her if she was engaging in sexual intercourse for the last few years. I also had no idea if she could enjoy the act. We were close, but I had not bridged this gap. I imagined that she had not had any activity and I knew that she was, by her own admission, a bit of a novice when she got married.

Again, I return to my prom analogy; the two kids in some ramshackle motel off Interstate Exit 43 and neither of them have any idea how to proceed. Wanting it to be good, wanting it to last, and hoping to please the other one. I wished that I had a bottle of cheap wine to make this all easier.

"You nervous, Clyde?" she asked after a long uncomfortable pause.

"Nervous, as hell, Bonnie," I had to be honest.

"Don't worry, babe," she reassured me. "It's like riding a bike. Or in my case; a cripple on a wheelchair."

I didn't laugh at this humorous comment. It was funny, but it made me sad. Again I felt like a predator.

"I love you," I blurted out before I realized what it was I said. Maybe I thought it would ease my guilt if I made it known that she was special to me.

"You do Clyde, I know you do," she said.

"I want to make love to you...," I said

"But?" she interrupted.

"No, buts," I said. With that, I walked over to her chair, crouched down and kissed her long and passionately.

"We can't do this here," she said as she motioned towards the camera in the corner. "I'm not a peep show for some security guard. Let's go to the bathroom."

So we went to the bathroom. Without giving the minute details of the activity, I will note that she still had the capacity and sensitivity to enjoy the act. We set the brakes on the wheelchair and I was the one in the seat of the chair. I was as gentle as I could possibly be and therefore went slower, which may have almost certainly prolonged and increased the pleasure. When we were done, we wheeled out into the room and I lifted her onto the bed and crawled in beside her.

"I love you too, Clyde," she said.

We lay in that bed until the break of dawn when she pulled herself up and eased herself into her chair with her incredibly strong arms.

"I will see you tomorrow, Clyde," she said after she wheeled herself to the door and turned around. "I just want to make clear that we violated no rules here. Sex is not frowned upon, but it has to be discreet."

I nodded to the darkness in the room and she let herself out.

This episode was not the climactic event in either of our lives, but a transitional one for both of us. She probably had not given herself to another man since her husband. Furthermore, she had caught her husband in the act. If her admission to pre-marriage inexperience hinted that she had a vulnerable side to her, then killing her husband in the act while trying to kill his lover revealed perhaps even an aversion to anyone who did enjoy the practice.

For my part, it had been a long time since I made love to anyone I loved sincerely. Mostly there were conquests and jaunts with women who I fancied or shared a bond with. Unquestionably, I wanted to spend time with them and enjoyed their company, but spending the rest of my life with any of these women was not possible unless one or both of us changed considerably. I did love my wife when we married, but I mostly felt that she was security and stability more than anything.

Probably the last girl I felt this way about was a girl named Stephanie who I met in my second year of college. I spent all of my time and money trying to please her and in the end, I just ended up broke with bad grades. It was one of those lessons that all young men must learn; love is not always reciprocal, nor ever contagious. Just because you feel that way, the other person may just be out for a good time. In other words, sex does not equal love. You can beg or con someone into bed, but love cannot be forced on anyone. I contend that love can only be shared.

With our life-altering coupling completed, I was wide awake in the faint daylight hours before my Tallhill day resumed. I sat up on my bed naked except for the sheet draped across my mid-section and looked into the camera, then looked down. I wondered if next time we should have an audience. It was such a revelation and a realization to both of us, which made me wonder that instead of using the bathroom, we should have done it in front of an audience at the Catharsis Center. I laughed out loud, shook my head, threw the sheet aside and headed for the shower.

****

I spent the rest of that day analyzing. It is what I do. I analyzed how this new event fit into my plans. I wanted to experience more of this, but I also wanted to get out of this place. I was not going to be one of these mindless drones clicking away at daily chores until feebleness rendered me useless. I was going to be free to decide what I would do with my time. I knew I wasn't crazy. I just needed less pressure.

I was in heady territory during this time. I was in a teenage love stupor while I was planning a great escape in a separate compartment in my mind. The tasks I performed on my job were mundane and repetitive enough that they didn't occupy much of my creative thought process. They barely even held my attention.

When I trimmed the trees on the corner of the fifth fairway, I was actually testing the angle of the camera. When I mowed the grass, I was looking for the best straight-line escape route and the closest building exit to that route. When I walked back to the equipment shed at the end of my shift, I was pacing-off the total distance from the building to whatever fence I had been near.

In between the complexities of my escape plan, I would bask in a sensation comparable to silly unvarnished puppy love. It was impossibly irrational of me to invite love into my plan. Simple horny attraction with a young vixen would have made things complicated; my soul mate in a wheelchair who had no reason to leave made things ridiculous.

So I would alternate between intensity and stupor. I was anxious to see Amos and find out more about the layout of the grounds and I was even more anxious to see Bonnie in order to explore the possibility of real love. Once again, I was making life unnecessarily complicated. I sometimes just wished that I could shut off my mind and be a drone.

My mind was always reaching for the next conclusion and approaching every angle to every problem. If I was an unlikely inmate, I was a master escape artist; at least in my mind. The details of my plan were slowly coming together in the vapor of unreality in my head. The plan's execution would obviously be more difficult because it depended on several external variables. So for those variables, contingency plans had to be developed.

One contingency plan was to shut the whole thing down. This could only be done in the early stages. Once outside the wall, this could only lead to trouble and possible discipline including a return to prison. The wall and the disabling of my bracelet were obvious points-of-no-return. I also had one date certain where I needed to be out and about and that date was December eleventh. The last concert in the Tallhill area was going to be December thirteenth in Chancellorsville. If I was out by the eleventh, I could be there within two days even if I had to steal a car. The Travelled were going to travel much farther west after the Chancellorsville show and there was the possibility of Canadian or even European tours. I could possibly get to Annette later, but that escape plan would have to be even more complex.

While my mind played with the possibilities of escape and destinations, it also played with plans to return to Tallhill to get Bonnie. I had not yet consulted her on this point. I suspected that she would need to fall deeper in love with me or come to realize that she was not the glue that held this institution together. Getting her out of Tallhill would probably be much easier, since her tracking device was on her wheelchair.

So my plan had the following objectives:

1. See Annette

2. Return to help Bonnie escape

3. Find our way to Naomi's Island

There could be no more complications than these simple steps. I had to memorize the plan, so groups of three it had to be. Objective one would have three steps and those three steps would each have three parts, I would check each of them off my mental list as they happened. So part one of step one HAD to be to get Tallhill's main power to fail.

Amos had already been an indispensable help in my plan. He seemed to know what I was up to, even though we never discussed escape in any way. However I had laid out several hints. He knew I wanted to see my daughter. He knew that I knew the concert dates. He knew I was at least passively interested in the security of the place. He was not one to tip his hand, but he was quite intelligent, his style of not directly confronting facts not only served him well as a defense mechanism, it served me well in not being asked a bunch of questions.

I learned that the location of the main power circuit breaker was in a tight security area. I would not be able to use this in my plan, so I would have to cause a power interruption some other way. It had to be the main power in order for the emergency generator to start and to cause the bracelet-monitoring system to become less effective and the cameras to be limited to half capacity. This was a major sticking point in my plan.

Fortunately, Amos came to the rescue again. One evening in mid-November, I was watching him study the inner-workings of the security system. He was very happy by now. He was a full-fledged apprentice and was talking about applying to be married. I found him in good cheer, by the computer in the break room.

"Clyde," he said to me. "I have applied for shared living quarters."

"Are you getting married?" I asked

"If she says yes, and Tallhill allows, then yes," he said smiling as he looked at me over his shoulder.

"I wish you happiness, Amos," I said. "No one deserves it more."

"Indeed, Clyde," he said as he returned his attention to the instructions he was studying on the computer monitor. "Indeed!"

Over his shoulder, I could see that he was studying instructions for generator tests.

"Interesting," I said. "Are they giving you a test on this?"

"Not really," he replied. "I just have to be ready to run a test on the generator."

"What kind of test?" I pulled up a chair next to his left side.

"On the third of each month," Amos said as he looked over at me. "We pull the main circuit breaker and the generator is supposed to kick on and I take some readings as the emergency power starts up various things. It happens at 2:00 a.m., long after lights out."

"So how long before all the lights are back on?" I asked.

"Oh, the lights are separate," he said "The emergency lights in the hallways, offices, and outdoor grounds have their own batteries and turn on automatically. The magnetic locks on the doors seal everybody in until the generator is full power."

"That seems like a fire code violation," I said.

"It might be," he admitted. "But it is very temporary."

Is sat there quietly as Amos studied the test levels of voltages and currents he was going to read and record as systems were turned on. The computers that controlled the security monitors were supposedly not going to be affected if they had a sudden power failure, but the radio receiver that received the ankle bracelet signal would suffer a temporary loss of efficiency. The extent of this loss of efficiency, I could not guess, but it was a promising opening. I now had until the evening of the second of December to perfect my plan. I would have to hide out for six days before I found Annette. It gave me time; almost too much time. But the news was good and my plans were progressing.

CHAPTER 31 – DEATAILS AND COMPLICATIONS

In my therapy sessions with Dr. Silk, I was actually feeling as if I was making progress recognizing my reality. My life and world that I had known was taken away by an act of my own. I acted out in hostility because life had become too much. It seemed that I felt as if there was very little give and take in my life. The people in my life took from me and gave very little. Even that little bit, though appreciated by me, felt forced and insincere.

I sought to test the strength of these people. I wanted to measure their dedication. I sought a different reality. The reality that hit me in the face was that very few stuck around for the fallout. Naomi was one of those few, but she was new to me and hadn't been worn down by my insistence that every day be examined to its fullest. She perhaps was a kindred spirit, but she was more likely a cynic who had been used and discarded. This was alright with me, because she was there when I needed her and she didn't abandon me.

Annette had not abandoned me at first. Even when she did, I was convinced it was because of bad advice. Besides, I was her father; she would come around in due time. This completed the list of my friends and relatives who had at least thought about me. It was a very short list, and this was a revelation. My new reality was, of course, the only actual reality. Dr. Silk had asked me to write of reality and I had obliged:

> *There is only one reality. There are, however, several types of realization. These realizations arrive mostly through time and experience, but these discoveries eventually add to a more complete picture of reality.*
>
> *The opposing side of realization is occupied by, among other things, denial and deception. Deception is applied by others, while denial is willingly performed by one's self. Realization overcomes these obstacles sometimes with great effort. Sometimes the realizations are significant; such as when a brush with death causes a realization of one's mortality. Sometimes they are minor, like a man realizing that he lives beyond his means. Perhaps a young boy realizes that he will not be a major league baseball pitcher.*
>
> *In old age, the realizations are ubiquitous; the limits are added almost daily. The promotion has passed us by; young people of the opposite sex do not seem to notice us as much. We can't eat what we want to. Eventually we lose physical abilities and mental acuity.*

People and their deceptions can delay all of these processes and the cleverer the deception, the longer the delay in realization. Like a journey to freedom, the journey to reality can be difficult, time consuming, and sometimes ultimately unfulfilling.

So was this the start of a new manifesto? A continuation of the old one? I really hadn't thought of it as anything more than a confession of my own limitations and the discovery that I had not really lost my mind in the classical sense. My theory is that I had arranged my situation to uncover reality. This was like an epiphany to me. I now found that I could continue and that a goal of true happiness was possible, but not necessarily on the exact terms I sought. Freedom was not in creating a reality, it was accepting and adapting.

Dr. Silk wanted to know what I meant in the last part.

"Clyde," he said as he sat on the leather easy chair in his five-thousand dollar suit, "what does freedom mean to you?"

I had to stop and try to determine where he was going with this analysis. I had not given away my escape plans, had I? After a pause, I answered.

"Freedom is being able to decide what mistakes I will make every day." It was the best honest answer I could come up with.

It was Dr. Silk's turn to pause. "You feel you have no freedom at Tallhill?" he finally asked.

"Well, Silk," I said. "Freedom can be a relative term. I am freer than I was in prison, especially in solitary. But I still have to be in certain places at certain times and I can't just stroll out of here."

"Have you tried just strolling out of here?" he asked.

I raised my eyebrow, "No. What do you mean?"

"Have you tested the limits of your freedom here?" he rephrased the question.

"I haven't," I said in puzzlement. "But I assume these ankle weights are going to give me away."

"You are probably right, Clyde," he said. "What do you think will happen?"

"I don't know," I admitted. "I guess they would catch me pretty easily and maybe send me back to prison."

"So the freedom you have here is just enough to keep you from trying to escape since it is more freedom than you had in prison." This didn't sound like a question.

"Doc, I just haven't thought too much about leaving," I fibbed. "I do like it here much more than prison bars and exercise yards. I have real friends here and…" I searched for the next words.

In the pregnant pause, the doctor cut in, "You were saying?"

I realized that maybe Silk was as smooth as his nickname implied and he was trying to get me to talk myself out of something he may have guessed I was planning. I swallowed hard and tried to piece together the possible ways he could have guessed my plans. I decided he was grasping at straws. Besides, if he suspected something, he would probably have me sedated or something.

Again, he broke the silence, "Clyde, you compare freedom to reality. What else do these things have in common other than the long journey and the possible unfulfilling nature of both?"

Without missing a beat, I answered, "I have always liked the phrase, 'perception is reality', I don't know who said it, but I believe it is accurate when one employs deception or is deceived. Freedom can also be perceived as existing where it really does not. Humans rationalize in order not to see the actual reality. It can be very traumatic to realize that you have no freedom or that your happiness is a sham; denial and deception, Doc; the twin impostors."

"So do people here at Tallhill engage in denial to compensate for their lack of freedom?" Silk asked.

"I have no way of knowing," I admitted. "I have a theory that most of them have made a trade that they are content with. They have traded freedom for security. The big world out there is a lot to handle sometimes. Certain people are always going to perceive that the world is always coming at them to harm them. Freedom to those people is defined by a different measure than what I would use. They might define freedom as freedom from fear or freedom from uncertainty."

"So your definition of freedom would be…?" He asked

"I want to have control. To me, control is certainty." I said this boldly and then felt as if I was letting the well-dressed doctor in on a secret. I wanted to add more to this statement because I felt strongly about what I said, but I stopped. My words just hung in the air for a minute while I literally bit my tongue.

"Very profound, Mr. Barrow," Silk finally said. "Unfortunately, we are done for today."

I sighed in relief as my brain spun into paranoid damage-control. I hoped I had not given too much information. I hoped I could still escape.

My relationship with Bonnie was blossoming into a full-fledged love affair. We didn't meet every night, but we were up to three or four lights-out sessions a week. It was the most fulfilling thing I had ever experienced. As I analyzed (like I do) this feeling, I supposed that it was so fulfilling because I was bringing such pleasure and joy to someone who had given so much to others. I felt I was helping her to get most of her guilt out of her system. Bearing the burden of ruining your family's life was too much and she needed to give herself a break.

I don't want to sound egotistical, but I think I put a bounce in her step. Well, as much bounce as one can get in a wheelchair. She was smiling more and so was I. At times I would see her when she didn't see me and she seemed more free-wheeling, if you can accept a horrible pun.

We did more than make love on those nights. We would discuss in frank terms the plans for our future. I say one future because to me, I could not comprehend not coming back for her when I escaped.

How she saw this, I did not know, because I couldn't let her in on my plans. One night in particular, we lay in my bed in the dark and clung to each other like we would never see each other again. I felt this way sincerely, as it was getting close to December 3rd and my chances to see her were drying up.

I had to broach the subject of freedom and futures.

"Bonnie," I said as her head lay on my chest. "Would you ever consider marrying me?"

"Is this a proposal, Clyde?" she asked as she pulled her head back to look at me.

"Call it a pre-proposal," I said.

"I am not sure they will allow me." In the dull light I saw her point towards the door with her hand.

"What if you are no longer here?" I asked.

"Wouldn't that be awkward?" she asked, "Unless we both got out?"

"That's what I am saying," I said. "But either in here or out there, we could stop being the midnight creepers."

"I will consider it, dear Clyde," she said. "I wonder how that would work in here."

"My friend Amos is marrying another member here," I said.

"So why don't you come out and propose?" She asked. "Make an honest woman out of me."

"Perhaps I will," I said. "But in my own way. I want it to be classy and romantic."

"Ah, my Clyde," she said. "You're just an old softy."

"Not yet," I said as I kissed her on the forehead… then the lips… then… well it went further.

* * * * * * * * * * *

It was the day of the twenty-fifth of November when I finalized my plan. I knew that the 2nd had to be a day that Bonnie was not with me. I could not involve her in any way other than leaving a note under her door. It wasn't that I didn't trust her; I just thought she might try to stop me. My plan for getting her out was going to be more carefully planned and I needed to get away clean if any of this would work. I had memorized my three parts of three parts of three parts plan easy as pie

I was going to wait for the generator tests to start before I would cut off my bracelet. Amos told me that that a very high pitched tone would sound when the generator was employed, but he would shut that tone off immediately. It was a 3 kilohertz tone; more of a whine, which is near the upper end of human hearing range.

I would appropriate a pair of garden shears from the garden shed for the purpose of cutting off my bracelet. A few weeks earlier, I had begun sharpening some of the garden tools. It was an unofficial job and only Martha, the garden tool custodian, knew I was doing it. I proposed this idea to her one day when I was turning in a pair of dull shears. She agreed to let me sharpen one tool at a time and I checked out those shears and a whet stone and brought back the freshly sharpened shears the next day. Martha was very pleased and since she liked me quite a lot, she let me do this a few times. Such was the way of Tallhill; we were treated as grownups until we proved that we could no longer be trusted.

Another item on my mental list was the magnetic door locks. Each major exit or entrance required an electronic key which opened magnetic door locks. According to Amos, these doors would be locked during the generator tests. In other words the magnets would be activated and the doors sealed even if someone with a key card tried to open them. This situation would last approximately two minutes.

I counted four doors that I needed to disable to get to my planned escape route. There was the door to my room, eighteen steps down the hall, the door to the stairway, twenty eight steps down, the door to the lower corridor, and then sixty-two steps from there, the outside door. I would disable the magnets with a piece of transparent packaging tape. This had to be done the night of the December 2nd and could not be discovered. If I was locked in, I would probably not be punished, but I would have to go back to the drawing board.

I also would need some civilian clothes. A few days earlier, I had procured one of Dr. Silk's finest shirts from the stand up closet in the therapy room while he was called away on some errand. I simply put the shirt on and pulled my green Tallhill uniform over it. He didn't notice. The shirt was white, which would make me stand out in the dark, but it was all I had. A few days later, I took a pair of denim work overalls from the garden shop and told Martha I was going to get the grass stains out ounce and for all. So my escape attire was going to be a $500 shirt and sloppy old pair of work trousers. Eclectic, to be sure, but at least it wasn't Tallhill green. These I kept under my mattress.

* * * * * * * * * * *

On December 1st, I had my last rendezvous with Bonnie. I hoped it would not be the last time I saw her and I tried not to allude to it in our conversation. Nevertheless, I could not help but to be sad and nervous as I talked about the future.

"I think we can make it," I said to here as we lay in the dim light.

"Make it where?" she asked.

"Wherever we want," I answered.

"I wish you could meet my father," she said out of the blue.

"I would like that," I said. "He sounds like a fine man."

"He's the only reason I even try," she whispered into my chest. "I would have given up a long time ago. He's like a king or maybe a knight. He lost his big job and just kept pushing forward."

"I want to meet him," I said. "I could probably learn a thing or two."

"Clyde, he would like you, I think," she said as she raised her head. "You have changed me too. I now think of leaving and having a life."

It was then I felt conflicted and almost told Bonnie that I was going to help her do just that. I had no plan beyond getting over the wall to the outside world, but I knew that I had to come back. If I escaped, Bonnie may be suspected of helping me, but I still didn't want her to know in advance.

So we clung together through that night and I listened to her breathe as she slept. I hoped that she was dreaming of our new life together. I eventually drifted off myself. I dreamt that I was in a large white room with dozens of doors of all different colors on all four walls and I could hear that sweet guide voice of Bonnie's once again. She was calm and reassuring as ever.

"Clyde, you have what it takes. You will not let us down. We will be together and we will be happy. Just go through the door. You can do it. But be smart and be fast. You have won me over. You are almost there."

In the dream I selected a pastel blue door and stepped through. The door slammed shut behind me. Suddenly really bright lights were in my face and I heard laughing. The laugh sounded familiar. It sounded like a fake southern cowboy hick lawyer. It was the laugh of Elvin Williams, AKA Tex. Then all I saw was teeth as he grinned at me. I awoke as Bonnie slid out of the bed to her chair. The sun was beginning to break through the blinds in the window.

"I gotta go, Clyde," she said. "We will be together soon. I love you"

She rolled to the door and then opened it and slipped out. I lay there bleary-eyed and numb. I was thinking things I could not say. I was hurting and nervous and confused. I wished to go back to sleep and understand what that idiot Tex was doing in my sweet escape dream. I tried to sleep, but couldn't.

Thus began the longest day of my life.

PART 4: THE TRIP OF THE DESCENDING KNIGHT

CHAPTER 32 – ESCAPE

As I have said many times before, Tallhill is an amazing place. I truly do think they did a lot of good for a lot of confused people. My amazement began the day I was taken there and grew daily. I eventually likened it to a bee hive, with drones automatically programmed to perform tasks and no real dissent. If there was violence, I never saw it or heard about it. If there was an escape, it was well hidden.

They recruited members like a college football team recruits blue-chip athletes. Like a football team, they went after prospects that fit their system. If I had to guess, I would say that most of the members had been shuffled through one system or another that had let them down. Some of the members had been abused and neglected, but were mostly non-violent on their own. This is where I didn't fit the profile.

But knowing why I was here was not going to help me escape. I suspected that in the initial surge of inmates from the state prison, they looked for the least violent among them. I may have had my run-in with my cellmate Clarence, but Tallhill's administrators must have realized that he was a nut who talked to toasters and that I obviously had acted in self-defense.

So the non-violent and contented population was not a threat to commit violence. I was not exactly content here, but I wasn't going to hurt anyone either. I am sure the doctors reassured the staff that I was not a threat, but they may have also suspected that I would want to leave at some point. Dr. Silk had asked me one time how long it would be before I became a trustee. I told him I had been there two months, so I guessed it meant four and I wasn't really sure. This was an answer I wished I hadn't given as soon as it left my lips. From my talks with Amos and other members, being a trustee was like being a made-man in the mob; it was something to strive for.

Perhaps Dr. Silk took my answer as modesty. At least I hoped so. The bottom line on December 2nd was I worried that maybe someone was on to me. My carefully laid plans were in my head and I had only dropped hints and suppositions to Amos, Bonnie, and Dr. Silk. Amos did everything but give me the blueprints to the security apparatus.

Before breakfast on my last day at Tallhill, I felt the need to write a note to Naomi. In the back of my mind, I had an idea that I might make it to that Caribbean island where she would provide a home for Bonnie and me. I thought it would be proper to let her know what I was thinking. She was a loyal friend, after all. Even malcontents like me know that those are hard to find. So I spelled out the situation the best I could on Tallhill stationery:

Dearest Naomi,

All of your letters caught up to me at once. There were 8 in total and they gave me quite a lot of information to digest. I read them in reverse order because I couldn't wait to hear the latest news. I am very pleased and excited to learn that your dream is coming true. I hope to see you on that island soon.

I have been transferred from prison to a private mental health facility called Tallhill. It is my great good luck to have landed here. I have made amazing progress and I have met some fine people. I am not necessarily happy here, but content with my past.

Most of the reason that I am unhappy is that I have become estranged from my daughter. The rest of the reason is that I am still not free. The remainder of this letter concerns the freedom that I seek.

By the time you receive this, I will have escaped. Hopefully for good. I have worked out all of the details and I know I can get out of here successfully. How long I can stay free and how far I can get away depends on several variables that cannot be predicted. But I hope to see you when I get out. Do not attempt to send me any mail at Tallhill, since I will probably be returned to prison or some other place if I am captured.

When I do escape I plan to see my daughter and discover what has caused her disdain for me. Once I accomplish that, I plan to return to Tallhill and help my good friend escape. She is in a wheelchair and is smart, bright, and has helped me as much as anybody ever has. She has a tragic story, but she stands undeterred. She has had her heart destroyed and has survived to helps others. She is just the kind of person that you should welcome on your island.

I will try my best to make it to where you are and I count on you to be there for me. I do love you and I feel that you have made my life better.

Sincerely,

Clyde

When I finished the letter, I put it in an envelope and put it in the pocket of my escape overalls under my mattress. I still had time before breakfast, so I wrote my little note for Bonnie. I could not give it to her until I was about to leave. My plan was to slip it under her door right before lights out. We had no plans to see each other that night, and that was mostly my idea. We had decided that every night in the sack was a bit too much for both of us right now. So I wrote a short note:

Bonnie- please read this and destroy it. I am escaping early in the morning. I will return for you as soon as possible. Be ready. I love you more than anything in the world- Clyde.

This note I carried with me. I wanted to make sure it was with me at all times. I took a quick shower and went to breakfast.

* * * * * * * * * * *

My December 2nd schedule had no mentoring session, so I had both a morning and afternoon work detail. My morning work consisted of taking care of trees. Upon inspection of some of the smaller saplings, I decided that they needed more support. The support for these saplings depended on stakes driven into the ground next to them. I went to the tool room and talked to Martha.

"Good morning, sweetie," I said with a flirtatious look in my eyes.

"What can I do for ya, babe?" she asked.

"I need some tape, Dollface," I said as I leaned forward with both elbows on the counter.

"You got it, Clyde Baby," she said.

"Don't you want to know what it is for?" I asked

"I'll just use my imagination," she said as she passed me a roll of red marking tape.

"Do you have any clear packaging tape?" I asked as I inspected the red roll of tape in my hand.

"Okay, Clyde," she said as she took the roll of tape from me. "You've piqued my curiosity. What do you need it for?"

I laughed. "I need to tape a couple of these saplings to the support stakes and that clear packaging tape doesn't bind too much, it just kind of breaks when it is stretched."

"Makes sense," Martha said as she turned around and walked back to the shipping desk near the big rollup doors. Once there, she opened a drawer and pulled out a new roll of tape and walked back to the counter.

"Here you are, hon," she said as she passed the tape to me. "Enjoy."

I took the tape from her with the most seductive smile a 45 year-old man can manage and turned to walk away. I stopped, then turned around. "Martha, my dear," I said. "I also need some of those stakes."

"Well, doll," she said, "those are kept in a closet down the hall." She smiled and reached under the desk for a key ring and pulled them out along with an electronic key. She walked over and opened the tool shed door and winked at me. "Follow me Clyde," she smiled. "And don't try anything." She walked forward towards the door that led to the hallway, "Unless you mean business." We both laughed.

We exited the tool shed area and walked down a long hallway, then turned right and walked down a short hallway with one door leading outside at the end. Before the end of the hallway was a door marked "Supplies". Martha unlocked that door and stepped inside.

"Wait here, Clyde," she said as she slipped into the supply closet. "The stakes are way in back and you aren't allowed."

While she was in the closet, I took the opportunity to pull the tape out of my side cargo pocket, peel off an eight-inch strip, stick it to my forearm, and pull my sleeve over it.

"Clyde, they come in bundles of twelve," echoed the voice from deep within the closet. "How many bundles do you think you need?"

"At least three," I said as I poked my head around the corner of the opened door.

Martha emerged from the supply closet with one bundle of four-feet-long stakes in her arms and handed it to me.

"Thank you ma'am," I said as I took the bundle in my arms. "Shouldn't we stack these outside?"

"Good point, Clyde," She said. "Way ahead of ya." With that she reached for the key ring on her belt that held the key card on a retractable string and passed it over the key card sensor for the outside door. The door clicked and I pushed it open with my shoulder. While holding the door open with my foot, I placed the bundle on the ground next to me and turned to see that Martha had disappeared to the back of the supply closet once again.

Taking this opportunity, I rolled up my sleeve, and peeled the tape from my arm. With little wasted motion, I applied the tape vertically over the magnetic locking mechanism of the door latch. A few seconds later, Martha was there with the other two bundles.

"Here ya go, Sweetie," she said as she pushed up against me to transfer the bundles.

"Thank you," I said as I took the bundle from her. She held the door open as I bent over to place the bundles next to the first one.

"I think I can just take it from here," I said as I stood up.

"Okay, Clyde," She smiled and winked at me as our daily flirtation continued.

Her eyes stayed on me as she backed through the door smiling as she let it close behind her. I waited a full thirty seconds for the lock of the door to re-engage. The door had no outside handles, so I attempted to pull the door open by digging my nails into a seam on the door's outer border. The door opened. I let it close again.

This was the only door of the four which I needed open for my escape which was normally locked from both sides. The hallway door and the stairway door were normally unlocked. My room door locked others out, but opened from the inside with my key card; which opened no other doors. All of these doors would be locked during a generator test, so I had to perform this taping operation three more times. The other doors would be easier than this. The best part was that I had proven that the tape would work. It was also not visible to the casual eye.

Satisfied with the results, I cut the string on the first bundle of stakes with the garden shears I had in my other cargo pocket and began whistling as I made my way towards the rest of my morning work.

****

I ate lunch alone on my last day. I ate lightly since I planned on eating a big dinner to store my energy. I ate little for lunch, but chewed slowly. While I chewed, I thought about my plans. I thought about the outside. I thought about transportation and the six days I would have to spend alone as I planned to see Annette. Lunch was like a torture session because of these things. Thinking about things tended to make me think about how things can fail. As I ate, I felt for the note I had in my pocket for Bonnie. It was still there.

After lunch, I had my usual one hour with Dr. Silk. I had no revelations. I talked about my isolated childhood for the millionth time as I realized how little I would miss having my thoughts picked apart. Freedom never seemed as sweet as it did in that therapy session. I lamented my lonely younger years and my distant fascination with the opposite sex. I wished that I could go back to those years of contemplation and solitude. I was free to speculate and nobody put any expectations on me. It was a world where I was pushed to the background and not even considered. It would seem tragic to some, but it was my comfort zone.

These thoughts never were expressed to Dr. Silk. I was careful to not give a clue as to my intentions that very day. If he already suspected my desire to leave, at least I was in control of the day I would leave. The session passed quite uneventfully. I left the session and headed to the gym.

My physical training for that day was yoga and that suited me just fine. My escape was going to involve some physical activity and possibly some endurance. Agility was what I needed and yoga was at least going to prevent me from pulling a muscle or straining a tendon. The stretching and centering myself allowed me to focus on my own strengths. I convinced myself that I was going to make it.

Back at work that afternoon, Charlie the groundskeeper assigned me to trim some of the trees on the golf course. It took this opportunity to measure the distance from the taped-open door to the nearest outside wall. I counted two-hundred thirty-seven paces from that door to the wall, which was right behind the tee box of the fifth hole. Two-hundred thirty-seven paces calculated out to around two-hundred fifty to three hundred yards and would take me around a minute in the near dark.

I had calculated that I would only be spotted on one camera, and that would be the fairway camera on the fourth hole if I ran in the direction that required the fewest steps. I knew from Amos that all of the external lights were on a circuit separate from the generator and those lights required only batteries. There was one very bright light pointing down the fourth fairway that lit the entire area. There was a tree near this light which required some pruning. It was not a real complicated task to get down on my knees as if I was pruning the tree and just to slip those giant shears down next to the wire that went to the back of the big square box that contained the light. I snipped that wire without much effort, and then returned to my tree trimming.

After my shift, I left my work area with the roll of tape in my left cargo pocket and the garden shears in my right cargo pocket. The note for Bonnie was still in my front pocket. I walked down the hallway from the garden shed after I turned in my other equipment. As I passed through the door that led to the stairwells, I looked first behind me down the hall and then into the barely-lit stairwell area. Finding no one approaching, I quickly peeled the strip of clear tape from the inside of my left forearm and applied it over the magnetic door latch. I climbed the stairs to the second floor and performed a similar task on that door with the tape peeled from the inside of my right forearm.

Personal time was spent mostly napping. I wanted to be alert when I escaped in the early morning. So I was groggy when I stumbled down to the cafeteria for dinner. I asked for the pork chops and I ate a generous garden salad while I waited. With the main course I ate three slices of homemade bread with butter and washed it down with a caffeinated cola. I had three slices of apple pie with ice cream for dessert and washed them down with two more colas. I was wide awake at this hour; fully aware that I would still take a nap soon because I had eaten so much.

I took the long way back to my room, wandering down to where the physical therapy rooms were located. There were four of these rooms, each with a small square window. I checked each until I reached Room 3. Inside Bonnie was sitting on a large padded bench massaging and stretching her legs. I could only see her in profile, but I could see the contortion of her face as she alternately put each leg through a series of long stretches. Fascination, pride, apprehension, and sadness took hold of me. This forced me to pull my face away before my emotions caused me to reconsider my plans.

All day I had avoided thinking about her as much as possible. I needed to focus on my night ahead. I stopped by her room on the way back to mine. I thought about waiting there for her. I decided against it when I realized a conflict or a long goodbye might attract attention. It hurt quite a bit to not see her, but I had to rationalize that I would soon be back for her. I looked around to see if I was being watched, then slipped the note under the door.

Upon returning to my room, I opened the door and walked over to my bed and lay down with my face buried in the pillow. I wanted to get every last bit of sleep out of my system in the seven hours that I had before the generator tests were run at 2:00 AM. Instead I remained awake for over an hour with a feeling of ambivalence. I had actually grown to like Tallhill and depend on the security and certainty it provided and now I was about to go into a world of uncertainty and confusion in spite of my best plans. In the institution there were few variables each day. Out in the big world, the variables were limitless.

I had lit the fuse and that fuse was burning. The steps I had already taken would be discovered at some point; the taped doors and the cut cables would lead directly to me. The fuse was burning, but it was not too late. The butterflies in my stomach would not let me sleep. It was still early evening and I knew that sooner or later fatigue would overtake the butterflies, but to my core I was still that misery addict that I have always been.

Unsurprisingly, I began to find fault with my plan and worry about how it might affect Amos and Bonnie and even Martha. These people helped me with good intentions and I was potentially making their lives more difficult. So I lay there with my face in my pillow with my thoughts churning up the possibilities of failure until fatigue did finally take over. I slept a dreamless sleep.

I awoke and looked at my digital clock next to my bed. It read 12:47 AM. I rolled out of bed and into the bathroom. After I relieved myself and splashed water on my face, I pulled the dress shirt and overalls from under my mattress and took them into the bathroom and put them on over my Tallhill uniform. In the dull light, I noticed a small piece of paper that had been slipped under my door. I walked over to the door, bent over and picked up the note, then walked into the bathroom to read it.

Dearest Clyde,

I want you to know that I love you with all of my heart. I understand why you didn't want to say goodbye in person. I may have tried to beg you to stay. But I know now that it is too late to stop you and I will not try. I wish very much to go with you, but I realize that I would just slow you down. Your promise to come back to get me is met with anticipation. I know that it may not happen, but I do know you will try. I will keep my window unlocked and even open if the weather is not too cold.

I wish you luck and more. I pledge my support. If you come back for me, I can help you in many ways. You are the best thing that has ever happened to me. I mostly put on a brave face for everyone, but the hope I show outwardly never really existed until I met you. You have changed me and I now know what real love is. It is more than words and good feelings. It is knowing that someone understands and builds you up instead of trying to take from you.

Even if I never see you again, I will always love you.

Forever Yours,

Bonnie ♥

Rare tears were pouring down my face as I read this note. I knew that we had a connection, but Bonnie had never put that connection in such strong terms. I had originally planned to come back for her, but now I would move heaven and earth just to see her face again. I put her letter in my pocket next to the letter I had written for Naomi. I stood looking in the bathroom mirror until my emotions faded. I had to be rational and calm. There was no room for irrational thought in what I was about to do.

I filled two water bottles and put them in the side pockets of the work overalls I was now wearing. I pulled a strip of tape from the roll and walked over to the door. In the dull light, I opened the door and applied the tape over the door latch. I quickly closed the door and walked back over to where I had the sharpened garden shears stashed under my dirty work uniforms in the clothes hamper. I sat the shears on a chair near the bathroom door and waited. The clock read 1:15.

In the next forty five minutes, I memorized the final details of my plan and allowed myself the luxury of planning my freedom. In my groups-of-three structure, I had broken my needs down to transportation, shelter, and money. The shelter and money could be had by going to the storage area that Annette had set up for me. I believed she had stashed some things of value. The problem with the storage area was that it was over two hundred miles away. I had no intention of walking that far and hitching a ride was out of the question. I had concluded long ago that I would have to steal a car.

While I assessed the pros and cons of the several scenarios which would allow me to steal a car, the time grew nearer. As the clock near my bed ticked away the time, my breathing became uneven. I wanted to be able to hear the alarm when it went off, so began to hold my breath for long periods as to not have any noise. The effect was futility, as I began to breathe heavier. Eventually I decided that I would sit cross-legged yoga style and try to focus on nothing. This worked to stop my erratic breathing and soon my clock read 2:00.

In mere seconds after I saw that the clock had changed, I heard a faint high pitched whine that lasted about three seconds. I also heard my door lock click. I sprang into action. I leapt from my bed and tested the door; it opened. I then grabbed the shears from the chair and sat in the same chair. I slipped the shears into where the ankle bracelet was weakest and began a rhythmic sawing. The bracelet cut quite easily.

In seconds, I was out of my room and walking quickly down the hall. I reached the door in eighteen steps and pushed the door open to the stairway. Twenty-eight steps down the stairs later, I opened the door to the downstairs hallway. I had not seen one person on my way, but I was sure that a camera was watching at least some of this. I turned right, after bursting through the door and walked briskly in the emergency-light glow of the hallway. Turning right again; I was in that short hallway by the supply closet.

In my head, I calculated that I had used up around a minute and a half. According to what Amos told me, the bracelet tracking system would become active after around two minutes. As I reached the outside door, I braced myself for a sprint of around three hundred yards. I knew that this would take around a minute if I didn't fall. It was also quite dark in this region thanks to my surgery on the emergency light overlooking the fourth fairway.

I sprinted; I sprinted as if the world was riding on it. I felt the stinging cold wind on that December night as I performed the ultimate act of a sane mind. I was escaping the fate of the crazy man. I was throwing off the opinions and judgment of those who thought me a danger and a risk. I was smiling as I reached the walls of Tallhill.

At the wall, I jumped to grab the top of the eight-foot wall, and then slung my right leg over the top in one motion. Gaining a grip with that leg, I rolled the rest of my body over that brick wall and dropped the ten feet to a ditch below. My feet hit and I tumbled down a slight embankment. Regaining my feet, I walked quietly for a long distance through a darkened meadow until I found a paved road.

I heard the sirens from Tallhill begin to sound. Instinctively, I ran at a stand of trees I could see in the distance. In about thirty seconds I reached the trees. I stopped there to catch my breath and decide my next move. There was an airport fifteen miles northeast of Tallhill. My plan was to go there. I gathered my bearings the best I could and started off in a slow jog in that general direction. Everything was going to be different from now on. But that was what I bargained for when I planned this escape. I felt more alive than I ever had. I was on the outside.

I was free.

CHAPTER 33 – THE TRIP OF THE DESCENDING KNIGHT

There's something about trudging across land in a cold and dark early December morning that brings out all of the demons. Not the monster movie kind, but the intangible kind, which can be scarier. The moonless night offered nothing but undefined lights in the distance. The blackness I saw before me was filled with contemplation of the possible outcomes of my actions. Of those outcomes, only a few were satisfactory. All of the satisfactory results involved seeing Annette and helping Bonnie escape.

Anything that didn't result in achieving those two objectives would be a complete failure. Even if I didn't make it to Naomi's island, I decided that I would get to some place where Bonnie and I would make a life and be happy. The details of this plan would have to be worked on later.

I moved as quickly as I could across uneven farmland. I guessed that the temperature was somewhere in the mid-thirties. The ground was not yet frozen in this rural area of the northeast, but it was chilly. I kept moving; not only to keep warm, but also because I wanted to get as far away from Tallhill as possible before daybreak. I had to keep heading northeast, having decided that three miles per hour would get me near the commercial airport in Lewisville sometime before the first light of morning. Airports were great places to find cars and other types of transportation. But stealing cars was also easier at night.

I would have to sleep in a stand of trees or a junk car, just anywhere, but I would have to be out of sight during the day. The demons in my mind conjured up bloodhounds and helicopters. I did not hear either of these at the moment, but I could see them in the near future. By now, I reasoned, my room was being tossed. I had taken the letters from Naomi and anything that could possibly give an indication where I might be headed. Perhaps they had discovered the taped doors and the sliced camera cable by now. I had seen bloodhounds in movies, but I felt confident that the local police, if they had them, would probably wait until the morning light to get those dogs on my trail. They might even find me. It was a chance I would have to take. Helicopters (if any) would also probably not start looking until they had some light.

These thoughts kept rotating through my mind, the plans and the possibilities mixed in with the perils and complications. It passed perhaps the first hour and a half of my travels across the farmland until I reached my first paved road. Until this time, I had no certainty that I had actually been heading northeast. So I turned right on the road and followed it for about forty-five minutes until I came to an intersection. The sign for the road I was on said that it was State Highway 307. The road that intersected it was County Road 2111. I had memorized the maps of the area and this information told me that I was roughly twelve miles southwest of Lewisville. I was not making great progress, but I knew that County Road 2111 led directly to Lewisville.

I had no time keeping device with me, but I reckoned that I had been gone from Tallhill for close to three and a half hours. This would put the time around 5:30 AM. The sun would be rising soon and the traffic would probably pick up before then. My plan was to scurry off the road at the first sign of traffic and lie down in the ditch. With all of that scurrying, I figured that I could walk another four miles before the sun came up, but I would stop as soon as I found a suitable place to spend the day.

The hour before the sun comes up is typically the coldest time of the day. This was true on that December 3rd. I was not dressed for the cold, so my defense was to keep moving and keep hydrated. I had a small supply of food that consisted of a stack of crackers and two small cans of fruit. I would consume those as soon as I stopped and I would save some water to wash these down. Soon I saw the sky begin to brighten in front of me. My goal now was to find shelter as soon as possible. I had passed five or six farm houses on State Road 2111, but they all seemed occupied. Even the barns seemed to be well used.

As it got progressively brighter out, I saw in the distance a large green combine harvester. I decided quickly that this would be my best opportunity. The season's harvest was over and perhaps the farmer was just parking it at the edge of the field. Maybe it was broken down and waiting for a repair part. I began a half jog towards the field where this piece of machinery stood at the edge of a stand of trees. Once I reached the field, I slowed to walk across the stubbly remains of corn stalks. In a few moments, I reached the big green combine and saw that it had a large flat tire.

I climbed up to the cab to find that it was unlocked. I opened the door slowly and quietly, and then climbed inside. As I cautiously closed the door behind me, I noticed a dark brown winter coat hanging on the seat. I folded the coat, put it on the seat, and sat on it to warm it up. I reached into my pocket for the first of my canned fruit cocktail as I looked out through the windshield of the combine towards the farmhouse in the distance. I was now at the mercy of the farmer who lived there and his plans with the large flat tire.

I ate the fruit cocktail lustily and followed it up with about five crackers. I took one generous swallow of water from one of my bottles. I then returned to staring at the farmhouse and wondering if these people would be alerted as to an escapee from Tallhill. I shrugged.

"If they catch me, they catch me," I whispered as I opened my last can of fruit and gobbled it up. I grabbed the coat I was warming with my rear end and put it on over my clothes. I looked out at the clouds now turned pink by the rising sun and then I slid down to the floor of the combine to sleep off the day.

Sleep did not come easy on that cold floor. My muscles twitched and my mind raced. I shivered quite a lot and I listened to the sound of the few winter birds awaking from their slumber. In a few minutes the light outside the windows of the combine became quite bright. I yawned and shivered, then slept. As I slept, I dreamed.

* * * * * * * * * *

In my dream, I was walking past a farmhouse similar to the ones I had passed on my escape journey. The difference in this house was that it was large and white and also quite shiny. One could say that it even glowed. It shone out of the darkness. I seemed to invite me in and the air was perfumed with the smell of fresh-brewed coffee. I approached the house in a sort of glide. The large picture window on the front first caught my attention. Looking in that window, I saw my old lawyer Elvin "Tex" Williams, sitting on a sofa with a TV tray in front of him. He was wearing that drug-store-cowboy outfit of his and looking as comical as ever with a stupid grin on his face. In a few seconds, my ex-wife Margie appeared carrying a tray with a teapot and teacups and sat them on the TV tray. They smiled and kissed and Margie sat on his lap. Sickened, I pulled away from that window.

I walked around the corner of the house to the next window. Inside the window was a group of beatnik musicians with their berets and goatees. They were on a small stage and sitting on a stool. Alongside them, sitting on a small wooden bench, playing a mandolin, was my sweet Annette. She had a large cardboard sign in front of her on the stage. The sign read, "Gypsy Rae. Will Sing For Food." There was only one person in the audience and that was my old nemesis Lenny. He was throwing money at the stage and shouting something I could not hear. I turned away in disgust.

Around the next corner, there was not a window, but a small peephole with a speaker next to it. I cozied my eye up to that hole and inside I could see Dr. Marlin and Dr. Silk sitting side by side. They each had their own big white easy chairs. Over the speaker next to my head I heard a seductive female voice. It was Dr. Monica from the state hospital. What I heard were words familiar to me; they were my words.

"Humans have all the logic and reason and we use it to rationalize our own selfishness and to exaggerate our own importance," she purred seductively. "I have boiled the human condition down to that one sentence. In fact, that has been my sentiment all along. I only fairly recently found the right words to express the sentiment succinctly. Pretense is not purely a human game. Animals in the wild are frequently deceptive. But for animals, the objective is mere survival."

My manifesto being read in such a seductive manner was a fascinating experience to me and it excited me. It made me want to stay at the peephole in hopes to see what she would be wearing. My enthusiasm was destroyed as both Dr. Marlin and Dr. Silk howled with laughter and high fived each other. Soon Monica appeared in front of them wearing a white nurse outfit with high heels. She stood in front of them with her back to the peephole and joined in the laughter. She then turned around and pointed towards me. Then the other two doctors also pointed at me and continued to laugh. I tore my eye away.

A little farther down on that wall I came to a small window. Inside was Naomi sitting on a chair made of straw and wearing reading glasses as she looked over a large table with engineering blueprints. On the other side of the large table were police officers wearing white uniforms with epaulettes on the shoulders and white shorts. They had handguns in holsters on each hip and they held shotguns. They both had ridiculous fake-looking beards. They both simultaneously cocked their shotguns and pivoted to face me. I skulked away from the window and around the next corner.

Inside the next window sat Bonnie in her wheelchair wearing a purple robe. She was sitting in a hospital room between two beds. In each bed was a child with no hair. Bonnie was reading to them. The name of the book was "The Little Engine That Could". I could not hear anything at first, but soon I could hear the children. A low murmur at first; soon they became progressively louder.

"I think I can, I think I can, I think I can," they chanted.

Then, "I know I can, I know I can, I know I can," they shouted as they each stood on their beds.

Then I saw Bonnie grab the side arms of her chair to brace herself to stand up. She rose up on unstable legs. She stood precariously for a moment and attempted one treacherous step. My mouth was dry as I watched this spectacle helplessly. The children provided no physical assistance as they stood on their beds clapping their hands and continued to chant.

"I know you can, I know you can, I know you can," they began to sound just like football cheerleaders.

Bonnie took one successful step without falling; then another, as her confidence improved. After four or five sturdy steps, she stopped. She shed her purple robe to reveal a light-pink ballerina outfit. She rose up on her tippy toes and danced to her right, then to her left. She then performed a pirouette, then three or four more. All were perfect; at least as far as I could tell. Bonnie performed several impressive ballet moves which I cannot identify but can surely appreciate, then came to rest on one knee with her left arm folded in front, and her right arm behind her. She was quickly showered with dozens of long stemmed roses and she took bow after bow. I pressed my face to the glass of the window and felt that I wanted to be in that place forever… but I woke up. It was still light outside and the windows of the combine were fogged up.

* * * * * * * * * *

I was chilly when I woke up on that combine floor. The cab smelled of corn and mold. The weather outside was too sunny for immediate eye-opening and a cold wind whistled through a small back window, which I couldn't quite close. So I lay there trying to get a grip on the situation and what was in my immediate future. I blinked my eyes and thought about the trail ahead. Blinking and thinking was my major activity for the next few moments. I was in a sort of shivering paralysis, as I was motionless waiting for some kind of sign indicating that I could move without being detected. Every little while, a shiver would be unleashed on my body and the floor would quake.

After maybe a half-hour, I decided to rise from the floor. I was getting colder and hungrier and I needed at least some crackers and a swig of water. I grabbed the side of the driver's seat and pulled myself up to peek over the dashboard to the right. To my amazement, the dashboard had a little digital clock. The readout, if accurate, said 2:15. I had no knowledge if the owner of this vehicle had adjusted for the end of daylight savings time, but if the time was even close to accurate, I had either two or three hours before dark and I figured that I had ten miles of walking in the dark in between bouts of running off the road when I heard cars approaching. It was a country road, but there was sure to be a decent amount of traffic in the early evening.

I had been a free man for about 12 hours and it actually felt good. I was even comfortable crouching behind the dashboard making a little circle in the frost on the window glass with my right index finger. I could stay here forever if Farmer Johnson (which I had decided to call my anonymous host) wouldn't mind. Through that little circle I could see the farmhouse perhaps three hundred yards in the distance. There was absolutely no activity there. I heard a dog bark somewhere, but listening from inside that cab, I judged that it could have come from anywhere. I decided that it could not be bloodhounds, but I did keep this possibility in mind.

I pulled myself up to sit in the driver's seat and sat down to absorb its coldness. My shivers, which had dissipated in my crouch position, now returned with a vengeance. I decided that if Farmer Johnson was going to come out and fix the tire, I would go quietly and maybe he hadn't been alerted about the escaped crazy man. I reached into my overall pocket for the crackers that I had next to Naomi's letters. I gobbled down the last of them and drank the last of my water.

"To Farmer Johnson and his hospitality," I said in a whisper before I drank from the bottle.

I sat back and waited for night and looked around my humble new home. I was quite impressed with the array of instruments on the super-modern dashboard. This was truly an amazing piece of engineering. It made me think of Amos and how much he would appreciate this machine. This thought made me sad. I was a little sad that I had perhaps compromised his happiness at Tallhill, and even more sad that I would likely never see him again.

I opened the glove box and found a thick owner's manual which covered all of the functions and features of this particular machine. Again, I was impressed as hell. I began wishing that I could buy one of these babies to give to Amos. I wanted something to read, but this was not the light reading I was looking for. I felt under the seat and my hand located some type of paper.

I pulled the paper out and discovered a copy of the Lewisville Times dated August 23rd. It wasn't the thickest paper in the world, but I figured it could keep me occupied until the light began to fade. It was only twelve pages and one of those was an advertisement for a local grocery store named Arnie's. Seems that Arnie had a sale on pork chops in August and Roses were really marked down at his florist section. This was not particularly compelling information, but it made me think of my former life and the mundane details which used to occupy a large section of my brain.

My brain: that wonderful and mystical tool that could coldly calculate how many different ways I could make things go wrong by one misstep had been formerly used to solve problems for customers and friends until that part of my psyche that fashioned theories and over-analyzed took over. It was stress that broke me, but the catalyst for the calamity that my life became was right beneath the surface all of the time. I was never going to be happy with the ordinary. Deep down, I doubted I would ever be happy at all.

At Tallhill, with Bonnie, I had discovered I could seek happiness that I had never considered. She had helped me uncover that small thread of hope and I believe I had done the same for her. I was her knight and she was my damsel in distress. She was the female equivalent of a knight and I was the male equivalent of the one to be rescued. As the fatigue of sleep left me, the clarity of my situation was realized; I had run away from the one I loved and I had almost no certainty that I was going to succeed in any way. I had held a fleeting happiness at Tallhill, and I had run like the wind.

I was either climbing to a greater plane of ecstasy or I was going to crash into a dark miserable place and complete my total collapse. I was either falling or climbing. I was ascending or descending. I was certain of neither, but I did know that the die had been cast. There was no going back. I began to read the front of the paper and the mundane news contained therein. The news just made me groggy. I yawned about a dozen times on the first story alone; something about a new industrial park going in next to the airport. *Maybe this was information I could use,* I thought as I yawned for a thirteenth time and then dozed off.

CHAPTER 34 – THE RUN

I woke to a light drizzle as the sun was setting. The drizzle was welcome since it might wash away my scent for those bloodhounds which might be on my trail. There was a concern in the back of my mind that the drizzle might turn to heavy rains or ice. But this thought was short-lived; I was going to continue no matter what the weather had in store. At least I had a nice brown coat to keep me warm.

In my groggy state, I decided to un-fog the windshield to see if I could better assess my situation. I made another circle with my finger where the previous one had fogged over. I saw that the farmhouse now had a few lights on in the windows and smoke was coming out of the chimney. So people were there and it would soon to be dark. I decided that my confinement inside the harvester had come to an end.

The grogginess still had a hold of me, but I decided that the cold and drizzle would do a good job of waking me up. I slowly opened the door as it again made no real sound. I hoped that the drizzle would prevent the people in the house from going outside. I peered out from over the open door to survey everything in front of me and around me. It was all quiet. I stepped onto the ladder that led to the ground and slowly closed the door and silently thanked Farmer Johnson for his unintended hospitality.

Smiling at my own weak joke, I descended the steps quietly to the moistened dirt below. I walked directly to the stand of trees and decided to take the wooded path to the highway. After relieving myself, I walked the four or five hundred yards through that thicket of trees along the field until I reached the edge of the road and sat on a large rock to await the darkness,

I sat for perhaps forty-five minutes on that rock under a large oak tree with my hood over my head and counted the cars that passed by on the highway. I counted seventeen cars including one brown Sheriff's deputy car. This did not provide me with a real accurate estimate of typical traffic for this road, since I figured that most of these people were probably going home from work. However, it did prove that this road could become quite busy at times. I decided that I would walk close to County Road 2111 in the woods until it was completely dark. So my journey re-started through the woods with the road in sight to my left at all times.

After another twenty minutes of slow progress, I decided it was dark enough to proceed on the highway. To my delight, I had only heard or seen three more cars in that twenty minutes or so that I walked. I crept up to the edge of the woods and looked left and right. I took one step into the ditch, then a few more as I climbed out onto the road. I figured that I had walked at least a mile in the damp barren trees, I had not hit any clearings in that time and the water had now begun to soak through my shoes.

So I picked up the pace; I walked very fast at times, but kept as alert as I could for cars in the distance. I had to scurry off the road about a dozen times that evening. The most perilous time was about two hours into my walk, when I was walking between two fields that each connected to farm houses. The house behind me to my left had a dog in the yard that had been barking like mad as I approached at my brisk pace. The dog must have been tethered to something, because when I reached the closest point to his barks, he failed to mount a charge. I braced for the kick in the groin I was going to deliver to that dog in the event that a charge did come.

At this point, I began to hear a second dog perhaps a half-mile ahead to my right. There was nothing but openness on either side and I chuckled quietly to myself as I imagined a coordinated ambush by these clever mutts. "They got me right where they want me," I whispered and laughed.

In perhaps ten seconds after my little joke, I saw approaching headlights coming around the corner ahead. I had no refuge on either side, so I dashed for a stand of mailboxes in the distance to my right. I dived behind the square wooden posts that supported the mailboxes and I remember being quite proud of my resourcefulness in finding cover where none seemed to exist. My pride lasted until I heard the approaching car begin to slow.

As I lay face-down in the dead grass and muck of the roadside, I heard the slowing car turn onto a gravel road to my right. In a moment, I heard a car door open, then close, and then footsteps approaching; closer, closer, closer, until they were almost on top of me. I held my breath. I lay motionless and certain that this person could see me. The next noise was the creak of a metal mailbox opening followed by the slamming shut of that mailbox.

I let small amounts of air out through my nose as holding my breath became impossible. I drew in dank air slowly through my nose as I heard a female voice humming some vaguely familiar classical music. She spoke between stanzas.

"Bum bumba bum bum, bill," she sang.

"Bum bumba bum bum, bill," she repeated.

"Bum bumba bum bum, bill," a third time.

Then, "Bum bumba bum bum, shit! I thought I paid that!"

Then I heard the sound of mud-muffled footsteps leading away from me towards the car. The car door opened, and then shut. I let out my breath. Next I heard the click of the car being shifted into gear and the car pulling away down the gravel road. The sound eventually faded until I heard the engine cut off in the distance as dog number two barked wildly.

"Shut up, you!" The female voice bellowed in the distance. All barking ceased. I scrambled to my feet, looked around me for cars or dogs, and then I brushed myself off. I looked around again and stumbled down the road still catching my breath.

* * * * * * * * * * *

Through the long drizzly night I kept up a good pace, even with my dives off the road as cars approached. I was easily surpassing the three-mile per hour pace I had planned. The drizzle had stopped and in a few short hours I could see the lights of Lewisville ahead in the distance. Lewisville was not a big town and as I got closer a flashing yellow light at the edge of town came clearly into view.

My heart was in my throat as I drew closer. I could see more cars coming my way, but I didn't head for the side of the road. As the volume of cars increased, I decided that it would be counterproductive to jump in the ditch every few seconds. If people in cars saw me, they saw me. I did keep an eye out for police cars and kept way off to the right side of the road. Luckily for me, no police happened by.

I had traveled this far through that early December dreariness for one purpose; to steal a car. From a few acquaintances in prison I had learned a few things about stealing cars. I was told that the easiest place to steal a car was at a gas station. Some people still got out to pay for gas and left keys in the car. This was considered low-hanging fruit to car thieves, especially if they had already had filled up the tank. There were perils with this also, since sometimes they had very little gas and sometimes these careless drivers had people in the car. Sometimes these people were small children whom you didn't notice unless you get right up to the car. These cars also tended to be reported stolen immediately and I didn't reckon I would get very far.

Another thing that my car-thief friends didn't consider was the new technology which allows the driver to pay at the pump. So if I was going to steal a car this way, I would have to wait for the right opportunity; I would need a lone traveler who had to go into the gas station shop for some reason while also leaving the keys in an empty car. This method did not suit me at all, but I did keep it as a backup plan.

My second backup plan was the long term parking at the airport. These places were guarded and fenced in, but I had learned from my frequent travels that the security was quite lax at some of them and an experienced thief could have his pick of cars. However, I was not an experienced thief. Even though I thought I could hot wire most cars, there were often alarms and security devices which could potentially trip me up. I decided that this was a poor choice. Besides, when I got to the gate I would have to pay the attendant and I had fourteen dollars on me and some of these lots charged that much for one day. I would need to find a car that was easy to start and had only been there a short time. I decided that this could be done, but it might take a while to find the right car and these lots DID all have security of some sort. I kept this option also as a backup plan.

My preferred plan was the rental car counter. At the bigger airports, they tend to leave keys in the car, which makes them easy to steal, but they also make you go through a gate with a security guard and unless you found a back way out, you wouldn't get far. Lewisville was not a big airport.

Smaller airports had rental counters that distributed keys and the renter had to walk out to find his or her car in a small lot. Typically these rental counters have one or two people working the late shift and these people tend to be younger. In my vast experience with traveling to these smaller airports, I had often found these places to be very lax with security. Sometimes they would keep the keys on shelves on the wall behind the counter. Sometimes they would keep them in the office in back. Other times they would just keep the keys on the counter to speed things up.

As I got closer to the flashing yellow light, the flashing sign on a bank a couple of blocks up ahead away came into focus. The time was 8:25 PM and the temperature was 27 degrees Fahrenheit and -3 Celsius. A large green sign ahead on the right told me that the next right turn ahead was Airport Road. I was tired and cranky at this point. I was also hungry and my escape had filled me with no real optimism. I felt guilt for leaving Bonnie and was increasingly discouraged that I could reach Annette before I was captured. The large green sign filled me with adrenaline at once and erased those negative feelings. I started towards Airport Road in a full trot to try to decrease my tension and dissipate the adrenaline.

When I reached Airport Road, I turned right and saw the control tower and the searchlights in the distance. This was a seminal event in my life. I stood at that intersection and observed those lights and that tower and decided that they were symbols of everything I had experienced up until now. Even though I was excited, I suppose I was pausing to make a deliberate observation and grasp at a real life.

I was searching for many things and one of the main things I wished to have was control. I stood there and wished I could be up in a tower where I could control all of what happened next. "What happens next" is what we all worry and stress about. It is out there waiting and millions of variables contribute to that future unknown result which may be profound or ordinary, but it is always an unknown and therefore out of our control. These thoughts were upon me as I stood at the corner of County Road 2111 and Airport Road with my arms folded. I took one long breath of night air, held it for a moment, exhaled, and then took a step.

"Time to take control," I said to no one as I strode down the road.

* * * * * * * * * *

There were three rental counters at the Lewisville Airport. They were all lined up along the same wall and each counter was attended by a single employee at the moment I strolled through the sliding glass doors at the airport terminal building. Without naming names, I will tell you that there was a red company, a yellow company, and a green company, identified by the colors on their respective trade-marks.

I walked briskly past these counters as if I had other business on my mind and took note of the situation at each counter on my way to the restroom which was located midway between these counters and the luggage carousel. Inside the men's room, I relieved myself and then cleaned myself up, splashing generous amounts of water on my face. As I toweled off, I evaluated my observations.

The green counter, the closest to the restroom, was busy with three customers in line. I noticed that the female behind the counter was reaching for shelves behind her to get keys. This was not the best target at the moment. The red counter attendant was a man who was currently busy on the phone. He had no customers and I could not guess where he had keys, if any. The woman at the yellow counter had one customer and was engaged in a conversation with him as I passed by them. This one had potential.

I walked out of the restroom and headed directly across the aisle to a large standing display of pictures and phone numbers of local hotels. In the middle of the display was a telephone. I picked up the phone and pretended to be talking to someone as I turned to look back at the rental counters. Green Girl was busy with a customer with another in line waiting. Red Boy was now busy with a customer of his own. Yellow Woman was nowhere to be seen.

Almost impulsively I hung up the phone and headed down towards the yellow counter. I did not make any effort to look at anything taking place at the other two counters. If yellow had no keys behind the counter, then I was off to plan B. I watched the yellow counter intently as a strolled towards the airport exit. I still saw no one there.

As I approached, I saw where she was; I saw the top of her head behind the window of the office behind the counter. She was talking on the phone and not paying any attention to anything. I walked up to the counter and looked down behind the countertop to the desk below. There were three packets lined up side-by-side with keys sticking out. I immediately grabbed one and strode quickly towards the exit. I did not bother to turn around to see if anyone even noticed.

The sliding doors opened automatically in front of me and I stepped through them into the brisk night air. When the door closed, I looked behind me to see no one in pursuit. I proceeded across the street to where the rental cars were parked and began clicking the door lock button on the electronic keys. As I got closer, I heard a horn honk ahead to my right. I pressed it again and saw lights flash along with that horn honking. I picked up the pace as I approached the source of the noise and light. I clicked the doors open and soon I was inside my new car, a green Mustang courtesy of the people at the yellow counter.

I stuck the key in the ignition and turned. The car roared to life and the gauges on the dash moved to various positions. The gas gauge read full, more excellent luck. I put the car in reverse with the lights still off and slowly backed out of the parking space. I shifted into drive and headed for the exit. My luck held up as there was nothing at the exit of the rental lot but a stop sign. I turned the headlights on and made a right turn onto Airport Road.

My destination that night was a storage facility over 200 miles away and I would be careful to not speed. I pulled off into the construction area by the airport and opened the hood. Upon opening the fuse box, I found some wires that looked out of place. These wires led to a small black rectangle with a red light and a green light. It was a tracking device sometimes used by rental car companies to locate their cars and keep a record of where the vehicle has been. After pulling the wires out of the fuse box and tearing the rectangle out of its Velcro cradle, I put the tracking device under the left front tire of the car. I climbed back inside. Looking in the rearview mirror, I half-expected lights from a police car behind me at any minute. The only lights I saw were those airport searchlights and the lights of the control tower. Searching and controlling, more metaphors. I put the car in drive and heard the cold crunch of hard plastic under the tire.

CHAPTER 35 – UNIT 11

Al's Self Storage was a series of six long skinny one-story buildings just off the interstate. It was rather big with an eight-foot chain link fence all around and rolls of razor wire on the top. It was about a mile away from my old house. I had to resist the urge to see who, if anyone, was living there. I even fell into an old habit of turning that direction after I left the interstate using the old exit I used to take. But I made the first U-turn I could and headed back towards the storage place. This would be my home for the next few days if I could swing it.

Soon I was in front of the main gate of Al's and looked at the impressive fencing and the razor wire and chuckled. The fence here to keep people out was more impressive and menacing than the fence built to keep people in the institution that I just escaped from. I rolled down the window of my new Mustang and punched in the code that Annette had given me. Coincidentally, it was her birth month and day: 0617. In the two seconds before the gate started, I flashed back on the twenty or so birthdays we had spent together, the cakes and the happy faces, the games and the joy and the promises of a love that would always be there. I instantly became profoundly sad, as if I had misplaced something that I would never find and had forgotten about.

I was startled out of this state by the humming of the cold electric motor and the low screech of the partially rusty gate beginning to slide to the right. I recovered and remembered the solemn duty of this mission was to try to recapture what connection I once had with that young girl with all of that promise. I would have time to think of the right words and gestures later. For this moment, I had to locate Storage Unit C-11.

I turned right as the Mustang rolled through the gate and headed towards building C while the gate closed behind me. The numbers on the storage units counted up from the front, so in a few seconds I was in front of Unit 11. I stepped out of the still-running car and worked the combination to the lock on the garage door on the front of Unit 11. After I opened and removed the lock, the door raised up to reveal darkness inside. I felt around the inside wall to my left and found a light switch, which I flipped up.

The illumination of the room revealed what material existed of my former life. There were two large bookshelves full of books. There was a foot locker full of mementos. There were two dozen boxes marked variously as CLOTHES, DISHES, PAPERS, CDS, and some just said STUFF. I decided that I had time to go through this stuff and some of the large appliances in the next few days. All I could really feel at this moment was overwhelmed and tired. A sudden cold and icy wind blasted through the open door and chilled the already frigid air.

I walked back to the car, climbed in, and turned on the heat full blast. I then maneuvered the Mustang to see if it would fit through the open garage door. I had maybe five inches to spare on both. I returned to the unit and moved most of the stuff against the walls. I put some of the boxes into the trunk of the car and some of the other stuff into the backseat, then I backed the car inside.

By means of stacking and unpacking a box marked CDS, and then using every available inch inside the car as extra storage space, I was able to squeeze the car into the unit and close the door. The heat inside the car was so intense that when I opened the door, the temperature inside Unit 11 went up noticeably. I was actually quite pleased with myself and how I had come to this spot. I would make my next plans tomorrow. For now, I needed sleep. I climbed into the driver seat and closed the door and reclined. Exhausted, I was sleeping within seconds.

****

I woke to a cold car and a dark storage unit. In the few moments it took for me to stir awake, I alternated between thinking this was a bizarre dream and thinking I was back in solitary confinement for some reason. I gripped the car's leather seats for assurance and I began to recall my journey and my situation. I was soon awake and quite hungry.

I knew there was probably no food in my boxes, so I resigned myself to the fact that I would have to spend some of my fourteen dollars on food. I still needed money for gasoline, but I figured I might have some stuff to sell. I would go through the boxes for valuables with the five days of time I had to burn while I plotted my confrontation/meeting with Annette. I really had not thought clearly about how I was going to approach this. I had made it to the storage facility and right now, I was the King of Fugitives.

I opened the door of the Mustang and the dome provided enough light for me to see most of my surroundings. The clock on the dash told me it was 11:45. I assumed that it was morning unless I had succumbed to some sort of coma. I stumbled to the garage door and opened it slowly. I was mindful of the fact that the facility had other customers and a manager of some sort, so I was not about to walk right out. This would most likely seem odd to anyone on the grounds.

Outside it was a decent enough day, partly cloudy and mid-forties. I decided to hang out close to my unit until I saw evidence of other customers coming into the compound. To take my mind off my hunger, I began to open boxes. In the back of my mind I hoped to find some kind of food, but I didn't hold out much hope. Maybe some canned or dehydrated food was in here somewhere, but it didn't seem likely.

Instead I found a notebook inside one of the boxes marked STUFF. I recognized it as one of the notebooks I bought when Dr. Marlin suggested I write down my thoughts. He suggested that I write down what happiness means to me. This was the writing I had started before I began my Manifesto. I momentarily forgot my hunger as I read my old words.

Happiness is an idea. Happiness is a wish. Happiness is a phantom. Happiness is a trap. Happiness is a journey with no destination while also a dead end with no beginning. Happiness is what is accepted for to-day. Happiness is a fool's mission and a target of a wise man's derision. Happiness is different every day. Happiness is finding a parking space. Happiness is paying off a debt. Happiness is the last drink of wine in the bottle. Happiness is holding someone you love.

The writing stopped there. The rest of the notebook was blank pages. I suddenly remembered the day that I wrote those words and the reason that I had stopped. I was writing at my desk when Annette arrived in the driveway in the car of a friend. I wrote the last part from my desk facing the larger picture window and saw her outside.

I put the pen down so I could greet her and hold her. The fact that I never returned to this notebook was significant; it meant that I had a very good idea what happiness was and I found no reason to explore it further while Annette was around.

In this moment, sitting in the storage unit, I questioned what I actually thought about my mental illness. I had completely destroyed my life and lost my freedom looking for something which did not exist. Maybe I did not really have it so bad in my mundane marriage. Perhaps I had the world on the silver platter and was a complete fool to expect more. Being alone in the storage room was causing me to analyze everything again and I was sure to do more in the coming days.

I had to get out and about. I needed money and food. I also was curious to know if I was much of a wanted man. I looked up from my contemplation to the outside world as a pickup truck slowly rolled past the open door. I snapped out of the analytical and into the practical. I knew that it was useless to try to change the past. I reached around inside the box marked STUFF and found a pen. Grabbing the notebook, I made another entry.

Happiness is freedom. Freedom is limitless.

I put the pen down and closed the notebook. I got up and headed out of the door towards the office.

I walked out of Unit 11 in full stride as if it is the most natural thing in the world to spend the night sleeping in a storage unit. The office was a tiny building, about the size of a guards' shack, near the gate with little spotlight on the top. Inside was an old man in a beat-up leather chair with his back to me; perhaps seventy years-old and he was chomping on a cigar and reading a newspaper's comic section. I walked up and tapped on the door glass, which startled him out of his contemplation of the predicament which confounded Dagwood and Blondie on that day. He turned around, unlocked and opened the door.

"Hi," I said. "My name is Amos." I used the first name that came into my head as I wondered if I actually looked like an Amos. The old man just blinked at me. I noticed the hearing aide in his ear and wondered if he heard me. But he HAD heard the tap on the door. I resisted the urge to shout. He just looked and blinked with his mouth slightly agape; perhaps he had seen my picture in the paper.

"I know you," he finally said. "You are that Johnson kid."

Good lord, I thought, *He's nuts.*

"No sir, my name is Amos Barrow," I assured him with my best Tallhill smile on my face as I stuck out my hand. I decided to use my last name to cover for the fact that Annette's last name was going to be on the paperwork for the storage unit.

The old man lightly grabbed the outer edges of my fingertips in some kind of handshake that left me feeling like an unwanted interruption to his day.

"Bert," he said as he turned to go back to his chair.

"Glad to meet you Bert," I said a bit more forcefully. This stopped him from going back to his chair.

"Listen, Bert," I continued. "I was thinking about selling some of the stuff in my unit. My daughter put this stuff in there after my divorce and I moved out of state. I have no use for some it."

Bert just stood there and from the irritated look on his face, I could tell he wanted me to go away and never bother him again. As the saying goes; if looks could kill… how does that saying go?

"What kind of things do you want to unload?" an irritated Bert growled at me.

"J… just a washer, a dryer, a microwave, and some other small appliances," I stammered. "Maybe some clothes and books, I still haven't looked through…,"

"My brother can sell those bigger things," Bert interrupted. "He owns a pawn shop besides owning this place. I need to look at the stuff, but if it is in good shape, he will give some cash and haul it away for you."

"Excellent," I said. "I will pull those appliances out so you can look at them then?" As I asked this question, I knew the answer, but I could tell by the look on Bert's face that he knew that I knew the answer and this irritated him quite a bit.

"What unit?" he barked out.

"C-11," I said.

"I will be there in fifteen minutes," he said. Then he turned around and sat back down on the chair with the newspaper he still held in his hands.

Back in C-11, I decided to not try to hide the fact that my car was in the unit. I had no knowledge of the rules of the storage facility. I probably should have picked up a brochure or read the rules or something. I just figured it was natural to store a car you weren't using. With this in mind, I located my tools in the box marked TOOLS and removed the license plates. I made a mental note to seek out and steal some plates, from a green Mustang if possible.

Twenty minutes later, the washer and dryer were outside with the microwave, blender, and toaster oven sitting on top. Bert came walking slowly up with a notepad in his hand. I waited patiently while leaning on the dryer. It took Bert a good long time to get there and I just stared into my storage area while he walked.

"Is this everything?" He asked when he got within a few feet.

"All the major appliances," I replied.

"I will give you 100 for the washer and 50 for the dryer. 20 for the rest," he said as he held out that exact amount of money.

"You have a deal, Bert," I said as I took the money.

Bert's head turned and he looked inside the rental unit. "Is that Mustang for sale?" he asked.

"Not yet," I said. "I might still get some use out of it."

Bert looked at me and raised his eyebrow. He then took off walking towards the back of the facility at the same slow pace. He walked a few paces, and then turned around.

"My brother will be here in a half hour to pick those up," he said over his shoulder. "Just leave them there."

"Okay," I said. "I'm going to get lunch. I'll be back in a little while."

****

Outside the gate, I walked down the sidewalk of the busy street towards the restaurants that I remembered from the days when I used to live near. There was a greasy spoon truck stop up ahead near the freeway exit that I used to always be curious about. I concluded that a truck stop was less likely to be frequented by locals who might recognize me and would be just busy enough mid-day for me to blend in with the undistinguished clientele. I had located some of my old musty clothes from one of the boxes because I knew that the truck stop had a Laundromat and showers. I carried these clothes in an old netted laundry bag. I wore one of my old baseball caps which I had rarely worn in my past life. I sarcastically chuckled at my mastery of disguises

My first stop was the Laundromat, where I paused outside to mail my letter to Naomi. I then opened the front door, stepped inside, and just dumped the clothes in a washer and went to the change machine to get quarters for the machines and detergent. As I fed a five dollar bill into the change machine, I noticed a newspaper machine underneath. After I started the washer and dumped in the detergent, I walked back to the newspaper machine and purchased the day's paper.

With my clothes in full agitate, I walked into the front door of Carl's and took a seat at the counter. I was not a spectacle or a curiosity to anyone as far as I could tell. I did not see a head turn as I sat down. I was just another mid-forties man, graying at the temples, with two-day graying stubble on my face. I continued to wear the cap along with the brown coat I had found on the combine floor.

I grabbed a plastic-laminated menu and began to look at pictures which all made me hungry. I do not mind telling you that I was a little tingly as I anticipated my first meal as a free man. My interest in the menu captured the attention of the waitress, who up until that point had been talking to a gentleman at the other end of the counter. She headed over to me.

"Hi, hon," she said. "Can I get you something to drink?"

I looked up at a young woman who looked to be in her early thirties with a little white waitress tiara pinned to her red hair and the beginning of crow's feet in her eyes. She probably looked older than her actually age, but I guessed she was not in her late thirties due to the presence of a small diamond stud in her nose. She had a wedding ring on her left hand where she held her writing pad. Over the left breast of the dark blue apron, which shielded her blue and white checkered uniform, she had a name tag which read Stephanie.

"Stephanie," I said as I looked up from my laminated menu. "I think I will start out with a cup of coffee and a glass of water."

I really wanted to order a ton of food, but I didn't want to seem as hungry as I actually was. Just the smell of burgers and fries cooking was causing my stomach to rumble, and I didn't want anyone to hear it. Although I suspected that Stephanie did.

"Do you know what you want to eat yet?" Stephanie asked with bright warm perfect smile.

"Call me Amos," I said, surprising myself.

"Okay, Amos," she said as she leaned on the counter with her left elbow and shot her right hip out in the opposite direction while she tossed her head and tilted it sideways in a semi-flirtatious pose.

I smiled back and placed the menu on the counter. "I would like a T-bone steak medium well, with French fries, please," I said.

Stephanie smiled and wrote down the order in her pad. "'Kay, I'll be back in a sec," she said and then went towards the back.

I opened the newspaper, which I had set on the counter next to me. Two nights had passed since my escape and I was certain that my home town paper would have news of my daring escapades, so I scanned the front page. There were articles about the upcoming Christmas parade. There was a weather report, which called for snow. There was a story about the city council putting in a traffic light somewhere. No news about Clyde- the escapee nut-job would-be bomber.

Maybe it was buried in the back pages. I thumbed through section after section and then did it again. It was not a big paper; twelve pages in total. There had to be something. I was big news when I was arrested. I made a third slow pass through the paper after my steak arrived. I sat and ate my slightly bloody steak as slowly as I could as I dripped catsup from my fries and juice from my steak on the pictures of the high school basketball game and the crossword puzzle. In my head I had a puzzle of my own; why no news of my escape?

After I finished my steak and left my tip, I went back to the Laundromat to move my clothes to the dryer. I scanned the pile of magazines and newspapers left at the convenience counter by the soap machine. I found most of the previous day's paper and leafed through it while my clothes dried. No mention of fugitive Clyde Barrow on the loose. My emotions became a mix of hurt feelings, optimism, and anxiety.

Surely my notoriety would have been noteworthy enough locally to be included in the news by the local newspaper editor. But it did relieve pressure on me to know that the general public was not aware that I was on the lam. The anxiety arrived when I realized that in my research of Tallhill and my personal experience at the facility had taught me that they tend to approach everything in an unorthodox way.

I suspected that Tallhill wanted me to feel relaxed and careless. This suspicion made me paranoid; therefore I decided to be even more careful. I sat there staring at the paper without reading it, while considering the possibility that a private security force was already hot on my trail and would logically assume that I was headed for my home town. It did not matter whether this made any sense, my paranoia was taking over and I remember wishing I had a fresh supply of Thorazine.

I folded the paper, placed it on the counter and headed back to Carl's. I sat down at the counter where Stephanie was cleaning up my area.

"I thought you left, Amos," she said with that delightful smile.

"Jest taking care of laundry, Steph," I replied. "Could you get me another coffee and a slice of apple pie?" I was still hungry and I needed to store up some calories for my planned overnight in the storage area.

"Sure thing, doll," she said, and left to get the coffee and pie.

After I ate the pie, I retrieved my laundry from the dryer and took a shower. I put on my clean dry clothes and bought some water and beef jerky from the truck stop store.

I walked back to Al's as the early December sun was finishing its descent in the sky. As I entered the compound, I saw that Bert was no longer at the booth/guard shack, so I decided that I could just cruise into my rental-unit lair and sort through the minimal treasures left from the charade that was my former life before I crashed for the evening.

CHAPTER 36 – OUTSIDE THE BUBBLE

If a thief or some treasure hunter came upon any of the boxes stashed in Storage unit C- 11 at Al's Self storage, there would be a few trinkets of interest and very little of real value. If I were to tabulate the total value of the clothes, dishes, CD's, and other assorted trinkets I would value the total at around a thousand dollars. One would be lucky to get one quarter of that at a pawn shop.

I fully intended to sell anything of any real value that I found in the boxes that Margie and Annette had packed and placed in this cold gray concrete and steel dungeon. I found some of my old shot glass collection. I located some knives and tools and decided that those would bring some money. It took all of the detachment I could muster to keep an emotional distance from these accumulated treasures of my former life.

The wind began to blow some cold rain into the storage unit on that December 4th. I closed the door and soon the sound of ice hitting the metal of the garage door could be heard. I knew from the forecast that snow would probably come later. This would put a layer of ice under the snow and keep the less ambitious people off the roads. I paused to think about whatever private security force might be searching for me. I imagined this weather would slow their progress and this pleased me.

Digging through one of the boxes marked "STUFF", I came upon one of those bubble blowing kits that we used to give out as gifts at birthday parties. The kits were cheap, maybe a dollar for a small bottle of a soapy concoction and three or four plastic sticks with circles, stars, or triangles on the end. I ripped open one of these packages while I considered the reasons why Margie and/or Annette would save this for me. I shook the soap bottle and twisted off the cap. I took the green plastic stick with the small circle on the end from the kit and dipped it into the bottle. I blew a bubble that was actually quite impressive, maybe five inches around.

The bubble floated for perhaps thirty seconds before it drifted into a wall and burst. I was left to consider the bubble. I considered it for a few seconds before I sent another off in its wake. I thought about bubbles and what they represented to me. This moment, alone in that cold storage unit with freezing rain pasting against the outside became a profound moment in my life. Like the searchlight and the control tower, I again was contemplating metaphors and symbols.

I had lived in a bubble for over a year now. I was protected from the outside world and the outside world was free of the menace I had become. What's more, not only had the institutions which held me served as a bubble, the life with a steady job and dependable marriage had kept me inside the fragile walls of a bubble of security. I had climbed out of that bubble and walked around on the thin walls of the outside until the bubble burst.

In the institutional bubble I was also not content with the security and predictability of the beehive of activity and certainty. I had to escape what I feared would eventually become the acceptance of ordinary performance of unchallenging tasks. The Tallhill smile symbolized that beehive/bubble acceptance. It was painted on the faces of the longtime members. They had traded uncertainty for security and a smile. They asked for little except what was given in exchange for their labors.

Taking whatever is given is a form of surrender and I was not ready to surrender. I likened Tallhill to a cult. Similar to a cult, the least able to cope with the outside world were the most susceptible. Tallhill received money for quality care and they provided quality care. I had no doubt that their methods were effective. I sensed no uneasiness or fear from anyone that I interacted with. The problem with all of this serenity and optimism was that I found it mostly unnerving. Accepting a situation without questions is just not in me. So I took a walk outside the bubble and I was once again tiptoeing on those thin fragile walls.

I kept blowing those bubbles and watching them burst. Without fail, they all burst. Some simply fell from the force of gravity and hit the floor. Some collided with the wall. Some burst from too much internal pressure. They all burst rather quickly except for the ones that were kept aloft by blowing air beneath them. These bubbles were only kept alive by artificial means. Observing this, I realized that the bubbles of Tallhill also needed artificial means and support to keep from bursting and that my former life needed accommodating circumstances and collaborators to keep that bubble from falling to the earth or colliding with a wall.

I kept my bubble alive because it was all I knew, safe in that artificially secure atmosphere, even though it provided no hope or comfort. I soon found ways to test the walls and the durability of the bubble. Cheating and sneaking and opening my being up to other people had weakened the walls and steered the bubble towards destruction. As the bubble headed for doom, I escaped and burst it from the outside.

I had no power to destroy the Tallhill bubble. Surely that all of the people I interacted with would notice my absence and would at least momentarily wonder about their own fate on the inside. However, that effect would be temporary for most. I suspected that most of them mistrusted the outside world. No, I couldn't destroy that bubble with my singular act of defiance. I truly didn't want to destroy their good work. I just wanted out and even if my voyage to freedom was ultimately futile, I wanted a chance to prove that we could make it somewhere. The irony of my plan was that my final goal was to escape with Bonnie to an island. On that island, we would exist in another kind of bubble.

* * * * * * * * * *

The days I spent living at Al's Self Storage were some of my most isolated while at the same time very enlightening. My last real isolation had been after my incident with Clarence in the state prison. At that time, I was worried about Naomi and losing her support. Even though I was as analytical as always, it was in a self-centered survival state of mind.

Since Tallhill and Bonnie had entered my life, I saw what happiness could possibly consist of. I was no longer reaching for the impossible dream of a much-younger heiress taking care of my needs. I never really was in love with Naomi and that dishonesty would doom us. I did care for her and cared about what happened to her, but I knew my role for her was to be a friend and possible mentor.

On the other hand, I was deeply in love with Bonnie and strongly suspected that she felt the same about me. She was a dozen years younger, but much closer to my age than Naomi and we definitely felt a kinship and connection. We were each other's other half and in the isolation of Storage Unit 11, I felt yearnings deep in me that I had really never felt. I had not seen Bonnie for two-plus days and I felt alone and confused about a lot of things. I would read her last note frequently to reassure myself about her feelings for me.

But I had run; I had risked losing her to see my daughter to ease my mind and re-connect. My plan included returning to get my true love, but none of this was certain. This uncertainty weighed heavily on my conscience for my entire stay at Al's. The inactivity while waiting made things worse. My future was either as a fugitive or as a prisoner. I could never go back to the security and certainty of Tallhill and late-night visits from my lover. These fears and this confusion manifested itself in my dreams.

In one dream I was locked in an institution where everyone stayed in one large room. The sign on the outside informed everyone that it was called *The Institution of Incorrect Behavior.* Nearly everyone I had ever known was locked up there and so were a lot of other people. Seemingly everyone was being penalized for doing something wrong. The only person who wasn't locked up was my brother Johnny.

Johnny was the third oldest of my brothers and always did everything that everybody expected of him. He was not exactly my antithesis, but I seemed to always want to do the opposite of him just to not be like him. People always seemed to approve of Johnny quite easily. He married the prom queen. He went to college and became a CPA. He worked for a large firm and he coached little league. In real life, I had not seen Johnny in about fifteen years. I rarely thought about him.

In the dream, he was visiting me in my large room of incorrect behavers and was coaching me on how to be upright and straight-laced. I explained to him that I was just being honest to myself and he confessed that he had been faking it for all of these years. He confessed that he had three other families with three other women and the strain was getting to him. This confession pleased me and I invited him to stay with me in my room of offenders. He accepted and told me that for once he truly felt happy. He felt free of burden even though he was now not free to go anywhere.

All of us inmates in the large room wanted out, but Johnny wanted in. There was no happiness or solutions promised to him if he stayed; he just wanted out of the mess he had made of his life. He no longer wanted to pretend. He was a symbol of all of the baggage that all people want to dump, but feel obligated to carry because of others' expectations. In the dream Johnny was happy, but the people in the room resented him. All of them, including me, wanted to leave.

I was not the type to be satisfied that people wanted to be like me. Instead of being happy that my life was someone's idea of a great life, I wondered what horrible thing might have happened to this person for him or her to aspire to my level of mediocrity. The dream with Johnny did amuse me. It forced me to admit that I was also envious of those who sought mediocrity. I wished I could be like those Tallhill occupants who found satisfaction with being told where to be and what to do every minute of the day. I wished that I could shut off whatever it was in me that made me want to seek fulfillment.

* * * * * * * * * *

On the 5th of December, I rose to seek out my fortune at Al's Pawn shop. Because of the ice and snow, I chose to walk. It was a challenging ten blocks, but driving risked an accident and accidents brought police. I had decided that I would only drive when I made my ultimate escape. My mission on this day required me to carry a lot of my trinkets. I had wanted to take all of them, but because of the snow and ice I had to limit things to a box of stuff I could carry. So I trudged off through the miserable conditions on a partly sunny day wearing my old clothes and work boots. Walking past the gate, I paused to note that the door of the guard shack was still frozen shut. This indicated that Bert had not yet been in that day.

I knew where Al's Pawn Shop was from the many times I had passed it on my way to somewhere else. With the three balls and the flashing neon sign in the window, Al's was a classically decorated place on 4th Avenue. By the time I got there, my load was becoming heavy. The storefront window displayed watches, cell phones, and other items that were once perhaps treasured gifts, but now trinkets to be discarded for easy cash to this local low-bidder. I paused only for a second to see if anything caught my eye. However, as my load was quite cumbersome, I moved quickly on through the door of the shop.

A bell rang as the door opened and quickly closed after me. Behind a glass counter stood a man who was the spitting image of Bert, the storage area guy. I almost called him Bert until I remembered that Al of Al's Pawn Shop was his brother. The old man just stared at me expressionless.

"Good morning," I said with a smile as I sat the heavy box down on the glass display full of jewelry and knives. The man just looked at me, lifted his reading glasses from around his neck to his nose, and shuffled over to inspect the box.

"My name is Amos," I finally said, extending my hand. I hoped this gesture would clear up my awkwardness at not knowing whether this was Al or Bert.

"What have we got here?" He said as he pulled out a giant K-Bar knife. I pulled back my hand.

"That's my hunting knife," I responded with enthusiasm. "I am trying to clean out my storage bin little by little."

"You're the guy with the Mustang," the man said. "My brother Albert told me about you." He stuck out his hand and I shook it.

"My name is Alvin," He smiled. "People call me Al and they call him Bert to keep us straight. We're twins, ya see."

I could tell Al was the friendly one of the two. This was not saying much. At least he didn't come off as a cold fish who wanted to back me down into a corner. If Bert had hung around me much longer, I may have confessed to something just to relieve the tension. Al wasn't Mr. Personality either, but at least he could smile.

"So you're selling?" Al Asked.

I nodded.

Soon Al was systematically taking every item out of the box. He had the knives, a dozen shot glasses, my pool cue, and my entire rack of billiard balls. He was typing numbers on a calculator after he set each item on the counter. After the last item, he hit the = sign and turned the display around towards me so I could see the results. The display read 42.00.

I was in no position to negotiate. "Deal," I said with a smile and Al went about the business of writing up a bill of sale for each item. He was meticulous in his work and he asked for a phone number where I could be reached. I gave him my old home phone which I knew was disconnected. He folded over the top page of the receipt pad and tore off the carbon copy below and handed it to me. He then opened the cash register and passed me two twenties and two ones.

"Thanks, Al," I said.

He nodded.

"I think I might need this box," I said as I grabbed the empty box from the counter. "I will probably be back tomorrow." Al nodded again and smiled. I nodded and smiled back as I headed out the door of the pawn shop and into the icy misery of that day. I was feeling good in spite of the weather. I was getting some much needed gas money and food money. Over the next few days I would unload my tools, most of my compact disc collection, picture frames, jackets, work boots, and other paraphernalia from the life that once was. Al didn't buy everything, but he bought most of it.

Outside of selling my possessions for travel money, my days were spent avoiding the semi-watchful eye of Bert. He may have suspected that I was living in the storage unit, but I was not going to worry about that. If he asked me to leave I would just move my car to the woods somewhere and hide out there. I just wanted to delay that situation as long as possible. On the sixth of December, I had purchased a small hot plate and I didn't want him aware of this either. I decided that eating out was risky, so my meals soon consisted of ramen noodles and canned foods.

In the evenings I would go through my dwindling possessions and decide their fate. I had four categories for each item; take with me, discard immediately, sell, and keep in storage. The items that ended up going with me either had sentimental value or were going to be useful in my travels. The things that Annette had made for me as a child were included in this group, as were the many recordings of her singing and pictures of her. I also took the newest thing of hers I could find; her gold ballet shoes that she used in her first semester of college before she decided to be a singer.

Among the useful items thrown in my old beat-up brown suitcase was anything that could be used in a disguise and my multi-tool. The multi-tool had four knife blades, two screwdrivers, pliers, and a bottle opener among other things. I had sold most of my other tools to Al, so the multi-tool was going to have to get me through.

The items that I decided to keep in storage were things like an iron and ironing board. There were some things that I had given to Annette as presents like dolls and games that I couldn't bring myself to throw away. I guess if she ever returned here she might want them. It is a foolish thought, but I wasn't going to sell these things or send them to the landfill. There was also a limit to what I would take with me. So these stayed in the boxes in Unit 11.

When I wasn't sorting through material evidence of my former life, I was rehearsing what I would say to Annette. My plan was to go to her performance and to try to see her afterwards. I had no idea how much time I would get with her before goons dragged me away, but I had to plan on a private conversation over coffee. I knew I had to play up the fact that it would probably be the last time she ever saw me because I felt that this would cut through the false wall that was now between us. Restraining order be damned! I was either going off to some island or I was going to prison for a long time.

So I would recite my words into the cold dark night in the storage unit like I used to in solitary while I was composing my manifesto. The words would echo off the sliding garage door and come back tinny. In those nights I would explain myself to the shadows. I recounted my reasons for my circumstance and the sorrow I felt at having been the absent inattentive father; the emptiness at being cheated out of time with my one creation. I rehearsed like a fine musician or an accomplished actor perfecting his craft. I wanted to not sound bitter or pitiful. Wanting to be contrite, but optimistic, the reasons were rationalized and the words were deliberated. Words spilled out of me a hundred different ways on those nights. I knew I would get the right words out if I could get her to listen.

My impending flight to my island of obscurity depended on her discretion and those around her not calling the police. I imagined that everyone by now knew I was on the run somewhere. If Tallhill had private security on my tail, they would have tracked down Annette by now. By now, her entourage was on the lookout for the desperate old man. I had to consider that I might have very little time in which to make myself heard. Therefore, by the time I started out on that day, I had fine-tuned my message. I had also taken on a strange companion that morning. It was my old nemesis and tormenter. It was a potentially lethal and always inconvenient feeling.

Once again, it was hope.

CHAPTER 37 – GYPSY RAE

December ninth was a crisp cold morning with five inches of fresh snow. The snow had been accumulating during my stay at Al's Self-Storage and Hideout. I had been careful not to move about much during the daytime. Only when nature called did I roam from my self-imposed confinement. I would brush over my tracks in the snow as I returned from the porta-potty in the rear of the compound and take a circuitous route around to the doors of other units so nothing led directly to my hole-in-the-wall. If Bert was suspicious of anything, he never let me know about it. I only saw him one more time during the last three days of my stay when he was knocking snow and ice off the guard shack on the morning of the seventh.

I left as soon as I could that morning because I had become restless and I wanted to get close to Maplewood as soon as possible. It was going to be around 150 miles of driving and I had my fill of talking to empty rooms and sneaking around. My anxiety was driving me crazier than the world thought I was. I packed all of the things I thought I could take with me into a couple of old suitcases. I slowly rolled out of Unit 11 and cranked the wheel hard left to clear the buildings on the opposite side of the alley. Once I was clear, I stopped the Mustang and got out to close the door of the storage unit.

I took one last sentimental look at my short-time home, pulled the door down and secured the lock. Before I got into the car, I inspected for defects that might get me pulled over. I had put the license plates back on the car. I was sure that it had been reported stolen and no plates (or stolen plates) would be just as likely to get me pulled over. Satisfied, I climbed inside the green Mustang, threw it into gear and slowly left Al's Self Storage. The guard shack was again empty as I pulled through the automatic gate in the snow.

The drive to Maplewood was uneventful and I obeyed the speed limit to the letter. I stopped at every yellow light and took my time. The possibility of ice on the road made me drive slowly out of necessity. I avoided the interstate highways since state police don't tend to patrol the outskirts and back roads. Every time a suspicious car pulled in behind me, I would turn onto another road or just pull over and stop. I did this quite often as I suspected every car. By way of this routine I arrived in Maplewood around noon.

Maplewood had a population of 13,235 people. That's what it said on the green sign as I pulled into town. There was only one venue in town which could safely accommodate a following as large as The Travelled consistently drew. That venue was called Dexter's

Roadhouse. Dexter's was at the intersection of 3rd Avenue and 3rd street, having started out as a humble tavern, but had recently expanded by adding a dance hall and regularly hosted concerts of local country bands.

I arrived via the main street of Maplewood, which was actually named Main Street, and turned left onto 3rd street. I followed 3rd street for three blocks until I arrived in front of a large old-west-looking building with a large white marquee sign above the front entrance. There was a man on a ladder leaning against the sign and another man supporting the ladder. The men were in the process of changing the letters of the sign. The sign read: TON TE TH TR VEL D on the first line, and ONE N TE NLY.

The man at the top was still putting the O in front of the last word, but the sign was easily understood. I sat in a no-parking zone across the street and watched them work for a few minutes until I decided that maybe it wasn't such a good idea to be in such plain sight. I decided to try to find any traces of Gypsy Rae and her crew.

The best hotel in Maplewood was called The Atrium. The online guides gave it four stars. It was a red-brick six-story building with a fancy façade which was highlighted by a nice portico that featured a green half-circle awning over the doorway. The name of the hotel was emblazoned on the awning and an actual concierge stood out front in dark green pseudo-military garb, with a brimmed cap and white gloves.

I sat in my car in the drugstore parking lot across the street and watched the magnificently attired young man as he greeted visitors with prompt courteous service. Was this a touch of class left over from a bygone era? Was it a special occasion? The answer was not clear.

I suppose I was staking out the place to see if The Travelled were going to stay there. It was only four blocks away and a safe bet. It was not vital that I knew where they stayed, but I wanted to see my little girl: the little girl to whom I once read books and sang songs to and with, the little girl who now found me to be a nuisance, an embarrassment, and an inconvenience.

Melancholia gripped me as I thought about what was so important in those days. I do not think that I was ever so innocent to think that the joy on a young girl's face can last or that happiness and warmth is intended to carry me through life. I just wished my memories were more than regrets compounded by mistakes. I could never undo the damage I had done and I had no intention to even try. I just had to see her, maybe for the last time, to try to set things on the right path. Annette had rare talent and she was going to be rich and famous. Perhaps in my mind I thought she could come and see me on my island sanctuary on some later date.

But as I sat in my stolen green Mustang, I began to sleep. It was not an especially cold day that December 9th, so sleep came easy. I knew that I would eventually catch up to her, so the urgency was not there. I drifted in and out of uneasy slumbers until sleep finally came.

I dreamed an uneasy blur of images of a small girl playing on a swing set and of a small girl giving a speech in front of a crowd. Every scene was her alone trying to perform some task. The girl was not Annette, but perhaps she was a symbol. In every blurry scene she was struggling.

In the dreams I was helpless to do anything to help the girl. I would frequently awake from the dreams and drift right back to sleep as I sat in that reclining front seat in that drugstore parking lot. I would drift off for a few minutes of edgy sleep only to be presented with the same little girl trying to get a kite airborne or attempting to tie her shoes. Each time I felt completely useless right before I was jolted awake.

It went like this for probably a couple of hours before I could no longer sleep. So I adjusted my seat upright and attempted to clear my head of the cranky frustrated feelings that had taken hold. I looked out towards the hotel in the fading light and saw a dark green bus parked directly in front of the entrance. "The Travelled" was emblazoned on the side. I sighed.

For good or for bad, I would see my baby girl on this night.

* * * * * * * * * *

Dexter's Roadhouse smelled like smoke. Not cigarette smoke, but hickory smoke. Their specialty was open pit barbecue and they supposedly packed in the customers even on nights when there wasn't music. The walls were plain local oak and pine wood with high rafters. There were peanut shells on the floor and dim lighting which added a tinge of ambience. I arrived early to avoid the cover charge and was seated at a booth near the indoor stage. A young stringy-haired blonde pimply-faced waitress named Violet took my order of all-you-can-eat ribs and a beer, and then strode off purposefully while I sat and absorbed the atmosphere.

The expectation and the rehearsed speeches in my mind mingled with the soft glow of the dimmed stage lights and the low murmur of the small dinner crowd. I suspected that this place really picked up at night and I was a few hours away from music being performed. I had only come in this early because I was quite hungry. I wanted to beat the crowd, but also blend in. I decided that a booth near the stage but in the relative dark was the best place to pass my time. I would eat the ribs slowly and drink the beer at my leisure.

I surveyed the room where the various autographed guitars, shirts, pictures, and other music memorabilia that hung from seemingly every square inch of wall space that wasn't already crammed by cables and sound equipment. The large wood-tiled dance floor in front of the stage was currently cluttered by several tables and at a few of those tables sat customers. I occupied my time before the concert slowly working through four entire racks of ribs and four large mugs of beer. The appetite of a fugitive was quite impressive.

In between bites and drinks I sat and watched a college basketball game. It was the University of Massachusetts and the University of

Connecticut and it went into two overtimes until UCONN won on a tip-in at the buzzer. The game and the eating passed the time nicely and as I downed my fourth beer, I noticed that tables had been cleared from the dance floor and that roadies were busy setting up equipment on the stage.

In a few moments I was treated to the sound of technicians and musicians tuning instruments and adjusting sound boards and microphones. Dexter's was beginning to fill with customers. This was welcomed by me, since I could get lost in the crowd. I was soon startled by two young girls wearing plaid flannel shirts and bandanas on their heads.

"Sir," said the one in blue-orange plaid and a purple bandana as she tapped on my shoulder. "Is anyone sitting here?" She asked.

"No," I said as I looked into her makeup-free pretty face. "You can sit here if you want," I motioned towards the bench on the opposite side of the table.

The two girls scooted into place on the opposite bench; which did not directly face the stage, but put the stage over their right shoulders at about a forty-five degree angle. My angle to the stage was better.

"You may have a better view over here," I said loudly as the developing crowd become louder. They looked at each other, then back at me with smiles.

"Are you staying for the show?" The one with the red bandana and green-red plaid asked me.

"It's why I'm here," I said as I smiled.

The two girls again looked at each other, shrugged, and then got up to sit on my side of the table as I scooted against the wall.

Both girls wore large hooped earrings, *Fans of Gypsy Rae? Is this how Annette dresses now?* I asked myself. I much preferred that they sit on my side of the table since I didn't want to spend the next few hours being self-conscious about looking at them.

The girl with the purple bandana sat closest to me and absolutely pressed her leg against mine. "So you are a fan of The Travelled?" She asked as I caught a whiff of cigarette breath from her.

"I know someone in the band," I answered.

This answer made her and her friend take notice. They both turned to face me and Purple Bandana Girl asked, "Who?"

"A… Gypsy Rae!" I yelled above the din.

"That's awesome!" said Red Bandana Girl. She probably said that a lot.

"My name is Candy," she said as she awkwardly reached her hand over her friend to shake my hand.

"Clyde," I said as I took her hand in mine placed a delicate kiss on the back. "Charmed," I said as I returned her hand to her.

"Melissa," said the one next to me. I repeated the hand-kissing gesture and an uncomfortable pause ensued which was mercifully broken by another question from Melissa.

"How long have you known Rae?" she asked.

"All of her life," I said.

This really impressed them. I was really growing in relevancy and esteem in the eyes of these young girls.

"Can you introduce us to her?" Candy asked.

"It depends," I said as a made an anguished face. "I haven't seen her in a while."

More awkwardness followed between the fugitive and the Gypsy wannabees until two young men who seemed to know these girls simply plopped down on the bench opposite of us.

They made some rude comment which I could not hear and Candy got up and told them something else I could not hear. Both young men shot incredulous looks in my direction. I smiled and resisted the temptation to tell them to go find their own fucking table. Instead I ignored them and pointed my face towards the stage where the emcee was now grabbing the microphone.

"Ladies and gentlemen," said an unshaven man with a cowboy hat and western shirt that hung over his vast and expanding belly. "I am Dexter, and I want to welcome y'all to Dexter's Roadhouse." He raised his hands and the assembled crowd exploded with cheers as if commanded by Caesar. "We are now calling last call on the all-you-can-eat ribs, but it's still two-for-one drinks for the next half hour." He raised his hands again to another smaller cheer filled with more hoots and whistles.

"Now," he started again after the crowd calmed. "Dexter's is excited and delighted to present an up and coming band that has been featured on television shows and has now released their first album of original material." More hoots and whistles mixed with cheers followed. "So without further delay, I give you The Travelled!"

The crowd went stone silent as a single acoustic guitar played a few beginning notes somewhere in the darkness. From my seat, which was slightly elevated from the dance floor, I could make out a silhouette on the right side of the stage. A spotlight soon shone down on that silhouette to reveal a young man in black with a black goatee, wearing a red fedora. He played slowly and precisely and he was soon joined by a sweet female voice which I instantly recognized. She sang, "Ooooooo…," for a good fifteen seconds before her spotlight was also lit.

There, on a raised stool, sat Annette. Not in some fake gypsy garb with hooped earrings, but in a long black dress that a torch singer might wear. Next was the sound of a stand-up bass being bowed. Then the young girl that the world knew as Gypsy Rae began to sing one of her own compositions titled "Napalm".

Your desire sticks like napalm to my heart
Needing high-voltage to restart
Damage beyond a function of life
Cutting deep as you wield the knife

Next to me with a love on fire
Heat is nothing I cannot take
Passion melting cold desire

Far too intense

Too hard to fake

Fools pretend to understand

The danger in that heat

Holding embers in hand

Burning moments of defeat

Climbing to what life can be

A little at a time

Clinging to pleasure almost free

On our climb

The stairway to nowhere

Mouths water and eyes dry

A little at a time

Hearts pound and seconds fly

A little at a time

It is folly

An error of comedy

Life not happy

Nor complete

The stairway to nothing

I may not be the answer to your prayer
'Tis not easy
Nor too clear
To brag, to tell someone
About this
About what I fear

Wrapping myself around a dream
Only a fool knows
Blistered walking
On broken toes
A stairway to no one

Brave new world
As far as I can tell
Braver than heaven
Much closer to hell

Your desire sticks like napalm to my heart
A cruel and wretched hoax, as we're apart
Burned-out husks of promises denied
Senses submerged in swallowed pride

These are mere words on paper and do not express the depth of emotion in her voice or the quickening of the tempo until it slowed again for the last verse. The interplay of the music with the singer allowed the singular instrument of that one human voice to dominate the slow but quickening march forward of the bass, guitar, and subdued snare drum. When the song ended, the crowd, who had been in rapt attention, exploded with cheers that sent chills down my spine. At that moment I felt the range of all possible emotions that brought everything boiling to the surface. Tears of joy and sadness ran down my hot red face as I tried to rationalize what had put me in that place in that time where I could not fully enjoy the triumph of the one gift I had given to the world.

I grabbed a cocktail napkin and wiped the tears from my embarrassed face, then looked around me. Candy and Melissa were also in tears. The young men across from me were misty-eyed. The lyrics themselves were open to interpretation; to me the song was about an uncontained, unexplainable, and doomed love. It was the voice and emotion that carried the song to the listeners' hearts. There were probably three hundred people at Dexter's that night and they all were still and silent while she sang. I believe that most of them would tell generations in the future about the night they saw Gypsy Rae when she was nobody.

Annette grabbed the mic.

"Thank you," she said softly. "Thank you," she repeated a little louder as the crowd continued to cheer. "Please," she said. "We got more." The crowd cheered again, then quieted.

I sat in the dark with my emotions churning and not prepared to take much more. Yet I knew there was much more to follow and I had to brace for the duration.

"Thank you," she said again to the quieted crowd. "These are our new songs. That was *Napalm*."

"This next song is called *The Fugitive*," Gypsy Rae said softly.

I slid down in my seat.

CHAPTER 38 – THE ALTAR OF BEST INTENTIONS

The run continues

Unbound and alone

The fugitive rides

A hero he is not

A battle is not won

The fugitive hides

For all that is gone

To all he's left behind

The fugitive knows

He won't be back this way

You won't get in his way

Where ever he goes…

Staring at a future of repaying
Things gone long ago
Nights are as long as they seem

Tomorrow's a day
The road is further on
The end is in someone else's dream

Just sending time down the line
To somewhere he will never be
Never by your side

Nor under a tree in your gaze
On a beach shading those eyes
By your walls he is not confined

While you curse fools
You surrender
To empty promises so easily

To endless pointlessness
Monotony replaced by confusion
Despair repaired by absurdity

So out there tonight
The fugitive hurls
Blistering questions to the sky

Why this place?
Why this time?
Ultimately, just why?

He moves through time
At the speed of flight
Hesitation is his crime
Redemption is his fight

It was as if I she had written an anthem for my predicament. As if Annette had a psychic connection to me. When the song was over, I looked down to examine my napkin as the crowd erupted into cheers again. The events of the evening were a major triumph of Annette's life. I could write about every song and every nuance. Instead, I include this fine article by the music reviewer from the *Style* section of the local paper, *The Maplewood Press.*

A Torch Song?
By John Gold
When: Friday, December 9
Where: Dexter's Roadhouse

Who: The Travelled

Gypsy Rae- Vocals, Piano, Mandolin, Harp

Roy B. - Drums and percussion

Jack Hale- All stringed instruments, Vocals

William Turner- Horns, percussion, piano, stand-up bass, backing vocals

Elvira Thornton- Horns, percussion, violin, piano, backing vocals

Eldin- Guitars

(Note: None of these seem to be their real names)

<u>Set One:</u>

Napalm

The Fugitive

Out of Bullets

Dignity of Unknown Origins

The Vine

Flies in the Face

Empty Arms

<u>Set Two:</u>

Paranoid

Born to be Wild

London Calling

Aqualung

Every Picture Tells a Story

Get Off My Cloud/Both Sides Now

Time/Time in a Bottle

All of the excitement surrounding this Folk/Rock band has centered on three things: first is their eclectic technique of turning well-known rock and roll songs into folk ballads that interplay a variety of instruments and tempo changes. The second feature of the band is the loyal devotees that follow them from town to town like latter-day Dead-Heads. These fans are even encouraged by the band to trade digital recordings of their concerts. These concerts are all unique in content. Although the new original material is featured nightly, even the new stuff often gets different treatments on different nights.

Their third and most important feature is a quiet, but thoughtful lead singer named Gypsy Rae. The beauty and range of her voice is only part of her repertoire, which includes a natural charm and flawless tact. She is at once unpretentious, proud, unapologetic, and respectful. I interviewed this girl with a mysterious past a few hours before the concert and she seemed to know what her place was and what is expected of her. When I asked her about the evolving success of the band she gave a long thoughtful answer.

> *"We are a band," she said. "We are not a family. If we pretend we are a family, then we will fall into the roles that will eventually lead to a split. I think success tends to make all people feel more important than they really are. But success happens, just like failure happens. I am here to express what is inside of me and that is all any artist really has. If my*

art becomes a commercial success, then that may lead to people demanding certain compromises. Compromises are a part of business, but the consumer of art must understand that art is not business. What worked yesterday to make money, may work tomorrow, but if you look at your music as a commodity, then you are lost."

This was a thoughtful answer from a young lady of an undetermined age. But if I had to guess, I would say that she has not yet reached 25. She continued her answer:

"But we are all susceptible to the big money grab at some point. Life is funny that way; young people like me have high ideals about the way we want things, then the handlers and the business people creep into our lives and begin to chip away at our integrity. We must be vigilant, as should all people."

So I took my seat at Dexter's Roadhouse on Friday night expecting to be surprised and impressed. The opening song was *Napalm;* this song is a simple straightforward ballad on their new album *Schizophrenic Sound Wave,* but this night it was a torch song that tore at the soul with its tale of anguished broken love. Rae came out in a long black dress and sang a song that soared into the stratosphere and pulled the 300-plus patrons of Dexter's with it. The crowd was polite and silent for the subtle music changes. This silence may have been so their digital recorders could get every note, but my better angels will contend that it was for the reverence they felt at witnessing this moment.

The entire first set consisted of new songs. It is hard to single out any one of them as being above the rest. The treatment all of the songs got on the stage was markedly different from the album. *The Fugitive* is a song about a drifter who is not necessarily a prison escapee and perhaps not even a drifter in the classical sense. This performance featured repetitive guitar chords that chopped behind each line. The bridge before the final verse featured a mandolin solo.

The next song was *Out of Bullets*, a song about someone out of answers and full of regret for the time wasted. Rae serenaded through the entirety of the song in a slow a cappella in the first run and then repeats the full song at twice the tempo sitting at a piano and accompanied by a harp and violin. She then repeated the final verse; again a cappella:

Leaving, I pause
Measuring grief
In stolen time
Myself the thief

The rest of the first set included the Gypsy Rae original compositions, *Dignity of Unknown Origins, The Vine, Flies in the Face, and Empty*

Arms. All of these songs are deep and passionate and are evolving as performances as The Travelled's exciting experimentation continues.

The second set included their by-now classic take of Black Sabbath's *Paranoid,* performed this evening by mandolin, piano, and tuba. The range of the lead singer's voice is complemented nicely by the virtuosity of all members of the band. Jethro Tull's *Aqualung* was sung as an operetta with Jack Hale, the guitar player, singing the middle part about December's foggy freeze in a pitch-perfect baritone.

The other classics were given a new and unique treatment which I am told changes with each performance. In fact, the classic rock songs change each performance. On this night, The Clash's *London Calling* featured a violin solo by a tall and striking woman named Elvira Thornton. Rod Stewart's *Every Picture Tells a Story* was just two acoustic guitarists (Hale and a man named Eldin) accompanying Rae. As she sang the verses, a projector flashed images on a gray curtain behind them. Each picture was a summation of the words she was singing.

The final two songs raised the ante on the eclectic scale and sent me looking for my Joni Mitchell LPs. First they combined The Rolling Stones' *Get Off My Cloud* with Mitchell's *Both Sides Now.* Rae sings of bows and flows of angel hair and ice cream castles then tears into the up-tempo Stones' classic and she tells that pernicious interloper to get of her cloud in a gravelly voice unlike anything we have previously heard. As she finishes the song, she is seated at the piano and once again singing lightly the first chorus of *Both Sides,* where she admits *I really don't know clouds at all.*

The concert ends with the juxtaposition of Pink Floyd's *Time* and Jim Croce's *Time in a Bottle.* These two songs are such a natural fit that I am surprised this combination has not happened sooner. The final verse of the Pink Floyd classic again finds the sweet-voiced Rae at the piano.

The piano fades to a mandolin and violin squaring off in a blur of frenetic activity that itself fades to the beginning strains of *Time in a Bottle* on acoustic guitar. Rae and crew completely and faithfully perform this song as written until the music fades and she is left alone and unaccompanied in a spotlight repeating the final lines over and over, but quieter each time.

The concert ends as the light fades with the music and the crowd explodes with applause and calls for more for the next fifteen minutes. I am left with an appreciation for what music can be and what a night of music should be. I predict superstardom for this band and I hope Gypsy Rae and her exquisite band can keep their heads screwed on straight and always give the crowd what they need and not just what they want.

****

I sat with my Gypsy Rae fans through the entire show. Only once did I get up, and that was between sets when I used the restroom. I returned to my booth to find a smiling Melissa and Candy. Their male friends were no longer around.

Melissa stood up smiling to let me slide into my bench seat. "We know where they are staying," she said as I brushed past her.

"You do?" I asked as I slid towards the inside.

"Yes," she said, talking over her shoulder as she slid in next to me. "They are staying at the Atrium, third floor. They each have a suite. Rae is in Room 311."

I smiled back. "How did you find that out?" I asked.

"We asked the door man and he went and looked it up behind the desk," Melissa replied.

"So what are you going to do with that information?" I asked.

"We were hoping to maybe stake out the hotel and maybe hook up with a member of the band... but now that we know you, we were thinking…" she paused.

"You think I can get you in," I finished for her.

"Well… can you?" Melissa persisted.

"I can get in the hotel easily, but Rae may not welcome my company," I said as the band began to take the stage for their second set.

"Well… what's the plan?" Candy shouted over the growing crowd noise.

"We need to leave right as soon as the show is over and not one second later," I said as Annette strode out into the spotlight.

* * * * * * * * * * *

An hour later, Candy, Melissa, and I sat in my car in the back parking lot of the Atrium Hotel. Candy was in the back and Melissa was in the front passenger seat. Mellissa had by now taken a keen interest in me. I did not encourage this attention, but it was not in me to create more tension than was necessary.

After a couple of minutes of waiting, a car pulled into the hotel back parking lot. We all got out of the car and made our way slowly towards the rear entrance. Melissa grabbed my hand as we walked three abreast. The young man from the newly-arrived car reached the door at nearly the same time as us and he opened the door with his key card and let us in without question. Once inside we headed for the stairwell and slowly made our way to the third floor.

As we reached the top the stairs, we began discussing what our actual plan might be.

"Do we just wait here?" Candy whispered.

"For a moment, I think," I whispered back.

"We can't just stand here," Melissa said loudly as she clutched my hand tighter.

"I think it will seem like an ambush if we just pop out," I said in a slightly louder voice.

"We could wait by the elevators," Candy added.

"We could ambush them there," I said with a laugh.

I began to think of the absurdity of the situation. I was in my mid-forties and I was staking out my own daughter with a couple of young star-struck twenty-somethings- one of whom was acting like my girlfriend; absurd and uncomfortable. We stepped through the door and into the hallway. The rooms at our end started at 301, so we were at the opposite end of the hall from the room where Annette would be staying.

We walked towards the elevator, which was midway down the hall. Opposite the elevator door were two chairs sitting on either side of a potted plant on a small table.

"I think you two should go sit by the elevators and wait while I stand down the hall by Rae's room pretending to be a hotel guest," I suggested.

"Why are we doing this?" Candy asked. "Does she not want to see you?"

"I am her father," I finally confessed. "We are estranged. I might scare her away if I jump out at her."

Melissa let go of my hand. "So you want us to scare her down the hallway?"

"Not exactly," I answered, "but if you take off the bandanas and flannel shirts, they may not think that you are a threat. They will just pass you by and I can introduce you once we clear the air."

"What if she doesn't want to clear the air and has her goons throw you out?" Candy asked skeptically.

"I guess we go about our business," I answered.

The two girls looked at each other and seemed to exchange psychic messages. They both took off their bandanas to reveal medium-length black hair. They then removed their hoop earrings, folded them inside the bandanas and put them in the pockets of their jeans. After they removed their flannel shirts and tied them around their waists, they again exchanged looks, shrugged and walked over to the two antique-style chairs to take a seat.

I stood and waited. In a few minutes, the elevator started to hum and the bell rang as it reached the third floor. I retreated down the hall and watched as an older gentleman in a business suit turned the corner and headed the opposite direction from where I stood. A new flaw in my impromptu plan was revealed.

When I heard the elevator close, I walked back to talk to the two girls.

"I think we need a signal to avoid false alarms," I said as I reached the elevator.

"I can whistle," Melissa offered.

"Too obvious," I replied.

"I can cough," said Candy.

"Better," I said, "but cough twice just in case you might really have to cough."

"How about I cough, then Melissa coughs," Candy said as she pointed to her friend.

"Perfect," I said as I ducked back into the safety of the hallway.

After two more false alarms and perhaps a half-hour, I finally heard the humming, then the bell, followed by the door opening, then two distinctly separate female coughs. I turned my attention to the door of room 314, which I had learned from my two new friends, was not occupied by any member of the band or its entourage. As I pretended to fiddle with the lock, I looked over my shoulder to see Annette dressed in sweat pants and sweatshirt, holding a bottle of water and heading towards me. Behind her were members of the band and next to her was a youngish-looking man wearing a slick business suit and small round eyeglasses. I stepped away from the door of room 314.

Annette, with room key in hand, stopped in her tracks. Eyeglasses Boy stopped and looked first at her, then at me, then back at her. She spoke first.

"Dad?" she said in a half-question.

"Hi Annette," I said.

"Sir," said Eyeglasses Boy as he walked towards me, "you are not allowed...,"

I brushed passed him as if he wasn't there. He tried to weakly grab my arm. His strength was unimpressive and I easily broke free. I embraced my daughter as tears formed in my eyes. She embraced me back. She then extended her right hand towards Eyeglasses Boy, who stood behind me.

"Open my door, will you Ken?" she said politely to Eyeglasses Boy.

I heard the click and whirr of the electronic door lock and the door opening behind me. We separated from our embrace and I looked down to compose myself as Annette guided me by the arm into her room.

"No visitors, Ken," she said. "I will call you if I need you." She shut the door.

* * * * * * * * * * *

The room that Annette had at the Atrium was completely unremarkable. It was not a suite as my new friends had suggested. It had one king sized bed, a small bathroom, an antique-looking chair and table, and an old tube television in an old console. She was unpretentious as always. She was a real person and not about to put on airs. The name Gypsy Rae might seem pretentious, but she had a legitimate reason to hide her identity: a crazy father.

She walked through the doorway behind me. "Make yourself comfortable," she said. "I gotta freshen up."

She slipped into the bathroom as I sat on the edge of the bed and tried to remember one damned word I had rehearsed only yesterday in Storage Unit 11. The time went quickly as I waited for the running water in the sink to stop, and soon Annette was back in the room with a towel around her neck.

"So you're out of prison?" she asked.

"Yes," I said.

"Parole?" she asked.

"No," I replied.

"Escaped?" she asked as she took a seat on one of the antique chairs.

"Not exactly…, well not escaped from prison..," I began to stammer unconfidently as I searched for any good words.

"It's okay if you don't tell me," she said. "I would rather not know."

"What I meant to say was that I escaped from where I was, but it wasn't a prison," I said uncomfortably as I tried to adjust to my child putting me on the defensive.

"But you are on the lam?" she guessed.

"Yes...," I said, pausing, "I am."

"You need money?" She asked.

"I do," I said candidly, "but that's not why I am here."

"You are taking a risk you know," she said as she walked towards the head of the bed and sat down. "Ken could be calling the police right now."

"He seems like a charming guy," I said sarcastically as I looked towards the door. "Is he behind the restraining order?"

Annette got silent. She slipped off her shoes and reclined back on the still-made bed.

"Did you go to the show?" she asked.

"I did," I said, absolutely beaming with pride. "I think you and your band are the best thing I have ever seen live. But I am biased."

Annette smiled. "Thank you," she said.

"I particularly like your new songs," I replied.

She then rolled over on the bed and began searching through a small backpack that sat on the nightstand. She pulled out an old red notebook, opened it and tossed it on the bed next to me.

I picked up the notebook and read the neat blocked letters written in my handwriting:

Dignity of Unknown Origins

In empty afternoons and nights of rage
In drunken stupor and in a grieving stage
Swearing to be what some would desire
It falls to me now to douse the fire
(chorus)
I don't want ribbons
Don't want a parade
Don't want to be forgiven
Won't be dismayed
I don't seek glory

Don't need love

Not in this story

I was thinking of

I am what I appear, but not in this place

A vagrant, a wanderer, a drifting disgrace

Here amongst the ruins survives a thread

Resolve not ruined; dignity not dead

(Chorus)

I don't have time

Don't have the look

The story is done

Finished the book

Won't be persuaded

By a few choice words

Nor casually invaded

On ordinary terms

As I rescue myself by the margin of a wire

Seeing you now revealed as a liar

Rejecting the contemptible words you speak

Confounding those who see me as weak

(Chorus)

Your words are not needed
Your advice is well worn
Your warnings not headed
Just greeted with scorn
Do not compensate me
For what I've been through
I don't want you to hate me
And I don't want you

I put the notebook down on the bed. "I knew that song sounded familiar," I said with a smile.

"Not just that one," Annette admitted as she rolled back over. "All of the new songs. I changed some words, but they are essentially the same. I have four notebooks' worth. Maybe four more albums in there." She pointed towards the backpack.

We sat in silence as the gears in my head began to mesh and Annette waited for the realization. I just stared at her face until the recognition was within my grasp.

"Hence the restraining order," I finally said.

"We really made a mess of this, Dad," she said as she covered her face with her hands.

"I am really not mad or anything," I said. "I mostly expected that you were embarrassed that I was a nut job."

"Well, there's that…" she said and we both laughed.

We laughed until it became uncomfortable and then laughed a little more. Then it became quiet for a moment.

"So why are you here?" She finally said.

"I am here to explain myself," I offered.

We were interrupted by a knock at the door.

Annette rose and walked to the door and looked through the peephole. She opened the door to reveal Ken standing with a pissed off look on his face. The poor guy looked like a he had been stood up for the prom or something. They whispered a few words to each other and Annette closed the door.

"Am I holding up your plans for tonight?" I asked.

"Not really,' she said, "He was just concerned about your..., um..., legal status."

"I will be leaving soon if you all are worried," I said. "I doubt that he calls the police. That would be bad publicity. Assure him that I will be moving on quickly."

"He's been really smart managing our affairs," she said as she sat down on the antique chair near the foot of the bed.

"I am glad he's giving me the opportunity to say what I have to say," I said as I turned to face her.

Annette just sat there as if she was waiting for whatever wisdom I was about to impart.

"For most of your life I have been gone," I began. "I traveled constantly and even when I was home, I was not everything I could be. I was always analyzing things and examining how I could make myself happier. Hell, I examined what happiness actually is. I still examine that to this very day. I have had a great many opportunities for this recently. The conclusions I have reached is that happiness cannot be achieved by scrutinizing every part of every decision."

I paused momentarily to gather my now fragmented thoughts into a coherent presentation while Annette stared patiently at me. I continued.

"I will never make excuses for my behavior or apologize for my belated realization. My work was never more important than you, even though I traveled. My introspection was a search for answers that I hoped would benefit all of us. I thought I could only help others if I understood myself. I could only help myself if I understood others. An analytical mind is a trap that has doors slamming on all sides and has no escape route. The only escape is if someone else crashes through those doors and destroys the trap."

"What does this mean?" Annette interrupted.

"I have fallen in love," I finally got around to saying.

Annette smiled, and then looked away.

"I guess I am happy," she said. "Who is it?"

"Bonnie is her name," I said with pride, "and she gets me as close to happiness as I think I am capable of."

"So she has destroyed your traps?" she asked.

"She destroys them daily," I said. "But, I reconstruct them."

"I see," Annette resumed, "you escaped to be with her."

"Actually, I escaped from where she is," I said.

"I'm confused," she admitted.

"We were both being kept in a place called Tallhill," I explained. "It is a minimum security place, a nice place too. But I could never be happy there."

"But you left the woman you love," Annette interrupted

"Temporarily," I said. "I am going back for her."

"Why didn't you bring her with you when you left?" she asked

"She's in a wheelchair," I explained.

"Holy shit!" she sprang out of her chair. "You are going to be on the run with her?"

She sat down. "Sorry," she said. "Bad choice of words."

"It's alright," I reassured her. "I haven't quite worked out all of the details, but we will make it work."

"So when do you go back?"

"Tomorrow night after lights out," I said "The security is lighter then."

"Where are you sleeping tonight?"

"In my new car," I said with a smile. "I stole a Mustang."

"Excellent," Annette exclaimed. She seemed to be enjoying this. "So you came to say goodbye?"

"I originally came here to explain my failures as a father and I may still do that someday." I said as I got up. "Right now I think I just need to make you understand that you are always in my thoughts and always will be. I don't know exactly where I will end up, but I hope it isn't prison. I will understand if the cops show up and Ken sends them after me...,"

"I will talk to him," she assured me.

"I can't tell you where I intend to go, but I will get word to you when I get there," I said as I walked towards the door.

"So you are leaving?" she asked in a kind of begging fashion I didn't really expect.

"Yes," I said as I turned around, "but one more thing."

"What is it?" she said as she got closer to me.

"There are two girls in the hallway who want to meet you," I explained. "They are nice girls; Melissa and Candy. They helped me find you. They are big fans. I am going to send them down here. Could you be nice to them?"

"Sure," she said. "Send them down."

I reached in my jacket pocket and pulled out a tiny black and white stuffed killer whale.

"Remember this?" I asked.

"I do," she said "You got that for me from Sea World."

"It was a trip that I planned to take you on, but you got the chicken pox," I said. "I never went to Sea World myself, but I got this at the airport." I handed it to her.

She grabbed the whale and tears began to form in her eyes.

I fought my own tears as I tried to explain, "I found it in one of the boxes in the storage unit at Al's. I wanted to give you something small to help you think of me."

"I love you Dad," she said as she opened her arms to embrace me tightly. "Be safe."

"I will," I said through my own sobs, "I love you and I will always be your biggest fan."

After about a minute and a half, the embracing stopped and we pulled apart slowly. I kept my head down and headed for the door. I let myself out without turning around. All I could hear were sobs. I walked down the hall as I left behind what was left of everything I had ever created. I turned the corner by the elevator to see Melissa and Candy faithfully waiting.

"Girls," I said, "she will see you, but give her couple of minutes. It was ... emotional."

I hit the elevator button. The girls got up and stood next to me. I looked to Melissa on my left and smiled broadly. I turned to my right and smiled equally at Candy. The elevator rang and the door slowly opened. Melissa stepped into the elevator with me as Candy held the door open.

"Clyde," Melissa said as she grabbed my hand, "where are you going?"

"I got places I gotta be," I said as I grabbed her other hand and held them in front of me.

"Can I go?" Melissa asked stunningly.

I was rocked back a little by this. I recovered to say, "Melissa, you have your whole life to find what I have only recently found and that is happiness. I doubt you would be happy with me for very long."

The elevator began to alarm and this caused Melissa to release my hands. She stepped from the elevator as Candy released her hold on the door. They both looked at me with sad smiles as the door gradually closed. I pushed the button for the second floor. When the elevator door opened again, I stepped out and took the stairway down to the ground floor. I slipped out of the back door and out to the parking lot.

I climbed into my new Mustang and fired it up. As I waited for the car to warm up, I reflected as much as I would allow myself. I knew I had not said all of the words I had rehearsed. In fact I had not even come close. What had happened was a change of my mood. Annette's music and talent and expression of my words fed back to me proved to me that she understood more than I could have hoped for. Words are wasted on those who already understand. I was comforted by this and found myself trying to reassure her that I was going to be alright.

By the time I had reflected on this, the car was warm and my thoughts were clear. My mission was the only thing on my mind. I checked off another box on my mental to-do list. I put the car into gear and pulled out of the parking lot and into the street. I drove into the night… in the general direction of Tallhill.

PART 5: THE ADVENTURES OF BONNIE AND CLYDE

CHAPTER 39 – POSSIBILITIES

In all of my dreams, Bonnie could walk. When she was just a voice, her physical limitations were of no consequence. That voice was always a power capable of forcing my will beyond what I thought was possible. Never mind that only when I met her and got to know her, did the voice take on a physical form in my dreams. She was incredible in real life, and that made the transition to super hero status in my dreams seem natural.

When we talked of the future, she always talked about walking again. To the casual observer it may have seemed wishful thinking or perhaps pathetic. However, the way she talked about it was not merely hopeful, but clinical. She talked of keeping her legs active and about how the joints and muscles that were long dormant would need to be prepared for the day when she started to walk again. A dance on the beach is what she promised me and I believed her. Modern medicine and tenacity were going to win the day. She was convinced and convincing.

Following her example, I treated her obvious real limitations as an inconvenience. We had overcome the sexual obstacles and my own mental block when it came to a wheelchair-bound woman being an object of desire. I had walked miles, stolen a car, slept in a tractor and in storage areas just to say my little piece to Annette. The bond between us was pre-ordained and easily explained; we were father and daughter. The situation with Bonnie was not nearly as natural. As I drove back towards Tallhill, the significance hit me. I was about to shatter convention to smithereens and stretch possibilities to beyond known limits for a woman I had known only a very short time.

If I fail to find the exact words to explain the unique bond we shared, I hope I can be forgiven. I have enough of a task just to explain myself and my behavior. It is possible that the voice in my dreams could have belonged to someone else and I have conveniently chosen to match her to that voice. Time has blurred what the voice really sounded like before Bonnie entered my life. This nuance has become trivial since she became that voice in my dreams and remains that to this day.

I was armed with my cynical defenses and my self-inflicted desperate situation. Her life story made me re-examine my examination of myself. The teams of psychiatrists who had treated me had merely dissected me. Bonnie mended me and made me feel significant. I felt almost lost as to what I would do to help her, but I swore I would try.

I thought these thoughts as I reclined in that green Mustang parked on an icy dirt road in the trees near a cornfield just outside Maplewood. I could have stayed in a hotel, or maybe wherever Melissa and Candy were staying, but I feared letting my guard down. I reclined in the front seat and tried to sleep as the sun came up. I smiled and felt a sort of perverse comfort that I had little chance to succeed in my audacious plan.

Sleep soon came and I dreamt the dream where Bonnie was a being hailed as not only a medical miracle, but also a dancing phenomenon. She was a roaring success and all of the black tie and tails folks in the upper crust of society approved and sought her company. They toasted her at banquets and gave her awards. All of the humanitarian people gave her humanitarian awards. The children's cancer people gave her children's cancer awards. Old obstacles were just distant memories.

There were no symbols or examinations needed for this dream. I was dreaming what I wanted for her. I was imagining what life should have been if that awful day had not happened a dozen or so years previous. Images were clear in this dream and people spoke concisely. I woke midday and could only absorb the enormous sadness of what life really was for this angel. I had no one to tell any of this to and no one with whom I would discuss the meaning. I had no comments to add or any reaction to share. I was alone.

So I sat and absorbed. The absorption took quite a while, perhaps an hour. I sat perfectly still and watched tree limbs buffeted by the cold winter wind. Once the full impact of the colossal sadness of her situation hit me, I cried like a baby: a helpless muttering mess of a baby. Once my blubbering stopped and my composure was regained, I vowed to myself that I would never fall apart like this again. Sadness was never going to rule me and I would never feel helpless again. I started the car and the heater.

I looked at the clock and it read 4:05 PM. I put the car in reverse and backed out of the stand of trees. I threw the Mustang into drive and pulled slowly out of the field and down the road to rescue that angel who had saved my sanity and had given me a reason to try anything noble again. I was noble and I was on a quest. I felt purpose. As any knight on a quest will tell you, the purpose is what you live for.

****

As I may have mentioned before, Tallhill was not an especially foreboding place. With its fruit trees and well-manicured shrubbery, it looked positively charming. To break somebody out of there seemed as hard as breaking someone out of kindergarten. But there were complications; there were cameras and lights; there were distances to be traveled by foot with and without a load. But I knew the camera and lights layout. I knew where all of the trees were and I knew where Bonnie's room was. I also had kept myself in shape by doing rounds and rounds of pushups and sit-ups.

I knew that only a few of the cameras had infrared and could see at night and I had memorized the locations of those cameras. I would lurk in the shadows and behind the trees where the regular cameras were located. It was my only chance if I wished to go undetected. I figured that I could accomplish the interrupted short dashes to the building in three to four minutes.

On occasion, there are those three minutes of your life that test all of your faculties and physical stamina. I say three minutes, but sometimes the length of time is much longer than that. It can be shorter also, but not by much. In any case, the length of time seems longer because of the increased awareness and perception. The mind's focus sharpens just in time to achieve that appreciation for the profound activity in which you are about to engage, 10PM on the night of December 10th was one such occasion.

I had parked my green Mustang- my faithful steed- on the main highway shoulder pointed towards the interstate. It was mostly out of sight next to a small bridge barrier. There was about a half-mile of woods to reach the fences of Tallhill. The spot on the fence which was closest to my car was also the spot that was closest to Bonnie's window.

While I planned to be careful not to be spotted on my way in, I was going to get out as fast as possible. There were cameras with infrared pointed in that direction and there were more lights here than most parts of the compound, but I had no intention of wasting time as I expected to not only have to carry Bonnie, but also any kind of belongings she was bringing.

Because of my increased awareness, the bite of a brisk winter wind blowing through my light overcoat seemed especially harsh as I darted from tree to tree. I would poke my head out occasionally to gauge how close I was and to determine if I could see any lights in Bonnie's room. In a few minutes I was at the last tree, which stood about 20 feet from her window, where I could see the faint lights of a television flickering inside. I dashed those few remaining feet and crouched down below her window leaning with my back to the wall.

The sharp cold wind took another bite out of my bundled warmth as I braced myself and began to shiver. I collected my courage for a minute and then stood on my tip-toes to place my face on the lower part of Bonnie's window. I knocked lightly on the window and then cupped my hands around my face as I pressed against the glass to see if my signal had been received. The blinds on her window covered all but the lower ten inches, but it was enough for me to see stirring on her bed and soon the blankets were peeled back to reveal Bonnie in the dull light; her shape defined, but her appearance not clear.

The silhouette slid sideways onto her wheelchair by the side of the bed. Her head turned to face me and I saw a flash of her black hair as it was caught in one of the small beams of light that streamed in from the outside. She then reached down to release the brakes. She turned the chair towards the window, rolled over and released the window lock at the bottom, then opened the window the ten inches that the blinds did not cover.

"Clyde?" She whispered.

"It's me," I whispered, my reply inches away from her face.

From that proximity, I could smell a fragrance that I had come to associate with Bonnie. The only way I could describe the aroma was clean and fresh. She always smelled like she had taken a bubble bath in some heavenly oils. It was enchanting and comforting.

"Wait here," she whispered.

She rolled inside her room as I crouched and reclined with my back to the wall again. In a moment, she was back.

"Take this," she whispered as she shoved a medium sized gym bag through the window. "I tried to pack light."

I grabbed the bag and stashed it next to the wall at my feet. Bonnie pulled the blinds all of the way up and opened the window enough to fit through. She lifted herself out of the chair and pushed up to sit on the windowsill; back facing out. I stood and supported her back under the armpits as she reclined into my arms.

In this moment, I felt as if my heart and head would explode as the danger, expectation, desperation, and passion fought for room in my consciousness. I held her firmly and returned to my crouch as I sat her on the ground. We kissed passionately for a few seconds and then released our embrace. I grabbed her bag and slung the large strap diagonally around my head and shoulders so the bag rested on my back.

"Are you ready for the run, babe?" I whispered.

"Ready," she said sweetly and confidently.

The run that I was referring to was not only the brief straining and surreptitious gallop across the grounds of Tallhill: it was not only the adventure we faced, it was also the challenges we would always face. I believe she grasped all of those meanings.

I gathered her into my arms and cradled her as she looped her arms around my neck. This was neither the most comfortable nor the safest way to carry her, but I decided that I would not carry her like an inanimate object by slinging her over one shoulder or even in the fireman's carry. This way would be more difficult, but at least I had been building the muscles I would need for this task. I paused and sighed knowing that this was as comfortable as this would get.

I took off at a slow jog towards the next tree as I allowed my body to get accustomed to the burden. I paused at the tree.

"Are you alright?" I asked.

"Yes," she said, "I think we need to make a dash for it."

"You're right," I said as I gathered her up in my arms and took off for the remaining distance to the fence.

In what seemed like 10 minutes, but was probably more like 2 minutes, we reached the stone fence. The muscles in my arms were burning as I paused at the base of the eight-foot wall. I set Bonnie on the ground and we both listened for the sound of alarms or any sign of pursuit. There was none.

"How do we clear the wall?" she asked.

"This is where we rely on your arm strength," I said.

I saw her nod her acknowledgement in the dull light. I took her bag from around my shoulders and jumped up and set it on the top of the wall. I then hoisted Bonnie up by her hips as I imagined many male ballet dancers had done in the past.

"I am going to jump," I said. "I will try to be careful not to hurt you, but I need you to grab the top of the fence and hold on as long as you possibly can."

I knew I could easily reach the top of the fence, but this was going to be tricky; I needed to get her over the fence without smacking her face on the stone and brick surface. I jumped straight up.

"Got it," she said with excitement in her voice.

As she dangled from the wall, I jumped to grab the top of the wall and then slung my right leg over the top; which knocked her bag down to the ground beyond the outside of the wall. Before I dropped the ten feet to the ditch on the other side, I worked my way over to where Bonnie was and threw my left arm over the wall so that the top of the wall was in my armpit.

I grabbed her left hand firmly in the grasp of my right hand as she let go of the wall. She grabbed my right forearm with her other hand and I pulled her upper body clear of the wall.

"I need you to put your arms around my neck," I instructed her as my burning arms competed for attention in my nerve center with the wall which was digging deeply and painfully into my ribs.

Bonnie put her right hand behind my neck and I moved her left hand to where she could clasp them together. With my right arm now free, I lifted the rest of her body over the fence and she was soon on my back with her hands around the front of my neck.

I repositioned my body until the fence was under both arms. I then pushed away from the fence and dropped down to the ground below. Bonnie let loose of my neck as I carefully backed up and sat her on the ground again.

"Maybe I should have dug you a tunnel," she joked as we both recovered from our mad dash.

I laughed briefly and we both listened for any sign of pursuit or alarm; still nothing. I stood and slung the bag over my shoulders again. Soon she was in my arms as I dashed towards the green Mustang. The run was much longer than the dash to the wall and by the time we reached the car, the accumulated fatigue and injuries began to take their toll.

Upon reaching the car, I could only manage to lay her on the hood before I fell to my knees in a heavy-breathing heap. My rest was brief however, as I realized that I had no time to relax. I quickly recovered and opened the door while sill on my knees. I stood up and threw her bag in the back seat. I grabbed Bonnie again, carried her over to the open door and sat her on the passenger seat. This time she kept he hands laced behind my head.

"I love you Clyde," she said and kissed me on the lips.

"You are what I have been waiting for all of my life," I said as we pulled apart.

I strapped her in her seatbelt and stood back up. I closed the door softly and ran around to the other side. I opened my door and listened again. No alarms. I climbed inside and closed my door. I started the car and rolled away slowly with the lights off. In a few minutes, I turned the lights on as we were pulling onto a state highway and on our way to somewhere uncertain and a life full of challenges.

But we were free and we were together.

CHAPTER 40 – THE FIRES OF EVOLUTION

There is something to be said for wisdom and maturity, but I like to take those two concepts and lump them into an overall process called evolution. There is the evolution of species that develop the best traits to adapt to their surroundings. This evolution comes into play when I speak of Annette and how she is hopefully better adapted to face the future than Margie and I ever were. Her upbringing, her intelligence, and her pragmatism may serve her well in that vast unknown she has entered.

Some of the mistakes we have made may have damaged her psyche, but may have also made her wary of the evils of the world. The lessons were there to be learned and if she learned them, she may well be better adjusted than me. At least her music provides an outward mechanism for her misery. I have convinced myself that this is the case.

What I have experienced in my life could also be classified as an evolution; the things I found important when I was eighteen seem foolish now. The traits I find important in people are different and the way I judge those traits have different parameters. For instance, as a young man I may have thought that physical beauty was the most important thing in a mate. While this may be the nature of most beings, it does involve compromise and deception. In being attracted to another person simply based on physical appearance, we can sometimes overlook or otherwise adjust to the things about them that we find less desirable.

As I made my case in my manifesto, I accepted a marriage of convenience and simplicity without realizing that this actually complicated things when my psyche developed enough to realize that I was not happy in this situation. I am not sure that this doesn't happen to everybody. I have conducted no clinical studies that back up this contention, but I think that this happens to people quite often. Divorce rates prove that people make very bad choices and that they get married for the wrong reasons.

It is my guess that physical attraction is number one or two on the list of wrong reasons. Money or perceived financial security would also appear near the top of the list. At least with money, there is that security, even if it is false. Money can fade with time, just like beauty. Sometimes it all goes at once. It took me only a few years of marriage to realize that we had made a mistake. The fact was that

Margie and I were incompatible. Then there was the added complication of having a child.

Subsequently, I found that I wanted things at age thirty-five that I had not previously considered important and had not even thought about in the early years of marriage. One of the things I wanted was trust, to trust somebody was important, but I wanted also to be trusted.

I found after a few years that my self-examination began to extend to Margie. I discovered that she had insecurities that I found foolish. She was indeed an attractive woman, but she seemed to think that I was always going to leave her for someone younger or prettier. After a while, people can paint their partner into a convenient caricature as a substitute for real understanding. That caricature becomes their point of reference and all things that run contrary to that paradigm will only cause conflict, confusion, and pain.

Returning to evolution, when I reached my forties, I was still attracted to pretty girls, but I only felt comfortable with women who shared my misery. There was an element of having failed to find a soul mate and an element of desperation. I felt the clock was ticking on both my physical attractiveness and my earning capacity. In desperation, I began thinking that the security of my job and my marriage were actually traps.

My true evolution only came when I interacted with others who had lost everything and in that I found an odd perspective. For Amos, he was sure that he could be happily married and inside an asylum. Bonnie also found a purpose in that place, but I always felt that she sought something more significant. It took very little convincing on my part to get her to leave with me. I think she realized that contentment was not happiness. She knew that she would waste away in an institution and that they really wouldn't punish her if she was caught escaping. She needed to experience love and freedom again. We both did.

The qualities that my evolved-self sought were not found in the miserable people who shared my despair and sought an even more exotic despair; the qualities that I grew to desire were those of a champion who had overcome long odds and persevered. What I had done with my bomb stunt was to quit and walk away from a bad situation. It was bold only in its misdirection and shock value. The real result was that it hurt people.

I was attracted to Bonnie's spirit and her optimism. Her intent to walk again could be seen as a childish fantasy fed by deception. However, during my long conversations with her, I learned that she was pragmatic about the challenge. She knew the odds were long, but she would always say that everything had a first time. To some, her attitude may have seemed like a deception or a charade, but to me it was welcomed tonic. When Bonnie said, "I will walk again," I believed that there was belief and determination behind the words. If she failed, she would probably not see it as failure, but as a temporary condition. Which one could also say about life itself.

The other thing that attracted me to her was the amount of soul searching she had done. She had done one bad deed, but she had spent most of her life trying to please other people, to be perceived as a good person. In one violent act, she had destroyed that whole persona. Her condition left her with many hours of silent contemplation. I knew exactly what that was like and I knew that regrets were always the stars of those contemplation shows. I knew that like me, she regretted the violence a great deal, but especially regretted the loss of self-identity that led to the violence.

Another person was living those years that led to it, not the person we had forgotten about while we went from day to day trying to please a world that would never care too much if we weren't in it at all. The stress accumulated and was caused by compromise. By not being our true selves, we suppressed our identities until they could no longer be contained. The doctors call this other identity the alter ego. In my case and in Bonnie's case, our alter egos had not only been kept locked up, they had been malnourished.

Once unleashed, our other selves struck back quite violently. In our soul searching, both separate and together, we have come to understand that we both feel the same way about this. We had learned to communicate less with words and more with feel. I found that I almost never had to explain myself to her. The mood I was in was understood and so was hers. I believe that it was the rarified air of finding a soul mate, even though those words were never expressed by me directly. The worst part was over now and we had evolved into something real, something that owed no apologies.

* * * * * * * * * * *

In the early morning hours of December 11, I was driving as far away from Tallhill as I could manage in one night and as much as my over-strained muscles and tired brain could handle. Bonnie was reclined on her seat with her head firmly on my shoulder as she gazed through the sunroof at the stars. The cold air rushed in and filled the car. I simply drove the speed limit with the heat running full blast.

She suggested that we head northeast toward a large city where we could get lost easier in the crowd. I shrugged, since I had no concrete plan, and did what she proposed. I turned the green Mustang onto the freeway as she tucked her left hand under my right arm and nuzzled closer with her head still pointed upwards. For at least a half-hour I drove through the night watching mile markers pass, assuming she had fallen asleep. I was just about to find a place to pull over to re-adjust her body to a more comfortable position when she spoke.

"When I first went to the hospital, I had a roommate," she began. "Her name was Roxy. She had just been discharged from the burn center and was put in my semi-private room to finish healing. She was a college student who was also heading for the loony bin. She was a pyromaniac who had torched her own sorority house and killed three of her Kappa Alpha Theta sisters."

"Hmmm," I said as I had no words to add to her story.

"She was quite insane," Bonnie continued. "But very in tune with the universe and nature, if that makes any sense. She was obsessed with fire, as I suppose all pyros are. It was all she would talk about. She would say that earth was created by fire and that it would be consumed by fire. The sun is just a giant flame that allowed life to exist and that there were bigger balls of flame in the universe and those were the stars we all see in the sky. She was right about that of course.

"This is all common knowledge and scientific fact. It wasn't any revelation or anything, but it did put things in perspective for me. So I asked my father to bring me books about the stars to my hospital room and I learned a bunch of facts and numbers about locations and sizes of stars. I learned about the composition of those heavenly bodies and I read up about recent discoveries of distant stars. All of this accumulated knowledge from centuries of scientists and guessers just led me back what Roxy had said; that fire controls it all.

"So now when I stare at those stars, I feel connected to everything… by fire."

Bonnie stopped talking and remained silent for a long time. I finally decided she was sleeping and closed the sunroof to keep out the harsh cold wind. Once the heat of the car became contained, I began to get drowsy. After several yawns, I started to look for a place to pull over to sleep off my fatigue. Eleven miles later, I pulled into a rest area along the side of the interstate. The rest area was full of trucks with their diesel engines idling and a few cars scattered near the public restrooms. As I parked the car, Bonnie awoke.

"Bathroom break," I said as she pulled herself over to her side of the car.

"Not a moment too soon, "she said.

I carried her into the ladies room and helped her to do her business, and then I carried her back to the car and sat her back into her seat before leaving her in the locked car so I could relieve myself.

"Be right back," I said as I closed the door.

In a few minutes, she was in my arms on the reclined passenger seat as we both looked up at the stars far beyond the cloudless sky. I like to think we were of one mind at that moment. I thought of distant fires. I thought of fires that had been burning forever and that would burn long after the Earth had gone dead and cold. I even thought about the heat in the center of the earth.

At that moment, Bonnie piped up, "There's a fire in an old coal mining town that's been burning since 1962."

"I've heard of that," I replied.

"Somebody thought it was clever to burn garbage in an old coal mining shaft," she continued. "But it got out of control and just kept consuming all of that underground coal. It got so nobody could live in that town. The ground was too hot, the air was too toxic. That fire may never go out."

"I heard it would spread to the neighboring towns."

"It will. It is going to consume everything slowly. Fire doesn't punch a clock, it is eternal."

She paused again until I was almost sleeping.

"Roxy ended up burning herself again," Bonnie picked up the old conversation.

"She had gotten her hands on a butane lighter somewhere and burned up her bed using an oxygen tank. They have lots of oxygen tanks around burn centers I guess."

"This happened while you were there?" I asked

"No, she transferred to another hospital," she replied. "Closer to her home town. I heard it from a nurse at my hospital. This time she didn't survive. But this is really how I decided that I was not crazy. I decided that I was redeemable. Because, as liberating as my actions were, I could never think of repeating them."

"Sad," I said. "She felt the need to end it all. She probably had a brilliant mind turned sideways. That's what I have discovered about most of the mental patients I have met."

"Interesting that you should say that, Clyde," she continued. "I think she analyzed things much the same way you do. In fact, before I met you she was the person who most knew how to get things down to the bare bones. I still think about her every day. I think about her wasted intellect. I used to dream about her all of the time. Every time I dreamt about her, she was near water and I always had the sense that she was going to do herself harm.

"She used to say that she was named after Roxane from the play *Cyrano de Bergerac.* But she saw that Roxane as superficial; she was attracted to a man for his appearance and Roxy claimed she was never like that. On the contrary, she was quite beautiful before she got burned up and had turned down many handsome suitors. She detested physical beauty and called fire 'The Great Equalizer'. I tend to think that the girls in her sorority must have been physically attractive, at least some of them.

"So she was sort of like Roxane turned on her ear. Whereas Roxane in the play saw the error in her ways and fell for the ugly man with every other desirable feature a woman would want, my Roxy decided to make all beauty equally grotesque. Although she thought of fire as the most beautiful thing in the world.

"I asked her about this paradox of fire creating such ugliness, she shrugged and said, 'Fire is always a paradox, it is everything; it is destroyer and creator.' Hard to argue with that logic."

"Indeed," I interrupted.

"I asked Roxy, that if instead of destroying beauty, she could have just found a man with qualities such as Cyrano's…,"

"I can answer that, Bon," I jumped in. "He doesn't exist."

"That was her answer," Bonnie replied, a little shocked. "She said ugly men thought ugly thoughts and pretty men thought ugly thoughts. Roxane was a simpleton to be bowled over by a pretty face and twice the fool to be swayed by words."

She paused.

"I still think about her all of the time," she yawned. "Goodnight, Clyde my love. My hero. My Cyrano."

To this, I had no response except to squeeze her tight and kiss her on the forehead. I dared not call her Roxane or Roxy, so I tried my best to quote from the play I had read in ninth grade and seen performed a few times since:

"And what is a kiss, specifically? A pledge properly sealed, a promise seasoned to taste, a vow stamped with the immediacy of a lip, a rosy circle drawn around the verb 'to love.' A kiss is a message too intimate for the ear, infinity captured in the bee's brief visit to a flower, secular communication with an aftertaste of heaven, the pulse rising from the heart to utter its name on a lover's lip: 'Forever.'"

"You are man worthy of my affections," Bonnie whispered as she drifted into slumber.

I loosened my grip on her, but not by much, as sleep also overtook me.

CHAPTER 41 – BENJAMIN PARKER: ATTORNEY AT LAW

The sign was wooden, hand-painted and hand-carved. It was painted in glossy gold and the artist actually took great care with the detail. The B in Benjamin started with a large swoosh and was connected with another large swoosh to the e. The n stood alone. All of the lettering was done in this same half-cursive style and the letters were all tilted to the right. It was all on display on a weathered-looking piece of what looked like driftwood. The sign was fastened to the left of the back door of a reclaimed old row house set amongst other row houses that had all been converted to businesses.

I had time to study the sign because I was standing alone on the back steps waiting for Bonnie to finish explaining herself to her father. We had arrived at his law office at 8:45 AM and hoped to get his attention before he walked through the front door. We didn't want to alert his secretary, his customers, or any other tenants that the old lawyer was being visited by his fugitive murdering daughter and her fugitive insane kidnapper boyfriend.

I had suspected that this was our destination when Bonnie suggested that we drive towards the big city. She had only given me details of her plan when we woke up at that rest area on the interstate.

"Clyde, I want to see my dad," she said, as my eyes opened at 7:15 AM to the first shaft of daylight peaking over the trees.

She was sitting in the passenger seat massaging her legs. I guessed that this was part of the therapy she had been going through in order to keep her leg muscles from breaking down. I rolled over to look at her and I remember thinking that I would give anything to see her dance again. She was always insistent that her goal was to dance and not simply to walk.

She looked over at me again while she rubbed and stretched. "He works less than an hour from here and he's usually early to work."

"I… I think we should go see him too," I said as I struggled to move my brain from its slumber.

So after a restroom break, we were on the road to the inner-city where her father had set up shop after he lost his job at the big important law firm. The drive didn't take very long and we were parked by the curb out in front as Benjamin came walking up the sidewalk.

"There he is!" She said as a tall gray-haired man in a long beige overcoat came strolling towards us with a bounce in his step one might expect from a younger man.

I suspected that Benjamin was in his early to mid-fifties since Bonnie was almost thirty-three and Benjamin was in college when she was born. From the looks of him, I could tell that he was the type of person I would want on my side. His career and family had come crashing down around him, and here he was arriving early at work at a place where most of his clients were poor. As he drew closer, he absolutely shone confidence. I could see where his daughter had inherited these traits. Bonnie told me that he rode the train to work every day and walked the remaining six blocks from the closest stop.

"He told me that he had his fill of rich people and their pretentious lifestyle," she said as we watched him walk up the street. "He says that it also helps him to understand the world his clients live in. Back in the day, he used to have a car service pick him up and drive him to work every day, and then take him home at night."

"Honk your horn!" she said suddenly.

I obliged. The brilliant-looking man in the long overcoat stopped walking about 25 feet in front of where we were parked. A flash of recognition appeared on his face and then he continued towards us, the bounce in his step now gone. In a few seconds, he was bending over next to Bonnie's window. He shot a look at me before he smiled and kissed her on the cheek.

"How have you been?" He said to her, as he crouched down next to the car.

"I've been great, Dad," Bonnie answered.

"I know that both of you escaped," he said as the smile disappeared. "I need you to pull around the back, Clyde," Benjamin motioned his right arm towards the alley on the left next to his office building. "The police have already been to my house."

He turned away from the car, carrying his battered black briefcase and headed for the front door of his building without looking back. I did as I was instructed and pulled into the driveway and down the alley next to the building. In a few seconds, we were in the small pea-gravel parking area behind his row-house office. Soon Benjamin walked out the back door pushing a wheelchair down a ramp. It was as if he had this planned. My mind jumped on the idea that maybe he did; maybe Bonnie did too.

He rolled the wheelchair clumsily across the gravel until he reached the rear of the passenger side of the car and stopped. I got out of the car, walked around the front, opened the passenger door, and lifted Bonnie out of her seat. She wrapped her arms around my neck as I carried her to the wheelchair. I sat her in the chair, but as I motioned to push the chair, Bonnie grabbed my arm.

"Clyde," she said, "let me do it. I haven't had to roll on gravel in quite a while."

I loosened my hold on the chair and just stood by the back of the car as she glided smoothly across the gravel to the ramp. Benjamin also just stood and watched with what can only be described as pride.

"I want to talk with her alone first," he said as he put his right hand on my left shoulder. "You understand?"

"Of course," I said hesitantly.

"You can wait out here," Benjamin said over his shoulder as he rushed to open the back door that Bonnie had already reached. "It shouldn't take too long."

So as I stood in the cold by the back door admiring the originality of the sign, I began thinking about all of the things that Bonnie had told me about her father. She spoke of him often, more than anyone else who had been in her life. Her mother was a subject that she avoided on a personal level, even though she did talk about her dancing career. Her father, however, was the star of most of her reflections about life.

"He is the reason I never gave up," she said to me once as we stared at the ceiling while lying in my small bed late at night. "To outward appearances, he has it all, a successful practice and a lovely wife. But people don't see all of the hard work and determination behind his success. His father worked at every job he could find to provide for his son. He had no mother for most of his life. I think he got everything from his father and I think that is true with me also.

"You never know about yourself until you are down and out. He used to say that to me all of the time. He said, 'Anyone can be ready for the world when everything is going right. But life just isn't that way.' He always said to not blame others for your situation and to never think that nothing can be done. If you see how I am and wonder why I never gave up, the answer is Benjamin Parker. He never just talked in clichés either; he would tell me stories about his father and how he overcame adversity.

"One time my grandfather fell off the ladder and could have just lay around and complained or made excuses, but got back to work as soon as he could get out of bed. His dad was a locksmith, but he was also the guy who would plow the snow out of your driveway or pull your car out of the ditch. He taught himself veterinary medicine and he helped several struggling farmers get supplies through some of his contacts in bigger cities. He would even hire temporary help from among parolees just to help them get back on their feet.

"Benjamin is exactly the same. When he was in college, he would tutor other members of the football team. He had to curb these activities when I was born, but he still found time to teach adults how to read and he always was showing me things his father taught him about cars, or animals, or how to pick a lock."

I remembered all of Bonnie's words about this man and I remember thinking that she absolutely glowed when she talked about him. I knew that I would take any advice he offered and do my best not to let him down. I also had a slight inkling that he might turn me in to the police. I think he knew that Bonnie would not be severely punished and that I would be sent away to some lockup and never put her in this spot again. I mostly trusted my intuition that he would see that she was deeply in love and not just out for cheap thrills. But the doubts and fear still began to eat away at that certainty.

So I alternated between looking at the wonderful sign and other features of the row house architecture and staring at the adjacent panorama of backyards. There were differing heights and conditions of all of the chain length fences. There were junk cars with graffiti. There was one house to the far left with a nice fence and a well-manicured yard with bird feeders. I instantly associated that house with an older couple who were too old to move out of this rundown neighborhood.

In my mind I began to fantasize about being part of that couple and having lived a fulfilled life and not having to explain myself to everyone I met. My short fantasy was soon interrupted by the noise of footsteps approaching the door and the creak of Benjamin slowly opening the door.

"Clyde, could you come in?" he asked politely as a he poked his head out the door towards me.

I stood for a moment on the top back step without any response. I finally just walked up to the door and followed him inside. We passed through a short darkened hallway while my eyes adjusted to the lack of light. We passed a bathroom on the right and an open door to a basement on the left. I followed Benjamin into his office where Bonnie sat right in the middle of the room. His office was decorated with pictures, diplomas, plaques, and trophies.

There was an impressive array of humanitarian awards and civic pride plaques. His law school diploma was on the wall behind his desk next to a framed picture of him shaking hands with a young man being supported by leg braces. His desk was neatly arranged with an In Box and an Out Box on opposite ends and the pens and pencils in proper circular holders. Other office supplies were lined up in neat order by descending height. I paused to look at a medal that hung inside a frame on the wall nearest to the door. It read: *Benjamin Parker, Urban League Man of the Year.*

The Urban League Man of the Year casually sat down on the right edge of his desk with one leg still resting on the floor. The look on his face was serious, yet kindly and receptive. He was not much older than me, but he seemed to me to have an air of sophisticated confidence which made it seem as if he had been around the world and back.

"Have a seat, Clyde," he said as he motioned toward the chair to the right of Bonnie.

I looked over at Bonnie and for the first time I realized that her face betrayed no emotion. I moved over to the chair next to her, sat down, and reached out for her hand. She clenched my hand and I looked into her eyes once more. Again there was nothing to betray what had transpired between her and her father while I waited outside. I turned my head towards the distinguished looking older gentleman who was still casually sitting on the edge of his desk.

"Bonnie speaks very highly of you," Benjamin finally said after I had settled in my chair. "She seems to know all of your secrets. She says that you are the genuine article and a man of substance."

He said these words with no irony, no sarcasm, and no bitterness. They were all matter-of-fact type declarations. I looked at Bonnie and she seemed to have become possessed by a new stone-faced demeanor. I did not find this development comforting.

"She is willing to follow you to wherever you go, Mr. Barrow," he continued. "Just where are you going?"

I paused as I realized that I had not considered that I may have to explain details of my impulsive plans to someone other than Bonnie. She had not really bothered me for details.

"I have a friend who owns an island," I finally said. "We will be safe there and beyond the reach of the law, if they bother to look at all."

"How will you get there?" he asked.

The trial lawyer was attempting to rattle the witness and the witness had very few answers. The entire escape plan existed only in my brain and even there it was spotty and tenuous. My answers were destined to be likewise.

"I stole a car, I will steal a boat," I said, as my grasping for answers latched onto this nugget.

"How far is this island from here?" The prosecution kept up the pressure.

"Close to 1,000 miles, but I intend to use the inter-coastal waterway...,"

"That waterway is patrolled by the Coast Guard," he interrupted.

"We will travel mostly at night..."

"And what about safety? Bonnie is not the best swimmer in her condition...," he said with a more confrontational tone.

"Actually, she is quite a good swimmer if it comes to that," I shot back and then looked over at her as she sat silent.

After an awkward silence, I decided to make my case.

"Sir, I appreciate your concern, but you do realize that the risk to her is not very great. If I am caught, I will surely go to a maximum security prison for a long time. If she is caught, she will just go back to Tallhill and live mostly like she was with maybe more monitoring. I don't know if you approve, but I do think that Bonnie is one of the finest human beings I have ever met. She is the one person I have had in my life who builds my confidence and gives me hope. What we feel about each other is genuine. While it may be hard for most people to conceptualize what we have, we actually can communicate without words at times. I feel lucky to have found her and I will fight if necessary to keep her by my side."

"It is exactly THAT desperation that concerns me," he said. "What if you decide that you will not go back to prison and it all ends violently? How can I be assured that she will not be hurt?"

"I guess you can't," I confessed. "It doesn't mean she shouldn't be given a chance at real happiness."

Benjamin looked unconvinced.

"Look, you can call the cops at any time and have both of us locked up. I will be sent far away and you can go back to visiting Bonnie in her asylum on visitor days. My words aren't going to change your mind about this, but maybe my sincerity will."

He stood up and walked around the front of his desk to the left side while he looked at the floor. He plopped down on the chair behind his desk, let out a sigh, and then scooted the chair up and leaned forward with his arms folded on the desk.

"Bonnie is my only child and has always been the light of my life," he began. "But she is stubborn and smart like her mother… and her father. Her marriage was a dream come true for all of us; I was going to be a partner in an important law firm and her mother's dance studio was doing brisk business with élite clientele.

"But her marriage was a sham," he continued. "For that, we are all to blame. I never once asked Bonnie if she loved Chandler. If I had, I probably would have detected a hesitation in her response. Even then, I would have ignored it. But at least I would have asked the question and I would be less at fault, as if that matters.

"Clyde, while you were waiting outside, I DID ask her that question about you. Her answer was immediate and complete and affirmative. Her eyes glowed and her face flushed with excitement. I know she wasn't trying to mislead me. I believe her and I think she deserves a chance at real happiness."

With that, Benjamin got up from his seat, walked around the desk, stood next to me and stuck out his hand. I stood up and firmly shook his hand.

"Take good care of her, Clyde," he said as his eyes moistened.

"You can count on me, sir," I said, fighting my own emotions.

I knew from my own recent emotional goodbye to Annette that I should probably leave the office. I looked back at Bonnie's now tearful smiling face and excused myself before we all broke down in a quivering emotional mush. I walked to the door and pulled it shut behind me. I stopped to use the bathroom before I left the building. After splashing water on my face and bracing myself, I walked down the hall and out the back entrance and waited by the hand-made sign.

After about five minutes, I heard the sound of the wheelchair coming slowly down the hall. The door opened and Benjamin pushed Bonnie out into the mid-morning sun. He looked up at me from his wheelchair pushing to notice that I was looking at the hand-made sign.

"Bonnie made that," he said as he stood straight up with a burst of pride.

"Somehow, I knew that," I said.

"I made that my first month at Tallhill," Bonnie added.

It was at this point that I realized that Bonnie had said nothing while in the presence of her father and me. She told me later that she wanted me to make my case all by myself; for her to plead with him would have made her seem like a petulant child. I agreed that the mature and responsible thing was for me to make my case alone and that it was the best way a lawyer could handle and process the information. It was very cunning, and in this case it worked.

"The wood is from the sign from my grandfather's old locksmith shop," Bonnie continued. "It was his office warming present when he moved here. This is the first time I have seen it displayed."

At this point, I could see that leaving was going to be awkward and difficult. I stood for a few moments trying to decide whether I should push Bonnie down the ramp or let Benjamin perform the task. This issue was resolved once again by Bonnie, who looked over her shoulder to her father and nodded. He let go of the handles of the wheelchair and she slowly guided herself down the ramp.

Benjamin and I smiled at each other. It was the first and only time this happened and words were not necessary. I sensed his approval of me and I stuck out my hand to shake. He did not offer his hand in return, but said, "Help Bonnie into the car, I will be right back." He then disappeared behind the back door.

I did as I was told and opened the door for Bonnie and helped her into the passenger seat. I closed the door, folded the wheelchair and put it in the back seat. As I began to walk around the car to start the now cold engine, Benjamin reappeared. I stood by the rear door of the driver's side looking at him over the car's roof. He motioned for me to get inside and I did so. I started the engine and in a moment, he was at Bonnie's window. I rolled the electric window down.

"This is all of the cash I had in my safe," he said as he passed a big wad of bills over to Bonnie. "I have paid for a room at the Heatherton downtown for one night. You are Guadalupe and Daniel Figueroa."

He reached into his breast pocket and pulled out four cards. "These are pre-paid calling cards," he said. "I give them to some of my clients in case they get in a jam. There's fifty dollars on each of them. Call me if… well call me if you get in a jam."

He stuck his upper body through the open window and hugged her as I sat uncomfortably. He shook my hand as the hug ended.

"Be safe, you two," he said and removed himself from the car.

We both watched as he walked away from the car. He stopped after a few paces, turned around, and walked back towards us.

"Bonnie, you might be thinking about stopping to see your mother," he said as he bent down again at the window. "I wouldn't recommend it. She will probably call the police."

He paused, stood up, and walked away again. Stopping to turn around once more, he yelled, "But you do what you want."

I threw the car in reverse and backed the car out of the alley. We pulled onto the street and into the great unknown with more trepidation than before. We had more money and we had more fear. On the other hand, our relationship had at least one approval, but I had to know what Bonnie had planned before I made any further moves.

"Should we see your mom?" I asked.

"They are getting divorced," Bonnie said as she fought through the emotion of the statement. "My fault too," then she broke down in tears.

I decided not to raise the subject again as she worked through the guilt and pain in her mind. I drove aimlessly in a large lazy square of right turns for about forty-five minutes while I waited for Bonnie to give me any indication of what we should do next.

"I need to go see her," she said finally.

My stomach sank.

* * * * * * * * * *

In the inner-city business district there were several tall buildings that had undergone a sort of urban renewal. They were all turn-of-last-century brick, mortar, glass, and steel structures. The bricks were variously colored brown-gray, or black-gray, or blue-gray, or gray-gray. The architects may have had something artistic in mind other that just large concrete rectangles, but that was not betrayed by the results. These were, first and foremost, functional structures. These were office buildings with businesses on the ground floor. On one block there were coffee shops on all four corners of the intersection. Next to one of the coffee shops was a dance studio with pink lettering and blue fringe on the window. It read *Rosemary's Dance Studio.*

We had parked three blocks away and we were lucky to find a spot that close. This older part of the city was beginning a sort of renaissance; many structures had scaffolding rising to work on various stages of restoration on façades and porticos. Windows were being hoisted and power tools performed a sort of construction symphony. It was an inspiring thought and it put me in a good mood as I pushed Bonnie down the sidewalk in her wheelchair. It was one of the few times she made this concession, but the rough terrain of broken sidewalks and electric cables made my help necessary.

We wheeled slowly down the street in a very awkward stop and go fashion until we eventually found ourselves in front of Rosemary's studio. The walk to the studio was not filled with anticipation or nervousness for me. I was too busy negotiating obstacles to think of anything else. Bonnie's thoughts were probably more disquieting and confusing. I assumed so and I didn't dare broach the subject. It was obvious and words were useless gestures when dealing with such feelings. So we stopped in front of the big picture window with the name of the studio on it.

"Do you want me to wait here?" I asked.

Bonnie didn't answer right away. Instead she wheeled herself over to the window and leaned into it until her face was pressed against the glass with her hands cupped around her head. I became curious about what she could see. I likewise pressed my face to the glass.

Inside was an older woman in a black leotard standing in front of a group of preteen girls. She looked exactly like Bonnie from this distance except for the gray in her hair. Her body was well maintained and she stood straight and still like a statue of a dancer. The young girls were being helped through their steps by young women in white leotards. There was the faint sound of piano music playing. Unsure what to do, I just stared at the scene that was playing out before me. The older woman would make hand gestures and the young women would pay strict attention. The older woman would start and stop the music on a small stereo sitting on a chair next to her. The little girls would turn, or jump, or pirouette one at a time as instructed. They would step and slide in groups.

We watched this scene for probably twenty minutes completely undetected by the people inside. Eventually, Bonnie pulled her head away from the glass and looked up at me.

"Let's go Clyde," she said.

I paused and blinked a few times then grabbed the handles of the chair so we could negotiate the gauntlet of potholes, workers, and power tools on the way back to the car. We headed for the Heatherton Hotel to spend the evening. Bonnie said nothing on the way there and very little that night at the hotel. The only words I can recall from that night were after I had turned the television off and the room grew dark.

"Gold shoes," she said, then cuddled up next to me as we spent one last night in a nice bed for what would be good long while. I left the words alone.

CHAPTER 42 – ACCORDING TO BONNIE

Bonnie kept a journal. It contained thoughts and observations about life that she had previously shared with no one. She eventually shared them with me, but only after she had pored through my manifesto and even then she had given me a very short time to read a few selected passages. It was only after we escaped that I was allowed full access to her most recent journal. It was the journal she began keeping in the early part of that year. She had sent all of her previous journals to her father for safekeeping. After we visited her father, she told me that he would send them when we got to our island.

After we left the hotel in the morning, we went to a small café for breakfast. It had only been eight days since I escaped from Tallhill and Bonnie had only escaped two nights before. Somehow it seemed much longer, but we were a little desperate and we were on the run. Time kind of undergoes a weird suspension in one's mind under these conditions. At least that is my observation. It seemed like a month to me.

Although desperate and anxious, we also wanted to live a little. We ordered a big breakfast in that café next to the five-star hotel and we took our time eating it. Bonnie ordered eggs benedict, with a large serving of bacon, and we both indulged in large stacks of pancakes topped with fresh strawberries and whipped cream. When we had finished eating, Bonnie reached in her messenger bag and passed me her latest journal. It had a dark green cover and in the spaces provided for name and date it read: *Bonnie Parker, The Future*.

I opened the journal and began to read the first entry. What follows are the selected readings of what I read over the next few days. Periodically, after we escaped, Bonnie would make new entries which are included in the succeeding excerpts:

March 9

I have now been at Tallhill for over seven years and I never get used to being alone at night. I was alone when I was married quite frequently. Even though Chandler was probably nailing some socialite during those evenings, I remember not being sad that I was alone, but grateful for the solitude. In my solitude, I could always put on some Tchaikovsky or some Salsa and dance in my giant living room. All I have now is this goddamned wheelchair.

I avoided prison of the four-walls and barred kind; I am confined to an even more oppressive place. I cannot feel below my waist and I cannot overcome that barrier. No prison walls ever built can contain a person as well as the loss of legs. It is a life sentence worse than any that can ever be handed down by judge or jury. In my case, it was handed down only minutes after my crime.

The loneliness is compounded by the fact that I cannot ever make things right for anyone. It is downright depressing to think of such things and I have had numerous doctors try to prescribe anti-depressants for me, but I have always wanted to get through this on my own. Like a brave soldier fighting a battle that no one will ever know about.

On nights like this, I wish one of those doctors was here for me. I would take the whole drawer full of Prozac or Zoloft or whatever magic mushrooms they had for me. I want to forget every damn thing that ever happened. I want to be Rosemary and Benjamin's bright-eyed little girl in the flowered dress. I want ponytails and ice cream. I want something besides this goddamned wheelchair.

March 28

The girl I was mentoring left Tallhill last night. Her rich parents transferred her to another institution. She is quite young and she is a cutter. Her name is Nadia and she has been slicing and piercing herself since before she was ten years-old. She was around twenty when she was sent here by her parents. I think she was making amazing progress at Tallhill. It is a real shame that she left. The parents really didn't give the administration a reason for taking her away. They really didn't need to; the reason was me.

Nadia's last name is Harrington. She is from old money; old snooty money. They are big friends with the Foxes. Lana Fox was the girl who was screwing my Chandler. She was the girl I slashed. It probably didn't take the Harringtons long to figure out that I was here and Nadia probably mentioned that I was mentoring her and that sort of thing was not going to sit well with these society types.

I am not even upset or surprised at this development. I suspect that I am just another in the long line of therapists, psychologists, psychiatrists, and counselors that this poor girl has seen. She had been here all of six weeks. When we first met, she was quiet, but not very outwardly troubled. Her file said that she had been on Paxil and Ritalin and all of the happy-time miracle drugs for young people with problems.

After our third session she began to talk badly about her mother. Not in wicked terms, but in a sort of dismissive way. She had not talked much at all until then. I cracked open that door when I asked very casually, "Tell me about your mother."

"Let's talk about something else," she said.

I have the notes from all of our meetings, so I can actually quote her word for word. During that meeting, I steered us in another direction, but later in meeting five, she opened up a little more about Mrs. Chelsea Harrington.

I know Chelsea a little bit; she was in my little social group, but always seemed to be a little above it all. She was nice enough to me, but seemed a little put off by my family pedigree. This attitude was not uncommon among the "old money" types, so I was not offended. Hell nothing these rich old bags did offended me at the time I was in their midst.

My research into cutters told me that some childhood trauma may have triggered some type of self-loathing. My job as a mentor was not to treat her illness, but to help her adjust to her institutional life and hopefully help her become productive in the real world. I knew that Nadia would always have money and servants and that she wasn't going to have to stay at Tallhill any longer than she wanted to. I decided I wanted her to know she wasn't alone.

"I know the world that you were raised in," I said during that fifth meeting. "That world did this to me," I told her as I motioned to my presence in the wheelchair.

From that point on she was an open book to me.

We even began to socialize a little. She worked in the bakery; away from sharp objects of course, but she baked cookies and bread for the kitchen. She even began to bring cookies to our meetings. Soon she was telling me about her mother's brutal treatment of her brother. She had a brother who was a tad overweight; not much, maybe twenty pounds, but Chelsea was always ridiculing him about his weight.

Chelsea was a looker. She had been a beauty queen decades ago, and she was twenty-five years younger than Caldwell Harrington. She was his third wife; the trophy wife. She bore him two kids: Gerald and Nadia. Gerald resembled her chubby daddy and Nadia was the spitting image of her beauty queen mother. Nadia was her pride and joy and Gerald's appearance was undesirable to Chelsea.

I think I quite correctly diagnosed her syndrome as being a sympathetic response to her mother's cruelty to Gerald. This was further bolstered by Nadia's reaction to being assigned to the bakery. Not only did she love to bake, she loved to eat. If I had to guess, I would say that she had gained around thirty pounds at Tallhill. I let it go. Some therapists might say she was trading one disorder for another. She was not cutting herself, that's all I cared about.

Besides, I'm not a therapist… and the cookies were delicious.

April 8

My condition is fair today. When I am between mentoring gigs, I read a lot. Most days when I am caught up in some really interesting subject, I forget to fill in this journal. The more I do this, the more I feel I am explaining myself. I do not like explaining myself to anyone. With wheelchairs, there is always the story that needs to be told; how did I get here?

Rather than horrify and scar them for life with a horrible story, I can look right back at them and say, "Never mind that, here's what I intend to do in order to get out of this."

Tabitha, the girl I mentored a year ago, had written a college thesis about the promise of embryonic stem cells. I guess she was inspired by me and wanted to give me some glimmer of hope. So I started reading about stem cells and their regenerative properties within the spine. I read that the less serious cases like mine were considered too risky for stem cells. The risk of doing worse damage seems too great at this time. The doctors who have used the stem cells have used them on quadriplegics. There seems to be no current rush to make paraplegics walk.

So I do all of the reading I can about the ways I might walk again. Stem cells seem to be the current rage, but I may need to go to another country to avoid the restrictions. With them I may walk, but without them I cannot walk. With them perhaps I can dance. I want to try.

July 4

Today we sat and watched fireworks. I feel sometimes like I am a little girl when I am told that I will attend the fireworks or miss out on the ice cream. I am now in my early thirties and I have not by any means given up my dignity, but I am subjected to these constant reminders that I will always be treated like a child.

This place makes any celebration of Independence Day seem ludicrous. I have not been independent since I landed between the sixth and seventh discs of my thoracic region. Even the able-bodied members are constantly monitored and told where to be. Every goddamned one of them has the same shitty smile that reveals nothing but what complete dupes they are. I know I could be in worse places, but I certainly do not feel independent on this day or any other day. The security of confinement is no place to tease people with dumb concepts like liberty. All smile at the fireworks, but if they are really that happy it would have to be without realizing the irony of the absurdity.

September 1

I got my new mentoring project today. His name is Clyde Barrow. He is the first man that I have mentored and he is older than me. He is being transferred from the mental ward in the old state prison. He's been in there less than a year, so I hope he is not a hardened criminal. I have folders and notes from psychiatrists to go through. He even has written his own manifesto. After reading most of it, I have decided that he is either quite brilliant, deeply disturbed, or both. Either way, the criminal justice systems seems to think he is not dangerous.

He attacked a co-worker and was found to be under quite a lot of stress. Perhaps they think that he was a one-time thing like me. The manifesto has been quite helpful in getting me acquainted with this fellow. In fact, I think I know more about him than I learn about most of my mentoring subjects after three months.

September 2

Clyde arrives here today. I find that I am anxious to meet him and talk with him. I even did something that I have never done before; I left him a note on his door. I did not sign the note, but I wanted him to know that someone was here to help. I think it also helps establish myself as his mentor. I did not sign the note; it was a suggestion from one of the other mentors here.

I also had to give a talk at the catharsis center. I talked about the little girl who I used to visit back when I was rich and powerful. Her name was Molly and she had a brain riddled with tumors. She died one day when I was attending her. Her mother held one hand and I held the other as she passed. Molly was probably the most important person in the world to me for a long time. I enjoyed seeing her bright smiling face and she taught me what it was to be dignified. She suffered her condition with such incredible grace that I find her example to be comforting until this very day. I told the catharsis group about Molly and we all had a good cry together. Most of the cases here are sad and some even hopeless. Far be it for me to tell people how to deal with their own mental illness. I just want to give them my perspective.

September 3

Met Clyde today; he is at once the most interesting, charming, and confounding man. He had piercing blue eyes and brown hair that is going gray. I let myself in his room to settle in. I didn't want him to feel he had to help me get in the door, so I got access to his room from the front office. They see no complications from me in my condition.

Clyde immediately impressed me and seems completely out of place in a mental institution He always seems like he's going somewhere. This place is just a stop along the way to him and I think he truly believes that. I don't know if I doubt him.

He was completely in charge of our first meeting after the first couple of minutes. I opened up to him almost completely. This is not my normal style, but I felt it was fair since I knew so much about him. There will be time to get his whole story anyways. I do admit to being slightly bewildered when I left. This kind of feeling is rare for me and I do think I should be careful with this one or I may get drawn in.

November 7

We made love last night; Clyde and I. It was an incredible experience. It was like the first time, but more exciting. It really was the first time in many years. It is very hard to find a point of reference except for the first time with Chandler. I remember being more nervous than anything on that occasion. He was a man of the world and I was a novice. I recall not wanting to disappoint him. I had even read all of the manuals and novels of the day. So that occasion and all of the early occasions seemed more like exams that I had to study for. On those occasions, the overwhelming feeling of apprehension followed by inadequacy afterwards.

With Clyde, I felt anticipation; almost from the first moment we met. I have been debating for weeks whether I should approach this subject with him. I know it must seem weird to most men to even consider sex with a woman in a wheelchair. There is some reading material out there on this subject, but I doubt that Clyde would be like young Bonnie of the past and treat the challenge like studying for an exam.

I had left Clyde a note on his door three nights previous, stating my intentions. I had no other way to approach the subject. I had tried a hundred times to come out with the words, but I always shied away. With Clyde's years of experience, I decided that I needed to be a little coy with my feelings and pretend that I was still in control. So I hit the ball into his court and really gave him no option other than accept my proposal or detail reasons why he would not be making love to me. In the end there was only one proper response.

I have suspected for some time that he felt much the same about me as I do about him. He was gentle and passionate. He was considerate of my condition and my feelings. I will not go into detail since I am not a writer of the types of books that I used to read when preparing myself for Chandler. Suffice to say that I could spend every night of the rest of my life exactly like last night with little difficulty.

December 3

Clyde left me last night or early this morning. He escaped and there is no reason to expect that he will return. I find my mind racing in a thousand different directions as I have no idea whether or not he will be captured or not. He will certainly be returned to prison if captured. Other attempted escapees were sent to maximum security prisons or more stringent mental facilities.

The alarms were sounded early this morning and I heard what must have been the security staff running down the hallway as the whole place went into lockdown mode. Lockdown mode was really no big deal since most members were sleeping. I hope I see Clyde someday, but I don't know how that is possible.

Her December 3rd entry was the last in the journal before her escape. The staff at Tallhill had confiscated her journal after my escape to see if they could find any clues as to what my plans were. The journal had been given back the day before I returned for her. There was not much detail about me that couldn't be found in Dr. Silk's notes or in my manifesto. Bonnie was coy with them the whole time and gave no indication that she knew anything about my plans. They decided that I had my separate reasons for wanting to escape. Just to be thorough, they decided to toss her room for further clues. She had already eaten the note that I left her.

Just like in the spy movies.

December 11

Clyde and I have escaped from Tallhill. He returned for me last night and we have been driving ever since. My head is filled with exciting new possibilities, although all of my past has come rushing into my consciousness. I think of all of the people in my past, like the family in the Midwest who had planned to come and see me, but now may never see me again. I think of the sick children in the hospital who helped me gain perspective.

Mostly I think about my parents. I will probably ask Clyde to take me to see Benjamin. I doubt he would refuse that request. He does love me. I also think about Rosemary. I have not yet decided if I actually want to see her. She has stubbornly refused to visit me at any time during my confinement.

While I do understand her sense of shame and disappointment, I am hurt and fear that a confrontation will not give any relief to my frustration. She is a stubborn woman and I understand from Benjamin that I have inherited this trait from her. This is a backhanded compliment, but he always adds that I have also inherited her talent and intellect.

Rosemary IS quite talented and quite brilliant. She had completely choreographed a ballet based on Cyrano de Bergerac. When she was reminded that this had already been accomplished, she replied that she did not like the way that it was interpreted. She spent tireless hours working on the project and she was planning to use the students at her academy in the cast. When she wasn't busy composing or choreographing, she was fund-raising. She had lined up several rich donors who were going to help her stage the ballet by renting the hall and funding for materials and promotion. She was even ready to set a date for the premiere.

Then I killed Chandler. All of that ended. There is nothing I can do to ever replace the lives and dreams I shattered. I just wish I had my mommy back.

I was still sitting at the café with my nearly empty cold plate next to my left elbow which supported me on the table. I closed the journal and dabbed my eyes with a cloth napkin as I looked out the window at the passing pedestrian traffic. I looked back at her smiling face with her head cocked to one side. In response, I looked down at the table.

CHAPTER 43 – THE DANCE

There were three of them; one very large, one quite big, and one about my size. I am not normally predisposed to violence; my bombing escapade notwithstanding, but these three men were all standing near my green Mustang, and one was engaged in some kind of rude behavior which did not seem to be very pleasing to Bonnie, who was sitting in the passenger seat with the window open. Her eyes looked desperate and scared when I caught a glimpse of her while walking from the convenience store.

We had stopped at the store at Bonnie's request. She decided she wanted to have a little fun and feel like a normal person before we again became fugitives. The big breakfast at the diner had kept us past noon. We hit the road reluctantly and Bonnie lazily suggested that we head towards the coast and I drifted in a somewhat easterly direction until I had drifted us to a wide corner. On that corner was one of those big convenience stores.

"I want a drink," Bonnie giggled as I pulled into the vast parking area.

I purchased three 40-ounce malt liquors and a bottle of Cabernet. Behind the counter was a clerk who resembled my middle-school English teacher. There was a flash of recognition for a second as he looked up at me while he went about his business. As he put my Cabernet into the paper bag, then set them both into a plastic sack, I became convinced that he really was Mr. Danning from 8th grade English. Ironically he was the one who had assigned *Cyrano de Bergerac* for the class to read so many years ago. I didn't know if he was an amazing look-alike or if Mr. Danning had retired and bought a convenience store near the coast just to enter Cyrano into my consciousness again.

Mr. Danning also would often quote Bob Dylan in class. I spent my time in line trying to come up with a way to make store-clerk-version Mr. Danning quote Dylan so I could prove he was really who I imagined he was.

Mr. Danning continued to pack my 40-ouncers into individual paper bags and then all three into a large plastic sack. The bill was twelve dollars and forty-six cents and I even threw the 54 cents change into the take-a-penny-leave-a-penny cup; a minor gesture that got a twinkle from Mr. Danning. I decided to take the opportunity to try to see if this was the actual Mr. Danning.

"Just in case someone needs eleven dollar bills and he only got ten," I said rather loud with a smile on my face.

This brought an immediate response from this once-renowned Dylan quote machine.

"Look out kid. It's somethin' you did," he replied with great enthusiasm and even let out a little laugh at the end.

I laughed too. I even had a bit of a bounce to my step as I came out of the store. For that instant I was not the fugitive lunatic, but that young boy who was interested in literature and poetry.

As I was bouncing through the door trying to remember the balcony scene with Roxane, Cyrano, and Christian, I noticed the three gentlemen I mentioned earlier. There were two by the pumps and the big one was over by the Mustang leaning all over the passenger side back door with his head cocked while he was talking to Bonnie. She shot me a look that made it clear she was not comfortable talking to this guy.

I glanced over at his buddies; the smallest of the three, the guy my size, was presently pumping gas into a motorcycle with a sidecar. He had no facial hair, but long sideburns and wore a sleeveless denim jacket with a logo stitched on the back that featured the devil in a circle with the word BADASSES stitched underneath it.

My guess was that he rode in the sidecar.

His partner, big and hairy, who was probably too big for the sidecar, was standing and smiling with his hands in his pockets as he looked on at the biggest one who was still leaning on the Mustang and saying something inaudible to my ears. Bonnie was not looking at him at all, but she would look over at me periodically as I approached from her right side. I decided to not head directly for the vehicle. The bounce was still in my step, but my smile had faded.

I learned several things in prison from real criminals; one of those things was how to win a fight against long odds:

1. Look harmless, even scared.
2. Hit the biggest one first and with everything.
3. Fight dirty and don't stop until they are all defeated or run away.
4. Superior tactics can defeat superior numbers.

I walked between the biggest one and the other two as if I was leaving the premises to walk up the sidewalk, the gas pumps on the left and the Mustang on my right. I passed all of them completely and kept walking until I reached the sidewalk. I never turned to look at any of them at the scene. At the sidewalk I turned right then looked back at the scene. The big gooney-looking one was next to his own bike, but leaning on my car and now he seemed to be stroking Bonnie's hair as he reached inside the passenger window.

I turned back towards the car and walked up behind him making as much noise as possible. I shuffled up to him as he continued to use my car as a leaning post. I cleared my throat. This startled the large man and he jumped a little as he straightened up and turned around to face me.

"Is there something you want?" he sneered.

I stepped back while looking into his face and brought the shopping bag with the three malt liquors up into his groin with as much force as I could muster. I was still looking into his face, but my aim was true. His curious eyes now took on the look of surprise followed by anger, and then finally closed tight in pain as the effect of my assault took hold.

His hands reached for his nuts as I brought the wine bottle up with my left hand to his chin. The bag in my right hand had ripped and now two of the 40-ounce bottles were rolling on the ground; one came to rest under the right front wheel of the Mustang and the other rolled towards his two companions. The bigger of the two at the pump picked up the bottle and began to walk towards me as the one my size began to circle around. The biggest one was on the ground moaning.

I held the wine bottle in my left hand and the shredded remains of a plastic shopping bag in the other. The paper sack containing my last malt liquor clung to the last remaining pocket within the plastic sack. I decided that I must scare the Badass who was coming at me with one of my forties. I looked to my left at the biggest one still on the ground next to his bike. I stepped towards him and struck the wine bottle on the gas tank of his bike. The wine bottle did not break, and in an instant the other two Badasses were upon me.

I suddenly felt a sense of being hopelessly outnumbered, so I figured I would even the odds a bit by taking out the guy with my malt liquor in his hand. The largest Badasses' bike, having been struck by my wine bottle, had by now fallen on him. The one who was my size had just kicked me in the shin when this occurred. He stopped doing that to attend to his big friend. This evened the odds for me. At least momentarily

The one with the malt liquor bottle had swung once at my head with it and was winding up for another try when I hit him flush between the legs with the unbreakable wine bottle.

Whack!

His face turned purple for a second, the he fell to his knees and seemed to go completely limp. I had very little time to enjoy this triumph because soon the big one was up again with the help of his little friend and began to walk towards me. I began to back away towards the gas pumps when BOOM! A shotgun blast shattered the drama.

I stopped in my tracks and looked over my shoulder towards the store entrance. There, wearing a sword that he kept in a scabbard on his belt, was Mr. Danning. He was also pointing a 12-gauge shot gun straight up in the air. As scattered birdshot rained down upon us, Mr. Danning stepped out towards us, pointed his gun barrel towards the biggest badass and said:

"Strike another match, go start anew. Because it's all over now Baby Blue."

I took this opportunity to get the fuck out of there. Fights sometimes meant cops and gunfire always meant cops. I had maybe minutes, if not seconds, to be on my way. I ran to the car with both bottles firmly in my hands and they seemed to help my speed somehow. Bonnie had worked her way up through the sunroof, but she began to climb down as I climbed into the driver's seat. I shoved the bottles into the back seat. I fired the engine to life and left the gas station slowly and carefully. By the time I had pulled back on the street Bonnie was inside the car. As we approached the first traffic light, she let out a yell that was kind of a Whoop!

It was a strange noise and I was about to respond to it with a whoop of my own when I saw the cop car approaching from the other direction. I began to feel a little guilty about what I did to those guys; I may have just assaulted the mayor's kids for all I knew. I got very tense very quickly. In a few seconds, I heard all three motorcycles start, and then the cop car lights turned on a second after that. Off he went in the other direction as the light turned red. Looking in the mirror, I saw the cop car pulling into the gas station as the motorcycles pulled out in the opposite direction.

I looked over at Bonnie and said, "We need to get far far away from here."

She looked back at me and said, "I wanna go dancing."

CHAPTER 44 – BLACK DIAMOND BAY

My former mistress Priscilla- she was the one who was an escort- once told me that people who opened up to other people only give the details that fit a certain narrative. She had heard the dark thoughts of many of her wealthy clients. She knew they were holding back details that would paint them in an even worse light. Her theory was that they were twisting things to make them more sympathetic.

"They always wanted to be little boys," she would say. "They wanted to be forgiven."

But, whatever their sins may have been, whether kicking puppy dogs or stealing from the collection plate, she felt they were hiding bigger deeper transgressions. I carried this bit of information with me whenever I talked to any of the inmates, mental patients, or Tallhill members I encountered. Whether it was Amos hiding the real weird stuff that landed him in trouble, or my crazy cellmate Clarence who talked to bugs, I could only imagine some of the bizarre things that they were capable of. I somehow had put these suspicions to rest when it came to Bonnie.

Bonnie was human and had human failings. I knew this, of course. However, I had somewhat blinded myself to this obvious fact. In my defense, my desperate situation and our mutual exuberance had made in-depth evaluation of personalities a luxury - something to be explored later. My keen awareness of her charms had covered over her possible quirks. This is where Black Diamond Bay Casino and its magical power of temptation enter the picture.

My own quirks are not mere obstacles to happiness. These idiosyncrasies inform me on the real trials and complications one can endure when overcoming a serious vice. In my case, the vice I had to conquer was not my misery addiction, but the way in which that addiction manifested itself. My vice was philandering. In retrospect, I may have rationalized my wandering ways by portraying my situation as desperate. In reality, I have always yearned to be wherever I was not. As long as my misery addiction was my own, I mostly just hurt myself. My philandering hurt others; it hurt people I cared about.

In Bonnie's case, her vice was about to be revealed to me and the occasion was an unplanned visit to a strange casino near the ocean, where I found myself caught off-guard by my own arrogance.

After the biker fight, we had driven for hours. One time, we paused by the beach as the sun set and the cold wind forced us to huddle together in our stolen Mustang. We ate at a seaside coffee house, and talked and laughed about the Badasses. We then went looking for a place to dance the night away. We ended up at a large casino/hotel called The Black Diamond Bay; it seemed perfect.

The outside lights of Black Diamond Bay were quite subdued for a casino. There was a tiny string of flashy lights below a modest neon sign over the main entrance that alternately featured a pair of rolling dice, a roulette wheel, an ace and jack of black diamonds, and a couple of drinking glasses clinking together. The not-so-subtle message was, "Come inside: drink and gamble".

Bonnie and I were already taking care of the drinking part. She had the bottle of Cabernet in her hand as I wheeled her through the crosswalk between the parking garage and the main entrance. We pulled up alongside the main entrance and she passed me the bottle as I leaned against the brown brick wall. A door attendant dressed in an all-green faux-naval uniform stood there with his blocked hat and his shoulder epaulettes and stared disapprovingly at our audacity. Bonnie laughed and sent out a salute towards the doorman befitting his rank and stature. This caused him to turn his head forward and scan the street for something else on which to focus.

Bonnie and I made quick work of the wine and then headed for the door. The doorman opened the door for us as he shot a disapproving look in my direction.

"Thank you, Admiral," Bonnie cackled in an increasingly slurred manner.

As we rolled inside the casino, we were presented with the standard cavernous, noisy, and intensely lighted room, a typical casino. As we pushed forward, smiling faces greeted us. Actually, I do not think that anyone even noticed me. They were all smiling at Bonnie. Perhaps smiling is not the correct word. They were beaming at her. This was our first real exposure as a couple to a large group and I was beginning to become uncomfortable and irritated. People smiling and gawking at my lovely companion in the wheelchair just turned up the heat on my irritation.

I pushed her right up to the edge of the carpeted slot machine area and let her have control of the chair. She pivoted in a slow circle as I did the same. On the outer reaches of the main floor were several restaurants featuring a multicultural variety of food. At the far end was a large flashing sign that read "Diamond Buffet". To our right, a Jazz combo was playing softly in a small bar, to our left was a disco called "The Bay". Large goons in black tuxedos stood out in front at the end of a velvet-rope corridor. They were checking IDs of the people who entered. Bonnie rolled towards The Bay.

As we approached the velvet-rope corridor, I glanced to my right. There, next to a twenty-five-foot Christmas tree, was a pedestal sign that read, "Poker Rooms on Mezzanine Level". There was a large red arrow at the top of the sign that pointed diagonally up a winding staircase. I noticed that Bonnie was also looking at the sign and she stopped at once and looked up towards the mezzanine in full inspection-mode. She pivoted in a half-circle to take in the full expanse of the mezzanine and then resumed wheeling herself towards the tuxedoed goons.

Once past the goons and inside the thumping noisy disco, the darker room mellowed the mood somewhat. However, my serenity soon turned into another emotion. I began to analyze what could go wrong and I started to worry.

"I want a shot and a beer," Bonnie said quite loudly between the pounding beat of the electronic funk music. She said this in those two seconds between songs, so a few heads turned towards us and several of them continued to look at us until I shot irritated looks in their direction. Some smiled shyly and returned to their own business. One man continued to stare at us.

I bent over to talk closer and to hear Bonnie above the din.

"Tequila," she whispered in my ear and kissed me on the cheek.

I stood straight and walked directly towards the man who was still staring at us. He was sitting at the bar and I guess I had decided that I wanted him to feel a little of the unease that was overtaking me. I squeezed next to him at the bar. He smelled of cheap cologne and cheap cigars and he wore about fifty pounds of gold chains. His shirt was unbuttoned halfway down to reveal his hairy chest and he had one of those pencil-thin mustaches that sat on the edge of the top of his lip. On his head he wore the worst-looking cheap toupee in captivity. He looked ridiculous.

As soon as I ordered my drink, Mr. Gold-Chain stood up from his bar stool and headed towards Bonnie. My head turned to follow him as the bartender poured the beer. He stopped in front of her. He held out his hand and she did the same. He bowed and kissed her hand. The bartender returned with the shots.

"Twenty-two dollars," he said.

I handed him a twenty and a ten and grabbed one of the shots of tequila and turned to see the progress of Mr. Gold-Chain as he put the moves on my woman. I slammed the shot glass down and felt it burn as my irritation grew into anger. I took the other shot and repeated this process before I remembered that it was Bonnie's drink. I ordered another shot and the barkeep poured one.

By the time I reached Bonnie, I had already drunk half of my beer and the interloper was whispering something into her ear. I put her shot and beer on the table and stood with my mug while I waited for Mr. Smooth to stop talking and straighten up. This did not happen as fast as I thought it should.

"Hey!" I shouted over the constant drum beat.

He continued his close-proximity interview with Bonnie and my tequila-fueled anger doubled. I tapped on his shoulder. He turned towards me and semi-straightened with a sly grin on his face. He then returned to talking to Bonnie.

"Hey, Fuckface!" I said in a quite loud manner. Some heads turned.

Unfazed, the intruder continued to talk whilst all in Bonnie's face. I swallowed the rest of my beer, slammed the mug on the table and walked to behind Bonnie's wheelchair. I grabbed the handles and swung her away from the large head of this weird bar creature. This task was made more difficult by the fact that Bonnie had set her brakes.

Mr. Gold-Chain actually grabbed her chair to stop me from this maneuver. I let go of the chair and that caused the chair to topple and caused Bonnie to go sprawling on the floor.

Realizing what I had done, I lunged to pick her up. At this point, I felt a large hand on my right shoulder. I turned to see one of the tuxedoed goons from the entrance. Behind him was another one. Soon one had my right arm behind my back with my hand pressed into the back of my neck; very painful. The second goon went for my feet and in quick order I was being carried towards the exit.

"Bonnie!" I screamed as the music stopped momentarily.

All I could see was a mass of people forming around where Bonnie and her disrupted wheelchair remained. The pounding rhythms returned. My shouts towards her became obscured as I struggled with the goons who were carrying me. The music continued and I heard a familiar singing voice serenading the clientele of the disco. It was Gypsy Rae, it was The Travelled; it was Annette. My Annette! It was a remix of one of her songs. I knew the words. They were my words. I remembered writing them as I sat in some hotel room alone and listened to a noisy party down the hall. The name of the song was *Empty Arms.* The words were out of order from the way I wrote them, but made even more sense to me somehow:

What I have...

Faded remains

Your beating pulse

Sound causing motion

Motion causes action

Action causes pain

Pain and desperation

In the way again…

The song faded as I was carried out of the disco and into the cavernous casino. The irony of the moment was only mine as I contemplated the situation I now faced. The goons' grip on me began to slip and I freed myself briefly, only to be dropped on the hard marble floor. This hurt tremendously as the shock traveled through my spine. Before I could gather myself, I was being carried through the main entrance and then unceremoniously dumped on the sidewalk next to the doorman. The doorman looked down at me with a smug self-satisfied smile and walked away as I groaned.

* * * * * * * * * * *

About an hour later, I sat in my Mustang in order to assess the absurd situation. I was still a fugitive and my co-fugitive was now missing. I had been thrown out of a disco that was playing a dance remix of my daughter's music after I picked a fight with a bizarre casino character. I did this within hours of being involved in a one-on-three brawl at a gas station. This type of behavior was just the thing that was going to cost me my freedom. I looked at the clock on the dashboard. It read 2 o'clock AM on December 14th. I had been free for eleven days. Bonnie had been free for barely three.

I had no idea where she might be or if she was even okay. Maybe she was hurt and had to go to the hospital? Ideas and possibilities flashed through my now over-analyzing brain. I listened for ambulances. I thought through the past hour and tried to remember if I had heard any sirens. I couldn't remember.

I had tried to go back into the casino front entrance immediately after being tossed out, but the doorman wasn't about to allow it. I kind of slinked away towards the parking garage to try to regroup and plan our next escape. However, my planning capacity was being depleted by anger and jealousy. I had no idea what the bar weirdo was saying to her and why she seemed to accept his general familiarity. Did she know him? I had no explanation; soon jealousy dominated my psyche. I needed time to compose myself.

After I had calmed myself and decided that she was still inside the casino somewhere, I began to make a plan. I would need a disguise and another entrance. I looked through some of Bonnie's belongings to see what she had. There were a few scarves and an eyebrow pencil. I figured that I could darken in my light brown/gray eyebrows. I found a Pittsburgh Pirates baseball cap in one of my boxes and an old pair of eyeglasses. These may have been Margie's or

Annette's but I had packed them in anticipation of needing a disguise.

After a few minutes and a change of wardrobe, I was a near-sighted, dark-eye-browed Pittsburgh tourist, with a gray windbreaker and a brown woolen scarf. I walked out through the side entrance of the parking garage so as not to be seen by the doorman. I walked to the end of the block and crossed the street, then continued until I was in the rear employees' parking lot. A biting cold wind made me glad I had worn the scarf.

As I approached the rear kitchen entrance, I noticed a wheelchair sitting out by the trash dumpster. I walked up and examined it and found, astoundingly, that it was Bonnie's chair and that one of the front wheels had come off. The wheel was missing a fastener and something to allow the wheel to glide smoothly.

Looking around, I saw that the only potential source of hardware around was a big smelly dumpster. Bracing myself for the stench and sliminess, I raised myself up and into the container and felt around for the bottom. I retrieved a handful of objects which I examined under the dim light. I picked out couple of washers and a paper clip. With these, I was able to rig the wheel to where it would not come off.

I found the kitchen entrance to be unlocked, so I pushed the door open and carefully looked around. I carried the wheelchair inside and set it up. I sat down carefully and tested my weight on the repaired wheel. It didn't collapse. I pushed forward slowly and awkwardly. It rolled okay. But how long would it last? I hoped just long enough for me to get close enough to Bonnie, grab her, and run like hell to the nearest exit. I had no plan beyond that.

I wheeled myself down the narrow hallway that led to the kitchen. I favored the left front wheel as much as possible. That was the good wheel. At the end of the hallway, the corridor split; on my left was the kitchen, and on the right was a hallway that led to a set of elevators. Beyond the elevators the hallway turned left and led to the unknown.

I headed for the unknown around that corner.

As I turned the corner, I saw the twenty-five-foot Christmas tree up ahead. It looked like the same tree we had seen earlier so I guessed that The Bay discotheque was directly across from there. I decided to not go directly into the disco. I figured I would observe from a distance in case the goons recognized me or the wheelchair. So I rolled right on past the tree and onto the carpeted slot machine area.

Once by the slots, I pivoted to look towards The Bay. Peering over the disguise glasses, I saw the goons who had thrown me out. I decided that it might be wise to let the situation settle for a bit and that Bonnie may not be in there anyway. She might be at the slots or playing blackjack. I wheeled myself out to take that tour.

After two slow and careful circuits around the floor and cursory glances into the restaurants and buffet, I concluded that she must be in the disco or somewhere else. Approaching The Bay's velvet corridor one more time, I saw that the goons were still in place. Looking beyond them, I saw a small café that had pictures of pie slices on large placards. I decided to wait them out. Bonnie would come out, or their shifts would end at some point and I would be there. I could not risk being thrown out again; it would probably mean jail.

So I rolled up to the place that was quaintly named The Bay Café and studied a big picture of pecan pie. Soon a pretty, late-forties-looking brunette waitress in a blue-plaid apron approached me.

"Sir," she said with a slight southern twang, "may I get you a table?"

"Yes," I said. "That one, please," I pointed to a table facing the entrance to the disco.

She wheeled me to the table.

"Can I sit on the other side, sweetheart?" I asked.

"You got it, hun," she said and wheeled me to the other side.

"Coffee, black, and pecan pie with a side of vanilla ice cream, please," I said as she slid me into place.

"Coming up," she said as she whisked away the menu and the place setting on the other side of the table and headed for the kitchen.

I sat there, removed my disguise glasses to look across at the goons. I was determined to wait them out as long as it took.

When the waitress returned with my pie and coffee, I asked her a question. "What time does the disco close?"

"Four-thirty," she answered. "Can I get you anything else?"

"What time is it now?" I asked.

"Two forty-seven," she answered.

"Thank you," I said. She walked away.

So I sat and slowly finished my pie and my coffee. Unfortunately, the pie and coffee did not have the effect I had hoped for… I was becoming sleepy. It had been a long stressful day and the toll of it was hitting me all at once. Part of my brain told me that a catnap would probably do me some good and that an hour nap would set me right at about 4:00 AM. The other parts of my brain presented no counter argument and soon I was sleeping in my wheelchair.

Bonnie was riding a horse and she was charging off into battle. She was Joan of Arc-like, her foes crumbled at the feet of her horse, and she rode on with her sword in the air and her black hair flowing magnificently from underneath her armor helmet. All at once, she stopped her gallop, turned towards me, and made her pony dance in place. She held her sword in the air and removed the helmet from her head. On her face was a determined and fierce look that I had rarely seen. In fact, I had only seen it once on her face. It was the dark cold look of a victor in a mighty struggle.

Then something in my mind snapped and I woke up to a realization.

I lifted my head and gathered my bearings. I was still in the café. I closed my eyes again and tried to remember that look on Bonnie's face. I had seen that look on Poker Night at Tallhill. It was the look on Bonnie's face as she vanquished all comers. She seemed to lose herself in the game and not realize that she was taking money from mental patients who were living on sometimes-small allowances. It did not matter to her.

To her this was her battlefield… her conquest.

Soon, several small realizations took hold in my mind. Poker Night used to be every Friday at Tallhill before my arrival, but some of the previous members had caused a ruckus of some sort and now Poker Night only happened monthly with strict betting limits and one could only play 5 hands and then sit out. I now suspected that Bonnie was the cause of the ruckus and the reason for the new rules.

I also remembered her bragging about her country club games where she would play all sorts of games like Bridge, Canasta, or whatever. She mentioned that she wanted to get them to play poker, but the more senior members shot down the idea. Suddenly, and perhaps miraculously, I knew exactly where to find her.

****

After I paid the pretty waitress at the café, I rode the elevator up to the Mezzanine. I could not decide which room I would find her in, so I would check them all. The Poker rooms were numbered 1 through 16; arranged by the minimum bet allowable. The ten-dollar rooms seemed a waste for someone out of circulation for so long. So even without knowing how much money her father had given her, I went straight to room 14, which was a $50 room.

The poker rooms had these huge wooden double doors with big ornate handles and they were not wheelchair-friendly. I struggled with one for a few minutes before an attendant from inside the room opened the door to allow me to wheel myself through. Once inside, I noticed that there were about a dozen tables and that they all seemed to be doing brisk business.

In the far right corner table, which was in a darker area than the other tables, sat Bonnie. She had her back to me, but I saw her jet-black hair peeking out over an official Black Diamond Bay wheelchair. I also heard her distinct voice. I slowly wheeled closer.

"Raise," she said confidently. Then I heard the sound of chips clinking together.

Groans were heard and one man's voice said, "Fold."

Another said, "Call," followed by more clinking.

Bonnie turned over her cards. "Three Ladies," she said; which caused the voice who had called to exclaim, "Damn!"

Bonnie leaned forward to pull her winnings towards her, but couldn't manage it all.

"A little help?" she said, in sort of an insulting fashion at one of the waiters who was nearby.

The waiter helped, and he was rewarded with a chip from her pile.

I sat through three more hands. Bonnie won one outright, then bluffed and won on the second, then folded early on the third. After the third, she excused herself to the bathroom.

"Don't deal me out, fellas," she said. "There's some of you I haven't fleeced yet."

This comment was met with nervous laughter as two of the men picked up their chips to leave. Bonnie poured her loot into a large bag marked with a $ and the letters BDB in green.

As she wheeled herself towards the ladies' room in the opposite corner, I decided that it was time for me to make my move. I doubted that the poker room people knew about my earlier tussle, so I figured it would be all right to get out of my disguise. So I wheeled myself into the men's room. I ditched the chair, removed my cap and glasses, and then washed off the eyebrow pencil. In a moment, I was outside trying to look like it was the most natural thing in the world to be leaning against the wall by the lavatories in a poker room.

As Bonnie backed her way out of the ladies room, I scurried to hold open the door for her. As she turned around and looked up, a devilish smile spread across her face. She didn't look surprised at all.

"Clyde," she whispered as she motioned for me to come closer.

I bent down and put my ear to her mouth.

"I am up over forty-thousand dollars," she said and then giggled a little.

"Holy shit," I whispered back. "We can buy a boat."

"I can win more…," she started, but I cut her off.

"We need to get far away," I said and got behind her chair and started pushing her towards the door.

Bonnie gripped the wheels hard and then set the brakes on the chair.

"Clyde, I have these chumps right where I want them," she was almost pleading.

I stood and contemplated. I really thought she was losing her grip on her addiction, but in the end I decided to compromise.

"As long as you let me keep enough to buy a boat," I acquiesced.

Bonnie reached into her sack and pulled out a few chips, closed the sack and shoved it into my hands.

"I'll start with five hundred," she said. "I can do it again." Then she wheeled herself towards the Texas Hold-em table she had just left. I have to admit that I felt a tingle of anticipation as I followed.

"I'm back, rubes," she announced once she reached the immediate radius of the table.

What followed in the next few hours was a clinic in concentration, obsession, and maniacal humor. Once she learned someone's name she would use different variations of that name. A man named Charles became Charlie, then Chucky, then Chuckles, then Chazz, then Chunky Cheese. It went on and on. A slightly chubby guy named Dan became Danny Boy, as in, "It's your bet Danny Boy." He was later Dano, Dan the Man, The Danster, Danko, Danielle, and Dumplin' Dan. Bonnie was hilarious and on a roll. The funny part was that nobody seemed to get mad at her.

Approximately thirty hands later, Bonnie decided that she was tired. I knew this time would come. Her adrenaline high had worn off and she had to crash. By this time she had built up another enormous kitty. I was delighted and tired. But mostly I was scared. As I stood watching the games, I became anxious about anyone who came through the doors of Poker Room 14. I suspected that the security video of me being carried out was probably legend by now amongst the casino goons.

As Bonnie continued to win, more goons seemed to be appearing. Perhaps they were going to ensure her safety. Maybe they had run my video through a wanted fugitive database and they were going to pounce when we made our move through the door. As the Poker playing went on, I started to sweat and my heart started to beat in my ears louder and louder. If Bonnie had waited any longer to quit, I may have decided to let her cash in her chips on her own.

As it was, I pushed her and her enormous bags of chips down to the cashier on the bottom floor. The security guards who followed made me nervous, but I just acted natural as possible. I decided they would be protection if someone decided to steal our bags. We wheeled down to the cashier's window while a barely-conscious Bonnie's head bobbed and her eyes blinked open occasionally. I just forged ahead and avoided eye contact with anyone, especially the two goons who were following me.

The cashier's window was manned by a silver-haired gentleman wearing a visor… classic. I grabbed both sacks and squeezed them one-at-a-time through the small opening in the cahier's window. The silver-haired man took each sack and slowly dumped them into a chip-counting machine. I watched the machine and waited for the results.

"Sir, that's seventy-three thousand, four hundred and fifty dollars," he said with a smile. "How would you like that?"

"Cash please," I said with a highly shaky voice. I was a little stunned that Bonnie could win more playing poker in few hours than I used to take home in one year of risking my life climbing towers.

"What denominations?" the silver-haired man asked.

The gears in my mind contemplated the usefulness of large denominations.

"Give us forty thousand in hundreds," I thought some more. "Give us thirty thousand in fifties and the rest in twenties."

The silver-haired man stared at me blinking for a minute and then set about his work. He walked back to a large safe and pushed a cart up next to it. A large security guard stood next to the safe and he made eye contact with me for a second, which made me avert my eyes immediately. My tension grew.

In a moment, the silver-haired man was back and he counted the money out to us slowly and carefully. Bonnie was barely paying attention and had started to chew her nails; something I had never seen her do before. Once the silver-haired man was done, I nodded to him and he put the cash into one of the sacks we had brought with us. He shoved the sack back through the opening and I put it in Bonnie's lap.

The man pushed a receipt through the window with a pen. "Sign please," he said.

I handed the pen and paper to Bonnie, who winked at me and scribbled *Guadalupe Figueroa* on the bottom. *Perfect,* I thought. I then began maneuvering her chair to find the nearest exit.

One of the goons spoke up. "Ma'am, would you like us to escort you to your vehicle?" he asked.

I didn't look at him and said, "We would appreciate it." I actually did think it was dangerous to walk around with this kind of cash.

"We could arrange for you to have a suite at the hotel…,"

"No thank you," Bonnie interrupted in her reasonable voice that had vanished in the Poker room. "We have a suite downtown."

"Very well," one of the goons said as he walked ahead of us to the automatic doors.

Going through the front door, we passed by our old friend The Admiral. The sun was up by this time, so he seemed to be working a double shift. His eyebrows rose as he recognized my face. I simply passed by, pushing Bonnie into the crosswalk towards the parking garage. Once we reached the car, I opened the trunk and made room for the sack under all of our other stuff. I then helped Bonnie into the car. I squeezed the BDB wheelchair into the back seat as our escort looked on with little interest.

As I climbed into the driver's seat, Bonnie looked over at me with her big dark eyes and yawned. Mid-yawn, she asked, "What kind of boat are we going to buy?"

She then turned her face into the seat and fell asleep.

CHAPTER 45 – ONE MORE CUP OF COFFEE

Everything has a frequency; vibrations caused by stimulus of some kind. Radios have frequencies of course, but so does light. Even trees, rocks, and water have frequencies. In fact, all of these things have several frequencies. Some of these frequencies are strong and stable and some are weak and unstable. Some of these frequencies are harmonics of a stronger frequency.

I make this point not to show off my scientific acumen, but to theorize what can be possible with the human mind. For if all things in nature have a frequency, by extension, human brains have a frequency, indeed several frequencies. Among these frequencies- both weak and strong- is what is known as a frequency of resonance. The frequency of resonance is the frequency that allows for the clearest and smoothest waves.

When frequencies of resonance are possible with the least interference or background noise, then better communications are possible. I believe that this is possible with the human mind. The human mind is a physical object that is stimulated by electrical impulses and chemicals. It is also affected by outside interference.

Using this as a baseline, it is my firm belief that a brain can function much like a radio. Radios have the advantage of knobs or buttons that can tune to a specific frequency with very little error involved. The mind, on the other hand, will send out several different frequencies at once. Depending on the focus of the mind and several external factors, there can be several frequencies generated that also change intermittently.

Conversely, a clear mind, a focused mind, should be able to operate consistently at a frequency of resonance and transmit information. This information could be received and deciphered by a similar brain with a similar frequency of resonance. Like a radio, it must have an antenna of sorts and also a receiver that is tuned.

What all of this means is that I believe that Bonnie and I shared at least one frequency of resonance that operated with the most clarity when we were sleeping. It didn't always work, but when it did, I am convinced that we were able to share in each other's dreams.

I brought this theory up to Bonnie after one of the first times we slept together. The fact that she understood exactly what I was saying- as she usually did- just confirmed to me that we were locked on the same frequency, at least sometimes. Unfortunately, it was not something we could control, at least not yet.

We had conducted an experiment where we would write down our dreams as soon as we woke up without discussing them with each other. The results were inconclusive. She was almost always in my dreams, even before I met her. I was less often in her dreams, but I did appear enough. When comparing our notes, we were almost always doing dissimilar things and acting in different ways. If I dreamed about us roller skating, she dreamed about us bowling. If I dreamed that she was the world's greatest dancer, she dreamed about her and her mother stuck on a life boat. After a few weeks we stopped writing down the dreams and even stopped talking about them. The incident at the casino made me think of this in a quite different way.

Instead of looking at the activities in the dreams or trying to remember the words, we should have instead looked for other clues and used different parameters. When Bonnie was of a singular mind playing poker for high stakes, her thoughts were an uninterrupted series of fierce determination. Her signal was strong. My sleeping mind had picked up those vibrations and had determined exactly what Bonnie was up to. I was even able to pick the right poker room on my first try. In this instance, she was the perfect transmitter and I was the perfect receiver. And we seemed to be always on the same frequency.

As we left the Black Diamond Bay Casino parking garage, Bonnie was asleep and I figured that she would sleep for a good long while. I turned onto the street in back of the garage and headed south along the beach road. I decided that we would stop and sleep somewhere along the beach. As I drove, I thought about my childhood and my loneliness. I searched for one of the sadder memories of my adolescence. I thought about the time a pretty girl pretended to like me just so she and her friends could make fun of me and insult me. I thought about how this further deepened my isolation and strengthened my independence.

This retrieval of a long-buried hurtful episode triggered my strongest feelings of cynicism, sadness and futility. None of these are positive emotions, but they are perhaps the strongest feelings in my psyche. If Bonnie was going to feel something in her dreams that I had transmitted, I decided that it was going to be these.

After about thirty minutes of driving south down the coastline, I found a beach parking area that was open. I turned left into the small parking lot, parked the car, and nuzzled up next to my sleeping lover and she gripped me tight in her sleep. I quickly drifted off.

When I awoke, the windows of the car were frosted over. Clearing a small patch with my fingernails on the driver's side window revealed that it was snowing outside. Bonnie was wide awake and eating beef jerky. She was calmly writing in her journal. I started the car in order to enable the heat and defrosters.

"I gotta pee," I announced as I opened the door into the bitter cold late afternoon.

We had slept most of the day away. At least I had, having no idea how long Bonnie had been awake. I instinctively knew not to interrupt her writing, just as I knew that she would tell me all about her poker adventures.

Being a gentleman, I first looked for an open restroom somewhere on the beach to relieve myself. I walked a short distance and scanned in both directions and saw no buildings within reasonable range. I headed for the ocean. After taking care of my business, I walked back to the Mustang and found the car to be quite warm and all of the windows cleared.

I put the car in gear and announced, "We will head south until we find warm weather and someone selling a boat."

Bonnie looked up and smiled. She fastened her seatbelt, sighed, and returned to writing. After a brief stop for gas and a restroom break for her, we were driving south and she continued writing. What follows is an excerpt from that day's entry.

December 14

I awoke from a deeply troubling dream; I was in a beauty pageant. The pageant was for girls in wheelchairs. I knew I had a chance to win the whole thing. I made it through all of the preliminaries and into the final 10. The final round was the talent completion. I was the first to go and I played piano. I was brilliant enough to receive a standing ovation. Then the next girl took her turn. She announced she would dance.

She got up out of her chair and began a complex and stirring dance routine. She even did a few spins using my wheelchair as a prop. Soon all of the remaining contestants were up and dancing as the audience howled with laughter. I was embarrassed and humiliated. I couldn't even bring myself to wheel off the stage. I just sat and cried and this made them all cheer more.

I was mortified.

I stirred from this dream to find Clyde driving in the snow. When his face was lit by approaching lights, I could see that he had a tear on his right cheek. This made me feel as if Clyde had influenced my dream. It was something he used to talk about all of the time. He felt that we were connected by radio waves and that if we made ourselves willing receivers, we could receive strong signals on the right frequency. I have been more than skeptical of this theory.

We had tried to sync each other's dreams before with mixed results. However, he may have influenced my dream this time. Pride prevents me from admitting that this was his handiwork, so I didn't bring it up right away. I just shifted in my seat and tried to dream something else. If I did dream again, I don't recall. In my total exhaustion I probably didn't dream at all. Why I am exhausted is another subject. Clyde has let me sleep with no questions about my night's activities. This is one of the reasons that I am so in love with him. Perhaps we are on the same frequency after all.

Clyde's behavior has begun to concern me. I have seen two instances in the last twenty-four hours of his over-protectiveness. During a rest stop at a gas station, he was involved in a brawl with some men with motorcycles who called themselves The Badasses. One of these men had come up to the car and was leaning on the door and asking me where I was going and where my "old man" was.

I was more uncomfortable and curious than scared since he must have seen the wheelchair in the back. I doubted he was much of a threat to kidnap me. I was only slightly flattered by the attention, since I had become a bit of an untouchable at Tallhill. When Clyde appeared from the store he used all available means to bring a halt to this offense on my vulnerability. He held off these ruffians with his own guile and a few choice blows to sensitive areas on the Badasses. As much as I am currently troubled by his recent outbursts, I am equally impressed by his resourcefulness and how much he is willing to put at risk to preserve my honor.

As I write this, Clyde and I have just left a large casino by the ocean called The Black Diamond Bay. My love of gambling has gotten the better of me. I had a few too many drinks before we got there and I succumbed to the temptation to gamble almost immediately upon seeing the interior of the place. I had intended to dance a little, but I ran into an old acquaintance within minutes of entering the disco inside the casino.

Ray Downs is a big horse track gambler who never seems to sleep. He always wears heavy cologne; my guess is because he thinks he smells of horses, since that's the only place I have ever seen him. While Clyde was buying drinks in the disco, Ray came over and started a conversation with me. He has a new job at Black Diamond Bay setting point spreads for the sports book. He says it's his dream job and that he can watch any race anywhere and that he really has to because it is part of his job. But he misses the track. He still wore the same cologne though, and plenty of it.

While Ray was getting close to me to talk over the loud music, I got to see more of Clyde's reckless chivalry. He returned with my drink and then started a tussle with my wheelchair before I could explain anything or introduce him to Ray. In the confusion I went flying to the floor and Clyde was escorted out. I didn't see what happened to him, but Ray apologized and got me a new chair to replace the one that was broken in the tussle. He told me that his bouncers had escorted Clyde out of the casino.

Ray asked me if I still played poker. I told him that I was worried about Clyde and that I had to leave. He told me that it was a shame and that Clyde probably needed to cool off. I thought about the fight Clyde had just been in at the gas station and I agreed. Besides, where was I going to go alone in a wheelchair? I decided that Clyde would find me. His determination was fierce. I had seen it in action.

I went with Ray to one of the poker rooms, where he sat in for the first few hands as we played against some of his cronies. He got up and excused himself, saying that he had to go set the point spreads for some college basketball games. After that moment, I do not remember much. I know I started out with two hundred bucks from amongst the money my father had given me. I know I won a lot of money and quite a few players came and went as I defeated them in quick order. I couldn't tell you my best hand or my best bluff. I guess I was in some kind of trance.

My trance broke somewhat when Clyde showed up, as I knew he would, but I talked him into letting me play some more and I don't remember much after that. I knew Clyde would be there for me and I grew even more confident. I won a lot of cash. We can buy a boat now instead of stealing one. Presently we are on our way farther south to find a boat and more favorable seas.

* * * * * * * * * * *

The middle of December is not a good time to find boats for sale in the northern parts of the United States. The ones for sale are typically nowhere near water and are probably not ready for immediate seafaring. So I drove south along the coast, looking for warmer weather and calmer seas and hopefully someone ready to unload a nice boat. I had thought about stealing a boat, but then I realized that stealing a boat is not like stealing a car. A car can be hid somewhere while they look. A boat on the open sea is going to be found by the Coast Guard or Customs or somebody. We had to buy a boat.

"Chandler was an excellent sailor," Bonnie said matter-of-factly as we drove down the oceanfront boulevard somewhere heading south. "He taught me some few things about sailing, nothing I can do in this condition, but one of the things I learned was making sure the boat was sea worthy. I did a lot of maintenance and cleaning. Grueling stuff."

"I guess that makes you the captain," I said with a hint of sarcasm. "For I know nothing of boats."

She let the comment go.

"I am pretty sure I could man the wheel in open waters," I added.

She appeared to be fuming. We drove in silence for some time afterward. I felt I had hurt her feelings with my flippant remark. I finally decided to apologize for my insolence.

Before I could speak she spoke first, "You know you don't have to fight everybody who speaks to me."

She had changed the subject to something more uncomfortable. But this subject I was more ready for.

"I am not normally like that," I stumbled. "But, but… I guess I never really felt this way about anyone."

In my mind I recalled the brawls I had been in involving Isabel. Isabel would flirt with virtually anyone and spark stupid fights. I really didn't feel jealous; I just wanted to cool off these potential Romeos. I felt protective more than anything. It was part of our mutual misery addictions; it was a game. Afterwards, we would occasionally end up making angry love in indiscreet places like the back seat of her car or a city park late at night. Danger and misery, it was on these tenets our relationship thrived. With Bonnie I really felt not only like protector and defender, I felt she had become part of me; a silly notion for my complex mind to settle on.

"I realize that I am wrong to treat you as helpless, but I want some kind of control," I let those words linger and waited for a response that was not immediate. Bonnie was going to make this as awkward as she could.

"I, I don't mean that I want to control you," I finally said. "I just want something besides being a fugitive in love with another fugitive. I feel like every slip-up will cause this whole thing to blow up and we go back… well you go back to Tallhill and I go to…" I was beginning to ramble and I wanted the awkwardness to pass, so I stopped talking.

The next hundred miles of driving down the coast seemed to take hours. When I finally pulled over in a roadside park, I was exhausted and Bonnie was sleeping. I pulled behind some trees and parked the car as far out of sight as I could.

At first light, I pulled out of the park, grateful that we had not been spotted by passing police on their rounds. We needed to eat and I needed to figure out where we were. I had steered us clear around the Chesapeake Bay and we were in a quaint little town in Virginia. There was still a bit of a drive ahead of us before we were somewhere warm by the ocean. Looking at my atlas I expected us to have to go all the way to South Carolina before we found decent seas. Perhaps we would have to go farther. I decided that the interstate was the best way to go. I could follow the speed limit and use cruise control all the way without arousing suspicion.

After about six hours on the road we found ourselves in a small town on the South Carolina coast. I had held to 60 mph for most of the trip. I was hungry and Bonnie had just woken up from a brief nap. She had been writing again for a good portion of the trip, so I had refrained from idle chit chat. I realized that she needed to put her thoughts on paper and that she would later let me read her notes. We were transparent to each other in that way, as I also held nothing back.

Upon reaching the ocean front, I turned right on the last possible street and began looking for any place to eat. The sun had gone down by this time and I just wanted a meal and a shower.

The mid-December coldness was evident even this far south. I decided that we might have to go all of the way to Florida, if necessary, to find good weather.

After about a mile of slow driving down the tiny seaside street, we came to a place charmingly named "The Bait Bucket" The OPEN sign shone in brilliant red neon in the huge dirty window on the front of what at first looked like a bait shop. I was about to pass it by, but I saw a sign on the glass door that said "Fish Fry Tonight." I parallel-parked in front of the place and walked around the car to help Bonnie out so we could shake off the road weariness.

There was no sidewalk in front of The Bait Bucket, just a patch of worn down dirt that led to a step-down that was made of misshapen rocks. Our borrowed casino wheelchair was hard to maneuver around these, but we managed. A gray-haired gentleman inside the place saw our struggle and held the door open for us. After our brief exertion, we were in a small room with about a half-dozen small tables.

There was another gray-haired man behind a small counter and the man who had helped us seemed to be a customer. They each looked as weathered as any veteran of decades of riding the seas would; cracked and gnarled features on their faces and tired-looking eyes.

"Here's the menu," the man behind the counter pointed to a black chalkboard that hung behind him.

Fish Fry (includes Fried Potatoes) $9

Baked Potato $2

Oyster Stew $4

Drinks $2

"We will have the fish fry," I said. "Do you have coffee?"

The man, who seemed to be a customer, had been staring at us the whole time. He resumed his crossword puzzle in the paper he had at his little table. The owner of The Bait Bucket brought out a pot of coffee and two small cups, and then retreated to the small kitchen in the back to start cooking our order. Sensing that these old guys knew everything about sailing and boats, I decided that I would start a conversation pertaining to the purpose of us being in this sleepy little village.

"I wonder if we can find calm seas," I said to Bonnie.

"Probably have to go farther south," she answered.

The old man looked up from his paper for a second and then resumed his puzzle.

"Probably right," I said.

"We also need a boat that can make the trip," she replied.

The old man at the table just sat there. In fact we all sat there in awkward silence for about 10 minutes until our meal arrived.

"Fish fry for two," The proprietor said as he set down a huge tray full of crispy fish and crunchy potatoes.

"Nestor, are we sellin' Cassandra?" asked the old man at the table.

"I always am, Calvin," replied Nestor. "She's been in dry dock for two years."

"More like five," replied Calvin. "Since Millie died."

"Ya, I guess," Nestor replied as he shuffled back behind the counter.

"Ketchup?" Nestor asked as he reached the counter.

"Yes," I replied. I got up to meet him as he started slowly back to the table. I retreated to the table.

"Tartar sauce?" Nestor asked as I sat down. Calvin let out a chuckle.

I looked at Bonnie who just smiled.

"Yes, please," I said, but this time Nestor had already reached the table with four small round containers of sauces.

"I like hot sauce on mine," he said as he touched Bonnie's hand and winked. He reached in his apron pocket and pulled out a small bottle of something called Fire Sauce and placed it on the table.

"Just a couple of drops on each fish," he said as he winked again at Bonnie and completely ignored me; which people tend to do when we are together.

"These folks are looking for a boat," Calvin said as he got up, folded his paper under his arm and moved across the room to sit by us.

"Nestor and I are brothers," he explained as he sat down and scooted his chair up next to Bonnie. "We have a nice big boat that hasn't seen the sea since his wife passed. He has a silly habit of holding on to useless things that only have sentimental value."

"Not true," Nestor interrupted. "She's been at sea a couple of times since Millie…,"

"Oh, yes, to scatter her ashes at Cape Hatteras," Calvin interrupted.

'Yes, and the fourth of July that year," Nestor continued.

"Yeah, I know," said Calvin.

"Is it seaworthy?" I interrupted their dialog.

"Should, be," Nestor answered. "I pay them to service the engine, she's been in storage."

Nestor paused for a few seconds, "Do you want to buy her?"

"We would like to see her, for sure," I gestured over at Bonnie. "She's the expert here. Hopefully, she can inspect it."

Bonnie was busy tearing through several of the fish as if she hadn't eaten in days. This wasn't too far from the truth; not a real meal, anyway. The fish was cooked just right and we both agreed later that it was probably the best we had ever eaten.

"So you are planning a trip?" Calvin asked.

"We are," I said between bites as I tried to get something in my belly before Bonnie left the platter bare.

"Are you going near Florida?"

"Ah, Calvin!" Nestor protested.

"Well," Calvin continued, "I guess I have never been one to beat around the bush."

"What is it?' Bonnie asked with her mouth momentarily void of food.

"Well, Nestor and I need to sell The Bait Bucket to the Marina Commission. They are going to bulldoze it and put in a bigger pier," Calvin got up and helped himself to a cup of our coffee as he continued. "I figure with that money and selling the boat, we can live pretty comfy down in Florida, since my daughter has a place there. The sea wore us out a while ago and some of us just can't accept the consequences," He shot a look towards Nestor.

Calvin pushed his chair next to our table, back-first. He sat down with his arms on the back of the chair and dropped his newspaper on the table face up. It turned out to be not a newspaper at all, but the latest copy of *Today's Detective* magazine. It was a cheaply-produced rag with black and white dot matrix words and pictures, but it had a large blaring headline on the front page: THE NEW BONNIE AND CLYDE? Under the headline was a picture of a very attractive, large-breasted blonde in a wheelchair wearing a bathing suit. On her lap was a handsome mustachioed gentleman smiling and waving a gun. These people looked nothing like us. But the picture and headline were made to sell magazines.

"Turn to page 8," Calvin instructed.

I flipped to page 8 of the yellow-tinged paper and began to read the story. At the top of the page was a picture of me from my work identification card. The picture was about ten years-old and showed me clean shaven with no gray hair. Next to that picture was a picture of Bonnie in her wedding dress. The story, which was written by one of the staff writers, was entirely based on interviews with a private investigator aptly-named Taylor Spencer. Spencer had been hired by the family of Lana Fox, the young woman whom Bonnie had slashed. It was an amazing story that contained some facts, but was very well embellished when it came to the stories of our escape and my incarceration. The story also included our real names, which I have chosen not to include for my re-telling. An excerpt follows:

Clyde Barrow is cold and calculating; he almost beat his cell mate to death while in state prison. He was inexplicably released to a minimum security private facility in spite of this. At Tallhill, he was mentored by Miss Parker whose charms are many. She persuaded Mr. Barrow to help her escape from the facility. Mr. Barrow escaped first, then returned a few nights later for Miss Parker, who although confined to a wheelchair, is young and surprisingly agile.

"Miss Fox rightfully fears for her life," said Spencer. "Miss Parker is clinically insane and may wish to exact more revenge. We have many leads which we are following up on."

The desperate duo is expected to be armed and dangerous. They are known to be violent on several occasions. If you see them, please contact the local police or Mr. Taylor Spencer.

A phone number was given for the private detective and the hatchet job article was complete. Bonnie, who was reading along with me as I looked over her shoulder, made no sound, but looked defeated as I sat down across from her. I didn't know what to think about Taylor Spencer. I supposed that he may have leads to go on; he said as much, but I knew that the time had come for us to get the hell away from the mainland.

Calvin got up, filled all of our cups with coffee and set the near-empty pot on the counter and said, "Let's drink up, while Nestor locks the place up. Then we can go back to my place and plan our escape."

Just like that, Bonnie and Clyde had become a gang.

CHAPTER 46 – WHEN THE SHIP COMES IN

Calvin was once a private detective. He had been a policeman in his younger days before he had fallen in love with the sea. He turned in his badge and joined the merchant marine and then quit them once he saved enough money to buy a boat along with Nestor. He spent the next 40 years taking tourists on chartered fishing trips and sight-seeing excursions. In the off-seasons and during down time, he investigated spouse-cheating and missing persons. He lived modestly and had been married briefly when he was in his late twenties. She ran off and he and Nestor's family had raised his daughter.

We knew all of this before we got to his modest apartment because he talked continuously on the way as he sat among our meager possessions in the backseat of the Mustang while we drove to his place. It was only after hearing him say he used to be a policeman that I realized that it may be a trap; there was a $25,000 reward for our capture. I decided to pretend that I missed the turn into the parking lot of his apartment complex and circled around the block to see if anyone besides Nestor was following us.

Bonnie probably picked up on this because she told me that she needed some female supplies. So I asked Calvin if there was an all-night store we could visit.

"You're not going to knock over another convenience store, are you Clyde?" He asked.

As he asked, he let out a little laugh. But I was by now well aware of the possibility of Calvin being anxious to get that reward. Even if that boat was worth more than 25K, it was easier money to just turn us in than to help us get down south. There was also the possibility of a number of bounty hunters on our trail. I pulled into the Gas 'n' Go and decided that I did indeed need gas just in case I had to make another quick escape.

I pulled up to the pump at the Gas 'n' Go and Calvin, being ever helpful, got out of the back seat with Bonnie's chair at the ready. He offered to push her to the store, but she waved him off. He decided to tail behind her. I kept my eyes on him as I pumped gas and scanned the streets for cars that might be following. Nestor's car, which was a giant old Buick LeSabre from the seventies, slowly chugged into the parking lot and pulled up beside me.

"Is everything alright?" Nestor said out of the half-open window.

"Bonnie had to get some feminine products," I said with great discomfort.

"Gotchya," Nestor said. Then he rolled up his window and pulled up to the front door of the store.

Calvin must have seen him pull in, because he was soon out front and talking to Nestor through his car window. I continued to scan for suspicious cars. I saw nothing. But the truth is that I didn't really know what I was looking for. I surmised that bounty hunters didn't just drive right up if they were tailing you. Perhaps they just drove a half-block away with their headlights off. Maybe Nestor had tipped someone off already. I began to get paranoid and worried.

Bonnie was the one that the reward money was for. Lana Fox had posted the reward and she probably couldn't care if I was caught or not. In my mind I decided that if the cops pulled in at that moment, I would try to escape alone. My anxiety led to impulsiveness and those two things had been my undoing in the past. But I knew that's what I would have to do. I continued to scan the immediate area.

Inside the store I saw Bonnie paying for some stuff and the pump had shut off as the tank was now full. I filled the tank with as much gas as it would hold. I joked to myself that it was "Freedom Juice". A dumb joke that I shared with no one, but it made me chuckle.

Bonnie emerged as I hung up the pump handle and walked towards the store. Bonnie waited for me. I handed the keys to Calvin as I walked past him.

"Can you help her out, Calvin?" I asked.

"Sure thing, Chief," he said.

This gesture of giving up control eased my mind and I think it may have had the same effect on Bonnie. She knew, as I did, that the reward was for her capture. If the bounty hunters were going to make a move, it would be now. They would get her and Calvin and Nestor would get the money. I would try to escape through the back or something.

I had no real plan.

As it was, I simply paid for the gas and headed back towards my car past Nestor and into a lively conversation about boats and sailing between Calvin and Bonnie. I got in and fired the engine and we headed for Calvin's place. My paranoia and anxiety began to fade.

****

"The ironic thing about Lana Fox," Bonnie said as I sat next to her in an easy chair back at Calvin's apartment. "She was screwing my husband for probably years, and she was sneaking and hiding. Now she has me sneaking and hiding."

I just nodded at this. I knew my words would probably be useless when added to such an accurate observation. Lana was lucky to escape with her life that day and should have gone quietly away.

Bonnie was no danger to anybody and I could see that this ludicrous bounty was beginning to play havoc with her psyche. For my part, I had no such bounty and it kind of seemed unfair. I had shown myself to be quite violent in the last few days and the cure for what ailed me seemed as far away as ever.

We were sitting before a nautical map spread out before us on Calvin's coffee table and Calvin was detailing our route down the Intercoastal Waterway. Nestor reclined on the sofa half-asleep. He seemed content to let Calvin do the planning.

"The route is all right here," Calvin said, "as easy as pie. I need to go through my other maps to find the route to your little island, but we have time. The boat will probably not be ready for a week and we have to buy provisions and take care of our business here."

"We have to get away soon," Bonnie said suddenly in a strange desperate voice I had not heard from her before. "There's a guy on our tail and he's got big money behind him."

"You can stay here, out of sight," said Calvin. "We can hide your car in the storage area next to the boat. Right Nestor?"

"Aha," Nestor moaned through partially shuttered eyelids.

"You see, tomorrow, that green Mustang will be hidden away until we leave. We have time."

"Maybe he's already on our trail," Bonnie said in that less-than-confident tone.

"If he is, then what difference does it make?" Calvin reasoned. "We need a plan and mine is the best one."

"They always win, ya know," Bonnie insisted. "Those people who control everything. They always win."

"Not always," I said. "They aren't even in the game yet as far as I'm concerned. But I am afraid they are getting in your head."

"That's right," Calvin said, "They haven't even seen the game yet."

"Don't you see?" She turned her chair around towards the bathroom. "They own the game." She wheeled herself away. "We play at their pleasure!" She yelled into the echoing tiles of the bathroom. "Their game, their rules."

Calvin just shrugged and reclined back on the couch next to his brother. I sat back on the easy chair and took a sip of the White Russian that Calvin had insisted on serving me. After a few moments, Bonnie came wheeling back into the room with a serious face.

"You want irony?" Nestor suddenly spoke up. "Calvin and I researched that private eye they hired, Spence, or whatever. He makes a living finding cheating spouses."

Bonnie let out a derisive "Ha!" and wheeled over to touch Nestor on the knee.

"Thanks, Nestor," she said, "I think I have a better perspective now. "Dark moods get ahold of me every now and again."

"I'm there all of the time," Nestor said. "When I'm alone and I think of Millie…" he trailed off.

Tears formed in her eyes again and she wheeled off to the corner. I decided that we had had enough of this stress. I got up and headed for Calvin's spare bedroom and made a come-along gesture towards

Bonnie with my head. She shyly excused herself from the present company and we all wished each other goodnight.

Bonnie had her heart shattered and her body broken by the same person. To add insult to injury, that person was now paying someone to track the stilted slow progress of her escape. The worst private detective in the world could probably track our wave of destruction through gas stations and casinos. I only hoped that we had put enough distance between us and them in our dash to the southern coast.

True to her need to put her emotions on paper, Bonnie sat up most of that night writing in her journal in the dim light of the lamp on the night stand. As I slid in beside her, I said something stupid that I instantly regretted.

"You're not going to stay up writing now?"

She just shot me a look of contempt and resumed her writing.

December 15

Like me, Miss Ellie used to write everything down. Miss Ellie was one of the first people I met when I got to Tallhill. He father had been in the Navy, a Captain I believe. She was an obsessive compulsive, keeping notes about everything. She wrote everything down. Her surviving relatives had institutionalized her many years previous as she had been diagnosed as an extreme obsessive-compulsive no longer able to care for herself.

I often had long talks with her and found I was one of the few she would open up to. The staff psychiatrists failed to break through her placid exterior and I never saw much of her relatives; there was a niece who visited sometimes, but Ellie told me that she was just after the money that they all thought she was hiding somewhere.

Ellie's father may have even been an admiral. Ellie just called him The Captain when she talked about him and she talked about him a lot. One of the things she told me about him was that he would show her everything about navigating and they listened to weather forecasts on the radio. She enjoyed every aspect of his naval career.

Ellie was an only child and her mother died or ran off when she was quite young. I was never quite sure which. Some of her so-called psychosis may have stemmed from this. But at some point she became obsessed with the tides. She began keeping a chart of high tide and low tide; since these occurred quite often, you would usually find her down by the ocean. At every one of her father's duty stations, she would faithfully chart the tides.

By the time World War II rolled around Ellie was enrolled at an Ivy League College, I forget which one, her father was stationed way up in the northeast. He was in charge of a program that was testing a new type of experimental landing craft. He was not the type to sit behind a desk, so he would go out with these craft and test the seaworthiness of the vessels.

During one series of night tests, there was a collision of some kind between some of the landing crafts and her father was lost at sea. They searched for days, but never found him. When this news broke, Ellie returned home from college and never went back. She took up residence at the little seaside cottage that she and her father shared and remained there for over 50 years.

During those years, she kept journals, charts, and notes for virtually everything; not just the tides, but every change in weather and air pressure. There were journals for every event that took place in her life. If she received a phone call, she would write it down in the log she kept. If she injured herself, she would record it. She kept a log of mail deliveries. She chronicled it all; yes, you could call her obsessive.

Her father's generous life insurance provided her enough money for living expenses and his will also left her with a small fortune that would have supported several Miss Ellies for many many years. She was an attractive young lady, but she shunned a social life and her only visitors were relatives checking in on her. Those relatives failed to understand her habits and most found them odd and even frightening. She would often stop in mid-conversation to record a hummingbird feeding at the window. After a while, most relatives stopped coming.

But she never gave up on her father. His body was never found, so without that closure, she would not accept that he wasn't around somewhere with amnesia, living a secluded life. She was often called by local police or the Coast Guard if an anonymous body would be found. She would go through the gruesome task of going to the morgue to look at the body of the poor soul. None of them ever was her father.

It was not her chart-keeping or note taking that landed her at Tallhill; it was a greedy relative. Ellie had taken most of her inheritance and invested it wisely in tax-free municipal bonds and government securities. This money was never touched, as her living expenses had been taken care of by the life insurance. Although the Navy had declared her dad officially dead early on, she feared that she would have to give that insurance money back once he was found. So the investments were never touched.

At some point, a great niece of Miss Ellie's mother learned of her enormous wealth and also figured out that she was her closest remaining relative. Miss Ellie was by this time in her 70s and the niece was in no mood to wait for an inheritance. There was also the possibility that Ellie would leave her fortune to some charity. The niece set about accumulating evidence that Ellie was not of sound mind. She eventually found a court that awarded her power of attorney over Miss Ellie's affairs.

Soon Ellie found herself in committal hearings in front of psychiatrists who diagnosed her with OCD and forced her to let the niece live with her. Not much longer after that, she was committed to Tallhill. The expenses for living there were covered by the niece when she sold Ellie's little cottage. Her journals and charts were destroyed and Ellie was packed away to be forgotten about.

I met Ellie and we became fast friends. She had a quick cold wit that you would miss if you weren't paying attention. She held no animosity towards the niece and she just went right on recording every event. Since she couldn't track the tides, she simply recorded whatever happened that day. She made her own weather forecasts and compared them to the TV guy's forecast. She was more consistent. This gave her great pleasure.

I learned from her to keep a journal and she told me to make sure that I sent them to someone I trusted. The only person in the world that I trusted was my father. Ellie is the reason I am always writing and she is the reason I am not as crazy as the world would like to think I am.

When Miss Ellie died, I was allowed to attend her funeral. I was the only member of Tallhill to attend who was not staff. If the niece attended, I did not notice, but an Honor Guard from the Coast Guard did attend. It turned out that Miss Ellie had been working for them for over forty years providing vital weather information. She had deferred her salary over all of that time with the stipulation that the money would be turned over to a charity that took care of service members' widows and orphans. She even got a 21-gun salute.

* * * * * * * * * * *

When Bonnie stopped writing, she scooted herself off the bed and into a wheelchair. This woke me up.

"Clyde," she said, "can you drive me to a phone booth?"

"It's 3AM," I said through the fog of half-sleep after checking the nightstand clock.

"I need to leave a message for my dad," she said. "There's an all-night diner that he uses as a message phone for his clients who think that people will listen in."

"Okay, sure thing," I said as I rolled out of bed and hurriedly dressed.

We drove around until we found a phone booth that would receive calls and she phoned the message phone at the diner using one of the calling cards her father had provided. She left a message for him to call the pay phone at 10AM and hung up.

When we got back to the apartment, Nestor was awake and making coffee.

"When you make a living serving coffee to fishermen, you tend to get up super early," Nestor said to us before we could ask him. He pulled up a chair to the small kitchen table.

"I have been listening to Calvin's stories of his private detective escapades for years since Millie died," he said as I wheeled Bonnie up next to the table.

"He reads those detective magazines forever, but he knows that the people aren't anything like those writers say they are. He's brought in several bounties and he gets to know them sometimes. He will follow them for days even, learning their habits. He treats it like a game. Also, since he works alone, he can't really do much for getting teamed-up on. He waits until they are alone."

"Anyways, I've been his wheel man a couple of times when he had to ride in the back with them. Most of them are nothing like the press wants you to think. We know you people aren't like that magazine says."

"It's true," Bonnie said. "We are nothing like that."

"Calvin already has called in some favors," Nestor continued. "He's had some of his friends call in false leads. Not too many. Just anonymous tips telling the cops or that private dick that you are in Key West or Canada."

After Calvin awoke, we all traveled to where they kept their boat. It was inside a larger storage area and off the ground. Calvin instructed the worker in the office to service the boat as soon as possible.

While Nestor drove Bonnie to the pay phone, I followed Calvin to the storage space where he kept Cassandra. Cassandra was a 1992 Flybridge 35. The 35 meant 35 feet long. She was quite seaworthy, Calvin assured me.

"We pay these guys for full service, so the fuel tanks are empty," yelled Calvin as he noisily raised the large garage door. "No old gas."

As a large pickup truck from the rental office-area began to back up to the boat, Calvin spoke to me more quietly.

"We are going to pull your Mustang in here and leave it," he smiled. "I know some guys who will turn it into parts within a few hours."

I opened the door to my green home on wheels and popped the trunk door open. Calvin and I moved all of my worldly possessions out to his car. I drove the Mustang into the garage and parked it.

"Leave the keys in it," Calvin ordered. I obliged.

"We will try to leave in three days," he said as I climbed into the front seat of his car. "Nestor needs to settle on his property over at city hall, plus the weather will be better by then."

The truck pulling the boat pulled out of the gate of the rental facility and as I watched the boat pass through the open gate, I caught a glimpse of Nestor's car pulling up by the gate. Calvin waved to him and he turned around and we all headed for the marina by different routes. Calvin took quite a circuitous route to the marina, so it was a good twenty minutes before we were seated in his car, watching Cassandra being backed off her trailer into the water. Five minutes later, Bonnie and Nestor had joined us.

"I don't think anyone followed us," Nestor reported out his open window as he pulled up next to us in the small parking lot behind his restaurant.

We just watched as the crew maneuvered Cassandra into her slip. They tied her off to the pier and the two men waved to Calvin as they climbed in their truck. They fired up the engine and left without a word. Only after the sound of the truck had faded, did we get out of the cars.

"Well, if you guys want, you can look at the boat while I heat up some cream of crab soup," Nestor said as he closed the door of his car. "We have to eat what we can of my inventory. The rest I will give to charity and I got a guy coming to look at my freezer and stove. It's all got to go now."

Bonnie, who had been sitting in the back seat of Nestor's car, opened the driver's side back door and pushed her Black Diamond Bay wheelchair out onto the ground. She slid from her side of the car until she was sitting on the edge of the seat with her legs dangling outside. She grabbed her chair and adjusted it the way she wanted. With the brakes set, she was able to lift herself out of the car and into the chair. Calvin and I watched with a kind of wonder and neither of us offered to help. Cassandra was next at the diesel pumps, so Calvin and I topped off all of the tanks and he paid the attendant.

I lifted Bonnie into the boat and she climbed up to the captain's chair.

"I can drive this," she said, "It has all hand controls."

"The cabin sleeps five comfortably," called out Calvin as he padlocked the gas pump.

Calvin handed me the wheelchair and climbed on Board.

"I have some fresh linens in the car, she's always ready to go, I pay the guy for that, but they don't do sheets," Calvin just kept filling us with information.

I just stared at Bonnie as her dark hair silhouetted the cloudy winter sky in a light drizzle. She was seated in the captain's chair and staring off into the distance. I believe they call it the Thousand-Mile Stare. Being an introspective type myself, I instinctively left her to her thoughts and went below to check the cabin.

CHAPTER 47 – TOMORROW IS SUCH A LONG TIME

December 16

Clyde Barrow is a cad and an opportunist. He is totally self-involved and vainglorious. He fancies himself a misery addict, but what he suffers from is the total disregard of consequences for his actions. He is brilliant enough to plan an escape and another breakout, but simple enough to get in two fights within a few hours. He seeks to be free from prying eyes, but draws attention to himself.

Clyde Borrow has violent tendencies. I read this in his file before I met him and I took this information seriously. When I got to know him, I didn't see this side of him. He seems generally in good humor, though constantly analyzing things beyond his control. I read the accounts of him attacking his co-worker and overpowering his cellmate and concluded that his violence was due to a lack of control.

When he was controlling the situation, he was pleasant to be around. When the control was lost, he snapped. With the motorcycle guys it was the same thing; loss of control. He flung himself at three men all for the purpose of regaining control. If not for the store clerk, he would have been pummeled.

His clumsy display in the casino club was another instance of control being questionable. The outcome was not as positive for him this time. He actually stood no chance and he should have known it. He explained all of his actions by saying he was instinctively protecting me. But I was never really in any danger. The guy on the motorcycle was not going to do anything but flirt and Ray was an old friend. Clyde's instinct is not to protect; it is to control.

We are currently in South Carolina looking to buy a boat and I have just gotten off the phone with my father. My father has had a few of his friends plant false leads to that private eye Taylor Spencer. Between the false leads planted by Calvin's guys and my father's friends, Mr. Spencer may take weeks to track us properly. Or he might be just down the street; there is no way to tell for sure. Such is life on the run. Any of the dozens of people we have interacted with may have him hot on our tail already. A bounty is a strong motivator.

My dad told me that his old senior partner Theodore J. Silkwood, was now brain dead with a stroke. Dad is friends with their maid, having defended her husband pro bono on a concocted theft charge. The maid had once found him in the arms of Lana Fox's ex-husband. They had been having an affair since he was a young paralegal at the firm and he and Lana were newlyweds. Everyone suspected he was gay back then, and we were not surprised that the marriage didn't last.

Dad happens to also be the gay paralegal's attorney; who, as Silkwood's lover, stands to inherit millions of dollars. Silkwood's kids are grown, rich and successful. His first wife died and his trophy wife took her prenuptial agreement money and left. The reason that my father betrayed his client/attorney confidence to me is that Lana and the supposedly gay paralegal are now back together. This could mean more money added to the bounty after the legal wrangling over the inheritance once Silkwood meets his final reward. I plan on being well hidden by then. For now, I am exhilarated and nervous. We have to hide the car for a while until we escape clean. I think we probably will make it to our destination by Christmas.

****

Calvin and Nestor left that night around 1:00 AM. Bonnie was already in the bottom bunk, so I crawled in beside her and snuggled as close as I could. We had a small space heater plugged into shore power, so the warmth of the berthing-area felt almost womblike. I wrapped my arms around her from behind in the spoon position. I cupped her hands in mine.

Bonnie, who had not spoken for the last two hours, kissed my hands and asked, "Why did you really assault Lenny?"

"I didn't like the way he treated women," I said without hesitation; startling even myself.

I proceeded to tell her the story about one of the old guys I used to work with. He was an experienced tower climber. I learned a lot from him. His name was Red for his rapidly-thinning red hair. He was most comfortable on the road and he treated women with contempt. He was ex-Navy and his first wife cheated on him, gave him gonorrhea, then left. He seemed to hold every woman responsible. After that, they were all whores to his way of thinking; the girl at the bar was the bar whore, the girl at the checkout counter was the store whore, the girl at the hotel desk was the hotel whore. One of his favorite terms was road whore. He used this term frequently at the start of a road trip.

"I got a road whore in this town," he would say.

I found out years later that Red was a bit of a child molester. It was not really surprising, from the way he talked, but it sure woke me up to the weirdness of the world, especially the road world. Traveling constantly made one tempted to sample the various indulgences of the world. Drinking problems develop, infidelities are engaged in, and marriages ruined. Red had his own story for the reason his marriage broke up, but I suspect that the wife just got tired of waiting alone. It also was possible that she was an actual whore. Red made no distinction. He even called his mother a whore for spreading her legs for his absent no-account father.

I heard every story about every road whore he rode, and how they all think he's something different. He told one he was a Broadway actor. He didn't intend on seeing too many of them more than once. They were whores to him, I guess. It got to be humorous to me. Then I found out about the kids.

Red had been molesting kids and taking pictures in different towns for over 40 years. He was not only molesting children, he was trafficking pornography at the same time. Some of his "road whores" were children, it turns out. I used to question myself about why I didn't realize what was going on sooner. In every town, we would check in a motel or hotel and Red would take the truck and disappear. I ate a lot of dinners alone at hotel bars and shithole diners. I socialized very little with Red, but met some interesting people on my own.

The shit came down on Red when he decided to take the company truck to a bar and park in a tow away zone. The truck was towed to a local lot, where a kid working as the tow truck driver's assistant stole Red's camera from the truck. The kid decided to get the film in that camera developed, with the result that the drugstore called him two days later and he was interviewed by the police. He told the police he had found the camera, but he was already kind of a shady operator, so they knew he stole it. He finally confessed to stealing it from our Sunrise Enterprises truck. The truck was registered to the company and they soon got a call from the same folks. Within hours they had decided that it was Red or me who had taken the lewd pictures found on that camera.

Searching my motel room, they discovered one marijuana joint, mostly gone. They bagged it as evidence. There were some other cops searching Red's room at the same time. They found porn. They found a lot of porn. They found his pictures and videos that he had been transporting in a hidden compartment in the rear tool section of the truck. Red was busted and I no longer had a climbing partner.

Enter Lenny.

Del, my boss, had hired his brother-in-law. Now I had heard Del complain about Lenny for years. Lenny was the Dead Beat who didn't want to do shit with his life. But years had passed and Del had advanced in the company and his wife was probably holding his nuts to the fire. So Del hired Lenny to be an apprentice of Red's. Lenny went out on the road a few times with Red and me. Lenny even tried to follow Red a few times. Red just drove around in circles. Lenny once told me that Red was boring and that his stories were bullshit.

"I followed him six different times," Lenny once told me, "the most exciting thing he did was go to church."

Of course, Lenny didn't know, but he sure ate up Red's stories of his road whores even though they were lies, but not for the reason Lenny imagined.

Red was a child molester and a truly evil person. He was also an experienced climber. Replacing him with Lenny was like replacing the fan belt on your car with dental floss. He barely cared about his job and he was afraid of heights. Red had trained him on the winch, but Lenny still hadn't got the hang of it.

If Lenny hadn't learned Red's work habits, he had inherited a lot of his unseemly behavior. He was out during all hours of the night and slept late. He was irritating at first, then funny, then sad, then irritating again. My own life at the time had taken a turn for the complicated. I had two female paramours who were challenging my every fiber of sanity as I was totally immersed in their lives. It was miserable to be without them and sometimes more miserable with them. But always gloriously miserable, if there is such a thing.

After working the road with Red for about a dozen years, I a developed a routine on climbs. I would finish the job safely and, if possible, smoke a joint after I had sent down all of my tools. Red didn't care either, he was already halfway down a bottle of scotch by the time my tools reached the bottom. If we finished during the day, I would stay up and watch the sunset clamped to a chunk of metal in the sky. If I had ground duty, I would wait for Red to descend before I sparked up. He always kept a small cooler with five or six cold beers that I would hoist up to him and he would drink a few, then climb down.

When I became the site supervisor, I decided that all drinks and smoke would wait until the job was complete. Lenny never succumbed to this rule and would usually be baked long before I descended. I could not tell Del about this, because Lenny would just tell him he learned it from Red and me. So I kept quiet. Besides, he was not much of a worker, even while sober.

This was all bad enough to make me want Lenny to quit or for me to quit myself, but for a few incidents involving women. I was a philanderer, to be sure, but if I was lucky enough to spend a night with someone, I would give her a gift or do something to make her feel like she mattered to me because, in truth, they all did.

Lenny, on the other hand, was violent and abusive. On more than one occasion, I was awoken by a ruckus in his room only to discover that he was not letting some poor girl leave his room. I would intervene, sometimes violently, to allow these girls to escape. Sometimes these girls were actual prostitutes and I was probably saving Lenny's life by helping them escape.

But Lenny never changed and never improved. He liked the word "whore" even more than Red did. When someone is as intellectually underdeveloped as him, they tend to just take the easy way to everything. So learning anything new was always a struggle. I tried to help with his emotional maturity by explaining my philosophy that treating people well was always the best course. He just didn't care, he was single, making good money, and he had almost no responsibility to anyone, including Del and his occupation.

I spent over a year trying to change Lenny and then I tried to tolerate him. But Lenny was constantly going to cause me problems and one of us had to go. If I had no other complications in my life, I could have simply found another job that paid well, but life is never that simple. Being pulled in ten different directions will take a toll on one's psyche and perhaps distort life's priorities.

"I think I understand," Bonnie finally interrupted. "I think in my brain, something similar happened. Years of sexual incompatibility with Chandler left an unexpressed gulf between us emotionally.

Bridging that gap became the focus of my mind for a while, but I never felt competent enough. He was kind about it, but never pleased. The fact that I was probably infertile was a strain also. For my part, I assumed he would get over this and accept it, but I don't know if he ever did."

Bonnie shifted and rolled to her other side, facing away from me and towards the wall. I pulled her close. "The rest of my life was almost as frustrating and unfulfilling; the friends I had in school were poorer and either didn't feel comfortable around me or just wanted money or to meet rich and famous people. My new rich friends were almost all raised rich and had no response to my common touch. My charity work with dying children brought insight and perspective, but mostly sadness. So yes, Clyde, I identify. We both wanted a whole new identity."

She grabbed my hands in hers and kissed them on the back.

"So we have them now," she smiled, "Me Bonnie, you Clyde."

I laughed heartily.

****

When it happens, it is an enlightening moment. Mostly it is unexpected, but not unwelcome. It is a moment of clarifying certainty. It has happened to me several times in my life. One such occasion was when I was in solitary confinement at the state prison. I sat alone with my bruised kidneys and my righteous indignation and listened for every noise while I memorized my latest lament.

I would listen to a constant dripping faucet in the adjacent cell. At first I found it annoying, but soon I learned to accept and appreciate the journey of those molecules of water forcing their way to freedom from the depths of the earth through valves and pipes to one last spigot: one last washer. Freeing itself, the drop of water is then dropped into a drain - plop! The droplet then takes a slow journey to a cesspool somewhere.

I equated it with my life in that moment of clarity. I made a metaphor for my life out of that faucet and that plop…plop…plop sound. One more life down the drain; life in prison.

As I lay with the now-sleeping Bonnie on a bunk below the deck of Cassandra, another one of those epiphany moments came. There was a steady drip by the stairs caused by the light drizzle. I thought immediately of that dripping faucet, then clarity arrived; I was no longer that miserable heap on the floor of that cell looking for the next piece of my misery puzzle. I had a beautiful woman who had decided I was worth everything and I felt the same about her.

I had planned and executed two escapes. I had a daughter who was a successful musician, with an album on the charts. In no way was there anything miserable about me; my manifesto be damned! But still…

Back to that droplet of water that forced its way free only to wind up in the cesspool; there was still a metaphor in that for me.

CHAPTER 48 – I SHALL BE RELEASED

D*ecember 20th*

We set sail today. It took an extra day for Nestor to settle on the sale of his restaurant to the Marina Commission. But he got his money and now he and Calvin will be taking us down to Florida. From there, Clyde and I will be taking over. Russell's Cay should be about 12 hours from where we drop them off.

Taylor Spencer, the private investigator, has been seen in South Carolina. According to Calvin, he was in Charleston asking questions of one of Calvin's friends who is still a private eye. The fact that he is closing in has forced Clyde and me to stay on Cassandra and barely even peek our heads outside. It was all romantic and sweet at first, but three days in, we are both ready for something besides hiding and sleepless nights listening for every noise.

Nestor and Calvin keep us in food and they say they know how to shake somebody tailing them, but I have no more stomach for this. I want to leave and never return. Clyde awakened something in me and I am not going to settle for anything less than freedom and walking again. The trials and tragedy I have endured have made me strong, resilient, and somewhat cynical about people's intentions.

Clyde told me more about Naomi the other night. He told me after we had made love in the lower berth. She fell in love with Clyde after only one night. She was not as experienced as Clyde suspected. Actually, Lenny had only recently taken her virginity, clumsily. Clyde, on the other hand, had taken his time and made her feel comfortable afterwards. Lenny had thrown up on her shoes.

Perhaps the knowledge that Lenny had deflowered the fair Naomi threw a switch in Clyde that set him over the desperate brink. Clyde already had a wife, a girlfriend, and a mistress. With Naomi, he had a damsel in distress; one deeply infatuated with the older man with the sex magic. I have counseled many such young girls.

Clyde was a hair trigger once he took her on. His act of aggression was not misdirected completely. Lenny was the source of a great deal of Clyde's irritation. His reverence for the females in his life had made him overly sensitive to anyone who was a perceived threat to womanhood in any way. It has manifested itself in violence on at least three occasions.

Lenny took the brunt of his first attack. Those three bikers were next to feel his wrath. My horse-betting buddy at the casino also presented a threat to femalehood and would have been thrashed were it not for security. Clyde really hates to see females in distress. He's like some kind of knight. Maybe he's not intended for polite society after all. Island life will be good to him.

* * * * * * * * * * *

I finished my manifesto the day before we set sail. I had to put the final touches on the theory I had begun to formulate. I realized that my so called "misery addiction" had become more of an explanation for my excessive behavior. I was always taking on more than I could handle. Most people find a hobby. I just got busy rescuing damsels in distress; sometimes it was holding my umbrella for the lady at the bus stop, sometimes it was trying to kick some guy's ass for touching Bonnie.

Below deck on the day before we sailed, Bonnie was cleaning out her knapsack that she had packed for her escape. She had her journals and she had other information from Tallhill in a small collapsible file box. I asked her if I could look at the files.

"Sure, those are notes on all of my mentees at Tallhill. I even got yours in there. The various doctors you visited sent summaries to me. Check out the notes from that Whipple guy from his hypnotism session with you," she said as she handed me a brown folder.

From the desk of Dr. Marlin Whipple:

Transcript of hypnosis session with Clyde Barrow.

Recorded September 2, 20—Subject: Clyde Barrow

Hypnotist: Dr. Marlin Whipple

Note: Subject has been hypnotized to go into character as a mercenary soldier when a trigger word is spoken. The following is a transcript after the trigger word:

I better lock the doors for before I start this story.

If they kill me now, it's because they record everything I do.

They even sent a dog.

It's kinda like a robot.

Yeah, he just stares at me out the window.

Very fierce dog, but very loyal.

Cowers to me though.

But watches me all of the time.

But that's just the dog, he's harmless.

Just another monitoring device.

They set me up in a job after the Marine Corps.

They set me up in a job and they clothe me and they feed my family.

They give me health insurance.

But they nail you to the wall and position you and influence you and control you until one day you look around you and all you did was sit still.

You fought for a little bit of ground.

And you haven't moved an inch.

You owe a lot of people money.

You learn a lot of lessons.

You probably won't get a chance to apply the lesson.

Even the hard lessons.

You touch a few people's lives.

You smile when you can.

Then you die.

But I've been owned for 30 years.

At this point… I speak the trigger word.

I ask Mr. Barrow about his job climbing towers.

Climbin'?

You want to know about climbin'.

You climb a tower.

You get up in that tower and you look at life below.

You sit there for a long time.

You are going to be there for a while.

Might as well get used to your surroundings.

Take a picture if you can.

But always take a mental picture.

[Long pause]

It is misery.

It is cold.

As cold as the biting winter wind on that tower.

The next note was on the letterhead of the state hospital.

From the Desk of: Dr. Monica Caulder

Chivalry:

He wants to defend women constantly, but also wishes to control them. He pleases them by bending to their needs and wants. This is intoxicating to a troubled woman who just needs someone to understand. The sympathy is easy in these cases and the "Misery", as Mr. Barrow calls it, becomes contagious. But he cannot even defend his treatment of his wife. In a cold marriage there is not equal blame. Mr. Barrow does admit to the majority of the blame for this cold relationship.

Mr. Barrow is also in possession of an almost irresistible charm. He seemingly can take any conversation anywhere and make it seem interesting. He is calm and confident. He does not judge nor take offense. But he is very unhappy. He wishes for humanity to know his condition and records his observations and theories to the best of his ability.

His chivalry manifested itself when he attacked a co-worker that constantly offended Clyde with his misogyny. Deep down, he considers himself a knight, and knights honor a code. Chivalry is part of the code. Rudeness to ladies is never tolerated and is only worthy of the commonest of men. This attitude runs counter to modern culture where equality is a popular cause. Clyde sees no one as his equal except those who would understand his misery at being miserable. He is let down like he knew would happen, i.e. a self-fulfilling prophecy; he snapped and fell and there was no safety net for him. He comes to me broken. I send him off to the unknown hopeful that this will be a growing experience.

My favorite summary was on State Prison stationery;

To the Custodians and Caregivers at Tallhill,

The prisoner that I release to your care, Mr. Clyde Barrow, shows absolutely no sign of any type of psychosis. He probably should be in some minimum security prison somewhere. But he will probably do well at Tallhill.

Dr. Pierpont J. Chulmsworth MD
Head Psychiatric Counselor
State Prison Facility Number 3

So I put a name to the face: Dr. Pierpont J Chulmsworth was the name of that frustrating shrink who dispensed the drugs with such impunity. The last note was from Dr. Silk.

Mr. Clyde Barrow came to this institution recently and has adapted reasonably well. He has made friends easily, but casually. He chats with members about all subjects. His observations about the Tallhill members are direct and humorous. He makes fun of our smiles, or as he says, "The fish with the hook in its mouth smile".

His mentorship with Miss Bonnie Parker has blossomed into a fledgling romance. This is not the intent of the mentorship program, but it is not unhealthy behavior.

In my sessions with Mr. Barrow, he has candidly recalled incidents in his life where he risked all for the honor of a lady. He had once been beaten to a pulp in a small Louisiana town because he didn't like the name some young tough guy called a young black girl. He is physically scarred from many of the fights.

Mr. Barrow's need for knighthood has led him to his quest of the ultimate damsel of distress. His mentor is one of the more accomplished and popular members at Tallhill; she is a paraplegic dark-eyed girl with the heart of gold. She is in no real need of rescue, but her situation in itself lends itself to sympathy and rescue.

* * * * * * * * * * *

Chivalry is what I call this madness; this obsession with correcting wrongs. An obsession that will ultimately be proven futile. Chivalry is my particular brand of misery. I have adapted ancient worship of the female above all other deities and I have made it my axe. Being a century out of step is one way to stand out in a crowd.

My parents were old when I was born. There was already a house full of children when they decided that twelve would be just the right number. One more kid, but an introspective one. Introspective Clyde with the socially awkward, but straightforward charm. An oxymoron; a dependable risk-taker. Old parents are not much fun when you are a kid. Life has taken a few pieces out of them, but maybe I inherited their life's experiences genetically. Maybe I was born with some information that some people need a lifetime to learn.

I have spent a good deal of time lately trying to get back to that kid I was before the world came into my life. I was eager, smart, friendly, and observant. I had no bad habits and I had no negative feelings to express and no hang-ups. I know I cannot be that kid again, but I think I can find his innocence and curiosity. Maybe I can put my violence behind me and act in a more civilized manner when confronted with bad behavior.

What torments me is the misguided belief that I have to change the way things are and to do it as quickly as possible. Did my father act like this when he was younger? I don't know, but he was too old to be a gallant knight by the time I arrived. None of my brothers behave like this, as far as I know. I do not know of any man who behaves as I do. Perhaps my methods cross the line, but my intent is pure. I defend honor and I defend the prize. I will defeat those who do not pay fair respect.

My assault upon Lenny and the Badasses motorcycle gang were instances of my manifesto being manifested. I could have calmly diffused the situation in each case; but I chose violence. In the case of Lenny, I was protecting decency. I was protecting my queen in the case of the motorcycle gang.

The fact that I was on the run was given only secondary consideration. It all felt so reflexive. There was a natural feel to my tactics in the fight and it felt good to be winning the battle at the start. However, if not for the store clerk, I would have been beaten and arrested.

But the knight rides one more time. He rides a boat into the unknown, where the dragons are not so easily identified. Sir Clyde was not Lancelot nor Galahad, but a keeper of some lofty purpose of human kind: a place above our nature. Sir Clyde was attracted to those who saw that possibility and then saw how futile the hope of that world had become. Looking downcast, we secretly hope for serenity and happiness, but see the fade of hope almost from the start.

We are big realizers; not accepters, and pointlessly we fight a battle against logic and refuse to accept our fate as ordinary. We are locked up, poked and pilled. Our analytical minds are analyzed. Our psyches are laid bare, then drugged into compliance.

At Tallhill, we succumbed to conformity and smiles by the mere certainty and security of the place. Our womb. Our cocoon. My decision to leave was based on there being limits assigned to me. I find these limits totally arbitrary since I am normally sane. My actions of violence were not without context and provocation.

They were acts of gallantry.

And people really don't care, they don't appreciate what you are. And there's nothing you can do about it. But does life really have to be like that? You end up taking a lot of unnecessary chances because you think it matters. I can't even justify all of the things I do. Many of them make no sense. My chivalry and my confidence lead me to do outrageous things.

Isabel and I would go on long drives in the country and sleep under the stars because it was fun. We would be happy and content and spiritual. There were no consequences and there was no fear. We understood that. But for some reason we returned to our miserable lives- as if programmed by some unseen hand- instead of doing what we actually wanted to do. We actually wanted to be together; at least we thought so, until we got tired of each other. If we didn't get tired, well that was okay too.

My menagerie of miserable people was not without its charming and interesting people. All of them were at one time the thrill of my life and my purpose for being. There was a happening there. We made something for a while. It just happened that I was born to be a rescuer, a hero.

Rapunzel was a fairy tale and Cyrano was a play. There was no girl in a tower. At least not one in any real danger. It was just one of my fantasies. I was consumed with my self-importance and looking for a way out.

Am I a hero or just a poser? I was self-absorbed and indifferent to the damage I was causing. I was just going after it for my reasons. But isn't that what everybody does?

Back to the accumulated stress that caused this. One day you look up and all of your obligations are fulfilled; you raised the kids and put them through college. You ask, "What's next?" The next thought in my case was that I had time for myself. Then I thought about running out of time. Things began to take on urgency; I wasn't where I wanted to be. I wasn't with who I wanted to be with. My wife, who was once at least partially accommodating to my needs, no longer even cared if I had needs.

So I searched for a purpose. Any purpose, really and for a level of importance. My career was not providing this purpose. In fact, my career frustrated me frequently.

So the chivalrous knight with the misery addiction nailed himself to the cross of selfless sacrifice, suffered and was condemned. Wrapped in a bow and delivered to a happy place and turned over to a damsel. She was a dark-eyed damsel with wheels and *she* rescued *him.*

CHAPTER 49 – THE FOOT OF PRIDE

"I named her Cassandra because of Millie," Nestor was shouting as we pulled into a marina somewhere in south Florida. He had piloted the boat most of the way, but had let me take the long dreary parts.

"Millie was always seeing the future and telling us how she dreamed stuff that would happen later," he continued.

I stood anxious and hoped he would let me steer the boat towards one of the piers.

"Sometimes there were calamities that would happen and she would claim that she saw it in a dream. Cassandra would always guide me to the good fishing spots and around storms when I took the tours out. So maybe the name fits. What do I know?"

We had left in the dead of night on the 20th of December. We made mostly slow progress along the coast. The cover of darkness allowed Bonnie and me some time above deck in the night air. I guess we felt more secure in the dark, but it probably didn't make any difference. For my part, I felt I had already succeeded. The law and/or bounty hunters had not found us and Nestor and Calvin were not going to turn us in. If they were, it would have happened already.

The remaining obstacles, as I saw them, were the unpredictable winter sea and my inexperience piloting a boat. I could do nothing about the sea and I practiced as many maneuvers as I could once Calvin turned over control to me. Bonnie also did her fair share of driving, being somewhat more experienced. We had skirted between the barrier islands of North Carolina and the mainland as the sun rose.

The long journey progressed at a snail-like 10 knots through the Intercoastal Waterway. We stopped once for gas somewhere in northern Florida. There were four large gas tanks in reserve to the main tank and this made frequent stopping unnecessary. Nestor had also packed as much of his leftover restaurant food as he could in the small refrigerator below deck. We moved cautiously and slowly towards southern Florida with high spirits and muted expectations.

There was a television below deck with a satellite receiver. Satellite television was not possible while we were tied up at the pier. Once we got away from the shore and obstacles to the signal, we had about 500 channels. A gyroscope compensated for the changes of direction. Even then, rougher waves and direction changes caused coverage loses. Bonnie had instantly been drawn to the news coverage. Because of this, we now realized how close our escape actually was. Major news networks had now picked up on the story.

Videos from the gas station incident and our casino adventures were now being played repeatedly on all of the 24-hour news networks. Bonnie became consumed with watching them and took fewer turns at the wheel. She had found an old video tape and began recording the news so she could find all available reports. A typical report from cable news went something like this:

Narrator: A modern Bonnie and Clyde with a twist; two fugitive escapees ride roughshod over biker gangs and casino poker players.

"Welcome to the nightly wrap-up; we are tracking the progress of two lovers who have escaped from a minimum security mental health facility." (My picture from my old Sunrise Enterprises security badge is flashed on the screen).

Narrator: "Good evening, I am Percival Crane. A nationwide manhunt has been underway for a fugitive couple who escaped from the Angelina Tallhill Memorial Wellness Center. Clyde Barrow is the infamous Back Pack Bomber from a few years ago and Bonnie Parker is the convicted murderer of her spouse a dozen years ago. Mr. Barrow apparently escaped from Tallhill earlier this month and returned to help Miss Parker escape a few days later."

The escape was kept quiet by Tallhill officials, but was leaked to the press by a victim of Miss Parker, who has hired a private investigator to try and locate the couple. That private investigator, Mr. Taylor Spencer, declined to be interviewed on camera, but did submit to a telephone interview."

Surveillance video appears on the TV screen. The narrator continues:

"Surveillance video from the Black Diamond Bay casino shows a woman in a wheelchair at a $50 poker table winning several hands after starting with next to nothing. She spent over six hours at the table only to be joined later by a man fitting the description of Clyde Barrow. The same figure appears to be in other security videos showing a man being carried and dumped into the street earlier that evening."

The woman is shown in the high definition video winning sometimes with a pair of twos or Jack High. She is later seen leaving the casino with the same man fitting the description of Barrow. One security officer remembered escorting them to their car and noting that they had a green Ford Mustang. There have been no credible sightings of the pair since the night at the casino, which initially led investigators to conclude that they might have settled in that area for the time being."

According to Taylor Spencer, they have been spotted in such diverse places as Key West and Spokane, Washington. Those were not solid leads, but he did say that he had something he was working on and did not want to comment at this time."

"These two have a calm demeanor, but on two occasions, have performed unprovoked violent actions in public areas, so we cannot verify if they are unstable. We have no knowledge of any medications they have been prescribed, but that could possibly explain their wild behavior," the voice on the telephone said.

Narrator: "That wild behavior was on display on a more-grainy surveillance video taken at a convenience store 45 miles away in the town of Chester. Channel 6 correspondent Chad Butler caught up to one of the witnesses to this incident."(While the narrator talks, a grainy video plays which shows a flailing lunatic swinging bottles and three pissed-off hombres who took the brunt of his frantic assault)

Percival Crane continued:

"We interviewed one of the victims of the assault at his home."

"He came out of nowhere," said the biggest of the Badasses. "The young lady in the Mustang asked me a question about my motorcycle. Next thing I know, he's swinging that wine bottle at me and gnashing his teeth like a wild man."

This would be typical of the news accounts of our escapades, with the television news and the local radio news seeming to take the law enforcement angle. At least on the radio stations we could pick up near the coast. The internet was another story entirely; the videos of Bonnie's poker and my gas station assault received close to a million views each. Television and radio news stories made it seem like there was a massive nation-wide dragnet searching for us. All of the comments by the talking heads painted us a desperados and dangerous.

A website was created that tracked our exploits. The person who ran the website investigated the crimes and sightings reported to local police and the hotline set up by Taylor Spencer. The home page showed locations where we had been sighted. The false leads planted by Bonnie's father and Calvin's moles had little colored dots all over the map. There were red and orange and pink dots. There were pink dots in Las Vegas and Seattle. There were Orange dots in Key West and Montreal. There were red dots in Texas and South Carolina. I never learned what the colors meant. But there was also a lot of support for us on the internet. We were folk heroes to some, especially Bonnie. Her beauty and her story provoked an abundance of sympathy.

One national television network trotted out Bonnie's mother. Her statement to the world was, "Please turn yourself in, my sweet girl. We have all forgiven you. This will only make things worse for you."

Bonnie's reaction was to scoff at her and deadpan, "How nice that you have forgiven me," she announced to the air in the room. "How hard it must be to come to terms with a monster for a daughter."

On TV, her mother continued, "I believe she is under the control of this dangerous man."

This upset Bonnie even more. "If you found the time to visit me, maybe you would understand who I am." But she didn't cry or tear up; she just watched the phony maternal concern and the manufactured melodrama.

Conversely, we found strength and encouragement from the internet. FreeBonnieandClyde.com defended Bonnie. The facts of the case were brought to light; it was a crime of passion and the whore (their words) who caused it was the one who hired the private investigator and she was the one offering the reward money. As far as her supporters were concerned, the paraplegic Bonnie Parker had paid her dues a long time ago.

The website also had a link to Taylor Spencer's web pages, so false leads could be planted. There were even faked pictures of women in wheelchairs in various places. We had a cult following… Actually Bonnie had a cult following. I was not revered like her, but not reviled either. No one really cared too much about me except I was helping her. I was the head coach of "Team Bonnie". Someone even offered a $50,000 reward for the arrest of Lana Fox for impersonating a human being.

For my part, I hoped that nobody would link Gypsy Rae to Clyde Barrow. The Travelled were currently on the top of the charts with their first album and had two singles getting plenty of airplay. But one other song had jumped out from the album; "The Fugitive" was getting nearly as much attention. Ironically, some blogger had posted a homemade video of the song with our pictures and videos and it instantly became sort of the theme song for FreeBonnieandClyde.com.

So on one hand, we were dangerous desperados, but on the other, we were folk heroes. Both versions made the whole thing seem romantic. In reality, we were trapped on a boat; we didn't dare peek out from the cabin while docked or even anywhere in broad daylight on The Intercoastal. Our slow steady progress down the coast was planned to not attract attention. We were pretty confident that Nestor and Calvin would get us south. The rest depended on mine and Bonnie's boating skills.

We could only get internet when we were docked somewhere. Along with several stops for fuel we would sometimes dock to wait out rough weather. Late December is not a time of calm seas, even down south. Our last docking for fuel was just south of St. Augustine on New Year's Eve. We did venture out of the boat on that occasion to watch the fireworks. The passage of time seemed a trivial matter; we both felt it was a fitting send off to our unknown new lives and our farewell to the country in which all of our lives had been spent.

It was farewell and all that mattered was the trip to Russell's Cay. If it took a week to get there, we were prepared. If it took a month, we were ready. The world outside our cabin was an amusement and a curiosity. Outside of our cocoon was a bunch of complications; complications that were other people's problems. We had only us, but we had a future. That future did not include prisons or asylums. Maybe we were desperados, but not the type that bounty hunters and private eyes wished we were.

The distance from southern Florida to Russell's Cay was approximately 135 miles. We were quite sure of this even though we could not find it on any of the nautical maps we had. But I had the latitude and longitude of the island and Cassandra had a GPS receiver. We figured 15 knots as a cruising speed and allowed for bad weather, we figured it would take around ten to twelve hours. On January 3rd we shoved off and left Nestor and Calvin at some small pier between

Fort Lauderdale and Miami. I was becoming more and more comfortable with the boat and I was about to test the open seas.

"Keep her away from land as much as possible and pay attention to the marker buoys," Nestor told me as he stepped off the boat with our large sack of money.

He and Calvin waved and Bonnie and I waved back, then I slowly chugged out of the small marina into the calm seas. It was twilight and we planned to be somewhere near Russell's Cay once the sun came up.

So with no fanfare, we motored away from the mainland, with no expectation to return. Bonnie was still facing the shore looking back at all she was leaving behind, either symbolically or literally. I just kept my eyes on the horizon. We were going to be at the mercy of the sea soon and perhaps rough seas. If the weather or the waves were going to do us in, I had no control. But if we did fail, I was convinced it was not going to be due to bad seamanship.

* * * * * * * * * *

January 3,

Clyde and I are celebrities. More than celebrities, we are cult heroes. We have fans and websites and news updates. We have bounties and haters and trolls of every type. Radio callers all have opinions about us. We are celebrities and we are on the run. I must grow comfortable with these facts; these are the facts of my life.

My former residence at Tallhill has come under a certain scrutiny. The news reports criticized their security, but I know for a fact that nobody had tried to escape for my entire stay. There was nobody unhappy, they carefully selected most members and the ones who left were the huge dollar clients who could leave voluntarily at any time.

Tallhill withstood the scrutiny because they were a success story touted by corporatists and privately-run prison advocates as a model of efficiency and by liberal activists as an innovative treatment for mental disorders. When you have those two groups going to bat for you, the criticism doesn't find a voice.

Clyde asked me why I would ever leave that place of comfort. I told him that it was just time to go. I had helped many people who were actually better off than me. They could walk, they could dance, and they could run. In fact, some of them could leave if they didn't like their treatment; some did just that. But I helped them all. I did my best and I poured everything into helping them.

While I wasn't mentoring troubled souls, I was reading to sick children. When I did have time for myself, I studied treatments for my condition. My life up until now has led me to where I can get treatment. I began corresponding with Naomi when I learned that she was quite benevolent and was hiring doctors with experimental therapies that were being held back by regulations. I sent her the names of the surgeons I had heard about. Furthermore, if Clyde wasn't going to help me get there, then I would get there some other way. But I owe Clyde my heart and soul; he helped make my pain and loss in this world bearable. I once married for the gallantry I saw on display in a social atmosphere. I married for that atmosphere. I loved privilege and prestige. In reality, it was money and power that were on display, and I mistook that for gallantry.

Clyde is like most men in many ways; he fears his masculinity will escape him at some point and insists on periodic displays of his virility. His sense of purpose is confusing and sometimes contradictory. On one hand he wants to be noble and forsake any happiness for himself. On the other hand, he laments his misery addiction as he sees no reward for his constant sacrifices.

I lost all of my friends, my dancing, and my mother when I lost use of my legs. After that, I had to find a purpose. I became consumed with helping others who had madness visited upon them.

As real as we are, we live in a mythical beast world in our minds. Clyde is the honorable knight of yore. I fancy myself as Roxane, the heroine of my Rosemary's never- produced ballet Cyrano. Roxane realized her love too late and was denied a certain type of happiness. A tragic heroine and a knight; we fit like hand in glove.

****

Day was breaking and foggy as I steered the boat towards where the GPS said I was heading. Bonnie was sleeping and that was fine for me. I wasn't sure how expected I was and who, if anybody, would be there to greet me. If it was the authorities, I would have to avoid any explanation as to my presence here. I had avoided the Coast Guard quite well that night and I was not going press my luck. I hoped that Russell's Cay would be laid back and breezy.

Russell's Cay came into view as a sort of glow in the fog. Slowly as we drew closer I saw lights take form and saw that all of the buildings near the shore were raised high off the ground. Only up on the hill, directly under a giant windmill, stood a huge green glass mansion with giant solar panels on its roof. There was a tiny harbor ahead of me with several boats tied to piers, so I headed in that direction.

The passage had been rough at times; we skirted the outer edge of a storm that was blowing down south and got some decent waves. But the rougher seas were a decent tradeoff for the lack of traffic. Guiding the boat through the well-travelled Intercoastal had been challenging when dealing with the giant container ships and the sometime narrow passageways. But waves were potentially life-threatening. We survived the worst with only minor seasickness and took on only a small amount of water that the bilge pumps dispatched with little difficulty.

We had given almost all of our money to Nestor for the boat. We did not have any use for money where we were going and perhaps we would have to live on the boat for a time while Naomi found us living quarters. We were prepared for this more than we were prepared for a possible clash of romantic interests.

I had spent a good deal of time on the crossing thinking about Naomi. It seemed like years since we were lovers. In reality, it was not even two years. Many things had happened to both of us. I wondered if she still thought I was going to make her life complete. I wondered if she was the jealous type. I wondered if anyone on the island would want the bounty money. I realized that I knew nothing about who would be on the island with her. Would they turn us in? I doubted that she would, but a bunch of strangers who may have their eyes on a reward gave me great apprehension. I knew Bonnie felt something similar, even though we didn't discuss it.

My doubts and concerns were real, but I didn't let on to Bonnie. I was going to hope against hope that Naomi would protect her and help her. I felt sure that Naomi would be welcoming, but she had thrown me a curve before. Once again, my loss of control of a situation was wearing heavily on my psyche.

****

January 4,

O Sea

My Journey is long

My bones weary

My eyes heavy

My heart restless

I am at your mercy

Be kind to my tired sprit

Allow me safe harbor

Guide my captain and keep him strong and safe

I beseech thee.

I spent most of the crossing to Russell's Cay below deck riding out the big waves and making sure that the excess water was being pumped out. It is warmer below deck and when calmer seas prevailed, I slept for a few hours. I awoke around 3:00AM and yelled for Clyde to help me above deck. Once in my winter coat, Clyde strapped me in my chair and lashed it to the deck so I could sit near the small heater at the helm near his feet.

It was foggy nearly everywhere, but occasionally lights and land were sighted at various points in the distance. Even though these were not our destination, they gave some glimmer of hope and comfort. These feelings rode with us for the whole journey accompanied by their close companions; fear and distress. We shared these emotions almost wordlessly as we held hands on our last dash towards our absurd refuge; towards rescue or perhaps capture.

Talking about it and analyzing it had become futility. The future was mostly out of our control. We could guide the ship into harbor; after that, we would be at the mercy of other people's good will and hopefully, at least, their good humor. So for the few hours before daylight we chugged at a slow 8 or 10 knots and contemplated our contemplations to ourselves and alternated holding hands and exchanging knowing hopeful glances. It was both the longest few hours and the easiest feeling to feel; relief and resignation to whatever was coming our way.

* * * * * * * * * *

Calm seas ruled as the sun came up and I saw a group of people gathered at the pier as we approached and some of them were loading a boat. There were still several patches of fog that obscured almost everything from time to time. After a particularly thick patch, the pier came into full view. I could see that there were seven people and one of them was Naomi. Even from a distance, I could tell by the way she carried herself. It was a proud walk that she had when I last saw her at the prison as she strode away certain that she had decided where her journey would take her.

She was directing men to load things into the boat and they were following her commands with little wasted motion. The scene captivated me. I kept the boat chugging along as I tried to decide what kind of mission she had assigned to these men. Suddenly, Naomi looked up in our direction and began to wave. I smiled since this brought me great comfort and satisfaction. It was a strange sensation, but it didn't last long.

A few of the men loading the boat also looked up and began to wave. This seemed strange, since I didn't expect any kind of greeting from these strangers. Suddenly I realized that their waving was not a greeting.

Their waves were all from their right to left; they were telling me where to steer.

In that instant of realization I also saw a marker buoy pass to my right. In my excitement I had forgotten Nestor's admonishment to steer clear of the buoys since they marked shallow seas; usually sand bars.

Unfortunately, this realization occurred too late. Cassandra came to a sudden and complete stop. Since I was standing and waving, I had one hand on the wheel. Soon I had no hands on the wheel, as I flew forward towards the bow. My attempt to grab at anything caused me to grab one of the supports of the boat awning.

My grip was not good on the cold wet metal and soon I was being propelled, spinning slowly sideways through the air. My last contact with the boat was when the lower part of my back hit the tip of the bow. I plunged helplessly into the water.

CHAPTER 50 – GOLD SHOES

As the brave knight struggled for certainty and control of the uncontrollable, the ultimate futility was realized, acknowledged, but ignored. Certainty: the beggar's quest, the fool's errand, the simplification of the absurd. It takes me for a ride, just to leave me standing back at the station.

This fourth dimension I seek, this sixth or seventh sense I speculate about; neither can I prove or disprove. My journey for all of the answers has led to something less than futility and yet something more than realization. Is it always thus when the reward is unattainable and unprovable?

Certainty is a trap in that it leaves nothing left to learn. It is the creation of the unambitious mind. When change is the only constant, when motion is the catalyst, nothing can be certain. At least not totally and permanently. The reason that a perfectly functioning mind does not learn or understand this is because it does not wish to learn or understand. But contentment to be in a trap is to be content with ignorance.

So I escaped the traps along the way. The stress that broke me free also propelled me into other traps and discoveries. I sought control and lost control. I gained structure and then escaped its certainty. The conventions and expectations of a world I did not invent could not contain me nor define me. To be what I am; a fugitive, a non-conformist, a rebel, and outcast, I have sacrificed all that others would find comforting, certain, and secure. And I have landed.

It has been three months since we landed here on Russell's Cay. I have had a lot of time to contemplate and write and analyze the current state of affairs. When my mind snapped and I did the deed; when I slammed Lenny's head into the work bench, I was not in that moment. I was off somewhere in a state of mind where my actions made sense. I liked being there; it was something other than a mindless march to the grave.

I returned to this state often afterwards when I was alone; whether it was in solitary confinement, in my room at the hospital, or my storage area. I would reach out for bits and pieces of my former shattered life and make them romantic and try to taste them somehow and bring that feeling back; any feeling of a real purpose.

I would think about my first trip to a big city when I was maybe 2 or 3 years old. I went with my mother to attend my much-older brother's wedding. His in-laws lived in an apartment in a tall building. The apartment had a smell and a taste, but most important, it had a view. One night, I sat and stared at those lights through a large glass patio door. Endless lights of all colors. I knew most of those lights were important. There were traffic lights and street lights and lights from homes. I imagined that all of those homes had happy families and important things in them.

Years later, when staying in hotels became the norm, I would still sit in the dark and look in wonder at lights. But the wonder had changed. I knew most people were no more important than me and life was a struggle and most of them were as lost as I was. The wonder that remained with me was why anyone was even trying. The whole charade seemed pointless; the acquisition of material goods that cost four or five months' salary, yet added very little to the overall quality of things other than to impress other people. I was ashamed to be a part of that.

The more I analyzed, the more I realized how right I was. Buying a certain car or a certain electronic device became a goal worth attaining at some point. I could not defend this behavior any more than I can defend slamming Lenny's head into the work bench; an empty accomplishment. Those nights alone on the road were nights I wished I could spend with Annette, I wanted her to see the lights and tell her. I did write my thoughts down, and I know now that she read them, but I wished that she could have been there.

So when a bittersweet smell triggers a misplaced memory, I think first of the lost opportunity to have someone share those moments. Even that little two year-old in the big city had no one to share it with. My mother simply sighed and went to sleep in the guest room while I sat on the edge of the sofa bed and stared at the big world that had decided a long time ago that certain things were important and I had no control over any of it. At that young age, I think I understood that it was going to be a lonely road if I insisted that I was just not going to accept that.

* * * * * * * * * * *

This is where Bonnie and I converge. She would not accept being marginalized. She came back fighting. She was determined to walk and I knew she would someday. As I sit here writing this she is on the beach with her physical therapist. Naomi had arranged for a neurosurgeon to be here, as she was fully expecting us. Bonnie had her surgery two months ago and she has been making slow and steady progress. Today she is going to walk without help.

It was her determination that saved my life. Three months ago, we came here with great excitement and anticipation. Our audacity at thinking we could escape and live a life of bliss and contentment came with a cost. My inattention to my boat driving was caused by this audacity and this presumption that we were home free. I had forgotten the lesson I had learned from my tower-climbing days; do one thing at a time and then move on. Skip a step and you may cause a calamity.

The calamity I caused was to come to a dead stop on a sand bar. The boat was not traveling fast, but it came to a dead stop and flung me through the air. I smacked the bow and then plunged into the water. As my lungs filled with water, I began to drift out of consciousness. The world grew dark around me and the bliss I was beginning to feel was interrupted by a strong arm around my chest. The last thing I remember is being pulled slowly up as air bubbles pushed out in front of my face.

Bonnie, who up until then was lashed to a seat on the boat, had dived in to rescue me. She had used one arm to paddle and one arm to pull me while keeping my head above water. She probably swam hundreds of yards until one of Naomi's boats reached her. Bonnie does not want to talk of this, but Naomi and the men from the boat talk of it often. They marvel at her strength and courage. The doctors and therapists marvel at her determination.

She is now on the beach with her therapists and the surgeon who performed her operation. They have wheeled her to a small brick path on the beach that has been constructed for this occasion. The path has been covered with some kind of matt. She is wearing the gold ballet shoes from Storage Unit 11. I am watching from the balcony of the main house, which is about fifty yards away. She has stood on her own recently but she has not tried to walk unassisted.

The therapists help her to her feet. Then they stand aside. Bonnie sticks both arms straight out. She looks down. Her right leg quivers, then moves ahead some; more of a slide than a step. Her left foot does something similar. One of the therapists moves in to grab her, but she pushes him away gently. I am filled with anxiety as I nervously chew my lip. I am watching with terror and fear for her. But I cannot turn away.

Her left leg moves now. The knee bent slightly. A real step; almost a full step. Her balance is amazing. She braces, then slides the right leg even. There she stands for maybe two minutes. I hear the therapists say something and Bonnie waves them off again. She takes almost a full step with her right leg, and then drags the left forward immediately. She takes a full step with her left leg, then a full step with her right. She is walking! She takes two more full steps before she collapses into the wheelchair that the therapists have been pushing behind her.

The therapists and the surgeons break into applause, as I also do as tears trickle down my face. I am delighted and excited for her. Very few things in this life are sublime, but this is one of them. My mind turns to her dancing and performing in the Cyrano ballet she wants to perform and I smile. I cheer and I yell. She looks up at me from her wheelchair and waves.

I wave back… from my own fully-automatic wheelchair.

****

At the end of the line, what it comes down to is that we are driven by selfishness. If we are not selfish we think of others who are selfish and tend to their needs. Even a long chain of selfless acts leads to an end user who is in some way very selfish. The true selfless act, therefore, is to remove one's self from the clamor for favors and deeds. The world of the recluse; the chamber where the give and take of chatter and commerce have no occurrence.

In childhood, alone as I was, my head contained the imagination to create a world of heroes that lived in my little cranium. I conquered worlds and sports and kept statistics for both. I accumulated all information as if there was going to be a test someday. I knew batting averages and home run totals on any given date. My mind was occupied with the banalities of details and facts. I averaged stuff and projected season statistics. I loved this world of numbered certainty that could win any argument.

So lonely.

We all define love and happiness in our own terms. We define every feeling in our own subjective lexicon. There really are no instructions and nothing is ever going to make someone else see what you see. Do most people even look? Do they even examine their own feelings? Not a soul anywhere in the universe will examine your feelings for you. To be alone is to be an outcast.

But the outcast has been joined; Bonnie and I are as connected and plugged into each other as is conceivable. We are sides of a coin, although the coin has flipped; she can walk and I can't.

I have nearly the identical injury as hers. The difference is my age, but I am in good physical shape otherwise. For now, walking is like a fantasy. But once again, I know I won't quit after having heard her voice in those dreams and seen her walk on a strange seashell beach.

An elevator takes me down to beach level while I look at my oddly-contorted feet. As sunset colors stream into view beyond the water, Bonnie is silhouetted against the sky and she is standing. She has her arms straight out and her left leg is bent at the knee and tilted inward. Her arms give her enough balance to hold this pose.

She holds that pose until the sun goes down; more than nine minutes. It was the time it took for my robotic chair to negotiate that seashell sand. But I make it to her and she collapses into my arms as the last of the big orange ball disappears behind the sign that reads:

TALLHILL SOUTH: SUNSET BEACH.

I negotiate a turnaround with my wheelchair's keyboard. I get her back to the elevator and she presses 2. This is the last time she will need my help. She will henceforth dance wearing gold shoes in the sand while I watch from a balcony overlooking our private beach. Contained and content in our new asylum. A slight breeze blows her curly dark hair into my eyes.

She kisses my cheek.

R. Jay Stewart has been a Farmer, a Marine, and a Radio Technician among other pursuits. A freelance writer, he currently lives in Maryland. This is his first published novel. Future novels in the works include *A Different Color Sky, Echoes of the Soul,* and *A Cataclysm in Repose.* His other writings and short stories can be found on his website/blog:

https://thebigfadeout.wordpress.com

Email: Rogstew2@gmail.com

Twitter: @rogstew2

www.ingramcontent.com/pod-product-compliance
Lightning Source LLC
Chambersburg PA
CBHW072007020726
47501CB00006B/1715
* 9 7 8 0 6 9 2 6 0 3 8 7 1 *